THE KING'S SUN
THE BRASS MACHINE: BOOK ONE

ISAAC GRISHAM

Cooper Blue Books, LLC
1112 W. Boughton Rd. #161
Bolingbrook, IL 60440

www.isaacgrisham.com

Edited, formatted, and book design by Kristen Corrects, Inc.
Cover art design by Dissect Designs
Author photo by Eric Mackiewicz

First edition published 2018

ISBN 978-1-7321406-1-5

for Justin

the dark-haired man

KITSUNE

Inari Palace had been the center of the Kitsunetsuki Kingdom for well over nine centuries. If its people always regarded it as a place to fear, Prince Kitsune could not tell. What he knew for certain was that his father, King Oni, was a powerful man who deserved the fear and respect given unto him.

Kitsune shared in the people's reverence of King Oni of the Asher lineage. Common gossip claimed Oni's father fell in love with and married one of the beautiful Yokai spirits that purportedly inhabited the land around Inari Palace. While Kitsune doubted such spirits existed, he understood the mythology of his people's religious beliefs. The offspring of such a pairing manifested heightened intelligence and magical abilities that increased in complexity with age. The motives of such individuals were a mystery, and their agendas were unlike those of ordinary people. This allegedly stemmed from a lack of human morals.

No one ever witnessed King Oni displaying acts of magic, but his wisdom and cleverness were renowned beyond the borders of Kitsunetsuki, as were his skills in war and battle. During his reign, the king and his armies had waged two successful military campaigns, resulting in the conquering of the Mogo Empire to the south and the Ruio Territory to the northeast. Preparations for a third were supposedly underway. Kitsune desired more than anything to fight alongside his father this time around.

Whether from the constant state of warfare or the demands of ruling the vast and expanding domain, King Oni was a man rarely seen by even his closest advisors. As a child, Kitsune looked forward to his birthdays not for the presents, but because they were the rare days his father would present himself—assuming he was not leading the military elsewhere. As he matured, Kitsune saw the king less often. Now he only knew his father existed from the messages, requests, and gifts sent via servants.

Such remoteness did not temper Kitsune's admiration of his father. It only solidified his notion that the judicious and dutiful king was uniquely qualified to handle the many obligations of running the kingdom. Understanding that such responsibilities demanded considerable time, Kitsune willingly accepted his position in his father's life. Though they both lived within the palace, it had been well over a sun cycle since they'd seen each other face to face.

This was why it came as a surprise when Kitsune woke late one morning to a servant knocking on his chamber doors with a simple message: *King Oni demands your presence immediately.*

*

Kitsune sat patiently in an opulent chair. He was in a large, luxurious conference area, one of four flanking the Boleyn Room. After hurrying down the curved hallways of Inari Palace, his long hair and heavy cloak reluctantly trailing him, he was still a bit out of breath.

By design, the place did not feature a single straight passageway. The rooms, furniture, and decoration abided by the same scheme. Nearly everything had curvature, and one would be hard-pressed to find a straight line within the stronghold. Built as a circular, layered pyramid, its base covering a sprawling fifty acres. Rich, green gardens spread across the outside rim of its ten layers, and ancient trees cast long shadows over the outer walls. From a distance, the palace could easily be mistaken as a small mountain.

The first Kitsunetsuki monarch designed and began production of the colossal structure. It took nearly a hundred sun cycles to complete, and its final form dwarfed the great pyramids found in the tribal lands and Odom's enormous castle fortresses. The project nearly bankrupted the new kingdom three times, but Kitsune's ancestors struggled through to completion.

Many believed Inari Palace's circular nature was more practical than aesthetic and that its purpose was to help focus the magical properties of the area. Again, Kitsune doubted anything supernatural existed, but he could attest to the mystical, if not slightly unnatural, feeling that emanated from the location. With its open, shaded terraces overlooking leagues of beautiful vista in every direction, it was hard not to get lost in fantasy. Plus, though having existed for nearly a millennium, the structure had stood up against the tests of time. The mortar contained no cracks, and water never leaked from any ceiling. Inari Palace always looked like its pristine finished condition.

Deep within his home was the Boleyn Room, an enigmatic space taking up several stories at the building's center. It was such a puzzle because, in all of history, none but kings and queens ever went inside. Even trusted advisors or family were unable to give accurate descriptions of what lay within. The four ancillary areas bordering the isolated chamber was as far as anyone got, as they were where the rulers sought counsel, met with foreign diplomats, or dined with kin.

"Kitsune, my son," boomed a deep, authoritative voice that reverberated off the walls.

Startled, the prince jumped out of the chair, taking a defensive position. He turned to see the heavy wooden doors leading to the monarch's private room had opened without a sound. Golden light emanated from within, as though the sun itself was inside, and his father's commanding silhouette was within the frame.

Immediately dropping to one knee, Kitsune said, "My king."

A long silence followed, though the prince could feel his father's eyes analyzing him. Eventually, King Oni stood to one side of the doorframe and, gesturing inward, said, "Please join me."

"Sir?" Kitsune said, not understanding.

King Oni stood motionless, continuing to point inward. A hint of impatience flitted across his face.

Like anyone else, Kitsune had only imagined the interior of the Boleyn Room. He envisioned an elaborately decorated space with tapestries of deep purple hanging from the ceiling, an ornate throne nestled at the top of a long flight of stairs, and rows of tables on which the king would lay out his battle plans. The truth, he saw as he walked in, was far more mind-bending.

Shaped like an elongated oval, similar to an egg, the room's floor gradually descended to the center while the ceiling tapered with a narrower design. The rounded surface shone with a golden brilliance that only magnified the most marvelous feature of the chamber: dozens of shining orbs floating through the air, apparently of their own accord. Some smaller spheres whizzed around the confines of the room; some medium-size ones moved at a more lethargic pace. Near the ceiling, an orb of colossal size floated stationary. It reminded Kitsune of planetary models the palace scholars often tinkered with.

No grand throne or tables lay cluttered with battle preparations. The only decoration was a portrait of a woman wearing odd clothing. Kitsune had never seen her before, and he did not see a family resemblance. Otherwise, only a single desk and two chairs stood in the middle of the room. King Oni gestured toward one chair, indicating that Kitsune seat himself, then sat down in the other. The prince took his seat, watching the spinning orbs with wide-eyed wonder. He did not want one to knock him to the floor.

Kitsune supposed this to be powerful magic. That thought, and his willingness to accept it as an explanation for this phenomenon, was a sudden and forceful strike at the foundation of his personal beliefs.

The enormous depth of what changed for him in an instant was dumbfounding.

"Kitsune, my son," the king said again, though this time his voice did not bounce off the walls. "I have asked you here today to send you down a new path. Your destiny, your purpose in life, is unfolding before you."

The prince pushed the shock of seeing magic out of his mind, replacing it with dozens of new scenarios, each more exciting than the last. Was the king about to launch his next military campaign and, as Kitsune had been hoping, wanted him to partake? Perhaps he even wanted his son to lead the campaign in his stead, giving Kitsune the chance to impress his father. This did not explain why King Oni granted his son access to the Boleyn Room. Many kings of the past bestowed such honor on to their heirs without doing so. Was the king abdicating the throne, or was he dying, soon leaving the kingdom in Kitsune's hands? The prince dreaded that thought.

"Yes, my king?" Kitsune replied with as much calm as he could muster.

Then his father said something he had not anticipated. Reality was unlike any of his fantasies, and the king wasted no time in revealing it. "I am banishing you from Kitsunetsuki."

Kitsune gasped. "Banished?" He felt his spirit being crushed into a tiny point in his stomach. "But why?"

King Oni stiffened for a moment, not used to his orders being questioned. Indeed, this was the first time in Kitsune's life that he hesitated at his father's demands. Now, as the king again analyzed him in silence, the prince battled his desires to obey his father while yet remaining near him.

"You are the strongest son born of an Asher monarch," King Oni said at last. "You have bested my most talented soldiers in arm-to-arm combat, dueling with a variety of weaponry, and in games of cunning. Your prowess may match—even exceed—my own, and I am most certain you have skills yet to learn. All this in such a diminutive body."

Kitsune wavered between pride and embarrassment at his father's comments. He spent as much of his adolescence studying all forms of combat as he did reading the volumes of books the scholars demanded he memorize. Having bested each of the military's generals, he could say he had outfoxed nearly all the kingdom's leaders, the exception being the king. Despite this and an honest effort to build muscle, the prince lacked the ideal chiseled male build. While not diminutive as the king described, Kitsune looked uncomfortably slender next to those he beat.

"I have given you every chance, opportunity, and even roadblock to help you become the finest ruler this kingdom has ever seen," the king went on. "I have sought the best teachers and trainers from even lands beyond the border of Kitsunetsuki so you would become strong and wise, leader of a force so vast you would eventually conquer those same lands. On top of this, I have showered you with gifts that would make a commoner satisfied for life."

With an imperceptible smile, Kitsune recalled his latest "gift," a pretty young lady he left behind in his bed.

"Despite everything," King Oni continued, "your one flaw is intolerable, and it is the reason you are being excommunicated immediately."

Even the hint of a smile disappeared from Kitsune's face, replaced by desperation and resoluteness. "What is my flaw, Father? Tell me, please, so I may remedy it."

Almost in a whisper, the king said, "The company you keep."

The prince sat still, frozen in his chair. His speechlessness was not due to shame but to confusion. Few cultures in the known world considered intimate relations with either a female or male abhorrent, and Kitsunetsuki was not among them. Kitsune was perfectly within normal social and legal constructs to invite anyone he desired to his rooms, many of whom had been men, and no one ever thought ill of him for doing so. No one except his father, apparently.

"I…I don't understand," he stuttered.

"I am on the verge of launching an assault on the lands of Gaav." The monarch reached out with one of his hands, summoning one of the golden orbs to him. He stared into it with a look so intense and emotionless, it sent a chill down Kitsune's spine. "Even before I dispose of their king, Marauxus, and annex Gaav into my kingdom, I will turn attention to the Kitsunetsuki code of law. It has not kept with the times, and it does not well reflect the current state and grandeur of this realm. My efforts will produce a more stable, peaceful, and economically sound dominion. Unfortunately, my son, your choices and actions do not align with what will soon become customary. I cannot in good conscience leave all of my work and my people in the hands of an individual with such a rebellious and unorthodox attitude."

Still unable to move, Kitsune hoped his face conveyed the same emotionless state King Oni's did, though his eyes stung with the threat of tears. He lived to serve his father, and now the king was rewriting the rules of society in such a manner that completely ousted him! While hating the juvenile feelings flooding through him, he was unable to keep from feeling helpless about the unfairness of those actions.

"The world is always evolving around us, impartial to the lives it affects," King Oni said as though reading Kitsune's mind. While staring from across the table, he continued, "I used to think life hated me, too. After all, your mother bore me you, then she promptly died. I've dealt with my lot, and so will you. It would please me if you would leave without any commotion."

Kitsune gulped, finding it harder to keep his composure after the clout of such harsh words. Both his head and heart pounded heavily, and the emotions boiling inside him clashed with the peaceful nature of the golden floating orbs in the room. "When do I go?"

"You leave immediately. There's a unit of soldiers waiting just outside. They will accompany you to your rooms, where you will gather whatever you need, then travel with you to the border. From there, you will be on your own." The light in King Oni's eyes gleamed brightly, and he suddenly seemed to take an interest in what he was saying. "I have not yet entirely given up on you, Kitsune. You should know there is a way to reclaim your future. There is one thing you can do to make me proud to call you my son."

Kitsune blurted out the question: "What must I do?" He would wholeheartedly focus on proving his worthiness to his father. His life need not be turned upside down.

The king gave a broad smile, revealing pearly white teeth. It may have been the first time Kitsune saw a genuine smile on his father's face.

"King Marauxus has successfully led Gaav for nearly twenty sun cycles, though I dare say this feat is not because of his own health or cunning. Rather, I believe it is Marauxus' son who is chiefly responsible for any of Gaav's achievements, whether it be militarily, economically, or socially."

Kitsune racked his brain for any information he had on King Marauxus and his son. While he studied the Kingdom of Gaav and was well-versed in Marauxus' victorious and celebrated reign, he could not recall anything about his son. He found this puzzling, for he remembered the queen had borne a daughter. Why would he remember one and not the other?

"I believe Marauxus' son is possessed by magic," King Oni said, interrupting the prince's thoughts. "It is for this reason I surmise Gaav's king has enjoyed so much success over many sun cycles and would explain why they have kept his existence a secret. The son stands guard over the father, keeping him safe and healthy, covertly directing the armies, wielding the magic possessing him for their own benefit."

A spirit of jealousy danced its way across Kitsune's mind. While he spent his entire life studying and training, another prince was experiencing family dynamics to a degree he had only fantasized. It wasn't in his nature to loathe others. Under the circumstances, however, he allowed himself this concession.

"You want me to kill the son of King Marauxus," he guessed.

"Only with him removed from this plane of existence will I have a chance of conquering Gaav," King Oni confirmed. "With the son removed, the father will become weak and vulnerable. The people will lose faith and possibly depose him themselves.

"So tell me now, my son. Will you undertake this mission?"

Kitsune had only to consider his options for a moment. Either be extradited from the Kitsunetsuki Kingdom, forever removed from his life and heritage, or displaced until he completed one task. He bowed before his father and said, "I shall succeed, my king, or I will die trying."

*

King Oni dismissed Kitsune from his isolated chamber without so much as a handshake or farewell. True to his word, an armed guard of twelve men waited for the prince just outside. Their captain was Saxma, a burly young man who had made a name for himself by rising quickly through the military ranks, led them. With Saxma at the lead, the group of guards guided Kitsune back to his rooms, four walking in front of him, four behind, and two at each side, as though making sure he wouldn't take flight.

Though he had no intention of attempting an escape, Kitsune was confident he could take the twelve by surprise. He might render four of them unconscious before the other eight realized what was happening, by which time he would be dashing down the hallway, slipping into one of the many secret passages plaguing the design of Inari Palace. As his father rarely allowed him to leave the palace, the complex was an extension of his physical self. Few knew its design better than he, especially now that he had been in the Boleyn Room. If he so desired, he could disappear within a few heartbeats.

Such actions, however, would not please his father.

Kitsune walked as slowly as Saxma and the guards would allow him, resolute in spending as much remaining time as possible here. Determined as he was to carry out his new task and reverse his banishment, he was reluctant to leave his home. He always knew his life would take him beyond the borders of the kingdom, but he had imagined being surrounded by comrades, hell-bent on a glorious cause. Instead, he was being forced out into a world he had never experienced, alone and rejected.

Despite his sluggishness, the group traversed the curved halls, climbing up to the prince's apartment on the eighth floor. It was a comfortable and luxurious suite comprising seven large, high-ceilinged rooms. Draperies of deep colors hung from the ceiling, covering the stone walls and splashing out onto the floor. If his spirit wasn't so restless, he could easily spend days locked away in there, basking in the glorious fact that he really had nothing to do.

Captain Saxma brought the group to a halt at the doors to Kitsune's rooms. The leader turned toward the prince, a strange smile on his face. Something about it chased away Kitsune's thoughts of his predicament and sharpened his focus on the present. He watched as the captain strode toward him with an irritating air of smugness.

Over the past few sun cycles, it had become an unofficial tradition for those being considered for promotion to challenge Prince Kitsune to a duel. While there stood little hope for winning such a skirmish, the goal was to last as long as possible. Saxma issued such a challenge before his promotion to captain. He fought well but did not come close to the record of forty-two resting heartbeats. Perhaps because Kitsune knocked his personal pride down a notch, Saxma issued a different and private challenge to the prince, one which took place on the other side of the doors in front of which they currently stood. He lost that challenge as well, though. Kitsune had enjoyed the duel immensely.

It occurred to Kitsune that Saxma might believe his perceived loss of pride negated by Kitsune's own indictment.

"My prince," Saxma said, his voice dripping with self-satisfaction. "You have exactly two tics to gather whatever you will need to survive your exile."

"Excuse me?" Kitsune asked, stunned by Saxma's statement.

"You have just under two tics to gather your things. After that, we will promptly begin our journey to the border." Captain Saxma turned toward the doors with a gesture that said Kitsune should enter, though Kitsune guessed the movement was really to show off the deadly sword attached to his belt.

The rest of the guards were now tense and alert, their hands inching closer to their own weapons.

"This is ridiculous," Kitsune muttered. He reached into one of his pockets, withdrawing a heavy key. Once the entrance was unlocked, he walked purposefully inside. No reason to stop and think about what he needed. Not only did his lessons teach him about the necessities of survival, but he often fantasized about being alone in the wild. He knew exactly what to collect.

The soldiers, pathetically small compared to the height and breadth of the rooms, streamed in alongside Kitsune. They watched his every move as he marched to his bedroom. The girl with whom he had spent the night was still in bed, and she squealed in surprise and covered herself as several men walked in and stood guard. She looked to the prince with frightened confusion, but he ignored her as he opened his closet and began removing items. Among them were a change of clothes, a traveling cloak, and a backpack to stash them in.

"One tic!" the captain called from the other room.

Kitsune cursed. He grabbed an emerald-studded silver chain off the nightstand, then ran out of the room. In the kitchen, he took only a loaf of bread, a hunk of cheese, and a glass flask of water. He would have preferred a canteen, but there was only enough time to find the last items he'd need.

Back in the entryway, his sword, a bow, and a quiver full of arrows hung on the wall. The weapons were not prominently displayed out of pride. Rather, it was an efficient place to grab them for a quick exit.

Kitsune was just gathering everything together when Saxma announced, "Your time is up, my prince. There's one more thing we must do before we leave."

Turning to the captain, Kitsune found the man was still wearing the smirk on his face as he ushered his soldiers back out into the palace hallway. They hurried to comply, their weapons clinking as they rushed out. When the last one exited, Saxma closed the door.

"What remains to be done?" the prince demanded, annoyed.

Saxma reached deep into his cloak and pulled out a persuader, a newer weapon that shot pellets or darts with the squeeze of a trigger. He pointed it at Kitsune and, without hesitation, shot him in the chest.

Kitsune stood still for several moments, his mouth opening in a silent scream. The sword and backpack slipped from his hands and clattered to the floor. Then his eyes failed him, and he crumpled to the ground unconscious.

BANISHMENT

Kitsune's ears rang, accompanied by an indistinct jumble of whispers, wind, and the hooves of horses. He perceived a dim light from behind closed eyelids. Sunlight warmed his face, and he knew it was around midday.

The prince felt like he was awakening from a midafternoon nap on one of the palace's shaded terraces. He would often doze off there after a hard morning workout and a good lunch. There was something different this time, though. His body hurt terribly, a result of being uncomfortably positioned.

Kitsune made to yawn, trying to shake the cobwebs from his mind. It was the surprising fact that he could barely open his mouth, much less breathe through it, that made his eyes snap open in alarm. If his lips had been clear of obstruction, he would have cried out in disbelief of his situation.

Since being in his rooms, where he vaguely remembered being shot, someone had stripped him naked and placed him upon a black horse. Cold metal shackles bound his forearms behind his back and connected his ankles by a chain running underneath the animal. A special mud the people called pakt covered the lower part of his face. Convicts and prisoners of war were often fully coated with pakt as a form of imprisonment, for once it hardened and dried, not even the strongest were able to break free without assistance. It was now drying over Kitsune's mouth, refusing to budge to his straining jaw.

Twelve horses, each ridden by a member of his armed guard, surrounded Kitsune and his mount. Captain Saxma led the group, and they all looked stoically forward as they traversed the cobblestone streets of Oinari, the capital city of Kitsunetsuki surrounding Inari Palace. Kitsune flushed with embarrassment as curious villagers, few at first, lined the streets, whispering questions to one another. More seemed to appear with every heartbeat, drawn by the increasing commotion. They poured out from their homes and shops and came in from tending their fields and gardens to stare at their prince, bound and silenced on a black horse like a common criminal. Their eyes filled with querying looks, pity—and, for a few, scorn.

Kitsune screamed for help and struggled against his restraints. The pakt halted his voice; the heavy chains hardly noticed his flexed muscles. Despite his best efforts not to become emotional, tears began to well up in his eyes as he looked pleadingly at the mobs. Nobody came to his aid, though. Such humiliation was a punishment reserved for the most heinous fiends found in the lands of Kitsunetsuki, people proven guilty of horrendous deeds. He was being forced to endure it, and they had no reason to doubt he deserved it.

The troupe made its way unhurriedly through the main streets of the capital, Saxma in no way attempting to avoid crowds. If anything, he seemed to want every man, woman, and child drawn out as witnesses. At points, the horsemen would be at a standstill among the people as they clamored inquisitively for answers. The soldiers had to block the masses as they tried to reach Kitsune, though they made no effort to stop the tomatoes that occasionally came hurdling toward him. It wasn't long before the sickly-sweet juices covered his body.

As the sun began its long journey toward the horizon, Kitsune tired of struggling against his bonds. Instead of wasting more energy, he concentrated on avoiding the fruits and vegetables. As he ducked and maneuvered in his limited capacity, he thought of only two things:

the motives behind Saxma's actions and King Oni's anger when he found out about them.

On the surface, Kitsune's current state appeared to be the captain's continued retribution. As though expediting his departure from the palace and belittling him in front of the other soldiers was not enough for the resentful man, Saxma was now multiplying Kitsune's disgrace by parading him around the city like a criminal. If this was true, it was a little heavy-handed after being fairly beaten twice!

As Kitsune thought about it more, though, he concluded that it made little sense for Saxma to initiate this punishment on his own. Once the king learned of it, the reprimand would be severe. There was a reason the monarch was so feared by his subjects. Saxma appeared to be ignoring the obvious consequences of his handling of Kitsune, which meant the actions themselves were purely emotional, lacking rational thought. This was not the way of Kitsunetsuki military officers.

Besides, if King Oni wanted this dramatic exit for Kitsune, the prince would have obliged. As always, he would gladly endure anything for his father. There had been no indication of such a desire during their earlier conversation, though, and Kitsune was skeptical he would have ordered this after the fact.

Before he drove himself mad attempting to solve the riddle, the group reached the main gate in the wall encompassing Oinari. Walled settlements were a long-held defensive strategy dating back to the kingdom's early days. Smaller villages had barriers made of wood, which made expansion easier. Larger cities commanded mason walls capable of repelling large armies. As the kingdom expanded, several kings started constructing walls encompassing the entire land. The results were haphazard, but the completed areas often incorporated the natural environment, such as mountains and rivers.

A gatekeeper manned each entrance of every wall in the kingdom. By tradition, this person allowed or denied passage through his or her gate. It was a powerful position. With it came the responsibility of granting only fellow citizens, traders, and diplomats access while keeping marauders out. One wrong decision had the potential to devastate a community. Gatekeepers commanded a large compensation, and the kingdom gladly paid. Villagers appreciated their watchful eyes and needed to keep them from being easily bribed by invading parties.

Saxma called out to the man who stood atop Oinari's wall. "Gatekeeper! I, Captain Saxma of the Kitsunetsuki military, led by the wise and powerful King Oni, request permission to exit the city so I may carry out my sworn duties."

The gatekeeper, a well-tanned, middle-aged man, stared down at the armed guard. With the sun behind him, it was difficult for Kitsune to read his expression. He seemed to consider their request for several heartbeats, but he was also conscious of the throngs of people around the troupe.

"I have watched as you paraded through the streets," the gatekeeper finally said in a deep, powerful voice. "I will grant you permission to leave Oinari, but you must first explain these sworn duties you speak of."

Many had asked similar questions over the past few hours as Captain Saxma and his men made their way through town. The troupe ignored all the inquiries. Kitsune had wondered why, as Saxma had a chance to create any story to further the prince's disgrace. The answer was now plain. An audience of hundreds of people, all silent and hungrily waiting for an answer, surrounded them.

"My orders were from King Oni himself, and they were quite clear. I am to escort this man to the Eastern Gate of Kitsunetsuki," Saxma declared, pointing to Kitsune, who flushed red. "He is now an exile."

"Prince Kitsune, an exile?" the gatekeeper said in surprise. It was abnormal for a member of the royal family—anyone, actually—to be trussed up on a horse. He seemed hesitant. "Forgive my impertinence, but I must inquire about his wrongdoing."

Saxma put a grim expression on his face. "I would like to know myself, gatekeeper, but it was not my place to question our king's orders. I dare say it must have been vile to deserve such punishment. There have been rumors within the walls of the palace, of course, but I would not relay such stories for fear of hearsay."

Murmurs erupted among the crowd, but the gatekeeper silenced them with a grunt from atop his wall. He crossed his arms, looking back and forth between Kitsune and Saxma. Kitsune recognized he, sitting naked and bound atop the black horse, must appear incredibly guilty of whatever rumored crimes anyone conjured up. Especially next to Saxma, who appeared sincere and respectable.

"I realize my answers are few and light," Saxma continued. "All I ask is that you open the gates so I may complete my assignment. However, if you seek the full truth of the situation, King Oni will address the people of Oinari from the palace grounds tonight."

The people burst into conversation again. King Oni had not addressed the public in person since the day he ascended the throne, choosing instead to speak through intermediaries.

The gatekeeper stared silently at Kitsune. Though the sun still obscured the man's expression, the prince perceived he was deliberating on the right and just course of action. Finally, ignoring Kitsune's pleading eyes, he said, "I reluctantly grant you permission. May the spirits bless your journey. We await your return." To Kitsune, he added, "May you survive your punishment beyond the borders of this kingdom."

The man disappeared inside a small enclosure atop the wall. A moment later a loud, rhythmic clicking noise sounded, and the gates opened. Saxma, squeezing the sides of his horse, led the soldiers through the opening at full gallop, Kitsune in tow.

Once outside the walls of Oinari, the group rode for nearly an hour. The path they traveled on turned east, taking them through rolling hills of green grass and fields of wheat and corn. Every once in a while, they would pass up a traveling band or a farmer, each of whom would cast curious looks but wouldn't say a word. No one questioned the king's men.

Kitsune, unable to handle the reins of his horse, squeezed his mount with his legs just to keep balanced. This, in turn, only made the black horse move faster, and he squeezed even harder just to stay atop. Before long, his muscles burned from exhaustion.

Just as the sun reached the horizon, they came upon a structure so foreign and unlike anything Kitsune had ever seen that at first he thought he was hallucinating. The building was famous, though, so he recognized it from descriptions passed on to him. It was two stories tall and constructed entirely of smooth, dark gray metal. With no windows or visible means of entrance, it looked like a giant cube. Against the green hills and blue sky, it was more than out of place. It demanded attention. The building's creators had obviously not meant to conceal it, but its purpose and origin were complete mysteries. The same went for its contents. Though scientists had studied it for over a hundred sun cycles, the thing was impenetrable.

Captain Saxma brought his steed to a halt and ordered everyone to make camp between the building and the road. Kitsune watched as the eleven other men scurried about, making four fires and rolling out sleeping blankets. They constructed a small tent for Saxma, one of the few commodities for a ranking officer on the move.

Once the group completed setting up camp and a patrol schedule worked out, one soldier approached Kitsune. He had a nervous, unsure demeanor as he removed the bindings from Kitsune's wrists and ankles.

Sliding off the horse, the prince successfully landed on his two feet. His fatigued legs immediately gave out, and he fell to the ground. The key holder gave an apologetic shrug and helped him to his feet just as Saxma approached.

The captain carried a large bundle in his hands. Kitsune couldn't identify it at first in the fading light, but then realized it was his backpack. More interesting, though, was Saxma's right hand, encased in a metal glove.

With a signal from his captain to move aside, the soldier let go of Kitsune. The prince wavered uncertainly, his legs threatening to give out again. He placed a steadying hand against his horse, determined not to fall.

Saxma stopped just two steps from Kitsune, giving him a quick look over. With a sneer, he threw the backpack to the ground by Kitsune's feet. "Pathetic." Then, with his gloved right hand, he punched Kitsune square in the face.

The pakt enclosing the prince's mouth shattered into thousands of tiny shards under the force of Saxma's metal-enclosed fist. Momentarily stunned by the impact, Kitsune fell over on his side. This time he stayed on the ground, crouched, alert, and ready to spring. He waited for Saxma to make the next move.

It seemed releasing Kitsune of the pakt was Saxma's only violent strike, though by the smirk he continued to wear, leaving his face a bloody mess in its wake was a bonus. Instead of moving to attack again, he pointed to Kitsune's backpack and said, "Dress yourself, then rest. We have a long day of travel tomorrow." Then, to the soldier who was standing off to the side, "Keep an eye on him."

As the captain turned and swept away, Kitsune reached for his bag. With the exceptions of his sword and bow, he accounted for the few items he grabbed from his rooms. He hoped Saxma would return his weapons at the Eastern Gate.

"Do you mind?" he snapped at the soldier, pulling his clothes out of the backpack. The man blushed, muttered an apology, and turned around as Kitsune dressed.

Once fully clad, Kitsune pulled the traveling cloak out of the bag. He doubted the soldiers brought an extra set of sleeping blankets for him, so he'd need it to fight off the chilly night air. Without the bulk of his clothing, the bag was light. All that remained was the food, water, and silver chain. Kitsune gently removed the latter, staring transfixed at the emeralds. He was only vaguely aware that his guard had begun talking.

"My prince, I know today must have come as a terrible shock to you—and you have every right to think of us with nothing but contempt—but I wish to convey that you still have the respect of most of the men here, including my own. If we were not bound by oath to King Oni, we would support and follow you." The soldier paused, waiting for a response. After receiving none, he turned back around, saying, "Prince Kitsune, are you still—"

The soldier stopped midsentence and, like Kitsune, stood mesmerized by the silver chain. The gems, intricately crafted into the piece of jewelry, glowed green.

"What was your name again?" Kitsune asked the guard, pulling himself out of his reverie.

"Hmm?" responded the other, struggling to take his eyes from the glowing emeralds. "Oh, my name is Mamori, sir."

"Well, Mamori," Kitsune said, fastening the chain around his own neck, carefully hiding the stones beneath his shirt. "I would ask that you tell no one about this."

"Certainly," Mamori replied, bowing his head. "May I ask what it means?"

"I don't know. It's never happened before."

The two were silent for a few moments while Kitsune secured his backpack over his shoulder. Then, looking about, he said, "So if most of the other men still respect me, they wouldn't mind if I slept by a fire?"

Mamori's eyes lit up like those of a child who had found cake. "They'd be honored! Well, most of them would be." He looked at each of the fires, analyzing which soldiers had grouped together, then led Kitsune to the one farthest from Captain Saxma's tent.

Three soldiers sat by the fire. They looked up as Kitsune and Mamori approached. A wave of excitement swept silently but palpably through them, and they got to their feet to welcome the prince. Two looked around nervously like mischievous school children keeping an eye out for teachers.

"My friends," Mamori said. "Prince Kitsune asks if he could join us by the fire for the night."

All three replied in a garbled mess of acceptances, jumping up to move their sleeping blankets around so he'd have a premium spot by the flames. Upon noticing Kitsune did not have any blankets of his own, one soldier insisted that the prince use his.

"Unnecessary, I assure you," Kitsune said. "But I am most grateful for your making room for me. My cloak will provide all the extra warmth and comfort I require."

As Kitsune set about spreading his cloak across the grass, he was acutely aware the four soldiers followed his every move. Their expressions were not of distrust and wariness, but rather of shame and fear. They were probably afraid he'd pull a weapon and exact revenge for their actions against him.

Once finished, Kitsune sat down, pulling the loaf of bread and cheese from his bag. He tore off conservative chunks from each and began to eat. The other four gradually calmed down as he chewed and sat with him. The ones he hadn't met introduced themselves as Nasuno, Tsuzumi, and Pan, and they immediately began asking questions regarding Kitsune's banishment. He replied honestly, retelling the morning's events.

"What do you suppose this all means?" Nasuno said, pulling a flask from beneath his uniform. With a quick glance around, he unscrewed the top and took a swig. "I mean, in the greater scheme of things."

"I'm not sure," Kitsune replied, which was how he answered a lot of their questions. He suspected there was much about which he was ignorant. How well could one understand a father or king when he had only the rarest of contact with him? The prince had not a clue his father was so opposed to relations between members of the same sex that he'd declare it illegal. "I don't know why the king would consider the kingdom's edicts and ethics to be outdated."

"I can understand trying to standardize laws throughout all the lands he's conquered," chimed in Tsuzumi. "But to condemn lifestyles that cultures have accepted everywhere for hundreds of sun cycles? Next, he'll be outlawing the eating of bread, walking on streets, or sex with women!"

"Like you could ever make it with a woman," Mamori joked, accepting the flask from Nasuno. He took a guarded drink, then passed it on.

Looking up at the dark sky, Kitsune said, "The king has either addressed the people of Oinari or is doing so now. Perhaps you will learn more of the details when you return."

Everyone remained silent for a moment, all knowing such revelations would not help the prince.

Pan, who had until now remained quiet, looked up at Kitsune. He was a small man for a soldier, and a few swigs from the flask loosened him up. "My prince, could you reveal to us what occurred after Captain Saxma dismissed us all from your rooms? You were in there for quite some time before the captain emerged, dragging you out in a rather, umm, bare state."

"I wish I knew," Kitsune said, looking down in uncertainty and indignity. He had a feeling—a mixture of intuition and a physical stirring in his gut—that Saxma had done unto him exactly what Kitsune once performed. "He tranquilized me with a persuader as soon as you all left. I didn't awaken until I was atop the horse being led through Oinari."

The four men didn't push for more information, opting instead for lighter conversation and a few drinks. Pan refrained from consuming any more, eventually getting up and taking his scheduled patrol shift.

"What do you think this building is?" Nasuno said, slurring his words a bit. The structure loomed above them a mere twenty steps away, a dark mass against the stars in the sky. "Anything the royal family knows that the rest of us folk don't?"

With a shrug, Kitsune responded, "If there is, I'm not privy to it."

"I've heard it's a relic from those who used to live in the Wastelands," Tsuzumi added. "You know…back before it was so wasted."

Kitsune, exhausted from the day's activities and unable to even feign interest in the conversation, began nodding off to sleep. He only just registered that they were trading theories concerning the metal building, each of which he had heard before. The last thing Kitsune remembered before slipping into unconsciousness was Mamori's declaration that he would stand guard over their fire in case another member of the troupe—someone with a different sentiment toward the prince—attempted an attack during the night.

THE EASTERN GATE

The night hours slipped by and the sun began its ascent far earlier than Kitsune would have liked. Even though Mamori had kept the fire stoked, the prince could see his breath in the chilled morning air as he emerged from under his cloak.

"Here you go," said the soldier, kneeling down and handing him a cup of hot coffee. Mamori looked as though he had kept his promise to watch over their small encampment all night. Dark circles ringed his eyes, and his head hung a little lower than the previous evening.

"You had some yourself, yes?" Kitsune offered the mug back.

Mamori barked a laugh. "I've drunk enough coffee in the last hour to piss this fire out of existence! Drink up, my prince. There's a long day of riding ahead of us. Captain thinks we can reach the border around nightfall. I don't believe he wants you as his charge any longer than necessary."

"The feeling is mutual," Kitsune said under his breath. He sipped his coffee, far more bitter than the variety he was used to, while watching the soldiers bustle about breaking camp. It wasn't long before one of them called the prince to mount the black horse again. He obliged, grabbing his pack.

That day's ride passed by uneventfully. They continued to travel southeasterly toward the Argent Mountains. The range ran southwest of their current position to the northeast, comprising the entire eastern border of Kitsunetsuki's lands. Two particular mountains, the peaks of which Kitsune had probably seen from the upper balconies of Inari Palace, grew ever loftier as the group neared.

The road upon which they trod eventually met up and ran alongside the Rout River, a wide waterway flowing from the unexplored territories of the far north down to the ocean on the southern side of the mountains. Both the road and the river had once been major trade and travel throughways between Kitsunetsuki and Odom, a kingdom that lay to the east. As Kitsune understood it, Odom slowed their trading when King Oni attacked Mogo, and they ceased most of their operations by the time Kitsunetsuki absorbed Ruio. Now the road was desolate and overgrown, used only by the occasional traveling band and soldiers.

Kitsune pondered his plan of action throughout the day. If they made it to the Eastern Gate by dusk—which at their pace seemed more than likely—he doubted Saxma would let him make camp with the troupe that night. The captain would instead opt to complete the primary objective as soon as possible, forcing Kitsune to find his own shelter. A glance skyward highlighted the importance of finding good cover. He knew weather varied dramatically around mountain ranges, but darkening clouds told him rain was imminent.

The next morning would be the beginning of his trek through Odom. It would be slow going, but he figured if he stuck as close to the mountains as he could and pushed the horse just short of exhaustion, he'd reach the Wastelands, a region forming the northeastern border of his homeland, in approximately ten days. The Argent Mountain range also ended at that point, so he'd then be able to travel due west. In time, he'd eventually come to the tribal lands, where he'd head southwest until he at last came to the Kingdom of Gaav, which lay on the opposite side of Kitsunetsuki. Then the truly hard part would begin: He'd have to hunt down and kill the son of Marauxus.

Despite increasingly gusty winds and a sky growing gloomier, the group made good time. It was barely evening when they came into view of the Eastern Gate. More a colossal wall than a gate, it completely overshadowed Onger, a small village that had once been a prosperous trade hub between Kitsunetsuki and Odom. The old settlement was now mostly a collection of dilapidated buildings. The few actively maintained structures functioned as garrisons for the military units stationed there. A tall stone tower was in the middle of construction by the gate, an odd sight among the otherwise weathered surroundings.

The gate itself, while perhaps not the shining splendor it once was, loomed nearly fifty footfalls in the air. Made of a combination of wood, stone, and metal, it stretched across the nearly thousand-step gap between two mountains, which included land and the roaring Rout. Metal bars had been ground into the riverbed beneath the wall, allowing the water to flow freely while making it impossible for anything larger than a fish to pass through.

The rocky slope of the southern mountain, which towered above the gate, had weathered and eroded into the recognizable silhouette of a human. Travelers could easily discern within the landscape a woman's face, hair, shoulders, and chest. Referred to as the Lady of the Mountain, she appeared to be lying back, sleeping peacefully. Stories alleged a traveling lady giant rested against the mountain, crushing a magnificent castle that stood there for hundreds of sun cycles, and had yet to awaken.

In keeping with tradition, the Eastern Gate's gatekeeper was technically not of the military. Still, the king tasked him with protecting his lands. This included keeping the wall closed to foreigners and expelling those who spent their lives delving into mischief and ill purpose. Perhaps because of the sheer magnitude of what he kept safe—an entire country rather than just a city—he was less thoughtful and forgiving than his Oinari counterpart.

"Open the gate!" the man barked from atop the wall after Saxma gave him the particulars on Kitsune's banishment. It hadn't mattered that it was a member of the royal family being thrown out. To the gatekeeper, Kitsune was but a cancer needing to be excised.

Gears, rusty with disuse, began to grind, and the gate opened just a crack. One of Saxma's subordinates came up beside Kitsune, grabbing the horse's reins from him.

"I don't even get to bring the horse?" Kitsune scoffed in disbelief. Though the black steed was a mark of humiliation, he had grown fond of it over the past two days. Without the mount, it would take so much longer to get to Gaav.

After being motioned to get off the horse, Kitsune hopped down, adjusting his backpack so he could carry his sword and bow. He saw that his entourage of guards, most of them still atop their mounts, had lined up alongside the road leading to the gate. Additionally, dozens of the men and women stationed in Onger joined the line, watching with interest. Saxma was at the front, closest to the gate, probably wanting to be the last person Kitsune saw before leaving his homeland.

Though the prince did not desire to step through the barrier, he wanted even more to cease being a spectacle to others. He hurried to the crack in the gate, subtly waving goodbye to Nasuno, Tsuzumi, and Pan. Mamori was nowhere in sight.

"What do you think you are doing?" Captain Saxma shouted from atop his horse, making Kitsune jump.

Kitsune looked up toward his nemesis, wondering what final degradation was in store for him. Surprisingly, Saxma was not targeting him. The prince turned and saw Mamori pushing his way through the line of horses and men. A traveling pack was slung over his shoulder.

"I'm accompanying him," Mamori stated.

Kitsune wanted to object, but Saxma beat him to it. "You swore an oath, soldier!"

"I am bound by oath to protect the king and his family," Mamori shouted back so everyone, including the gatekeeper, could hear. "In turn, the king's duty is to protect his people! In my eyes, King Oni is failing to do that. Whatever this man here is, whatever he has done, he is still my prince, and he will need protection outside of this realm."

"I should have you hanged here and now!" Saxma barked, his face red with anger. He moved as though he were about to give that order. Then a thought seemed to occur to him, and a cruel smile crept across his face. "That would be a mercy, though. I'll let the good folk of Odom do that for me. Besides, your prince might enjoy your company."

Kitsune's face grew hot with anger at what Saxma implied with sarcasm. He forced himself to calm down and, in doing so, questioned Saxma's previous remark. Why would the Odoms hang them? Even though they had been the ones to cease trading with Kitsunetsuki, they still sent emissaries from time to time. Kitsune never attended a diplomatic function, but he wasn't aware of a growing animosity toward the royal family, especially himself.

With his shoulders squared, Kitsune marched toward the gate. Despite the appearance of his dirty cloak and matted hair, he hoped to pull off a confident and dignified exit. He locked eyes with Saxma. "I will see you again."

"No, you won't," Saxma muttered, shaking his head and looking smug.

Looking back one last time, Kitsune took in the village of Onger, the surrounding mountains, and the rolling hills in the distant west. It was beautifully green, rich land. Even if it hadn't been, it was his home. Before his emotions got the better of him, he marched through the crack. Mamori, not used to being the target of accusing stares and jeers, stepped through. There was an ear-wrenching mechanical clanking sound, and the gate swung shut behind them.

As the sun had already reached the horizon in the west, it was far darker on this side of the high wall. Instinctively expecting it to be cooler, too, it surprised him when a wave of heat washed over his body. A cursory glance at their surroundings revealed why.

Rhinecourt, Odom's sister village to Onger, would not be providing any shelter to them that night—a fire had burned it to the ground. Where once stood homes, markets, barracks, and a town hall were now piles of ash and charred wooden fragments. Embers still glowed from within the piles, and pillars of smoke rose and dissipated into the sky, revealing the fire had been recent.

"Do you think there might be survivors?" Kitsune asked, squinting.

With a sad shake of his head, Mamori said, "This place was abandoned sun cycles ago."

The soldier urged Kitsune forward down the main concourse, littered with debris, all the while glancing upward. Large storm clouds gathered over the looming head of the Lady of the Mountain. The wind became more aggressive, blowing acrid smoke into their eyes. Water droplets, arriving too late to save the village, pelted their faces.

"My prince, we must find shelter. It is unwise to be walking about in this poor light and weather, and these ruins are inhospitable. It's too likely you'll twist an ankle or worse."

"Or yourself," Kitsune said defensively. He wanted to add more, but the air was making his lungs burn. They each pulled their cloaks over their noses and mouths to filter out the smoke, continuing to make their way through the burnt remains of Rhinecourt.

The town was not large, and only a few blocks remained to traverse before they were in the clear. Still, it was slow going. Piles of ash hid charred logs easy to trip over, and hot embers threatened to burn through the soles of their shoes. The wind continued to pick up smoke and dust despite the rain, reducing visibility.

Finally past the borders of the abandoned settlement, they got their first good view of what lay before them. The Rout River continued on, dumping into the distant ocean. It was Kitsune's first glimpse of such a large body of water, and it was an awesome view even in the fading light.

Against the southern mountain on the other side of the Rout, Kitsune saw a collection of boulders that could provide enough shelter from the wind to build a campfire. A bridge, miraculously intact, crossed the river a short walk from their current location.

As they strode toward the overpass, Kitsune's mind cleared. Able to focus, he asked the questions he hadn't a chance to earlier. "Why did you come with me, Mamori? Why would you choose this path?"

"You are my prince," the soldier stated, wiping soot from his face. "It is my duty to protect you."

"I've been banished from our land, meaning my titles and rights have been stripped away. I am no more deserving of your services than any other citizen of Kitsunetsuki, and your oath does not dictate such action."

"The banishment of a royal is unprecedented," Mamori said. "There is no actual protocol for it, just as there is no protocol for taking away what intrinsically defines a prince. In the past, heirs have tried to sidestep ascension to the throne or even abdicate. However, they could not escape what they were born into, and I believe the same applies to you. So no, I do not think your banishment negates my duty to you."

"Were you paying attention when I explained everything last night?" Kitsune argued. "I was banished because I have taken other men as partners. This is in direct conflict with the new statutes of the king, the very man you swore an oath to!"

Mamori shrugged. "My sister lives with another woman, and they are happy together. It is not for me to judge. It is not for anyone to do so, not even King Oni. It is a part of who she is. A part of who you are. Intrinsic, like being a prince. That has been the sentiment of our people for ages. There is nothing wrong with it."

"You violated an order! You have forsaken your duty!" Kitsune exclaimed. He felt justified in his perplexity at Mamori's actions. Though the prince could have escaped and eluded his punishment, he strove to obey the monarch. That anyone would not do the same baffled him. "Just as you say a king or prince cannot escape what defines them, as a soldier, you are to follow the orders of your superiors. It doesn't matter what you consider to be right or wrong."

"I clearly don't make as excellent a soldier as I believed," Mamori said with a slight smile. "My prince, I did what I thought was right. Was it the best decision for either of us? I don't know, but I cannot go back now. Like yourself, I have been exiled for my actions."

Kitsune grunted his resignation to that fact, and the two of them walked alongside each other until they came to the base of the mountain. They spent some time examining the large boulders strewn about the ground before deciding to camp next to one that jutted upward at an angle, providing a modicum of protection against the wind and rain.

With more camping experience under his belt, Mamori concentrated on gathering wood and building a small fire. Kitsune rolled out the other's sleeping blankets and laid out their provisions for dinner, some salt pork Mamori managed to grab before crossing over into Odom. That would liven up Kitsune's bread and cheese.

Later, as they huddled by the fire, their stomachs grumbling for more food, Kitsune muttered, "There will be soon."

"Pardon me?" Mamori mumbled, leaning back and pulling his blankets over himself.

"You spoke earlier of your sister and her partner," Kitsune said, staring into the flames. "That neither you nor the rest of the kingdom finds anything wrong with them. Though I do not yet comprehend the king's reasoning behind enacting new laws, he will do so soon. Once done, your sister must change her ways to avoid the consequences."

No response came from the soldier, and Kitsune knew he had fallen asleep.

"There will be soon," he repeated with a remorseful sigh. He wondered if this was what his life was to be from now on. Was he doomed to roam the lands, regretting his nature and loathing himself? Would he fall asleep each night by a new fire to the memory of his father looking at him in disdain, pointing out his one flaw and how the kingdom would not tolerate it?

As he rolled over, bundling himself in his blankets, Kitsune rejected that fate. He decided he would change his ways, intrinsic or not. Like Mamori's sister and countless others would eventually have to do, he would adapt to the new expectations. He would do that, and he would kill Marauxus' son. Then he would be living up to what his princely position demanded of him, and his father would welcome him back.

THE LADY OF THE MOUNTAIN

Even as he slept, Kitsune felt the rain splashing against his cheeks and the cold seeping its way toward his bones. The pitiful fire Mamori had somehow mustered earlier was now a soggy pile of ash. His cloak, wrapped around his frame, provided little protection against the elements. Though asleep, he was miserable.

Kitsune's dreams were similarly mocking. The vast ocean by which he camped threw its body against the shores, the spraying mists hissing in his ears. As his unconscious mind watched the tumultuous waters churn, he saw water droplets weren't the only things falling back into the deep. At first, pebbles showered down upon the surface from the sky. Then chunks of rock began falling, displacing the water enough to cause additional waves.

A thunderous crack rang out from above Kitsune's position, as though lightning had jettisoned right out of the mountaintop. He leapt up just in time to see a great boulder tumble down the slope and crash into the ocean, causing a tidal wave that nearly reached his camp. Above him, sheets of similar giant rocks gave way and skidded into the ocean. It was dark and he couldn't be sure he was seeing correctly, but it looked as though even more material was breaking away from the mountain and drifting up into the sky.

The moon found a break in the rain clouds, illuminating the area just enough for Kitsune to understand. The massive silhouette of the Lady of the Mountain, as obscure as it was before, grew more defined as rock fragments fell away from its face and neck. Shoulders and arms appeared, bracing against the side of the mountain, pushing upward. Amid a deafening noise and a continual shower of stones, a chest, abdomen, and legs formed as the Lady disentangled herself from her rocky bed.

Kitsune stared into the sky in disbelief. The Lady of the Mountain was alive! She towered above him, taller than the mountains themselves. It was a sight that would have scattered entire armies, yet Kitsune could not tear his eyes away for even a moment.

The Lady's massive head angled downward, and Kitsune thought for a moment she was looking right at him. That would be impossible, though. He was but a speck of dust on the ground compared to her gargantuan size. He'd be less noticeable than the boulders strewn about the ground.

A blinding flash of green light, coupled with an explosive sound and concussion wave, knocked Kitsune off his feet. He hit the ground hard, his head bouncing off one of the many rocks littering the terrain. Stars danced in his eyes, and he shook his head to clear them. This he regretted at once. His head swam with pain and nausea nearly overwhelmed him.

While he waited for his vision to clear, Kitsune closed his eyes. He realized how quiet it had suddenly become. Boulders no longer smashed into the ground, and the crashing ocean waves had stilled.

Then he heard the approaching footsteps.

Instead of the crashing steps of the rock giant he expected, these footfalls were soft. Kitsune guessed by the sound that the owner was about his size or smaller, most likely female, and was graceful, sure of her footing.

Kitsune was still debating on whether he should pretend to be unconscious or if he should jump up defensively when a cool hand pressed down on his forehead. The pain in his head eased and the blinding stars in his vision subsided. He opened his eyes.

The Lady of the Mountain stood before him, looking down at him with an expectant look. No longer a rocky monstrosity, she was the most entrancing creature he ever set eyes upon. Thin, fit, and trim, he would have guessed she lived her life mostly outdoors. Her skin, however, was pale and flawless, showing no age or damage from nature. Long black hair, stick straight, fell wispily past her shoulders. She wore a dark green dress made of a light flowing material. It fluttered to the side in a warm breeze, showing her bare feet.

Kitsune stood up carefully. Once surefooted, he gave a small bow to the Lady, speechless.

The woman stared at him for a moment, looking as though she was examining him in ways he couldn't imagine. Then she returned his short bow and said, "My greetings to you. I assure you we are quite safe."

"You are certain? I suffered a blow to the head, but I am most certain you were a gigantic rock monster just moments ago."

"Please accept my apologies for the injury sustained by my previous form," the Lady said, bowing her head. "I have done my best to repair any damage."

Kitsune remembered her hand against his forehead and the pain disappearing.

"You have done me a great service," the Lady added, pushing forward. "I must ask, though, did you not come in search of me?"

"Pardon?" He scratched the back of his head in confusion, noticing no cuts or bruises. What had she meant by that? What had he done for her?

The Lady pointed at his neck. Kitsune moved his hand to his throat, his fingers brushing against the chain he wore. It felt warmer to the touch than usual.

"You carry a hoshi no tama."

"I do not!" Kitsune objected. "This was my mother's!"

"It is a hoshi no tama, and it is what has awoken me."

"You are of the Yokai?" he asked, surprising himself for voicing it.

"I am."

Kitsune was speechless. Yokai mythology was a major facet of Kitsunetsuki culture. Most everyone knew the recorded stories by heart and strove to live a life worthy of the respect of the Yokai. Kitsune had always regarded the mythology as just that. Here, though, right in front of him, was a living example of what his people revered, worshipped, and prayed to. She was real.

According to lore, the Yokai were mystical creatures. Despite being referred to as spirits, they were actually physical, intelligent beings, possessing magical abilities that increased with age and wisdom. Their natural form was like that of a fox, though literature claimed one of their powers was shape shifting. They purportedly enjoyed taking the form of humans, which backed the fanciful claim Kitsune's grandfather married a Yokai spirit.

Some animal forms, like a human, were ill-suited for the souls and magic of the Yokai. To deal with this, they stored a great portion of themselves in a hoshi no tama, jewels of colored fire. The owners of these precious stones kept them close, guarding them with their lives. Separation from one's soul and power for too long meant death. If another individual gained possession of a hoshi no tama, they held great sway over its Yokai.

"This chain awakened you?" Kitsune asked.

"It awoke what little of me remains. Any hoshi no tama would have saved me, but this was the first one to pass through these mountains in many sun cycles. I sensed it from leagues away, and I grew stronger the closer it got."

Kitsune found himself sitting by his fire, though now it was roaring with a renewed intensity and giving off a pleasant warmth. The surrounding devastation caused by the rockslide had completely disappeared. Another of the Yokai's myriad powers, he remembered, was the ability to manifest themselves within a person's consciousness in a kind of manipulated dreamscape. What occurred in these imaginary realms could or could not impact the physical world, depending on the desires and intentions of the individual Yokai.

"I'm still asleep, aren't I?"

"It was the only way of reaching out to you now that I can no longer take physical form," the Lady said apologetically. "Again, I thought you came for me."

"While my quest was not to awaken you, I am glad it brought me here to end your slumber." Remembering himself, he said, "My name is Kitsune."

The Lady of the Mountain appeared to look inward for a moment, then a troubled expression crossed her face. "I have been without a name for so long I cannot recollect how others referred to me. Alas, as I am no longer whole, there is not much I can remember. My memory is fragmented, and I can recall but pieces."

"Do you know how you came to this place? How you became a part of the mountain?"

The Lady's eyes blazed. "I can recall some specific details about that day. I can relay them for you, if you care to hear. It shouldn't take long to recount, and there are still a few hours left in the night."

Kitsune leaned back against a rock, settling in and getting comfortable. "Please, do tell."

*

It was early in my life, what you might call adolescence, that I first encountered humans. They were miners or lumberjacks, pushing their way farther into the mountains where my family resided for more resources. Contrary to what I believed of their kind, they were respectful of nature and their surroundings. They exhumed no more from an area than it could withstand and attempted to give back to the earth for what they took. These endeavors were not always well-grounded, as men do not understand the ways of the natural world as the Yokai do, but they were gestures of good faith and taken as such.

As these humans would not purge the earth of all its life and properties, they were nomadic. Apparently, they moved through the lands, sending what they extracted back to their native country. It wasn't long before they left the mountain area my family and I inhabited. Still, they had been present long enough for me to develop an avid curiosity about their kind.

An entire age passed before I succumbed to that inquisitiveness and, against the advice and wishes of my kin, I left the mountains in search of the homeland of those gatherers long past. It took many a sun cycle, as it was my first time traveling, and about everything I came across fascinated me. If I saw a trail, even a deer path, I needed to see where it led. There were many adventures and encounters during this time of my life, not all of them pleasant, though all worthwhile learning experiences.

During my travels, I unwittingly journeyed too far north and then to the west until I happened across a large river flowing south. The ferocity of the waters grabbed my attention, and I was but helpless to follow. I danced upon the waters for what seemed mere moments. Then, after an ungraceful tumble, I washed up on the sandy riverfront of a great human settlement.

For as long as something remains of my consciousness, I will remember this image: a grand mountain dominating the landscape, the sun setting upon its left slope. Evening rays of golden light spilled out over the dwelling places of the humans; the cobblestone streets dotted with those returning to their homes. Some shops were still open, their owners watchful for the chance to earn a bit more coin before the sun officially ended that day of business.

Carefully tended fields of corn, beans, and pumpkins were closer to the river. Fences and roads broke up those fields. The largest street ran straight to the river where the largest stone bridge I had yet come across stretched out over the water, connecting the land on both sides. It was a marvelous, magical scene for me.

There was a sudden rustling in the nearby underbrush. As I was in an aquatic form most humans would not know of or be accustomed to, I changed my shape into something else, taking the shape of a human female. No sooner had I done this and turned toward the disturbance than a man stepped out from the shrubbery.

While humans commanded my thoughts and forged the path of my life, this man instantly brought forth a sense of immense attraction completely alien to me. Here was a lordly man, aged mid-twenties. He was tall and broad in stature, with a *square face and thick, dark curly hair falling over his ears and forehead. Though a cape mostly obscured his body, I knew he was muscular.*

It was the light green eyes of this man that captured my attention the most, however. They were piercing, calculating, and extraordinarily sad. The sorrow emanating from them was palpable. It washed over me with his gaze. My heart responded to this wretched melancholy, and the desire to heal this man of whatever was inflicting his heart and soul overwhelmed me.

I took a step forward but paused again when the man's mouth opened slightly. He seemed at a loss for words and fixedly clenched his jaw shut a moment later. Then, striding toward me, he swept off his cloak in a single graceful movement and draped it around my bare shoulders.

It was only then that my nakedness seemed concerning. I remembered that, while all of nature was naked, humans dressed themselves. I looked up at the man and said, "I apologize for my appearance, and I thank you for your assistance."

He cocked his head at me as though finding me odd. "You looked cold," he said in a beautifully rich voice. He took my hand, the sorrow in his eyes clouding over just the slightest, and led me away from the river.

We met up with his troupe, me at first discreetly hiding on the outskirts of their camp while he gathered some appropriate garments for me. That night there was a festival there in the fields, and I got drunk for the first time. While the concept of joy was not foreign to me, it may have been the first time I had "fun." Every one of the humans accepted me, loved me, and treated me as one of their own.

The alcohol had a hazy effect on my mind and memories, much like how I now feel when trying to recollect the past. It is difficult for me to remember much more than snippets or vague constructs during the time after that first encounter. I continued to see the man regularly; I was intensely happy. There was the first kiss I received from him and the eventual realization I was in love. The sadness I saw in him seemed to emanate from his soul, and I made it my purpose to help rid him of it. This played a large part in my acceptance of his proposal of marriage to me mere weeks after our initial encounter.

Despite my joy, I struggled with many things, such as whether or not I should reveal to him my true heritage. That decision made itself the first time we lay together. The ecstasy I experienced in human form made it far too difficult to concentrate, and I was just barely able to keep myself from fully reverting to my natural state of being. Something else happened during our first time, and I felt it almost immediately. New life had sprung into existence, taken hold, and was growing within me. I knew it was possible for the Yokai and humans to have offspring, but my being the host for such a creation caught me off guard.

Neither the revelation of my background nor my pregnancy fazed or detracted the green-eyed man, as it was only a few days later that he proposed.

There is not much I remember of the wedding itself except that it went well for the little time we planned for it. He did not wish to wait longer than necessary. My recollections of the honeymoon, as the final months of my physical self, are fairly coherent. The celebration was to last a full sun cycle, and we started off on a tour of the countryside, stopping at villages along the way. We tasted new foods, he drank too many beers, and we danced many a night away by the light of the moon. As the months passed and I grew larger with child, I saw my new husband's mood lifting to even greater heights, and I reveled in the fact that I was the cause.

On our journeys, we happened across Castle Verde, an ancient structure that, while known in even the farthest lands, stood empty for as long as anyone remembered. I knew from my own teachings it was a natural focal point for the magical abilities of my kind. Accordingly, many religions held this location in high regard. The closer we got to Castle Verde, the stronger my energies and power became in my body and in the hoshi no tama I wore around my neck. It did not take much urging to get my spouse to spend a few days relaxing in the vast and empty halls.

Whether or not my new husband knew of the castle's preternatural environs, it was only then that he dropped his mask and I saw him for who he really was. He was no mere human. Magic imbued at least half the blood flowing through his veins. It was a kind unknown to me, as it was not of the Yokai, but the power it bestowed upon this man was fantastic.

Magic intertwined the sadness and anger I always sensed in him. It is likely there had been a particular event from his past, an event powerful enough to continually evoke those emotions. His power probably began to manifest itself at that point, much like how potent occurrences are often the trigger in the offspring of a

Yokai and human pairing. Thus, they grew and matured together, making the other stronger.

While motivations were a mystery to me, the lack of love in his cold green eyes and his impassive face told me it was no accident we came to such a deserted location. He was after one thing, and it wasn't me, my body, or our unborn child. He was after my magic.

Before I processed all these revelations, he snatched my hoshi no tama away from me. I watched in horror as he drained the jewels of my magic, absorbing it into himself. I did not know it was possible to take another's powers, but such notions were as reprehensible as rape and murder.

"No!" I cried out, falling to my knees in weakness. "You can't! I will die without it."

"You are as good as dead," he said with such impassivity that it froze me. He tossed my hoshi no tama, now devoid of the magic I stored in it, to the ground. His body trembled viciously and perspired as it tried to reject a magic not its own, but he closed his eyes in concentration as he worked to overpower and exert his will over it. In proof to how strong his own powers were, it took him only a few heartbeats to incorporate them.

Once again under control, he opened his eyes and turned toward me. He looked me over, his normally controlled face shone with a wild greed that shocked me. He muttered, "More."

He reached both hands toward me, and before I even thought to react defensively, my mind tore open. It felt as though it was exploding in slow motion as he ripped from me the very fibers of my being. Light blinded me, or perhaps I was losing the abilities to perceive sight as he tore away the last vestiges of my being.

He gave a maniacal laugh as his body took on twice as much power and knowledge than it had before, and it hurt me even more that it was the most joyful I ever saw him. He ripped me of my heritage, determined on leaving me with nothing, until I was empty, naked in the dark.

I lifted my head, intent on asking him why, but it was the last physical thing I would ever do. My human body, barren of the power that held it in that form, shattered in a mighty display of energy and light others could have seen from leagues away. My destruction tore the castle from its base, decimating it and the surrounding

41

grounds. In the wake of such devastation were two things. The first was an empty shell of myself. Devoid of my magic and most of my soul, my scattered remains joined with the mountain itself, taking the form of what would become known as the Lady of the Mountain. There I have remained to this day, knowing nothing but the sorrow of being betrayed—

*

The Lady of the Mountain stopped speaking, and Kitsune opened his eyes.

"What's wrong?" he asked, seeing a concerned look on her face. She was glancing all around as though she sensed something amiss. Everything appeared fine to him, but he reminded himself that what he saw was not real.

"Someone else has arrived," she said in a whisper.

"Probably just my friend, Mamori," he responded in a reassuring voice.

"No. There are others." She spun around toward him, looking panic-stricken. "You must wake up now! You are in danger!"

She rushed toward him as though pulled by some mechanical means. Her hand reached out and, before he could move, grabbed him by the throat. It felt as though she were fumbling for something and choking him at the same time.

"Wake up!"

*

Kitsune snapped into the conscious world amid a flash of green light that knocked a man back from Kitsune's throat.

The surroundings disoriented him. The fire had gone out, and the rain had not abated as in his dreams. If anything, it fell even harder, obscuring his vision.

What he could see was not encouraging. Mamori, unconscious with a large bloody gash along the side of his head, was slung over the shoulder of another man.

"Oh, no. Magic of some kind," said the first stranger. His speech was slow, but the accent belonged to Odom. He reached into the folds of his jacket and pulled out a persuader. "I'm not messing around with that."

"No, Jimmy!" the other hissed. "I just got us these things. Do you have any idea what the darts alone cost? We've already blown through most of the coin paid for these two rats."

Kitsune took their argument as an opportunity to attack. If he disarmed the one called Jimmy, pushing him to the ground, he might gain control of the persuader. Then he could bargain with the other man to put down Mamori. Afterward, he'd shoot the man, then finish Jimmy in hand-to-hand combat.

Jimmy, however, was also not hesitant and did not care about what costs went into procuring the weapon or its ammunition. As soon as Kitsune made a move toward him, his finger tightened over the trigger. A dart flew forth and caught Kitsune right in the neck.

The prince gurgled a curse. In just a matter of days, he had been banished from his homeland, likely physically violated, paraded naked through the streets of his own city, and taken down by a persuader twice. He was used to being impossible to beat or overtake, and this string of events was more than just humbling. It was humiliating.

His eyes rolling back into his head, he slid to the ground, joining Mamori in unnatural sleep.

SAXMA

It was possible to describe Portley's Pub as a lively hangout for those desiring a drink and conversation, but that would be misleading. Crowds often filled the bar, especially during the planting and harvesting seasons, every seat taken by a man or woman with a drink in hand. After long days in the fields, patrons would haul their exhausted bodies into Portley's for a respite. Unlike most pubs, Portley's was a quiet and peaceful place.

The atmosphere in the tavern was also due partially to its construction. The black oak trees that grew in the surrounding forests served as the primary component for the floors, walls, and benches. A well-used fireplace and a multitude of candles sporadically placed about on tables cast murky shadows against the already dark wood. If a patron did not wish to take part in any of the hushed conversations that dared rise above the clinking of beer mugs and dinner plates being washed in a tub behind the bar, he could easily disappear into the shadows.

It was in one such dark corner that Captain Saxma sat alone. He hovered over a fresh mug of beer, staring across the room into the fire blazing in the hearth. He had frequented Portley's since being promoted to captain, believing those in positions of authority should not cavort with subordinates. He enjoyed leaving the confines of the barracks he and his two hundred soldiers occupied, and as his men favored the establishments providing particular brands of entertainment in addition to drink, Portley's suited him perfectly.

Saxma's mood was darker than normal. Usually, he would sit back, enjoy his ale, and strategize on how to further his career. He attributed his success in rising through the ranks to this little hobby. Tonight, though, his thoughts dwelled on the events that had transpired over the past week. No matter how hard he tried to focus on the benefits he had and would continue to reap from his actions, their troublesome nature continually surfaced in his mind.

Several days ago, Saxma's immediate superior officer sent for his audience. Saxma fretted the colonel was dissatisfied with his performance as captain, though he had only increased the efficiency and effectiveness of his company. The meeting, however, was only to inform him that King Oni was demanding his immediate presence. This was a shock, as the king only conferred with the generals, and even those occurrences were rare.

Saxma could only think of a few things that would bring him to the attention of King Oni. His quick promotion to captain was one, as well as the rumblings he was being considered for promotion to major, an honor normally not bestowed upon an officer until he served at least ten sun cycles of military duty. Saxma seriously doubted his king wanted to meet an aspiring officer. Most likely, he didn't want to meet any officer. It was not in the monarch's nature.

Prince Kitsune was the only other reason Saxma could conjure up. They were approximately the same age and attended many of the same military classes and training while growing up. While they were never friends or even held a meaningful conversation, it was the only direct link to the royal family he could think of.

In truth, Captain Saxma did not care for the prince. While the former heir to the throne continually demonstrated his aptitude and intelligence in schooling and military exercises, he seemed stricken with an inability to properly respond to those around him with the appropriate emotional temperament. Not that Kitsune lacked empathy. He got along with nearly everyone, finding a way to relate to them, and he was almost unanimously liked and appreciated. He didn't withdraw from social situations or look down on others as Saxma knew some royals were prone to do. Rather, he was easily accessible and appeared to regard everyone as an equal.

Put like that, Kitsune sounded like a well-adjusted individual, and Saxma continually had issues grasping exactly what it was about his prince that rubbed him the wrong way. There was something in the fashion Kitsune acted toward other people, something that set him apart. It was as though he could see right into those around him, appreciating and understanding the intricacies of human interaction, yet he had problems exhibiting or reciprocating those same emotional constructs.

If King Oni suffered from the same limitations, Saxma did not know. In contrast to the amicable prince, the king's persona demanded fear and respect from his subjects. Saxma did not disappoint in that duty, and he bowed in the customary formal fashion when he came before him in one of the conference areas lining the Boleyn Room.

"Have you been able to ascertain why I asked you here?" King Oni inquired, casually gesturing Saxma to sit adjacently. There was an amused gleam in his eyes as he sat back in a padded chair, as though the idea of a critically thinking soldier was humorous.

"No, sir. I have not," Saxma replied. A quick, small smile flashed across his king's face. While it was one of satisfaction, it did not contain the smug arrogance Saxma expected.

"Splendid. The security measures I have taken have been effective." King Oni paused for a heartbeat, but Saxma dared not speak unless requested. He had heard what could happen to those who spoke out of turn. Without a tongue, they'd never speak again.

"There has been cause to take military action against one of our neighbors. It will be some time still before we launch this new campaign, but the generals and I have been covertly making preparations." The king sat up straight and looked directly at Saxma as though he was finally taking the officer and the conversation seriously. "There are a few...errands...we must attend to now if we are to be successful in this new endeavor. I would like you to carry out these tasks."

"I live to serve, sir."

"Although he does not yet know it, I have found Prince Kitsune guilty of crimes against our kingdom. For this, I will banish him in two days' time. You are to personally escort him to the Eastern Gate and be sure he crosses over into Odom."

It took all of Saxma's training and willpower to keep his jaw from going slack. He had never cared for the prince, but he still would have taken an arrow for him. His purpose, after all, was to protect and serve the king and his family no matter his personal sentiments. Besides, he would never have considered Kitsune to be the traitorous type. It shocked and sickened him to learn he was.

"No harm is to come to him while under your care," King Oni continued. "That does not mean you need treat him as you would a true prince. He is a traitor, and the people of Oinari must understand that. Aside from the death we afford most turncoats, you are to handle him as such."

The king's green eyes fixed upon him with an icy stare. Saxma nodded in understanding. "Yes, sir."

"Before the sun sets today, you will dispatch some of your men. They are to cross into Odom and seek at least one mercenary. Preferably more. The mercenaries are to capture the prince and take him to their capital, the city fortress of Huem. Just outside the castle gates is a stockade, a warning against those who would threaten their people. There they are to hang the prince."

"Sir?" Saxma spoke out before he could hold his tongue. These new orders were perplexing, though his tactical thought patterns were already at work. It all had the makings of a setup. "Are we going to invade Odom?"

Isaac Grisham

Thankfully, King Oni did not seem to mind the question. He leaned back in his seat, looking to be deep in thought. "No. Not yet, anyway. I highly doubt the mercenaries will succeed."

Saxma bit his tongue before he could press his luck with more questions. Why would the king expect failure? What was the purpose of hiring mercenaries if he did not anticipate success?

"Report back to this chamber midmorning in two days. Be prepared for your journey east. The prince will meet you here, but grant him a few tics to gather some supplies," the king said.

"Yes, sir."

"This assignment may seem like a small chore, but I would not trust the proper treatment of the prince to a lesser soldier than yourself. Even so, a successful outcome will secure you an immediate promotion to the rank of major, and I will put you in charge of a special project underway in the north. Failure, though unlikely, will result in your execution."

The northern project was one of the monarchy's worst-kept secrets, at least among those in the military who paid attention to the goings-on around them. It was difficult not to notice an entire regiment of soldiers being sent to the remote northern regions, massive amounts of building resources being redirected, and rumors of the sheer number of Ruio villagers being forced from their homes for labor. Saxma had barely enough time to recover from the shock of a potential promotion to register the implications of the existence of the project or even the threat on his life. Before his mind could catch up, the king stood and dismissed him.

"That is all."

*

With a clunk, the barmaid set down another mug of beer without his asking for it. Saxma frequented Portley's often enough that they knew to do this for him until he showed he was through for the night. He drained the last few drops from his glass, then handed it to the young woman, who took it and disappeared into the shadows. Reaching

48

for the new one, he fell into his normal routine of staring into the fire over the top of the mug.

Saxma did exactly as ordered. Upon returning to the barracks, he sent two of his soldiers to Odom. Before crossing over, they were to change into plainclothes—anything identifying them as Kitsunetsuki military was not to be on their persons. Once in Odom, they were to seek as many mercenaries as possible with the amount of money with which Saxma supplied them. It was a difficult balancing act. They had to carry enough to spark the interest of those looking for work yet not enough that others would kill them for carrying a small fortune. Furthermore, they had to promise an additional sum for the successful completion of the mercenaries' job, an incentive for them to follow through with their task.

Then, two days later, he took eleven of his subordinates with him back to Inari Palace. A few tics after arriving, Prince Kitsune emerged alone from the Boleyn Room, his expression a combination of hurt, distress, and determination. It surprised Saxma that the prince had been inside, as he believed only kings and queens saw its interior. Even more mysterious was the golden light emanating from behind the door, but his training and position demanded he not ask questions and do as directed.

Prince Kitsune acted as though lost in thought as they escorted him to his apartment. Saxma and his men kept a brisk pace. During that walk, an idea began to form in the captain's head.

A few months ago, back when Saxma was being considered for promotion to captaincy, he sought to increase his chances for success by challenging Kitsune to a duel. Such trials had become an important custom among the men. Somehow, despite the little chance of winning, it built morale. Something about the prince taking part in the exercises or the chance to look him in the eyes face to face.

Saxma witnessed many of the duels, and now he believed he had found a way of defeating Kitsune. Most others fought with either swords or fists. The prince beat most within thirty heartbeats. Saxma thought this was because both methods were advantageous for a smaller person, allowing him to maneuver.

"Wrestling," Saxma announced at the duel, which took place just outside of the barracks as the sun was sinking. Strictly speaking, neither the military nor the king sanctioned the fights, so they were not to take place on official grounds.

"Wonderful," Kitsune replied. Instead of surprise or anxiety, the prince expressed a pleased look, like he was looking forward to a different kind of challenge. Saxma was furious. He was much larger than the prince in height and muscle, striking fear in the eyes of all those who faced him.

As it turned out, his height and muscle hadn't meant a thing. Within the usual thirty heartbeats, Kitsune had him pinned to the ground. Others described it as a lamb overpowering a lion. Even though he knew better, Saxma could not help but feel humiliated.

Later that night, while Saxma nursed his wounded pride over a red ale at Portley's Pub, he came to an uncomfortable realization: He hadn't been angry at the prince's reaction to his wrestling declaration. Rather, it was his own response to the prince's smile, which had elicited lustful thoughts from him. The feelings were not of the romantic variation. Instead, they stemmed from more basic needs. The same needs his men had at the whorehouses.

Lust—romantic, basic, or otherwise—was a distraction Saxma did not want, which is why he found the realization so discomforting. He had seen other soldiers injured during battlefield exercises because the focus of their minds and genitals were elsewhere. He'd be damned if something so mundane extinguished his career's momentum.

Kitsune had seen the momentary carnal glimmer in Saxma's eyes. As he often took duel mates to his bed—both women and men—Saxma hoped the prince would give him the opportunity to assuage the lustful desires that had emerged before they became distracting. After the duel, though, Kitsune had walked away without a word, which Saxma took as both a professional and personal slight. It was as if nothing mattered to the man. The soldiers didn't, and certainly not Saxma.

More than anything, Kitsune's cold attitude ate away at Saxma as he sat in Portley's that night and drank mug after mug of ale. At some point, somewhere between the waitress giving up trying to understand his slurred words and him going out back to piss for the sixth time, he had the brilliant idea to go straight to Prince Kitsune and demand he take care of his lustful urges.

*

Saxma sighed, settling into the seat and deeper into the shadows. The encounter was the most impulsive, irresponsible, and potentially career-destroying move he had ever gone through with. As with all spontaneous endeavors, he carried it out without a proper analysis of the consequences. The ease of entering the palace and slipping past all the guards, even in his drunken state, had not helped. Thanks to a high metabolism, much of the buzz dissipated as he made his way through the halls and stairwells to the eighth floor of the royal home. Even as the alcohol wore off, his boldness grew. He got this far. Might as well go the entire way.

Before long, Saxma was knocking on the prince's apartment doors. Several moments passed before they swung open to reveal Kitsune, wearing only a pair of lounge pants. The windows were open, an attempt to lessen the thickness of the unusually warm and humid spring air. A thin layer of perspiration, glowing in the soft light, covered Kitsune. It made Saxma, more or less drenched in sweat from his drinking and sneaking about the palace, feel momentarily self-conscious.

"I've been expecting you," Kitsune said with a sly smile.

"I doubt that," Saxma countered, irritated at how the prince could assert such a ridiculous claim. Kitsune, standing there half naked, his long blond hair gently drifting in a breeze from the open windows, did not have a calming effect. Instead, Saxma felt himself responding to the sight of the man. It was hard not to imagine licking that layer of sweat off the other's flawless skin.

"So you're not coming in?" the prince said, almost as a pout.

"Oh, I'm coming in," Saxma replied, stepping forward and pushing Kitsune into the room. He followed, closing the doors behind him. "I'm gonna put the little prince in his rightful place."

Turning around, he saw the prince was once again standing calmly, his hands on his hips. The pants had slipped downward a bit, revealing more lean muscles. "Another round of wrestling, then?"

As if being granted permission, Saxma stripped off his own sweat-soaked shirt and advanced. Kitsune walked back toward the bedroom, eying him with the approval Saxma had expected earlier after the duel. The captain undid his trousers, indicating his partner should do the same. "Let's see what the little prince has got."

"You will have to remove these pants yourself if you wish to see," Kitsune said with another one of his sly smiles. Teasingly, he pulled his pants up higher around his slender waist.

"With pleasure." Saxma again moved forward, pushing the prince back onto his bed. Kitsune, who was looking at his naked body, reacted positively. Saxma crawled onto the bed, starting near the bottom by Kitsune's feet. As he worked his way up the other's body, he could feel the heat emanating from his perfectly smooth skin. In particular, he enjoyed the heat and stiff movement he detected as he moved past the prince's groin.

With his fine hair spilt out across the sheets, his eyes closed as though he was sleeping, and his lips slightly parted in a contented smile, Kitsune looked angelic. A gasp of pleasure escaped his mouth when Saxma pressed his body down on top of him.

Then the would-be captain made a tactical error. He reached down with his hand to tug off the prince's pants. Before he even got a good grip, though, one of Kitsune's hands flew down and took hold of his wrist. The angelic face twisted into an expression of desire, and a wide grin spread across it as Kitsune shook his head as though telling him no.

With surprising strength Saxma had not experienced from anyone of any size, Kitsune tightened his grip on Saxma's wrist and yanked it between their bodies. The force of the movement flipped Saxma off of the prince's body nearly full circle so that, before he even knew it, he was face down on the mattress.

Quick and light as a deer, Kitsune jumped from his spot and was on top of Saxma. As he realized what was about to happen, Saxma began to struggle, rolling from side to side. Still gripping his wrist, however, Kitsune maneuvered the soldier's arm behind his back into a position that made struggling hard to do without causing pain. With no apparent effort, Kitsune reached out and grabbed Saxma's other wrist, twisting that arm into an identical position.

Deftly holding both of Saxma's wrists in place with one of his long-fingered hands, Kitsune used his other to shimmy down his pants. Then he whispered into Saxma's ear, "I suppose you don't get to see what this little prince has in store for you. You might want to relax now, or else this will hurt a lot more."

*

Saxma's blood boiled in remembrance, and he took several long gulps from his mug. It had been embarrassing to lose his own challenge—again—in the same day. Not that he hadn't enjoyed it. Though defeated, he lived up to his part of the unspoken agreement, moving his body in conjunction with his opponent's. In the end, they were both satisfied.

Afterward, Kitsune rolled over and drifted off to sleep, seemingly indifferent whether or not Saxma stayed. Saxma did not, instead choosing to grab his clothing and leave.

In the following days, Saxma's humiliation diminished. He was angry about losing, but what was he to do against the prince—the future king? He chose instead to look at it as a lesson from which he could better himself. With a sober mind, it was painfully clear how his emotions dictated his actions. Yes, it had been a goal to conquer the prince physically for career advancement, but history and statistics were against him. Any good warrior would realize that. To conquer him sexually, though, was a desire born from that lust he preferred to ignore completely.

Emotions, if well understood and carefully used, could be a powerful ally to a soldier. A true warrior, however, never let those emotions rule him. He since strove to make sure his actions had clear meanings and attainable goals. He never again wanted to respond to things so emotionally.

The revelation that Kitsune was a traitor struck him dumb. It was hard not to let the new flood of fury and shame sweep him away. He could not come to grips with his lusting after an enemy of the kingdom, much less being beaten so easily physically and sexually. His honor screamed for immediate retaliatory action. He got his chance, and the king's orders defined and sanctioned his actions.

He remembered standing at the apartment doors as the prince darted about, gathering supplies. It occurred to him that, with a loaded persuader, it was the perfect time to exact the revenge for which his honor begged. He took a moment to review his plan of action, making sure it wasn't being ruled by his emotions. True, his desire to humiliate the prince stemmed from lingering anger, but humiliating traitors was routine. As the king said, he was not to afford the prince any leniency. Saxma had already intended to parade Kitsune through the city, but there wasn't a reason not to start his punishment early.

So he ordered his men from the rooms, shot Kitsune with a tranquilizer, then dragged his limp body back to the bedroom. There was a girl in the bed, shaking in fear and too frightened to do anything. Saxma hadn't recognized her, meaning she was nobody of importance. With large eyes filled with tears, she watched as he carefully undressed the prince, folding the clothes and placing them into the dropped backpack. Then, after having a nice long look at both the girl and the prince, Saxma drew Kitsune close to his body.

Saxma had never been inside another man, and he couldn't say he preferred it one way or another. That may have been because Kitsune was limp. Bodies that didn't respond didn't provide much fun. Still, especially since he could simultaneously grope the girl, the experience had been pleasurable. It satisfied his need for revenge and his more basic urges.

Afterward, Saxma threw the prince out into the hallway, ordering the men to prepare him for his parade through Oinari. Some took to the task enthusiastically while others seemed dubious about the accusations against the royal. Either way, they all complied.

The ride through the streets went better than expected. It seemed as though every citizen came out to the streets to see the prince's punishment, and Saxma knew he had properly admonished and humbled the prisoner. Tears were even streaming down Kitsune's face. It was a good beginning, but not enough for a traitor.

After leaving the city, the only hiccup had been Mamori. Not only was it a strike against himself that one of his soldiers deserted, but the fact that Mamori was a trained soldier put the rest of the king's plans in jeopardy, decreasing the chances Odom mercenaries would successfully capture the prince.

It had only been since his return to Oinari earlier in the day that recent events began to unsettle Saxma, that their troublesome nature bubbled to the surface of his thoughts. This was why he had more than his usual amount of drink so late into the night at Portley's, thinking of things beyond the advancement of his own career. Others enlightened him what King Oni revealed to the people. The details behind the declaration of new laws and moral codes, especially how they had been used to define the prince's behavior as traitorous, made the righteous zeal with which Saxma carried out his orders fade. After all, he himself was now guilty of the same offense.

There had been intimations at new military action during the king's speech, but it mostly focused on the unruly and barbarous nature of the Ruio and Mogo people and how the new laws would bring them enlightenment and civilization. Saxma knew declaring outright war on a neighboring realm was unwise without completion of proper preparations and planning, but not once during his address did Oni mention the mysterious project in the north. He had previously confirmed its existence to Saxma, and the soldier now wondered exactly how displacing strong and healthy villagers and forcing them to work would deliver enlightenment to them.

And what was the project? No enemies resided in the north, no natural resources to mine, and there was nothing of great value to protect. Yet the materials supposedly being taken there suggested the construction of something of such magnitude that it put Inari Palace to shame. The number of soldiers redirected northward would usually constitute a colonel or general, not a mere major. A general would attract more attention, though, and it seemed the monarch was keen to avoid that.

Not that Saxma would receive the promotion or project. He had yet to hear from his superior officers, but he doubted they would take the desertion of Mamori lightly. He wasn't sure he wanted to know any more about what was happening in the north. In his opinion, it all sounded like an extremely wasteful endeavor.

A potential war was at hand, a project consumed massive amounts of resources, new laws and morals were being put into effect, and the prince was just excommunicated. It was so much for a kingdom to handle all at once, even one as prosperous and unified as Kitsunetsuki. The breadth of the king's plans for the realm were grand and bold, but they somehow seemed a smokescreen for something else entirely. Something sinister.

Within the scope of things, Saxma himself was one of the antagonists.

The barmaid set another mug of ale down, taking away the glass he just finished. He hadn't even recalled draining the last drops, but he stared appreciatively into the new frothy liquid. As he did, the concerns and troubles he felt throughout the evening began to slip from his mind. His usual confidence, sense of duty, and loyalty to the king replaced them. He sat there and hoped to become a major, beginning to strategize his way to colonel. How many sun cycles until he could make it to general?

From his dark corner of Portley's Pub, Saxma stared over his beer into the fire, dreaming of his future.

A HISTORY OF ODOM

Nearly a day and a half after the attack, Kitsune awoke, his body aching and feeling terribly sick. The combination of the horse-riding, beating, and persuader chemicals pumping through his veins was taking its toll.

He let his other senses paint him a picture, not wanting to open his eyes just yet. He could hear lapping water in the distance. The sound differed dramatically from the rapid movement of the Rout River, and the air had a brackish scent, so he guessed it to be the ocean. Besides salt, a strong scent of hay filled his nose, and his sense of touch confirmed he lay on a thin bed of it. Beneath the hay were planks of wood, and judging by the amount of warping, the boards were fairly old. Between his being jostled about and the sounds of hooves and wooden wheels, it was simple to deduce he was in the back of a small horse-drawn cart.

Two men, most likely the ones who had captured himself and Mamori, sat at the front of the cart, chatting as though nothing unusual had happened.

Slowly, Kitsune opened his eyes. What he could see confirmed most of his suspicions. Additionally, he saw Mamori, still unconscious, was in the cart with him. The cut on his companion's head looked swollen and angry. He attempted to reach out and feel Mamori's forehead, fearing he had developed a fever, but found he couldn't move. Aside from his eyes, his entire body was in a complete state of rest.

He was paralyzed.

Kitsune tried to stay calm and not let hopelessness overwhelm him, logically assessing the situation. As he already determined, he could feel everything his body was touching. Physiology was not his strong suit, but he remembered enough from his studies to believe these were good signs his paralysis was not permanent. That meant his captors probably dosed him with yet another chemical that would eventually wear off. He would just need to wait out the effects, assuming his captors didn't dose him again. Unfortunately, seeing that rope or metal did not bind him and Mamori hinted that they would.

Even if the two men hadn't drugged him, Kitsune doubted he'd be able to properly defend himself against them, much less mount an effective offense. His mouth and throat were parched, possibly worsened by whatever they poisoned his body with, and hunger had long been gnawing at his stomach. His last good meal had been the night before the king banished him. The few scraps he got a hold of since had kept him going, but he recognized the fatigue that came from malnutrition.

As the tics dragged on, Kitsune halted the encroaching fear by focusing on the conversation of their captors. From the familiar way they spoke with each other, it was clear the two were related, most likely brothers or close cousins. After a bit of eavesdropping, it was also obvious one was far brighter than the other.

"How long until we get there?" asked the one Kitsune recognized as Jimmy.

"I've told you twice already. It's a five-day journey, and we're only into the second day. These two fellows won't be giving us any trouble so long as we continue doping them up every few hours. Just remember to keep an eye on them so you'll know when the effects begin to wear off. We'll need them lucid enough to choke down some bread and water once or twice a day."

"But Benjamin, what if they need to piss and shit?"

There was a pause, as though the one Kitsune now knew as Benjamin was trying to be patient. "You've been under the influence of the same tonic, Jimmy. You know full well that if their bodies need to expel waste, they're just gonna do it. There's no waiting until you can dig a latrine."

"Won't they stink?"

"No worse than you."

They chuckled, then fell silent for a while, leaving Kitsune to ponder over when he'd be involuntarily soiling himself. It was not a thrilling thought to the prince. Nor was the consideration that he might have already done so.

Just when Kitsune thought boredom would kill him, Jimmy piped back up.

"Tell me a story, cousin."

"Aww, jeez, Jimmy," Benjamin said, exasperated.

"How about our history? The history of Odom?" Jimmy pressed.

"Last time I tried to tell you that one, you complained it was boring. Said it made you sleepy, and I will not sit here and talk to myself while you snooze away on the job."

"It's a little boring at times," Jimmy conceded. "Not at others, though. Maybe you can just skip the slow parts and stick to the action?"

"I can try," Benjamin said with a sigh. "You'll be missing out on some of the political intricacies that have led our realm to its current state."

Jimmy gave a little snort as though he knew he'd never be able to fully grasp anything so complicated.

"Long ago, back when the Kitsunetsuki Kingdom was less than a third of its current size, Odom was the economic force in the region. We were a prosperous people with fertile lands, rich mineral deposits, and productive cities. Nothing as industrious as the civilization that brought the Wastelands into being, but large textile mills and the like.

"As you know, the royal family of Odom lives in the capital, Huem. It sits squarely in the center of Odom and is still the largest city in the realm. While Huem is a solid military fortress, it also sets the standard for upper class living. Those who can still claim to be rich reside there, hoping Patriarch Kirby, our wondrously ineffective head of state, will keep them protected.

"Most of the other large cities in Odom are situated around grand fortresses. They were originally for the lords and committees governing the various provinces. As the royals shored up their power, however, these cities gave way to other purposes. Those closer to the borders served as military stations while the castles farther inland served their communities.

"Anyway," Benjamin said, apparently realizing the history of castles and their purposes would probably put his cousin into a catatonic state, "Odom's misfortune began some twenty sun cycles ago when Prince Oni's wife was brutally murdered. Oni swore up and down Odom spies were to blame, and he convinced his father, the king, to send spies of their own into our lands to investigate."

Kitsune reeled at what his captor was saying. His mother hadn't fallen victim to murder. She died during childbirth. King Oni had been fond of recounting that fact each time he appeared at one of Kitsune's birthday celebrations, adding dryly he was happy his wife was at least able to produce an heir for him.

How was it these men thought she was murdered? Was Benjamin just embellishing the story?

"What the spies of Kitsunetsuki found did not please the prince. The riches of our country were so vast it allowed us to train and maintain a grand standing army none could possibly oppose, much less consider attacking. There was no way Prince Oni was going to avenge his wife's death through military might.

"Instead of confronting Odom by traditional methods, our neighbor waged a different kind of war. Over the next couple of sun cycles, the Ashers discouraged trading with Odom. They placed ever-increasing taxes on imports until it only made sense for Kitsunetsuki markets to find their goods elsewhere. The Argent Mountain Passageway was eventually closed to most travel.

"The closing of the mountain pass was significant: It effectively cut off our trading with the lands of Mogo and Gaav. It's been argued we should have constructed merchant ships to sail around the mountain range. We have never been a seafaring folk, though, and to start at that point would have been a costly investment with no guarantee of monetary return. Aside from a few fishing operations, people and businesses gradually abandoned the coast and migrated northward toward the land of Ruio, the last accessible route for trade."

"If we were such a rich people, with fertile lands and mines of gold, why did we depend on others?" Jimmy interrupted. "How could we not be self-sufficient?"

"Good question," Benjamin replied, his voice conveying appreciation for such a critical question from his cousin. "I'm no scholarly economist, and I do perhaps oversimplify how the commercial machine of all the lands works. There are items we trade for that we cannot find or grow here in Odom. The marble floors of our castles originated in Mogo, as there is no marble to be mined here. And strawberries only grow in Gaav. Remember strawberries, Jimmy?"

"Just barely, but they were delicious," he replied longingly.

"Marble and strawberries are items we could live without, but I rather suspect folks get used to a certain standard of living. People come into this world, work hard to sustain themselves and their families, and try to live a little better than their parents. The thought of losing your progress, let alone that of many generations before you, can cause an unreasonable panic. Ruio represented a means to continue a better living, so many moved north.

"That is when the final gauntlet was thrown. The king of Kitsunetsuki died under mysterious circumstances. Prince Oni ascended the throne. Angry and grieving, he claimed agents of Ruio were responsible. The people loved Oni's father and wife, and they rallied to him in response. He led them in war, the result of which was the annexation of Ruio.

"With Ruio now a part of Kitsunetsuki, all of Odom's trading with the western world came to a halt. Passage through the Wastelands was not an option, so we couldn't even do business with those in the tribal lands. Merchants finally gave serious thought to building ships, but by this time there remained neither the money nor resources to do so. All the manpower was in the north, and the lumber required to construct ships still bore roots, limbs, and leaves."

Jimmy growled, interrupting his history lesson. "I think the one dressed as a soldier is coming off of his drugs."

"Gas them both up, then!" Benjamin said happily. A moment later he made a swallowing noise, and Kitsune guessed he was wetting his throat with some water from a canteen. It made him realize again how thirsty he was.

The cart ground to a stop.

"It's midafternoon now," Benjamin said. "We'll let them have a drink next time around."

Kitsune saw Jimmy lumber into view. He watched through squinted lids as the man reached into a wooden box and pulled out a dusty red bottle. Clumsily uncorking the flask, he dumped a generous portion of its liquid contents into a dirty, stained rag.

As if realizing what was about to transpire, Mamori let out a pained moan and twitched. With a clucking sound, Jimmy grabbed a handful of Mamori's hair and, lifting him up, covered the front of his face with the rag. Forced to inhale the vapors, Mamori's body gave an involuntary convulsion, but then fell still again.

Jimmy carelessly dropped his charge's head to the floor of the cart and turned to Kitsune. "Time for your medicine," he said with a little too much delight in his voice. Kitsune wanted to cry out in pain as the man grabbed his long hair and hauled him upward, but only a low, unintelligible groan escaped. The captor firmly placed the rag against the prince's face. Though Kitsune fought hard not to inhale, his body ignored his desires and continued to breathe as normal.

The effect of the vapor hit him immediately. While he didn't pass out, his recognition and understanding of anything real around him faded. He was aware his head, which Jimmy had been holding, was set free. He could see the air itself as his face cut through it, beautiful in its rainbow of pastel colors. Then came a sensation he knew was pain as his head smashed into something solid, though he didn't hurt. Instead, the colorful rainbow dazzled him as it exploded into a million specks of bright white light. The impression was like flying through space and stars, and it reminded him of being drunk. He wouldn't open his eyes even if he could, for he thought his vision would spin out of control.

*

Only gradually did Kitsune's mind return to a state of normalcy. His eyelids cracked open, and he watched as the red sun made its slow trek toward the pink and orange horizon. He marveled at the scene's beauty. Then he became aware that he was still in a cart, that Mamori was next to him, and that they were still moving.

It was a while yet before the full truth of their precarious situation settled in again. Benjamin's soothing voice didn't help. He spoke about the great bandits, mercenaries, and thieves that arose in the wake of Odom's economic fall. As the realm's infrastructure crumbled, crime became rampant. It was not uncommon for those like him and Jimmy to live on the outskirts of society.

"It's not like our way of life is particularly discouraged," Benjamin reasoned. "It's said the royal family has hired mercenaries to hunt down their adversaries. They have probably attempted to have King Oni assassinated, though that has accomplished little."

In his mind, Kitsune smirked. If he couldn't get to his father, ordinary filthy criminals had no chance.

"There are also those like you and me who will work for the coin of other countries. Like this job with the prince."

"I didn't like the guy who paid us for this," Jimmy said. "For someone wearing such disgusting clothing, he seemed to think awfully highly of himself. I wanted to cut him open, take his jacket, and steal all his money."

"Also not something beyond those of our trade," Benjamin replied with a derisive laugh. "The man was obviously military, though, and I'm sure there were others of his kind waiting in the dark in case we made such a move."

Kitsune's mind spun with this new information. Their captors knew who he was, and someone had hired them to kidnap him. Saxma came to mind immediately as the scheme's architect, but that made little sense. There would not have been time for the captain to pass through the Eastern Gate and find some random mercenaries while Kitsune and Mamori rested. More likely, another force planned this well in advance.

"Tell me what we're to do with them, cousin!" It was obvious Jimmy already knew the answer. His glee was practically orgasmic.

Benjamin was short in his reply. "We will kill them, you idiot. We're to take them to Huem and hang them by their pretty little necks."

Despite the drugs, Kitsune's eyes bulged open. Anger boiled in his veins and pounded in his ears. He concentrated on what they were saying, hanging on to every word. Their ultimate plan was to take their lives, and he couldn't allow that to happen. He couldn't die. Not before completing his father's mission!

How, though, if he was incapacitated?

"Why have we kept them alive so far, then?" Jimmy inquired. "Why not just kill them back at the gate and transport their corpses to Huem?"

"Have you ever smelled a corpse before, cousin? It's not the most awful odor your nose is likely to encounter during your pathetic life, but it's far from pleasant. I'd rather not travel the countryside with the scent of their festering carcasses in my nasal cavity. Besides, as requested, their deaths need to be a result of hanging. We'll do that at the stockade just outside of Huem, then amble into town to ask about the two young men hanging around!" Benjamin rocked back in his seat, laughing at his own joke. Jimmy joined in, though probably in imitation and not from understanding.

"Who we gonna kill first, do you think?" Jimmy asked.

"I'm not sure yet," Benjamin mused. "There are advantages to both. Kill the Kitsunetsuki prince first, and the idiot soldier has to watch his charge die. Ultimate failure on his part. On the other hand, kill the soldier first, and the royal one sees his last loyal subject murdered. I'd like to see the realization on his face that he was utterly alone."

Kitsune seethed in rage. Not only were these men hired to kill them, but they relished in spilling blood. They lived for it. He wondered how many innocent people they had already murdered.

"In the end, it doesn't matter," Jimmy said. While Kitsune couldn't see it, he could imagine the big happy grin on the man's face. "Their bodies will just be hanging by some rope around their broken necks and we'll collect the rest of our money."

No! No! No!

Just as Kitsune's fury reached its boiling point, a bolt of green lightning skewered the darkening sky, contacting the ground just left of the cart. All of their bodies flew from the wagon, Kitsune's and Mamori's limp limbs flailing like rag dolls. Remarkably, the horses seemed nonplussed and stopped after trotting forward several more footfalls.

"Magic," Jimmy sputtered, spitting out a mouthful of grass as he got to his feet. He looked up at the sky, where greenish storm clouds billowed. "This is magic!"

"Calm yourself, cousin," Benjamin said.

"No!" was the ardent rebuttal. Jimmy started spinning about, looking for something to concentrate his fears on. Bouts of rainwater began to fall. "I will not have magic! I will not have it! It must be…"

Jimmy's voice dropped off as his eyes fell upon Kitsune. More specifically, it was the chain clasped around his neck that caught the large man's attention. During his tumble, it had worked its way out from beneath his shirt.

"No rope for you," Jimmy grumbled, moving forward through sheets of rain with his arms outstretched. "You die now."

Without warning, Mamori leapt from the side, tackling the large man. Between the head injury and drugs, Kitsune hadn't thought his friend would be capable of consciousness, let alone moving. Yet here he was when he was most needed, bravely performing his duty.

Under Mamori's unexpected impact, Jimmy staggered back, tripped over his own feet, and fell to the ground. The side of his head landed upon a sizeable stone with a loud, wet cracking sound. When Mamori grabbed him by the shirt, lifting a fist to strike him, there was no resistance, no voluntary movement whatsoever.

"No!" Benjamin screamed. The horror in his voice indicated he knew his brother would not rise again. "What have you done?"

Mamori staggered back to his feet, the toxins still making him sluggish. Rainwater streamed down his face, mixing with the blood that had crusted over his wound. He muttered, "You can kill me, but you may not have Prince Kitsune."

"I was not paid to keep either of you alive," Benjamin said, striding over to Mamori. "I will have you both."

Benjamin drew a sword in a quick, fluid movement and jabbed it forward. Kitsune watched helplessly as the blade disappeared inside of his companion's chest as though it were a giant loaf of bread. Mamori looked down disbelievingly and even made to grab hold of the blade with his hands. Benjamin gave it a sharp twist, though, and Mamori's head jerked up as he screamed in a pain Kitsune never thought existed.

Benjamin yanked the sword out, and blood immediately soaked Mamori's shirt. The soldier clutched at his chest for a few moments, looking to Kitsune with a pitiful expression of shame and apology. He fell back limply onto Jimmy's body.

Despite the horrific scene taking place and a violent shivering that racked his body, Kitsune found it difficult to fight a sudden fatigue and darkness threatening to swallow his consciousness. As Benjamin turned toward Kitsune, the prince saw the murder of Mamori did nothing to lessen the anger and bloodlust in his eyes.

"Now it's your turn," the mercenary growled, walking forward, the bloody sword positioned for a downward jab.

Then he stopped short, and a surprised look crossed his face. Kitsune had to squint—his vision was going blurry—but he thought he saw something sticking out of Benjamin's chest. It looked like the tail end of an arrow.

A second projectile lodged itself in the mercenary's torso.

The man staggered back, dropping his sword.

"No," Benjamin mumbled, spitting up blood. He fell to his knees, then to his side. It appeared as though he tried to draw breath to let loose another curse, but the effort proved too much. His body twitched, then was still.

Kitsune struggled to reach out to Mamori, though he already knew the soldier was gone. Unable to move, Kitsune's body wasn't even able to draw up enough energy to call out in anguish. With imminent danger gone, the only thing it could do was slip into unconsciousness.

*

The rain strengthened to a downpour as the last vestiges of daylight slipped away. With four bodies strewn about the ground and covered in blood, it was a desolate scene. The only movement was from the old horses tethered to the cart. They glanced around, nervous now that all the activity had died down.

A figure emerged from the shadows, a young man with a bow in his hand. He passed by the horses, taking a moment to pat their necks and soothe their anxious spirits. Then, stepping into the middle of the road, he took several long moments to scan the area with careful eyes hidden behind the large hood of a cloak. Eventually, he moved to each of the bodies lying upon the ground, checking for pulses.

Blood still flowed through the veins of the last figure he checked, though weakly. He caressed the man's face, brushing back long blond strands of hair. The skin was cool to the touch, and he feared the man's core body temperature was falling.

With all the rain, building a sustainable fire was out of the question, and there wasn't a village or roadside inn within short distance. He acted fast, stripping himself of his cloak and covering the man's body. He searched the cart, finding additional coats and two thick blankets. Though they were waterlogged, he spread them out on top of his cloak. The waterproof barrier would prevent further cold water from leaching more body warmth.

He crawled underneath the layers of cloth, finding the other's body and pressing himself close. The icy cold was hard to ignore, but he focused on the short, shallow breaths the other man took. Wrapping his arms and legs around the unconscious body, he let his own warmth stabilize then increase the other's temperature. After a while, the shallow breathing normalized.

The newcomer eventually drifted off to sleep, joining the other in dreams.

MYOBU

Kitsune stood alone in the middle of a vast forest of tall redwoods, feeling particularly miniscule. Despite the sun directly above, it was dim under the canopy of the trees, the surrounding colors cool and muted. He saw no footpaths around him, and the grass and leaves littering the ground remained undisturbed. He wondered how he arrived here.

It also made him question if anyone lived in the cottage before him.

Nestled on the side of a hill, the warm and welcoming house seemed almost organic, like it had grown right up out of the ground. The windows were closed and shuttered, though, and no smoke issued from the chimney. It appeared nobody was home.

Yet Kitsune knew, or at least somehow instinctually felt, someone was inside the cottage, waiting for him. Or had the prince been the one waiting to enter?

The individual was a man in search of love. The jolting certainty of that fact startled Kitsune, as did a powerful belief that if he stepped foot inside the home, the decision would work to define the path of his life. This frightened him—letting another man affect him in such ways contradicted the edict given unto him by his father. He began to turn away, to run from the warmth of the house and his destiny, set on remaining true to his father's will. Then he saw the Lady of the Mountain now stood a few footfalls from him.

He stopped short.

"It is all right," said the Lady, her straight black hair and green dress rustling in a wind Kitsune did not feel. Her presence did not surprise him. She had been with him and protected him since she first drew him into her dreamscape back at the Eastern Gate, hanging around his neck in the hoshi no tama. In one sense, she was his guardian. In another, like now, she acted as a spiritual guide.

The Lady continued, "You can go down this path. It doesn't change who you are. You can go inside."

Pointing to the cottage, Kitsune said, "I don't know who that man is, but I perceive he is desperately looking for love. I have never desired the type of union he seeks. My needs are more...basic. Regardless, both needs are shameful things." He lowered his head as he remembered his father's stern, disapproving gaze. The king turned him away because of what he was, and others died. "I am a shameful thing."

"No, Kitsune," replied the Lady. She appeared in front of him, down on her knees and stroking the side of his face with her hand. He wanted her to stand up, knowing he was not yet worthy of such affection. "You are beautiful and perfect and deserving. What I say is true, and you should trust in me, for you are of me."

"I know," he replied to the last statement. They stared at each other, wondering where the revelation came from. It was as though she plucked the fact right out of the fabric of the universe, the knowledge natural. Without knowing why, he added, "Grandmother."

Confusion crossed her face, but her usual air of serene clarity soon replaced it. They nodded to each other in mutual understanding. Not everything made sense yet to Kitsune, as facts didn't quite line up, but he recalled the stories of his grandfather having met and married one of the Yokai. The tales never explained how his wife died—or if she had passed on at all—and did not reveal the past king to possess the cruel nature that would lead him to murder. If it was true, though, it would help explain why his own father, with the blood of the Yokai running through his veins, was so intelligent yet emotionally distant.

"Go and speak with him," said the Lady, turning him toward the cottage and giving a gentle shove. "Simply meeting with him does not constitute a sinful nature in anyone's eyes. I will speak with you soon."

Kitsune felt like he had made a grand decision, and with it a great burden lifted from his soul. In its place fell a wave of giddiness, and he barely kept from sprinting across the forest floor up to the cottage entrance. He looked back, finding the Lady had disappeared from view, a ray of dusty sunlight illuminating the area where she had been standing.

Turning back to the door, he placed one hand against the wood, pleasantly warm to the touch. With a turn of the handle, he pushed it open and walked through.

*

Kitsune opened his eyes, finding himself lying in a bed stuffed with old hay, cloaks and blankets spread across his body to keep him warm. Though makeshift, he was more comfortable than he'd been in some time.

His surroundings confused him. The room looked more like a banquet hall than a bedroom, complete with rows of tables and benches for dining, two enormous fireplaces to keep the room warm, and an area devoid of clutter for mingling and dancing.

The hall had witnessed many celebrations. Kitsune sensed gaiety lingering in the air. It would be a long while before it would happen again, if ever. By the looks of things, the structure had been empty for several sun cycles. The roof at the far end of the room had collapsed, letting in glorious rays of sunshine. Birds nested in the rafters above. They and other rodents taking up residence left a mess strewn about the floor, though it appeared someone recently swept aside much of it.

A clunking sound emanated from inside one fireplace, followed shortly by a long string of curses. Kitsune froze, half expecting Jimmy, back from the dead, to come stumbling out, cradling an injured thumb.

Instead, a young man close to his own age emerged, tossing aside a pile of charred wood.

The fear of his previous captors dissipated, but Kitsune still stood frozen in place. His eyes widened and his chest constricted. Though he had never seen this man before, he had the distinct notion he knew him.

He couldn't be sure from this distance, but Kitsune guessed the man to be a hair shorter than he. His dark brown mane was on the shorter side, though thick and disheveled. It framed a heart-shaped face with a strong jawline and high cheekbones. Several days' worth of facial hair sprouted from tanned skin, accentuating his masculinity. The absence of a shirt further helped this, and soot smeared his chest and abdomen. Like Kitsune, he wasn't incredibly muscular, but the prince saw the strength was there, as well as the will to use it.

The man picked up a fresh bundle of tinder, then disappeared out of view into the cavernous hearth.

This was the individual from his dream, the one inside the cottage waiting for him. Kitsune was unsure how he recognized this with such certainty, but it was as clear and true to him as the air he breathed. This dirt-covered man was his path.

Kitsune shook his head, reminding himself that his path may have led him to this man, but the journey must not end with him.

A sudden burst of flames roared from the hearth, and Kitsune heard the man yelp in surprise. In a flash, the prince leapt to his feet, ready to run to his aid. It proved unnecessary, for the other retreated from the now-roaring fireplace a moment later, wiping smoke and soot from his face. After a few moments of rubbing, he looked up, revealing soulful brown eyes.

And they were locked on to his.

"Good afternoon!" said the man in a soft but confident voice. He flashed a smile full of white teeth that shone brilliantly against his tan and soot-covered skin. He cocked his head toward the hearth. "I, uh, got the fire started."

"Who are you?" Kitsune asked. His heart found it a rude start to conversation, but his logical, well-trained mind fought for dominance. Despite what he understood of this man, he had to guarantee his own safety first. He did not want to be caught off guard again.

"I am Myobu," he responded. Then he pointed shyly at Kitsune. "The air is chilly, and I'm sure you're cold. I finished washing all your clothing. They are outside drying right now. If you would like to grab your cloak from the bed, you can sit here by the fire while I prepare us something to eat."

"Pardon?" Kitsune said, confused by Myobu's averting gaze. Then he looked down at himself and saw he was completely naked. Heat immediately exploded across his face, and he knew he had turned bright red in embarrassment. Instinct demanded he jump back into bed and hide himself from view. Instead, not wanting to fully reveal how flustered he had become, he casually reached back and picked his cloak up off the bed, wrapping it about himself. "I had another set of clothes in my pack?"

Myobu shook his head. "Everything was completely soiled. I took the liberty of cleaning your weaponry, too." He pointed to a table where Kitsune's sword and bow lay, looking as pristine as the day the Oinari weapons master crafted them. "Your hoshi no tama is the only item I didn't scrub down. That seemed personal."

Kitsune's hand reflexively went to his neck, where he fingered the jeweled chain. It was warm against his skin. Inside the emeralds, the remaining fragments of his grandmother's consciousness dwelled.

The chain didn't seem dirty. Certainly, *something* had cleaned it. But how could that be, if it was the only thing not scrubbed down?

As he came to a stop by the hearth, a few strands of his hair fell forward. They were so bright and clean they reflected light from the flames. Then the truth occurred to him, and if he had still been walking, he would have fallen over in shock.

Myobu bathed him!

Kitsune sat down on a bench, turning away from the other man to hide his flushing face. He took in a deep breath, trying to remain calm and logical. Myobu only did what was necessary, taking care of someone in need. Yes, he had undressed him and seen him at his most vulnerable and pathetic, something any healer would do. Perhaps Myobu was a healer by trade.

"Where are we?" he asked, attempting to focus on something else…anything else.

"I'm almost positive we're in Castle Nogare," said Myobu, watching him with an amused expression. "I can't be too sure. Looters have pillaged most of the items that would have born the place's name and seal. The location seems right, though."

"I'm not familiar with the area," Kitsune admitted. "I'm not from around here."

"We're a few leagues from the coast, then. Would have traveled farther, but I wanted to make sure you and the horses were well."

All that had transpired suddenly came to the front of Kitsune's mind, and guilt over not considering it sooner riddled him. He faced Myobu. "My friend? Mamori? Is he really…"

Myobu looked down, answer enough for Kitsune. He murmured, "I buried him by the beach. I made sure to lay his body to rest with his head to the west and feet to the east, in accordance with your culture."

Kitsune almost asked how the other knew they came from Kitsunetsuki, then remembered Mamori wore a military uniform. "And the others?"

"I took all their possessions and left their bodies for the wolves."

"Good," Kitsune said, weary again. The certainty that this stranger Myobu posed no threat to him remained, but the giddiness the dream filled him with had evaporated in the wake of remembrance. Mamori had been a good soldier, a loyal citizen, and in their short time of company, a real friend. It was Kitsune's fault he died. If he hadn't been the way he was, his father would never have banished him, and all would be well.

It might have been his imagination, but he was sure the hoshi no tama vibrated against his skin as though it disagreed with his train of thought.

Myobu seemed to realize Kitsune needed to mourn and excused himself to go find some dinner.

*

Just outside Castle Nogare's ruined front entrance, Myobu stood in wonderment. He observed how filthy and covered in soot he was, and he hoped his new companion had not noticed. Myobu spent a lot of time living outdoors and in the streets, so he was used to the dirt. Never before had he cared what others inferred by that. Why did he now?

The answer to his question was obvious. Fate had planted the seeds the night he crawled under the blankets to keep the stranger warm. Probably long before that, if he meant to be honest with himself.

Bow in hand, Myobu moved forward into the woods. He crept by the tethered horses, not wanting them to stir. Their nickering or stamping about would scare away potential dinner prospects, and hunger gnawed at his stomach.

Thankfully, it didn't take much walking before he heard a rustling in the nearby underbrush. Imagining he smelled rabbit, he sat on the ground. Careful not to snap any dry twigs, he leaned up against a tree and waited.

After raising his companion's fallen temperature that night, Myobu awoke the following morning to find him feverish. Fearing for the man's life, Myobu dragged him to a nearby creek and submersed him. He hoped the cooling waters would bring down the stranger's temperature. As days' worth of grime washed off the man's face and clothing, Myobu thought he'd make a stunning presence to be around—at least once conscious. He had fine features with long blond hair that drifted in the water like strands of silk.

Myobu's idea worked and, with the stranger's fever at least partially abated, he moved him to what he calculated to be Castle

Nogare. There he stripped the man, tossing the dirty clothes aside, and gave him a proper bath. He considered a clean body to be an essential step toward healing.

It was then that he saw the hoshi no tama hanging from his neck. He had been around the Yokai enough to conclude two things: the glowing emerald gems housed magic, but that magic did not belong to his companion. The man possessed magic of his own, that much was for certain, but he was not one of the Yokai.

A large rabbit hopped out of a bush, and it and Myobu froze. He watched as the animal moved its head around, its large eyes attempting to discern sources of danger. Myobu's bow lay on the ground next to him, but the movement of picking it up, not to mention nocking and drawing back an arrow, would alert the rabbit and send it darting away. He had other methods. He just had to be patient.

As the stranger rested and recovered, Myobu found his own thoughts to be distracting. At first, he thought it was because the man carried a hoshi no tama that didn't belong to him. To steal one filled with magic gave the individual great sway over its owner's actions and was thus taboo. However, scenarios other than thievery could have brought the stones into the man's possession.

And if Myobu's suspicions of the man's identity ended up being true, it was highly unlikely he had taken the necklace with malicious intent. The man's father, though, was more than malicious.

No, it was the stranger himself who so distracted Myobu's thoughts. Tending to the sick man gave him ample opportunity to admire his physique. He had seen men and women with slender builds, and he had touched skin soft and unblemished. His new companion did not stand apart from any of them. In fact, he preferred a little more meat on the bone than this one had.

The hair especially kept drawing Myobu's attention. It was long and so blond, neither of which were common where he lived. Once cleaned, the light reflected off the individual strands, almost as mesmerizing as the hair itself. Myobu daydreamed about it more often.

While lighting the fire in the hearth earlier, he pondered the sensation of running his hands through that hair.

Quick as a fox, Myobu reached out and plucked the rabbit from the ground. It gave one shrill shriek before he broke its neck. He stared at his kill for a few moments, determining it to be fat enough to feed two.

After retrieving his bow, Myobu stood up and made his way back to the castle. He listed other ingredients he'd need to make a proper stew, hoping to prepare something to the stranger's liking. The man's awakening pleased him, especially after the shape he'd been in initially. There was a time or two when Myobu didn't think the blond man would make it. Even more pleasing were the man's words and actions. Yes, they were those of someone disoriented, embarrassed, and somber. However, they did not reveal a selfish or entitled person, traits Myobu didn't care for.

Myobu glanced in one of the building's windows. The man still sat by the fire, mourning his soldier friend. Myobu found himself eager to distract his companion from his pain just as the blond man had done for him.

*

"Once I fed and watered the horses, I turned my attention to you. I needed to be sure those men hadn't injured you any more than what was visible."

Myobu handed Kitsune, now fully dressed, a bowl of stew. He joked it consisted of the vermin he had chased from the hall. Kitsune didn't care either way—the food smelled heavenly, and it'd been too long since he had eaten solid food. His stomach audibly growled for sustenance.

Dusk had fallen, and the two of them sat down on opposite sides of the fireplace. With the firelight casting dancing shadows and the stars visible through parts of the roof, Kitsune remembered camping just outside of Inari Palace as a youth. It was refreshing.

"Oh, so the horses took precedence over me?" Kitsune replied with a smirk. While his appetite had returned, so had his spirit.

"Truly? You were like a mule! As the drugs the mercenaries gave you wore off, you pushed and swatted at any attempts to move you. Quite obstinate."

"I am not obstinate!" he exclaimed, throwing a chunk of bread at Myobu.

"Well, you were, though whether it was you or the fever, I can't say. I simply don't know you well enough yet. Thankfully, aside from a few scrapes and bruises, you were unharmed. You were dehydrated and falling terribly ill. At one point your skin burned so hot I submerged your body in a creek."

"How long did I sleep?" Kitsune asked between mouthfuls of stew. He recalled from his studies that some contagions were isolated geographically. Scientists directly observed and studied this when the Eastern Gate permanently closed. He was aware a person could contract an illness just by drinking the water of another land or coming into contact with foreigners. Rarely having left the palace complex, he was probably abnormally susceptible.

"It's been three days since I stumbled across you. You probably could have awoken yesterday, but I got you to drink some herbal tea to help you rest. I wanted to be certain you had plenty of time to recover." Myobu's voice became soft. "I wasn't sure how you'd react to your friend's death, so I needed to be certain your body was strong."

Kitsune leaned forward. "Mamori was a recent acquaintance. Still, he was a friend, and he made a great sacrifice for me. Eventually, I will have to find his family and give them the terrible news and express my gratitude for his heroism and sympathy for his passing. Meanwhile, I can only thank you for saving my life, both from my captors and from illness. I am in your debt."

"Well, you can start repaying that debt by having a second helping," Myobu replied, ladling more stew into Kitsune's bowl.

They sat quietly for a while, polishing off their dinner. With a full belly, a warm fire, and the sound of crickets in the background, Kitsune relaxed for the first time in what seemed like ages. Though he had been unconscious for a couple days, he knew he'd sleep well tonight. Tomorrow he'd be ready to do…what exactly? What were his plans? How did Myobu fit into those plans, as his dream and grandmother seemed to imply he would?

He stole a glance across the hearth, catching his new friend staring openly at him. "What?"

"You're pretty," Myobu said, the lights of the fire reflecting in his eyes.

Kitsune was taken aback, assuming Myobu meant the comment to be an insult. He struggled with a retort. "Well, you've…got small hands."

Myobu held his hands up, gazing at them in a ponderous fashion. "I think they're all right. They're quite capable."

Capable of what? Kitsune asked himself. He couldn't take his eyes off Myobu's hands, now held up prominently for display. They weren't really that diminutive. Perhaps a bit smaller than average, though Kitsune's own long, slender fingers dwarfed them. He resisted the urge to reach out and touch them.

"I did not mean to be offensive," Myobu continued, lowering his hands. "About your being pretty, I mean. It's your hair. Blond hair isn't common where I'm from, and longer hair isn't in fashion for either men or women. It looks good on you. Very…pretty."

"Where are you from, exactly?" Kitsune asked, eager to take the attention off of him. His slender body had never truly been an issue for him, as he normally dispatched anyone who challenged him to physical combat with ease. Often, as with Captain Saxma, his combatants would face him in the bedchamber as well. Unless he took a fancy to being amenable, he usually came out on top of those altercations.

"I'm from way west of here. Gaav is where I call home," Myobu replied.

The self-doubt evaporated from Kitsune's thoughts in an instant, replaced by his duty and mission. "Truly? That is my current destination!"

"You've got quite a journey ahead of you," Myobu said with a knowing look. "Where do you hail from within Kitsunetsuki?"

As the name of his kingdom, which begat his own name, rolled off of Myobu's tongue, Kitsune realized he had not yet reciprocated the other's introduction. The thought flitted through his mind whether he should keep secret his identity. Myobu was likely playing coy, possibly having gleaned from him the information of his name and home while he was feverish. Plus, he preferred not to lie. Not that he had persuading moral issues with it. He couldn't come up with a single past situation when he had the cause to lie, and he wasn't sure he'd be able to effectively do so now.

Besides, the truth might be impressive.

"I come from Oinari. More specifically, Inari Palace. I am Kitsune of the Asher line, former prince of the kingdom." He said it casually, giving himself no pomp.

"Former prince?" Myobu asked, raising an eyebrow.

"Banished," Kitsune said as explanation.

"Well, Former Prince Kitsune," Myobu said, bowing his head slightly in respect, though Kitsune was sure he saw a hint of teasing in the other's eyes, "what takes you to my homeland? For such an arduous journey, it must be of great importance."

Kitsune considered his response carefully. He stuck close to the truth, revealing he sought a male member of King Marauxus' family, possibly his son. The plan to kill said family member remained under wraps, however. As a citizen of Gaav, Myobu might be fiercely loyal. Duty might compel him into actions that would prevent Kitsune from achieving his goal.

Brow wrinkled in confusion, Myobu responded, "Gaav has no prince. King Marauxus is rumored to invite other women to join him and his wife in the bed, but that is purely fanciful conjecture. There were no reports any lady birthed him a son."

"Whether or not the one I seek is the king's son or related by blood, I was told the king has kept his existence a secret."

"Why would they do that?"

"It's reported he possesses great magic." Kitsune remembered when his father stated this in the Boleyn Room. The reality of magic was just revealed to him, and he had been awestruck. By now he knew powers of such magnitude were truly something to be feared. He would eventually have to figure out exactly how he was going to carry out his intentions undetected.

Myobu's mouth dropped open in surprise. "You don't mean Marauxus' son! You're looking for the King's Sun!"

It was Kitsune's turn to appear surprised, especially as Myobu pointed up toward the sky with one of his beautiful little hands.

"The nickname of Marauxus' closest advisor is the King's Sun. Gifted with mighty powers, he can apparently exert his will over flame. Our researchers postulate the sun is composed of flame, which is how he gets his nickname. Otherwise, he's referred to as Ninko."

"Ninko," Kitsune whispered to himself. "Where would I find this man? I assume he'd be in the company of King Marauxus."

Myobu shrugged. "Ninko is an honorary citizen of Gaav, as he was born elsewhere. Part of his office, and perhaps a stipulation of his when accepting it, is traveling. He is absent for long stretches of time. Sometimes a full sun cycle. He departed on a mission about the same time I left Gaav. Probably won't return for quite some time. Why do you wish to speak with him?"

"I believe he can assist me in finding a way of ending my banishment," Kitsune replied, proud that this answer contained no lie.

"I'm certain he'll try to help you in any way he can."

"For what purpose are you traveling so far from home?" Kitsune said, changing the subject again.

"That's a tale I will reserve for our travels tomorrow," Myobu said, a mischievous look in his eyes. "I don't want to give away all my secrets in one day. Otherwise, you'll be bored of me before you know it!"

"We're traveling tomorrow?" Kitsune smiled inside, feeling strangely content that Myobu was planning to stay with him.

With an exaggerated yawn, Myobu said, "Yes. Not too far. I won't test your newfound strength. We do need to start moving, though. Someone might eventually come looking for your friends."

"Where are we heading?"

"North." Myobu said it with a hint of finality in his voice and got to his feet to emphasize the point. "For now, we need to get some sleep. You might not think you're tired, but I'd be willing to bet you'll sleep soundly tonight."

Truthfully, exhaustion was claiming victory over Kitsune. The information on the King's Sun, not to mention being in Myobu's presence, thrilled him. That excitement did not translate into energy, though. He knew if he closed his eyes and allowed his mind to calm, sleep would overtake him within heartbeats.

After insisting Kitsune once again take the bed, Myobu stretched out over one of the tables, wrapping himself in his cloak. In bed, Kitsune watched as the firelight danced over the other's figure. He was only slightly disappointed Myobu hadn't offered to sleep next to him…just to keep him warm. He would have declined, of course, but he dreamily considered pretending to be chilled and asking for such a favor. Then he lay back and tried to clear his mind of all distraction.

After a few tics, from across the room, Myobu whispered, "Kitsune?"

Only half awake, he responded, "Mhmm?"

"I don't care if you're a prince or banished or whatever."

"Okay."

"You're still pretty."

Isaac Grisham

THE ROAD NORTH

"Why am I here, Major?"

It took a moment for Saxma to recognize the title as his own, and he turned to face the small man standing at the entrance of his command tent. "I pulled a lot of strings to get you this promotion, Captain Pan. I would sound a little more respectful if I were you."

Pan stiffened, considering his next words more carefully. "I am grateful for your confidence in my abilities, sir. I didn't know you thought so highly of me. I didn't think you gave me much thought at all."

"Tell me," Saxma said, moving to a table in the center of the tent. Stacks of maps, reports, a lantern supplying the dark enclosure its only illumination, and a flagon of wine cluttered its surface. He reached for the drink. "How has your command experience been since we left Oinari six days ago?"

"It's been difficult, sir." Pan looked down, averting the major's eyes. "The company is disrespectful and doesn't approve of my being its commanding officer. The soldiers follow orders, but they do so slowly and sloppily. They've also taken to playing pranks on me."

Saxma smiled wickedly. "You put it like that and it seems you are failing the confidence I supposedly have in you."

"Sir?"

84

Saxma sat down in a chair behind the table. "The truth is I don't think highly of you, and I certainly don't like you. In the time since we've left the capital, your skills at command have proven abysmal, though I expected nothing more from you."

In truth, Pan proved even less capable of leadership than Saxma imagined possible. The company couldn't get past his short, unimposing stature. Neither could the new captain, it seemed. On more than one occasion, Saxma questioned his own decision of selecting Pan.

For that matter, Saxma could barely believe his own promotion. With Mamori's treason, he did not expect the promised reward for successfully concluding his directive. King Oni remained true to his word and granted him the rank of major the day after his return from the Eastern Gate.

The news, delivered by Saxma's colonel as he was still recovering from his long night of drinking at Portley's Pub, came with details of his new responsibilities in the north and orders to immediately depart from the capital with five hundred of the battalion's men. Saxma balked at leaving without being properly prepared to move such a large group on what would probably be a ten-day ride in the late summer heat. The colonel, passing along these instructions from his own superiors, hadn't budged.

Along with the usual perks that came with a promotion, such as a larger and better equipped tent to command from, the colonel granted Saxma permission to pick his own captain. This was a rare privilege, probably compensation for sending him to the outskirts of civilization with little notice. With only hours to consider his options, he requested the promotion of Pan.

"Which brings me back to my question, sir," Pan said, looking back up reservedly. "With all due respect, why am I here?"

Saxma took a long swig from the flagon, motioning for his subordinate to sit. "Proper command is a skill, Captain. It's obvious it won't come to you naturally. You clearly never observed how simple it was for me to lead the unit before you. With my guidance, I can help you gain their compliance, if not their respect.

"I may not like you, Captain, but I don't like any of my subordinates. To like them would be akin to friendship. Aside from leading your friends into deadly battle, it is hard to discipline them for disobeying or disrespecting you, even though you must punish subordinates who display such traits. Can you imagine yourself sentencing Nasuno or Tsuzumi to the cell boxes? You probably couldn't stomach it, but doing so would only help your image. Putting one of your own friends in a box for just a day as we travel through this unbearable heat would ensure the rest of the men never gave you problems again."

Pan looked ill at the thought of putting anyone, friend or not, into a cell box. Built out of thick planks of wood, they were only large enough so a single person could fit inside if they sat cross-legged and bent over. Small holes dotted the sides, meant to let in just enough air to survive.

"How would I get a man into a box? No one would voluntarily submit, and others would be slow to help."

"That's why I issued you a persuader," Saxma growled, choosing not to expand upon the subject. He reached for a glass, poured some wine into it, and pushed it toward Pan. "As much as watching you suffer at the hands of your own men has amused me, there's an actual reason I wanted you as my executive officer."

Shocked at being offered a drink, Pan only mustered, "Sir?"

"Conversation," Saxma whispered. "Discrete, hypothetical conversation. While I may not think too highly of you as an officer, I believe you are one of the more thoughtful men in the company. I suppose it's something to make up for your lack in stature. Also, I suspect, if given a choice or opportunity, you would align yourself with the former prince as your friend Mamori did."

Saxma saw the brief anger flash in the other man's eyes—anger directed at him and King Oni. There was also suspicion, and that distrust probably kept Pan from responding at all. Others had used such tactics to ferret out dissenters.

"I am a simple soldier, not a thinker or philosopher. I require your help in discussing particular subjects to better understand them and their implications," Saxma said, speaking carefully to protect himself in case Pan did not agree to his planned arrangement. "In return for such candor, I can help with your transition to captaincy. By the time we complete our project in the north, the men won't only respect you— they will *die* for you if you ask it of them."

Just as Saxma hoped, his statement grabbed Pan's attention. Few could resist the temptation of such power. The new captain seemed to toss the idea around in his head a few times, considering the pros and cons as well as the risks of such a deal. Finally, with the glass of wine in hand, Pan sat back into the chair, looking up with a slightly increased air of confidence, as if conversing was something he knew he excelled at.

"What do you wish to speak of today?" Pan asked in a level, confidential tone.

Saxma questioned the king's intentions ever since returning to Oinari. The idea plagued him that the monarch's words were not entirely true. In truth, what Oni announced did not seem beneficial for the kingdom or its citizens.

Mamori's words often echoed in his head: *I am bound by oath to protect the king and his family. In turn, the king's duty is to protect his people.* The soldier believed the king failed in his duties. Saxma now wondered the same thing, which would follow with the conclusion he was an antagonist working on the behalf of his leader, an adversary to the people Oni ruled over.

Any time Saxma reached that point, beginning to ponder what he should do to correct matters, an overwhelming urge to disregard such traitorous thoughts washed over him. Those impulses lessened since marching north, giving him a clarity of mind he hadn't felt since childhood. He was beginning to understand himself, for better or worse, and for the first time appreciate Mamori's political concerns.

Saxma knew he wasn't a good and honorable man. Good men didn't rape unconscious prisoners while fondling the breasts of a petrified young woman. There were codes he lived by and respected, though. His oath and military duty were but two of them. They gave purpose and direction to his life, as well as food in his belly, clothes on his back, and coins in his pockets.

While moving his men north, he started to see the world on a broader scale. He wondered if his oath and duty were to the king himself or to Kitsunetsuki as a whole. Previously, his answer would have been to Oni. Only now did he lean toward the latter. The kingdom surely didn't exist to stand up and support the monarchy. Rather, the monarchy was there to maintain its lands and citizens. If one king passed and another ascended the throne, Saxma's duty didn't die with the previous monarch—it transferred to the next one.

If these ideas were true, he rather suspected he was being used to carry out a devious plot. While he may not be a good and honorable man, Saxma would be damned before becoming a traitor to his oath.

It occurred to Saxma that he was turning his analytical mind toward other things than his own career advancement. Before reacting emotionally and possibly destroying that career, he knew he needed to step back and gain a better understanding of the issues at hand. Only through comprehension could he justify any course of action.

"King Oni gave a public address shortly after we left the capital with the prince," Saxma started, sitting back in his chair. "I assume you've informed yourself of its content. In your own words, summarize your understanding of the speech and the intentions it laid out."

Pan looked into his cup, gathering his thoughts. "It was purportedly an eloquent speech, a reminder of how personable and charming King Oni can be. He started with how proud he was to be the head of such a great realm and respectable people, and he was more than satisfied with how the military accomplished his goals over the sun cycles. There were just the slightest of hints further expansion was imminent and the people should be ready to act if called upon."

Pan's eyebrows drew closer together. "The speech apparently took a drastic turn as he spoke of the conquered lands of Ruio and Mogo. He referred to their inhabitants as savages in need of enlightenment, indicating that need as a primary reason we marched against them. Now that we are all under one banner, that of Kitsunetsuki, we can bring civilization to them."

Saxma held up a hand to pause Pan's monologue. "I heard similar reports. How do those statements strike you?"

"I agreed with the assessment at first," Pan responded. "It seemed only natural to do so. However, as I've pondered the matter since we left the capital, the more...ridiculous it became."

Saxma leaned forward. "Why is that?"

"I was too young to be in the campaigns against either nation, and I've never traveled there independently, but I sure spent a lot of time studying them in school. Mogo and Ruio were not like the tribal lands, unruly and unorganized. They had highly advanced societies on par or even exceeding our kingdom. Due to our close proximities, our cultures, beliefs, and customs were similar, which was probably why we existed in peace for many hundreds of sun cycles. The only recent difference was the size of King Oni's military."

"I had a similar reaction," Saxma said. "I took everything at face value. It was only later as we left Oinari behind when I remembered traveling to Mogo as a child. Having seen their high standards of living firsthand, I question the king's words. They do not fit."

"I do not understand," Pan began. "Why would the king relay such fallacy, and how did neither of us notice it immediately? I have heard no one else speak similarly, but I seriously doubt the two of us were the only ones to suffer such a lack of the obvious."

"While your questions are pressing, the answers are beyond my grasp. I suggest we question some other soldiers to ascertain how widespread the condition is. Discreetly, of course," Saxma said. Then, thinking a moment, he added, "If anyone else has noticed discrepancies, I'd be curious when they noticed."

Pan nodded enthusiastically, and Saxma made a mental note not to give the man wine before discourse again.

"What else did the king relay regarding Mogo and Ruio?" Saxma pressed.

"The king claimed annexing the barbaric lands had an unanticipated effect. We brought civilization, culture, and high morale to their people since conquering them," Pan said with a hint of disdain only the well-educated could pull off. "As if we could instill such things within a generation."

Saxma silently agreed. He recognized he was not the most civilized or cultured person in the land. He was gruff, drank bad beer, and ate half-cooked meat. He also knew how unlikely it was anything would change his ways and habits. They may be backward, but they were simple and familiar. He imagined it would take many generations to alter the ways of an uncivilized people. If they were barbaric to begin with.

"Supposedly, some of their more unsettling behaviors permeated back into the heart of Kitsunetsuki," Pan continued. "The king said, in retrospect, it would have been unlikely that we did not assimilate a few of their fledgling rituals. The ones that had, though, absolutely must be weeded out. That process will begin with a new set of laws and a formalization of morals and ethics. There will be an itemized list of what is or is not allowed, the applicable leniency, and the level of punishment for not obeying."

"The *leniency*?" Saxma said, blinking.

"Take murder, for example," Pan responded. "It's a serious crime with a severe punishment. There are circumstances, however, where leniency can be applied. As soldiers, we are charged with protecting the royal family. In the line of duty, we may have to kill a would-be assassin. Technically, that's murder, but the situation leads to little or no investigation or punishment."

"Yes, yes. That's why we have courts and judges. What is new about all this?"

"Two things really. The first is the audacity to dictate morals and ethics. To say what is right and wrong for one person absolutely must be the same for another. Society is too complicated an organization for such an idea to be practically implemented. Also, it's just wrong. It's an immoral plan."

"This is a directive from our king," Saxma argued, though he wasn't sure if he was arguing against Pan's point or for his own agreement with it. "So it must be right, and shouldn't we all strive to follow?"

"There's a small religious sect west of Oinari," Pan said, changing tactics. "They believe drinking wine is an act of depravity. To them, imbibing is a sin that taints their souls. About four hundred sun cycles ago, a king went mad. Among many of the crazy ideas he proposed, he demanded that all meals include a cup of wine. All citizens would have to comply or face execution! It would have placed those people in a situation to either die or, in their eyes, commit a heinous act. It would have been wrong.

"Conversely, it would be wrong for that sect to enforce their ideals on others." Pan raised his cup. "You and I, for example, would find it difficult to obey. Not only that, but entire industries involved in the production of wine would go under. Jobs would be lost. Economies would suffer. On and on."

Saxma nodded in understanding. "The abolition of wine is a ridiculous notion, though."

"It is!" Pan exclaimed. His cheeks flushed red, the wine now visibly affecting him. "It's good you realize that, because the idea is truly no less preposterous than some of the laws the monarch is about to enact, which is the second part of his new plans."

"For example?"

"Sex," Pan said, alluding to what Saxma believed to be a core issue. "I'm not speaking about whoring or what some soldiers might indulge in as we pass through lonely villages. King Oni presumes that he can tell others who they can and cannot love, believing he can restrict and regulate it like an industry. It's like putting a cow in the middle of a green pasture and saying it can't eat grass. It's not realistic, and it will result in many people being exiled from Kitsunetsuki."

"Just like Prince Kitsune," Saxma said, avoiding Pan's brief look of anger.

"Don't get me wrong," Pan continued. "I've reviewed the preliminary list of new laws, and there are many that will better the kingdom. In my humble opinion, though, for every good one, there's a snake ready to rear its head."

"Why any of this?" Saxma said. "What's the goal of this restructuring if it's not to bring civilization to new territories or excise practices that came into our own? I can't imagine the entire scheme is to justify banishing Prince Kitsune, as there would be easier ways to be rid of him. As I understand it, the prince is devoted to his father. Kitsune would have fallen onto his own sword if the king asked it of him. No, there's something else at play as a driving factor."

The two fell quiet for a bit in consideration, sipping their drinks. Pan's head began to droop, and Saxma was afraid he'd have to drag the man to his own tent before long. In a moment of clarity, though, Pan looked up and said softly, "We must take into consideration the old rumors of Oni's parentage. That his father married a Yokai spirit. Legends say the fruit of such pairings are incredibly intelligent, seeing things on a different plane than most others. This makes them and their actions extraordinarily difficult to understand."

"If the spirits are real, and Oni is the product of such a union," Saxma started, "we must also consider the possibility he has some control over the supernatural."

Pan finished Saxma's thought. "Which could explain why we, and assumedly everyone else, were so agreeable to his pronouncements no matter how contradictory they were with what we know."

"We have a lot to consider."

"Agreed," Pan said, stumbling to his feet. "Although if I have another drop, I won't remember a damned thing we discussed. With your leave, sir, I'll go and sleep this off."

Saxma took a gulp of his wine as he watched the other man leave the tent. He knew he should stop drinking for the night as well. A soldier in the field was never truly off duty. The mention of supernatural dealings, however, had him on edge.

Aside from his uncharacteristic acceptance of the king's statements and perhaps the mysterious golden lights coming from the Boleyn Room, Saxma never knowingly experienced anything otherworldly. He still wasn't convinced, though he didn't discount it. Like most of the military, he claimed to have no fear of the unknown while actually having a healthy dose of respect for it. One could never know for sure.

As for the Yokai spirits, he never questioned their existence. He never gave them or King Oni's parentage much thought. He'd never had to. Rather, he assumed the rumors were just the commoners' fears of the intelligence and power of people in better positions than themselves.

Saxma sighed, looking down at the maps strewn across the table. He absentmindedly moved some about with a free hand, not seeing what was on the paper. Instead, he imagined the road north to their destination. His colonel had briefed him on the project he was to oversee, though the details were slim. It still seemed a strange place to send such a large contingent of men and an even stranger area for massive development. He had been told it was ambitious and grandiose, words he usually translated into worthless.

He couldn't shake the feeling that, as a pawn having fulfilled its purpose in Oni's ultimate game plan, he was being shuffled off to the sidelines. On top of everything else, he didn't care for that one bit.

It would make for an interesting discussion with Pan during their next meeting.

MAGIC

The sun shined bright, the air dry and hot. Still, the white sand beneath Kitsune's feet did not burn. The ground was cool to the touch. The Lady of the Mountain was lying in a poised position, staring up at him. Her face had the usual calm exterior, though she displayed a hint of a smile in one corner of her mouth.

"What?" he said playfully, sitting cross-legged next to her. He looked out across the land, seeing nothing but rolling hills of sand so purely white it could have been mistaken for snow. Aside from the blue sky above, mountains in the distance were the only focal point on the landscape. They were distinctly different from those in Kitsunetsuki. With harsher edges and taller peaks, these appeared to be newer formations.

"What color are his eyes?" she asked.

"A beautiful dark chocolate brown," he answered, a broad smile breaking out across his face. It felt good there.

Despite the dire events having transpired of late, Kitsune found he was smiling more often than not. These dreamy getaways with his grandmother brought him immense comfort. It was a place where he easily forgot his worries and fears. He could get used to it, though there remained two reasons he could not remain in the dreamscape forever, other than the fact that his physical body needed sustenance. Myobu was one such reason.

The other, of course, was that his father was counting on him to complete his mission.

"Does he like you as much as you like him?" She said it in the same serene voice she always spoke in, but Kitsune recognized that she was teasing him.

"I'm not twelve, Grandmother!" He paused, realizing what he felt for Myobu was an entirely new emotion to him. There was nothing for him to compare it to. Despite his best efforts to conform to his king's new code of ethics, he admittedly wanted Myobu. It was an urge he had around any man or woman as attractive as this dark-haired man. What he truly desired, however, was for Myobu to stick around. To stay with him.

Kitsune was aware people tended to pair themselves. While he had observed and understood it his whole life, it never crossed his mind to partake in the custom. He shared his bed with several since discovering the joys of sex and continued to enjoy the company and conversation of those he'd been with, but not once had he considered staying with just one permanently.

That changed in the four days of traveling the pair now shared. Kitsune wanted this new companion as a whole.

"I've never experienced this sensation before," he continued. "It makes me feel like...when he and I are together, there are no limits to what we might accomplish. Everything in the world seems right."

"You have not answered my question."

Kitsune drew random lines in the sand with a finger, not knowing how to answer. In truth, he wasn't sure. Not much had changed between them during their travels. Kitsune grew more confident as time passed and his full strength returned, and he no longer acted like a prepubescent adolescent stumbling over his own words. Myobu remained his usual charming, slightly flirtatious self, always assured and always flashing a brilliant smile.

What he wanted to find out, though he wasn't yet sure how to inquire without insult, was if his inability to quash these new feelings resulted from the Yokai blood he had inherited from his grandmother. There were stories in which members of her kind developed rapid, close bonds with humans. He could not afford to become so enamored.

"Give it time," the Lady said wisely. "The creation of a true relationship can take many sun cycles. It's like a piece of finely woven magic, and you don't want to rush it."

Kitsune didn't quite understand that, but it made him recall something else concerning magic. "I never thanked you for saving me from Benjamin and Jimmy."

She rotated her head toward him, replying, "I do not understand what you speak of."

"The lightning that came down from the sky. It knocked us all from the cart, giving Mamori a chance to take down Jimmy..." He didn't continue, not wanting sadness to well up within him. "The lightning was green, just like your hoshi no tama. I assumed it was you, reaching out from the emeralds with your magic."

"You must remember I have no magic in this world left to me, grandson. I could not produce lightning of any color outside of this dreamscape." She pushed herself upward to sit across from him. Her body did not disturb the fine granules of sand, as though she were hovering just above the ground. "The lightning you saw was of your own doing."

"I did no such thing!" he countered, shocked at what she implied. The only times he had done anything remotely similar to producing lightning was to shock other people on contact after walking across a rug on particularly dry days—which was always just as surprising and painful to himself as it was to the other person.

"You may not have thought, *Lightning, come forth from the sky and strike these men down.* Tell me, though, were you in a state of great distress and need, searching for a way to save yourself and take control of the situation?"

The crisp desert skyline began to blur, the jagged mountain peaks becoming less defined, as though they were mimicking Kitsune's thoughts. He reached back through his hazy, drugged memories, remembering one of his captors unveiling their ultimate plan. The agenda involved the death of himself and Mamori. Even now, the memory brought up the engrained nature to defend himself. He had been angry and scared, and he vaguely recalled searching for something within himself for protection.

"Emotions play a large part in magic," his grandmother continued. "Especially for those like yourself who are the offspring or descendants of the Yokai and humans. Sometimes the talent within such an individual is apparent from a young age, and an elder can teach them to control and use that power. More often, however, these persons will never realize their hidden potential. If it is at all discovered, it is usually through great emotional upheaval. Emotionally distressed beings with newfound magical abilities can provide a disastrous result, which is why many people fear all magic."

During his childhood, Kitsune often dreamed of being granted mystical powers and saving the world from beings with the evilest of intentions. Legendary tales fueled those fantasies. Great leaders defeating massive armies against all odds, building entire cities within a day, and curing deadly plagues. He recalled stories of dark individuals who manipulated entire countries into malevolent actions, cause terrible climactic events, and erupt volcanos.

As he matured, Kitsune focused his dreams on more realistic goals and accomplishments. Even those crumbled, becoming harder to attain than he ever expected. He must not let his imagination run wild with his newfound gifts, if they were gifts at all. He looked intently at the Lady. "Wouldn't the inherent abilities within Yokai and human offspring be less than that of a full-blooded Yokai?"

"That is usually the situation, yes," the Lady conceded, looking into his eyes as though she were reading his thoughts, which she probably was. "It is not always how nature works itself out, however. Magical abilities among the Yokai vary, and it differs in their hybrid children. Some of the most powerful creatures to walk these lands result from these pairings.

"Keep in mind," she added, her voice taking on a mixture of warning and scolding, "the fables you grew up with are just that: make-believe. I have never heard of anyone slaying an entire legion of men with just a sword. Nor is it recorded anywhere that someone buried a city under volcanic ash just because they thought it so."

"I know. I'm just…overwhelmed by this. Before coming across you, I never would have believed any person held control over the supernatural, or that there even *was* a supernatural to control. Now I have done so myself without realizing it. Knowing I haven't even begun to understand what I'm capable of doing and how such power would help me and others…is exhilarating and terrifying."

She put a hand on his shoulder. "I just don't want you putting yourself in dangerous situations, thinking you can rely on magic to save you. What you need to do is begin training. Only then will you start to understand your own specific power and the force with which you conjure it."

"You said the magic within people differs?"

"Not necessarily the magic, but the power it imbues them with. Individual minds all lean in a slightly different direction. Just as those variances affect the personalities, mannerisms, and choices people make, they also point toward different aspects of power. Healers are but an example. Conjurers another."

"What was your particular power?" Kitsune asked.

"I had the unique talent of bringing life back to things lifeless."

After a few moments of silence, Kitsune thought she would not reveal more. Then he noticed the sand beneath her body rippled outward in concentric circles. Small seeds, long beyond their ability to germinate, made their way to the surface. As he watched, they sprung roots and leafy stems. The roots embedded themselves in the ground, in search of whatever sustenance the dreamscape supplied them. The stems grew upward, sprouting additional leaves and eventually exquisite flowers.

"My power was a dangerous one, requiring great wisdom to even practice. Without proper forethought, acts of beauty such as these flowers could end up having dire consequences. Because of this, I rarely used it."

"How do I find out what my particular ability is? What does training entail?"

"Uncovering your unique talent should not prove to be difficult. The lightning you have already produced will aid in your discovery. As for training…I'm no expert. I've never studied or taught anyone who was learning their own powers, but I would suggest starting with meditation."

"Meditating?" Kitsune said incredulously.

"Magic is not fun, and it certainly is not a toy," the Lady said, this time really scolding him. The sand leveled out as if to emphasize her point, burying the plants that a moment before had been thriving. "Are you aware of how much damage a single bolt of lightning can do? You must tread carefully lest you injure yourself or those around you."

"Of course, Grandmother," he said, admonished. "What should I contemplate upon?"

"Meditate on what brings out the strongest emotions in you. Think of joy and sorrow, peace and anger. Then consider how those things affect you and your environment, if at all. Much as how a person's mood affects others close by, the effects of magic can be contagious. Focus on lightning and what it relates to. It is possible that you wield control over the energy contained within lightning, storm systems, or over entire weather patterns. Eventually, you will find how your emotions affect your power, and you can use them to manipulate the latter."

"Can you walk me through it?"

"I would love to, grandson, but someone is calling to you now."

"Huh?"

*

Myobu glanced over at his traveling companion to find Kitsune nodding off again. The prince looked so peaceful, the cares of the world having slipped away. He wanted to study the man. Examine his skin up close. Feel the blood pulsing underneath it. Run his hands through that long, blond hair.

Heat was building up inside of Myobu, and he shook his head. He looked forward at the hindquarters of the two waddling horses in front of him, pulling the cart inherited from Kitsune's former captors. He had to focus on the path. The horses certainly didn't. If he continued to fantasize about being close to the prince, he'd get lost in thought. That would leave them vulnerable to a new group of would-be captors.

It had been hard to keep his distance from his companion ever since Kitsune regained consciousness. He would never do anything inappropriate, but he had constantly been by the prince's side until he'd been well. He bathed the man and wiped away his feverish perspirations, seeing him at his most vulnerable. Not that he wanted Kitsune to remain unconscious, but Myobu enjoyed the sensation of touching the other man's skin.

"Kitsune!" Myobu said. He tried his best to strike a calm pose and bemused look. "Wake up, Kitsune!"

The prince snapped awake, immediately crouching low in his seat. He glanced about their surroundings, attempting to identify any lurking dangers. Myobu watched as recollection flooded the man's eyes, then their gazes locked on to one another. Kitsune looked as though he wanted to be irritated but could only find calm in what was before him.

While pleased he inspired serenity in the one he daydreamed about, Myobu questioned if it was for the best.

"You're supposed to be keeping a lookout for mercenaries, not napping," Myobu said with a grin. "It's the middle of the day, anyway. How can you be tired? We get plenty of sleep."

"I haven't slept well these past few nights," Kitsune admitted.

Myobu wondered how he failed to notice, and he grew concerned for the prince. "Why didn't you tell me? Are you well? We should stop and rest right now."

Kitsune waved away Myobu's fears. "No, I haven't felt this good since I left home. Better, probably, to tell you the truth. You've done a splendid job nursing me back to sound health and mind. I should really reward you."

"You can pull double duty for a bit," he replied, handing Kitsune the reins. There were many other rewards he would have preferred, and he briefly entertained mentioning one or two of them lightheartedly, but the last thing either of them needed in the middle of rural Odom was for him to make things awkward. "You make napping look amazing. I just hope I don't drool like you!"

Kitsune gave a laugh, though it sounded somewhat hollow. "I won't be cleaning it up if you do!"

The day's travel and hot sun made Myobu drowsy, though he didn't think a nap would do him much good. He'd probably only dream of his companion. He'd instead pretend to sleep yet in actuality keep an eye out for thieves. At least he could continue to surreptitiously steal more sideways glances at Kitsune that way.

*

The next hour was like triple duty for Kitsune, not double. For one, he had to keep the horses on the road. The beasts were elderly, probably having changed hands and designations multiple times, and Kitsune had not the heart to burden them with new names. The horses were affable but not bright. While wagon trails marked the path and the animals most likely used to long days of walking, they would trot in a straight line right into a river if left to themselves. Still, he was growing fond of them.

His other duty, as Myobu pointed out earlier, was keeping an eye out for danger. The farther north they traveled, the more people they came across. Most were friendly, honest folk trying to eke out a living in Odom's bleak economic landscape. The pair spent the last few nights visiting campfires, trading goods and regional news. As the travelers looked out for one another, the chances of falling victim to mercenaries like Benjamin and Jimmy lessened. Still, they never ascertained who hired those two, as was the potential for future attempts to complete their botched job. Also, amid talks of large raiding parties, Kitsune grew acutely aware the darkness of night was the perfect cloak for thieves.

The final and most troublesome job was attempting to keep his wandering eyes on the trail and not Myobu's sleeping figure. One moment he was steering the horses over a hill and the next he was examining the man's side profile, admiring the shape of his nose or wondering over those long, thick eyelashes. He fought down the urge to straddle him across the lap and wake him up by kissing his soft lips, something he would have done with no hesitation in Oinari.

The cart lurched, snapping Kitsune out of another reverie. He brought the horses back into line, risking a quick glance over at Myobu to find the mishap had not awoken him. The prince chided himself, fixing his eyes ahead, determined to stay focused.

This had been how the past couple of days transpired. When he wasn't stealing sideways glances at Myobu, admiring his smooth, tan skin, he was conversing, soaking up all the knowledge he could about his new friend, trying hard not to sound too much like a fool in return. No matter how much information Myobu divulged about himself, which he seemed to give away freely, he still had a shroud of mystery about him. He answered most every question Kitsune threw at him, but those responses only birthed new lines of inquiry.

"We're traveling north," Myobu had answered the morning they left Castle Nogare. Kitsune asked him again where they were heading.

"You said as much last night. What is our actual destination?"

"We're going into the tribal lands," Myobu responded. "You should be able to get answers, or at least a direction, from the Harbinger."

"Isn't a harbinger someone who can see into the future, like a forecaster?" Kitsune asked. "Don't we need someone who is more of a clairvoyant, who can see what is? Or maybe an augur, who can do both?"

Myobu rolled his eyes, but there was a small smile in the corners of his mouth. "It is just what she calls herself. Her real name is Kyubi."

"Well, how can we trust someone who hasn't properly titled themselves," Kitsune teased. "How would you like it if I revealed I was a cook, despite my title of prince?"

"You can bring it up with the Harbinger when we see her!" Myobu said, giving him a playful shove. Kitsune hammed it up, rolling off the side of the cart and feigning injury. "Besides, I'd like you no matter what you did or what your title was."

Kitsune's mouth went dry, and he wondered exactly what Myobu meant. He hadn't raised the question, afraid the answer wouldn't be to his preference. Perhaps more afraid it would be. After climbing back into the cart, he returned to the point by asking, "So who is the Harbinger, or Kyubi, and how can she help us?"

"She's one of the Yokai spirits. Possibly the oldest of her kind alive, though you wouldn't know her age except that her hair is completely white. As they grow older, the Yokai gain the abilities to see, hear, and comprehend anything happening in the world. The oldest have infinite wisdom and can answer any question presented to them."

"Like where I'll be able to find Ninko," Kitsune said, catching on. He wondered that, for not believing in the Yokai for his entire life, they seemed to be all around him.

"That, and so much more." Kitsune noticed a touch of sadness in Myobu's voice.

"You have seen her yourself?"

"I have!" Myobu replied, the melancholy evaporating.

"What did you ask her?"

"Generally, how best I might serve Gaav."

"And the response?"

"She pointed me in the direction of Kitsunetsuki's Eastern Gate," Myobu said. Then he gave a big smile. "And I came across you!"

"Ah, so that's the reason you've been nursing me back to health! It's for the good of your king! Here I thought it was because you liked me." They chuckled, but Kitsune's stomach sank. What Myobu had to do for his own kingdom was not in the best interests of Gaav. If the Harbinger was wrong in pointing Myobu toward him, how could he trust her with his own questions? Whether or not her answers proved helpful was irrelevant, though, as they had to travel through the tribal lands to get to Gaav.

If Myobu seemed keen to avoid any area of conversation as they rode north, it was his childhood. Again, he would answer any question Kitsune posed, but kept replies short and succinct. It was as though he himself was trying to remain distant from the answers.

From what Kitsune stitched together, Myobu's parents died during some kind of battle when he was young. He had since lived in Hawte, the capital of Gaav, near the homes of the royal family. It surprised Kitsune to learn Gaav's leaders lived in a specially designed community of homes as opposed to one grand structure, a trait inherited from their nomadic days when building ostentatious permanent structures was not feasible.

Myobu grew up as a homeless orphan in Hawte, finding shelter when and where it was available. He always tried to stick as close to the leaders' community as possible. When the royal family needed help, they gave the unemployed chances to work and earn generous wages, and he was always in line to serve. He was familiar with all aspects of the royal community, having helped with building construction and maintenance, preparing and serving meals at diplomatic banquets, and security. They used his skills so often he had the coin to rent a room for more permanent lodging. Myobu seemed to prefer roughing it, however, remaining easily mobile.

"I like to travel," Myobu explained. "While I call Gaav my home, I was not born there. As often as I can, I will run diplomatic packages for King Marauxus. It pays well, and it gives me the chance to see new places."

That sounded appealing to Kitsune, who had spent most of his life inside of Inari Palace. He always knew of the greater world. An encyclopedia of knowledge about it resided in his brain. His banishment opened his eyes to how big it was, though, and he realized he needed to experience such things and not just read about them.

*

"What's on your mind?" Myobu asked.

They had made good distance that day. Night fell, and they made camp amid some trees. With the horses fed and watered, Myobu built a fire while Kitsune gathered leaves and spread out their cloaks and blankets for bedding. The prince knew the nighttime temperatures were sure to fall as summer gave way to autumn, and he wondered if they should attempt to procure better sleepwear for their travels.

Kitsune looked up from the fire to see Myobu staring at him. As usual, the prince's breath caught in his throat. "I may have the ability to wield magic."

The words tumbled out of his mouth, and he thought the other man might consider him stupid. That alone was preposterous, as Myobu had admitted to traveling great distances on the word of the Harbinger, a Yokai spirit. Still, Kitsune was relieved and surprised with the response.

"I know with a great deal of certainty that you have such abilities."

"You do? How so? It's only occurred to me recently." Kitsune may have only realized it today, but he knew he should have considered the possibility the moment he recognized the Lady as a blood relative.

"It's all about you," Myobu said, his face scrunching up as he tried to verbalize his thoughts. The light of the fire exaggerated his features.

"Some people have an air of power about them, like kings and queens. Others have an infectious laugh or persona that draws others in. You…you have a different type of energy. It gives you an aura of power and still manages to put others at ease."

"How would you know I put others at ease?"

"I've seen you interact with others on the road. You speak to them, and their faces—downcast and weary from days of travel—light up in an instant. They hang on to your every word, finding comfort in your assurances about the safety or warnings of danger on the path ahead of them."

"That's just coincidence," Kitsune said, exasperated. He didn't need to know about his personality. His teachers had taught him to be diplomatic, courteous, and an understanding man of the people. "That's just who I am. There are scores of others out there with the same qualities. It requires nothing special."

"I disagree with that," Myobu said in a rebuking tone. "Nevertheless, there is still the matter of the green lightning you called down. I've never seen a non-special man do such a thing."

"You saw that?"

"How could I not?" Myobu exclaimed. "It was the largest bolt of lightning I've ever seen, though that may have been due to my proximity. Still, the thunder knocked me off my feet!"

Kitsune didn't remember any thunder, but he had been so close to the source, so ill, and so dazed. "If this capability is within me, I need to properly harness it. I shouldn't be accidentally drawing upon it, but that kind of power would be incredibly useful. I need to figure out how to use it, which will require training."

"Do you know how to do that?"

"I guess I should begin by meditating," Kitsune replied, copying his grandmother's advice. The doubt in his mind must have shown through his voice, though, because Myobu gave him a look.

"Meditating is precisely the best way to train for the use of magic. It can teach you patience and help you uncover new facets of yourself you never thought were there. You can learn precisely what your gifts are, how to harness them, and when not to use them," Myobu explained. "You may think meditating sounds dull, but it doesn't have to be so. I do it all the time."

Myobu stood up, his feet crunching the leaves and twigs on the ground. He held out a hand to Kitsune.

"You know an awful lot about meditation," Kitsune observed, taking Myobu's hand. He enjoyed the warmth as the other helped him to his feet. Not wanting to relish the sensation too much, he took back his hand and followed Myobu into the trees.

"I've been around magic for most of my life. King Marauxus considers those with the gift to be special, so there's always one or two Yokai descendants around the neighborhood. I've picked up a few tips from them, and I'm more than happy to pass them along to you now."

They came into a small clearing, and Myobu brought Kitsune to a standstill. Then he turned and walked a few footfalls farther. Away from the warmth of the fire, the chill of the night air hit Kitsune. It was not yet uncomfortable. On the contrary, it awakened his mind and senses. The air was still, so the trees, branches, and starlight looked like one magnificent tapestry.

"Not all those with the gift display the same abilities," Myobu said, unknowingly paraphrasing the Lady of the Mountain. "Generally, though, magic draws upon or is influenced by emotions, making it vital that you can control them. This can be especially difficult when the sentiments needed to produce a desired action contradict the situation. For example, say there's an enemy soldier in your palace intent on killing you."

"I pity him," Kitsune murmured.

"Hush. Furthermore, let's imagine your talents leaned toward influencing others' feelings and actions. To stop the soldier, you might attempt to fill him with love, compassion, and the desire to defect."

"Or I run my sword through him," Kitsune interrupted.

"It's just an example," Myobu exclaimed. Kitsune thought he saw the man roll his eyes. "Anyway, producing such feelings requires those same emotions within you. That might be difficult to accomplish, however, considering you're being hunted down. The natural reaction is fear and anger." After a pause, Myobu continued, "Imagine a confrontation on a battlefield. You've lost your weapons, and the only tool at your disposal is your magic. Your rival is probably a good man forced into another's war, and you don't hate or fear him. The only emotion you have in connection to him is devotion and loyalty to your king, for whom you fight. How would you use those against your opponent?"

Kitsune confessed he did not know.

"While learning to control one's emotions is a worthy endeavor for those endowed with magic and those who are not," Myobu went on, "one of the first steps in mastering your unique talents is discovering exactly what they are and which related emotions are necessary to summon them. Only after that is complete should we attempt anything more complicated."

"How do I begin?" Kitsune replied, taking the exercise seriously now.

Myobu gestured for Kitsune to close his eyes. This was something he'd rather not do, not wanting to cut his senses of the other off, but he obliged. "Empty your mind of the thoughts and ideas you constantly dwell upon, then fill it with one thing you are passionate about. It should be simple. While I know your father and the mission he has sent you on elicit powerful feelings, they are complicated and intertwined with many aspects of your life. Picture instead something more akin to the love a parent has for their child. It's natural and pure."

As Myobu alluded to, it was more difficult than Kitsune imagined to experience an uncomplicated emotion, especially in relation to family. His loyalty to the king was complex by the fact that they shared the same blood. He would put down his own life for his father, but continual disappointment and adolescent anger had mired the purity of the relationship. While he had been in contact with his grandmother for just a short while, even that familial tie was multifaceted. It threw into question who his grandfather was, why no one told him this horrid history, and his own Yokai heritage.

Without meaning to, Kitsune's mind settled on Myobu. His thoughts cleared and became overwhelmed with singular passion. So many tangles still existed, like his father's disapproval of his being with another man or whether Myobu suffered the same giddy infatuation, but the emotion was as raw and pure as Kitsune could imagine. Disappointment would inevitably carve into the emotions as Kitsune trained his mind to conform with the new laws, but for now it was real and true and exactly what he needed to progress.

"I have something," Kitsune said, breathing deeply as he embraced the strong sentiments making his heart quicken and his stomach dance.

"Good," Myobu whispered, his voice low and raspy. "Now for the hard part. You need to uncover exactly what your magical talents are. This usually takes months to figure out, even many sun cycles. Knowing you can harness the power of lightning gives you considerable direction. Even so, do not get frustrated if it takes you time, as that erodes the raw emotions you need. Even if an emotion does not relate to your magic, you can still meditate on how it affects you and others."

The wind picked up a little. Branches creaked above them and dried-up leaves rustled along the forest floor. Despite the chill in the night, Kitsune's thoughts had warmed his body, and the breeze livened him. He responded in a husky voice, "I never believed in or expected to hold such a thing as magic, and I do not assume to master it quickly. I have other skills with which to defend myself and complete my goals. And I have you. I will not be frustrated."

"Perfect. Now, as you keep that one thought alive within yourself, consider your surroundings. Know what is around you, both alive and inanimate. Discern how they make you emote and contemplate on the ways with which you relate to them, especially in how it correlates to the concept your mind is focused on. How would you like to interact with or through them? What would you like to make them do?"

Kitsune's hair whipped about as the breeze grew stronger. He couldn't help but smile at the thought of how he'd like to interact with Myobu. He clung to his deep emotion, almost wishing his talent was influencing the actions of others. If he forced Myobu to embrace him just by willing it…

That wasn't right, though, even if it was within his power.

"As an example," Myobu continued, raising his voice to keep above the noise of the wind and leaves. "Let's say your current emotion was hot anger. Let us also pretend, for I certainly hope it is a pretense, that you really hate me. Lastly, say your talent is solely the conjuring of bolts of lightning. It would be possible to channel your anger into creating such a strike at me, a source of said anger."

Kitsune nodded his comprehension.

"I will be silent for a while," Myobu said. "I want you to meditate on what we discussed. I'm not going anywhere, though. I'm right here if you need me."

Kitsune struggled to identify his churning emotion. He knew it wasn't love. Not yet, anyway, for despite their time traveling together, he hardly knew Myobu. Still, it was more than simple lust. He had desired many of the soldiers or servants he'd encountered at the palace. Those feelings were more basic, miniscule compared to what was coursing through him now. He was enamored and infatuated, just short of euphoric. That would come only if Myobu reciprocated and Kitsune had the freedom to explore the hypothetical bond.

It occurred to Kitsune that pinning down his emotion was too restrictive, and he instead let the feelings define him. Sure, part of it was uncertainty and doubt, but it was mostly good. He never felt so elated in all his life, despite the dire circumstances in which he found himself. The thrill and joy coursed through his veins and pounded in his heart with such ferocity he thought he would explode.

The prince's attention turned to his surroundings, and he used his hearing and memory to identify what was around. Aside from the wind, which continued to grow in intensity, he sensed trees and other plant life, Myobu's fire crackling in the distance, and a few cautious nocturnal animals. He attempted to relate to each of these things in turn, wondering if he should concentrate on their individual joy or the joy they elicited in him. Did trees and animals have such emotions?

Kitsune focused on the surrounding woods, the trees reminding him of the large black oaks growing upon the terraces of Inari Palace. He loved it when their leaves sprouted in the spring, harkening warmer weather and the gorgeous colors signifying life. With his mind, he reached out and identified individual trees in the area just as though he was seeing them with his eyes. As it was only the tail end of summer, most still held on to their leaves, which were healthy and green. A few young saplings grew under the canopy of their elders, dying from a lack of sunlight. He wondered if his magic would let him breathe life into them.

A twig snapped somewhere in front of him. Kitsune was about to open his eyes, bring an end to this silly exercise, and assess the situation. He would not let an attacker catch him off guard because he was attempting something as asinine as meditation! He stopped when a familiar scent filled his nose—it wasn't strong, but it was the smell of something he spent a great amount of time in proximity with. Someone he paid a lot of attention to. The smell was that of Myobu.

Kitsune was opening his mouth to ask what Myobu was doing, but the touch of the other's lips upon his stopped him short. It was a cautious kiss, one he tentatively returned. Then Myobu's hands timidly ran through his hair, eventually coming to rest at the back of his head.

The prince dared not raise his eyelids, fearing that doing so would break whatever spell had fallen upon the night. Instead, he returned all of Myobu's advances with equal or greater zeal. With both hands, he reached up and caressed the sides of the other's face, pulling him forward into an even more ardent kiss.

Tongues, wet lips, and exploring hands drew the two of them closer together. Kitsune had kissed several men and women, but it was always a pretense to something else. This, here and now, was brilliant passion. It was no pretense—it was all for and because of the dark-haired man with smallish hands.

"I didn't make that happen with magic, did I?" Kitsune asked after they pulled away to catch their breaths.

"No," Myobu returned, panting, a sheen of sweat on his brow. "That's something I've been wanting to do for days. I didn't want to be presumptuous, in case you didn't feel the same way. You were too irresistible here in the moonlight, though, with an earnest look upon your beautiful face as you concentrated. I couldn't help myself, thinking I had to reward you for your effort."

You can use that as a reward every time was what Kitsune wanted to say, but the realization of what just transpired fell upon him. He had fallen to his own weakness, given in to his shamefulness. He pulled away from Myobu.

"Let's go back to the camp," Myobu suggested, looking a little perplexed. He reached out for Kitsune's hand.

"Myobu, there is something I must tell you. A few things, if I am to be honest," Kitsune said, keeping his hands by his side, balled up into fists. "The first is that I cannot—"

From a distance, a shrill scream of terror cut through the frigid air, silencing Kitsune's words.

SWORD AND ARROW

Hidden in the tree line, Kitsune scanned the open road before them. He paid close attention to the north where he believed the bloodcurdling scream originated. He clutched his sword in his right hand while Myobu, standing next to him, held a bow.

Kitsune looked inquisitively at his partner. With a nearly full moon shining brightly overhead, he should have been able to find the source of the commotion. It couldn't have been far from their position. No sign of trouble presented itself, though, and he wondered if the sound had been an unfortunate animal falling prey to another.

Myobu squinted as he stared into the dark. After a moment, he raised his hand, pointing northward up the road.

Not seeing anything at first, Kitsune soon realized Myobu was indicating a much farther location. At a distance he guessed to be about a thousand footfalls, just over the crest of a hill on the far side of the path, he made out the faint glow of firelight. It had been easy to miss with the moon illuminating the landscape, and Kitsune wondered at how his companion spotted it so easily.

Before they could devise a plan of action, another scream pierced the night air. Without a doubt, it came from the direction of the firelight. The terror composing its notes was definitely human, not a wild animal. The two of them sprang into action, sprinting toward the source through the tree line.

Anxious and concerned, Kitsune was nonetheless exhilarated. Here he was, outside of Kitsunetsuki, using the skills he grew up honing. His feet danced deftly and silently across the ground, careful to avoid snapping twigs and leaves that might give away their position. His eyes scanned their path for signs of others, especially lookouts that could surprise them from behind or alert others to their presence.

The weapon in his hand solidified his confidence. He was a master swordsman. At the very least, no one at the palace had defeated him in sun cycles. It wasn't so much a point of pride, but in the wake of banishment, captivity, and the revelation that he wasn't quite human, the sword gave him the assurance he could protect himself and others.

When they could not continue to their destination under the cover of the trees, they darted across the road, heads down. The two dove into the underbrush on the other side, then crawled up the small hill on their bellies. As they neared the top, the sounds of commotion reached their ears. Kitsune identified male voices, the nervous shuffling of a horse, and the crying of children.

When they reached the summit, the two peeked over to take in the scene. It was just as Kitsune feared. Two individuals had set up camp here. One was a slender, dark-haired girl a few sun cycles younger than himself. She had most likely been the one to sound the alarm. The other was a small boy, probably her brother, who was trying unsuccessfully to rein in his sobs.

The two campers were on the ground, backs to their fire, bullied by a large man wielding a knife. Another bandit was unsuccessfully attempting to calm a horse tethered at the edge of the camp, going after its saddlebags. Two other men dug through packs found in a small tent.

"There's nothing here!" one thief exclaimed, tossing a bag aside. "How can they be traveling with no valuables?"

"Where's the gold?" said the man with the knife, waving it closer to the captives' faces. This elicited a fresh burst of tears from the boy.

After letting out a small, frightened squeak, the girl replied, "We have nothing except food and water. Take those if you will, but leave us be!"

"We could always ransom them," called the man trying to calm the horse. It sounded like a reminder, as though he had suggested it many times already.

"We're not going to ransom them," spat back the one who'd tossed aside the bag. By his tone of finality, he was probably their leader. "That's a surefire way to get us hanged. It's unfortunate there isn't a decently sized city nearby involved in black market trade. They'd make good coin on the slave market."

"Please!" the girl tried again, looking frantically from man to man, hoping to find a spark of pity. "Just leave us alone!"

"Kill the boy now," the leader decided. "We'll stay the night here. Take turns with the girl. She can join her brother in the morning."

The young boy began wailing and the girl's eyes opened wide in shock. The color drained from her face as the knife-wielding thug turned toward them. He stepped forward, reaching to grab a handful of the younger one's hair.

Kitsune glanced over at Myobu, who nodded back at him. In that gesture, they understood exactly what they had to do. They worked well together as a unit.

Kitsune and Myobu jumped up from their hiding spot, screaming to divert attention away from the captives. Sword in hand, Kitsune sprinted down the side of the hill, covering the short distance in a moment. Myobu remained at the top, an arrow nocked in his bow. After taking careful aim, he loosed it. The arrow flew true, whistling above Kitsune's head by just a hair's width, and hit the knife-holding bandit square in the chest just as he was turning to face the newcomers. The man stumbled back, tripped over the girl as she scrambled out of the way, and fell into the fire.

Within the next heartbeat, Kitsune reached his own targets, the two who had been rifling through the traveling packs. The first man was defenseless, and he looked almost apologetic as he put up his hands to show he held no weapons. Kitsune cut him down with a single slash of his sword. He made his way to the leader.

The man held a sword, though it was unlike Kitsune's in almost every way. Whereas the prince's was thin, light, and elegantly simple in its design and construction, the bandit's was long, heavy, and ornate. Its maker had crafted it to visually impress and intimidate. Unfortunately for the man, it had also been originally forged for a far stronger individual than himself. It took him so long to draw the weapon that he barely had enough time to block Kitsune's first attack.

While the man may not have been quick to unsheathe his weapon, he was not afraid to use it. Both hands gripping the hilt, he slashed horizontally at the prince. Kitsune, not wanting to risk chipping his sword against the behemoth, easily ducked under the blade. With a grunt of effort, the leader then lifted the sword upward, preparing to bring it down diagonally.

In a sudden swish of displaced air, Kitsune watched as the man's eyes grew wide in the realization that an arrow passed within a finger's length of his left ear. The projectile had not been for him, though. That insight came to him as the remaining bandit, who had been attempting to mount the horse and escape, screamed in agony as the arrow pierced his spine. Fear finally shone through the swordsman's expression.

The bandit leader was wide open for attack. In the time it took him to bring the sword up, Kitsune could have killed him three times over. The prince's teachers had trained him to take advantage of the precious few moments other men wasted. Still, he wanted the man to know his error. With the fear blossoming in his eyes, that time was now.

Stepping forward into a crouch, Kitsune thrust his sword upward through the man's ribcage and into his heart. The leader let out a confused, high-pitched squeak, looking down at the blade protruding from his chest. His sword, now far too heavy for him to hold, dropped to the ground with a dull thud. The man slid backward off the blade, joining his weapon in the dirt.

It had all transpired in ten heartbeats, but it felt like so much longer to Kitsune. He had just killed two men—his first kills—in battle. His pulse thrumming from exhilaration, he scanned the surrounding area to verify no other thugs hid in the shadows.

"Clear," Myobu said, heading down the hill. The two looked to the fire. Flames engulfed the body of the man who had fallen in. The sounds of his skin cracking open filled the air, as did the smell of cooking meat. This didn't seem to affect the two children, though. They remained still and quiet on the ground, examining the newcomers, waiting to see if they had come to save them or take what was being taken.

"You are safe now," Kitsune said softly, sheathing his sword to show he was no threat. He knelt, holding his hands out palms upward. "My name is Kitsune, and this is my friend Myobu. We heard you scream and came to help. Are you injured? Did they hurt you?"

The children remained silent, but Kitsune saw in their eyes they were sizing him up.

"It would be best if we left this site immediately. Our camp is close by, and we could keep you safe through the night. If you would rather us leave you alone, we shall take our leave." He really had no intention of leaving these two youths open for another attack, especially not in the wake of such carnage. Still, he thought it best to let them think it was their decision.

In a trembling voice, the girl said, "No, please don't go. Not yet."

"What are your names?" Myobu said. "Are you certain you're not hurt?"

"I am Allison," the girl said, standing up and flexing her limbs. She offered a hand to the boy, who grabbed it. "This is my brother, Joseph."

"Look," Kitsune said, trying not to sound pushy or hurried. "We have a small camp down the road. It's in the trees, out of sight from the path and prying eyes. You are welcome to join us there. Myobu and I will take turns keeping watch so you can sleep."

Allison gazed at Kitsune thoughtfully, all fear having vanished from her face. He thought it odd she regarded them with so little caution. Perhaps it was his and Myobu's smaller builds and less haggard faces, or maybe it was that aura Myobu claimed to see in him, but she appeared to trust them with little reason...other than the fact they saved Joseph's life and her dignity. After what seemed a lengthy consideration, she asked, "You say your name is Kitsune?"

"Yes."

"Then we will join you." She indicated the ransacked camp. "Should we gather our belongings?"

"I will take care of that chore," Myobu said, waving them away. "I'll collapse the tent, gather everything strewn about, and be right behind you with your horse."

Myobu gave Kitsune a silent look that told him the bodies would also be disposed of.

Allison looked dubious, but she allowed Kitsune to shepherd her and Joseph away from their ruined campsite.

Though Kitsune would have preferred to retrace his original steps, he ultimately thought the children would make too much commotion stumbling around in the trees and brush. He did not want to draw any further attention to themselves. Joseph was also having difficulty staying awake now that the excitement had passed. The prince soon had to carry the boy, who began snoring softly.

"I know who you are," Allison whispered after they walked down the road a few tics.

"Hmm," he replied. He wondered why he hadn't thought to introduce himself under a pseudonym. It seemed like an obvious thing to do while traveling through foreign territory, especially with a recognizable name such as his. He might want to consider a new name and backstory.

"Exactly what is your purpose for being in Odom?"

Kitsune motioned for her to remain silent. They reached the point where they needed to enter the woods to get to his camp, and he wanted to be sure no stray thugs were pursuing them. How he wished he possessed Myobu's keen eyesight now. Finally convinced they were alone, he carefully guided Allison through the trees. While supporting Joseph's sleeping frame with one arm, he used the other to point out fallen limbs and clumps of leaves.

Both he and Allison gave a sigh of relief once they reached the campsite. Kitsune tucked Joseph beneath a few blankets, then added a few logs to the fire, which had reduced to embers from neglect.

He recalled the stories Benjamin told Jimmy regarding Kitsunetsuki. There was undoubtedly a communal anger against King Oni and his part in Odom's economic downfall. It was plausible those negative feelings extended to Kitsune, if only by association.

At last he turned to Allison and, hoping to allay any fears he was here to stir up new chaos, said, "Myobu and I are only traveling through Odom. We are en route to the Wastelands."

"Does that mean you'll be passing by Sandya?" she said, crawling under a blanket next to her brother. Without waiting for an answer, she added, "Would you allow us to travel alongside you? It should only be a day's journey from here. Maybe two. I know our father would be eternally grateful for your saving our lives and delivering us safely."

"Why is your father not with you now?" Kitsune asked. "What are you doing out here alone?"

"Joseph and I are traveling to meet the rest of our family in Sandya," she said. "We had another with us—an uncle. Bandits ambushed us along the way, though, and he died. We've been traveling alone for three days."

Kitsune thought it a wonder they had survived three days on their own. Building a large fire out in the open showed they were unaware of the dangers lurking about or did not truly understand them.

"I'll speak with Myobu about this when he returns," he replied. He tried to picture a map of Odom, having memorized the land and its cities a long time ago. He recognized the name of Sandya and knew its general placement on a map, but he couldn't quite reconcile its exact location with the path of their journey. "He knows these parts and our direction far better than I. Rest well, though, and know we will make sure you make it to your father safely."

*

Myobu watched as the trio disappeared into the night. When even his eyes could not find them in the darkness, he turned to the ruined campsite. The children's clothing fluttered about the ground. The horse was cantering about nervously on the outskirts, though he was thankful it had not fled into the wilderness. And there was blood. So much blood.

Death was something Myobu had become accustomed to. His parents had been murdered when he was young. He remembered their spilt blood all too well. Shortly after that, he almost caused the demise of another—accidentally, of course, but it was enough to send him on a long journey ending in Hawte, where he made his home. Even there, living out in the streets, he saw his share of death and blood. Now it was a part of who he was.

Myobu moved to tether the horse, shaking the thoughts from his head. He didn't like to dwell on such matters, one of the many reasons he avoided speaking of them with Kitsune. As his old street friend Tod would say, ruminating on such matters did no one any good, dead or alive. For a crotchety man, he could be surprisingly wise.

With the horse secured, Myobu collected more wood and stoked the fire. As it grew brighter and hotter, he gathered the bodies of the three unburned bandits. One by one, he rolled them into the flames, joining them with the remains of the fourth criminal.

Myobu knew Odom had strict laws concerning attacks upon and plundering of others. Code required victims or witnesses report such crimes immediately to the closest constable. He also knew the nearest such person was a day away, and they were probably so burdened with matters closer to home that it would be many more days before they'd get around to investigating this incident. Disposing of the bodies himself and in this manner was not legal, but it derived a particular level of satisfaction—just a little, for it was still more than they deserved.

As the fire burned through its new fuel, he took down the tent and gathered the children's scattered belongings. He secured them to the horse's saddle, seeing nothing of any value. He wondered why the thieves were convinced there had been gold.

Howls echoed in the distance. Myobu thought he should put out the fire and leave it to the wolves to devour and scatter the rest of the remains. Instead, he sat and stared into the dancing fire, remembering how the light reflected off of Kitsune's hair as the prince himself danced through the night, sword in hand and anger in his eyes. The men had been relatively easy to take care of, but Myobu recalled every heartbeat of the skirmish. The way they communicated without words. How each of their weapons acted in sync with Kitsune's movements. The prince's easy transference from warrior to diplomat, easily earning the children's trust and convincing them to move to a safer location.

Myobu held a hand close to the fire, feeling the heat against his skin. It mirrored the heat he felt within him, the heat he had been unable to resist when he kissed Kitsune. It had been a bold move—not that he was averse to taking such risks, but so much remained at stake.

The Harbinger revealed to Myobu the path he must take to best serve Gaav. That path led him to Kitsune, whom he was all too quickly falling in love with. Nothing Kyubi said made him think the prince would return those feelings. That kiss, though, had been the most passionate experience of his life. And he had plenty of experience.

Myobu moved his hand closer; the flames now licked his skin. Not for the first time since he began his adventure did he wish he could take it all back. Kyubi revealed more of what was to come, and he now knew horrible events would have to transpire if his efforts to serve his home were to succeed. He had no idea what he was supposed to do, and acting passively in the flow of events was not his preferred way of living.

This was the downside to seeking the advice of the Harbinger, Myobu supposed.

Myobu got to his feet and smothered the fire with dirt and ash. As the heat began to dissipate, he howled into the dark sky, hoping nearby wolves would come and investigate. Then, mounting the horse, he rode off into the darkness to join the others.

*

Myobu arrived back at camp later than Kitsune expected, looking tired and distracted. Kitsune did not wish to keep him from resting, but he asked about Sandya. Myobu nodded his consent to the plan of accompanying the children there. Not only would it be unconscionable to leave them alone out here, but the city was just a day's ride away and on their path to the Wastelands.

After breaking camp the next morning and getting out on the road, Myobu offered a few additional details on Sandya. He explained it was a newer city, founded when merchants rerouted all trade through Ruio. It housed a castle fortress of such magnitude some of its outer limits were still under construction.

"How can the royal family continue to pay for such monumental building projects when the country is in such financial despair?" Kitsune asked, pulling his cloak tighter to fight off the early morning chill.

"While the royals may sit in and govern such fortresses, they did not solely finance the building. The remaining elite families pay massive sums of coin for security," Myobu explained.

Turning to Allison, who was looking tiredly out into the passing landscape, Kitsune asked, "What exactly does your father do in Sandya?"

"He's an administrator," she said with a shrug. She apparently never took an interest in what her father did to provide for them.

Allison and Joseph fell quiet during the day's journey, Myobu steering the cart while Kitsune rode the youths' horse. Other than the occasional comment or polite question, they exchanged few words.

Kitsune would usually find this behavior odd. Children, especially those of Joseph's age, found royalty mesmerizing, especially those from foreign lands. They were capable of asking endless strings of questions, unable to keep their mouths shut for too long. The previous night had been terribly traumatizing for these two, however, and they were undoubtedly still processing the events.

Strangely, Kitsune thought little of the men he had slain. They were his first two combat kills, and he felt almost nothing.

Thoughts flooded Kitsune's mind. Even if the bandit attack the previous night didn't faze him, he had much to think of. There was, of course, the kiss he and Myobu shared. More than anything else that had transpired, that kiss was a defining moment for him. An energy moved between the two of them, and it felt as though that energy made the air around them sparkle in ecstasy.

He didn't want to stop it, to cease the progression of what was growing between them. That Myobu shared Kitsune's feelings was of much comfort. Ever since he stood outside the strange cottage in his dream, his stomach queasy with anticipation, he had been consumed with odd, energetic feelings that left him disoriented and confused. He never felt that way for anyone, had actively fought against the feelings for Myobu, and he had wondered if his head was broken. He knew things like that happened to some people after traumatic incidents. What Myobu said the previous evening—about not wanting to sneak a kiss unless he was certain Kitsune shared the same feelings—now made Kitsune think his head was broken before and not now.

Though he understood the mechanics of relationships, Kitsune was still unsure of how they progressed on a natural level. He'd always been an observer of such coupling customs, not until now having the urge to participate in one. His mind and body urged him to possess the other with a great fierceness, but he knew he could never let that happen.

Over the shine of the giddiness, the eyes of Kitsune's father glared at him. It encouraged a sick, sinking sensation in his stomach that originated from the realization he would have to come clean about his mission to Myobu. He had not lied about why he was seeking the King's Sun, but he had not been entirely forthcoming. He was dead set on taking the man's life. Even though he didn't desire to do it, his love and devotion to his father, his family, demanded he carry out the actions no matter the personal consequences. Myobu, who thought so highly of Ninko, would most likely think ill of Kitsune for planning such an act. Disclosure of the full truth might result in his departure. However, Kitsune knew enough about how people operated that if he continued to use the source of his infatuation to lead him to the target, Myobu would end up despising him. Kitsune would despise himself.

"There it is," Myobu announced, interrupting Kitsune's musings. He pointed to the west, where the sun was disappearing behind the mountains.

Just as Inari Palace could be mistaken as a mountain from a distance, an untrained eye might misinterpret the castle fortress comprising Sandya as being part of the mountain range it nestled against. It took Kitsune's sharp eyes several moments to recognize towers, walls, and the main keep. It took even longer to distinguish where the mountains ended and the fortress began. This illusion had been purposeful, constructing everything with materials gathered from the Argent Mountains themselves.

As gargantuan as the fortress was, sprawled across dozens of acres and towering six or seven stories, it took effort to find signs of habitation. No flags flew from any of the towers, and he saw no signs of smoke. Windows were difficult to make out, and if they contained glass, they somehow did not reflect light. Water was most likely collected from streams coming down the mountain. So long as citizens stowed away ample stores of food, he saw limited reasons for them to exit the city walls.

Kitsune knew the fortress' designers meant to keep an enemy guessing at the city's strength, population, and fortitude, but he still wondered at all the effort that went into concealing a city everyone knew existed. A company of soldiers stood just outside the main gate, and even their uniforms and encampment materials were dark and matte to better blend into their surroundings.

One of the few obvious indications of constant human activity was a well-worn path branching off from the main road toward Sandya's entrance. Kitsune and Myobu steered their horses down the path toward the guard. In turn, the soldiers organized into a defensive pattern. The site of so many men and women taking up arms made Kitsune cautious, and he reached for his own sword. Allison and Joseph, either not noticing the tension or not giving heed to it, jumped down from the cart and ran straight toward the encampment.

Myobu appeared attentive but unfazed, so Kitsune continued forward at the same lethargic pace. He doubted the soldiers would attack two children, especially if their father was an administrative official, but he didn't want to tempt any negative reactions by galloping after them.

The two watched carefully as Allison appeared to introduce herself and Joseph to the first battle-ready men they reached. Hesitant, the soldiers looked back. A woman stepped forward, clearly their superior, and demanded something of the girl. Allison reached into her satchel and pulled out a dagger.

The weapon put Kitsune further on edge, but the soldiers immediately dropped their defensive attitudes and took on a more formal air.

"Lady Allison! We have been worried. You were expected to arrive yesterday," the woman exclaimed as Kitsune and Myobu brought their horses to a stop just behind the children. Kitsune got a better look at the sheathed dagger in Allison's hand, a piece clearly ornamental. The hilt gleamed with gold, and several jewels sparkled luminously. In the middle was a circle with a *K* carved into it. He guessed the blade to be shiny and sharp, never having cut or sliced anything.

"We were delayed," Allison replied, replacing the dagger into her satchel. She pointed behind her. "These men risked their lives to save ours. They are welcome within the city walls."

The captain looked over the two men with a keen eye. She seemed to consider what Kitsune himself would suspect in the same situation: that whatever had befallen the two youths had been an elaborate ploy to gain their trust.

"Please," Allison continued, "would you be so kind as to immediately escort us to my father?"

"You must leave your weapons here," the woman said after another considering look. "We don't allow them into the city."

Kitsune hesitated, not wanting to part with what he considered extensions of himself. He almost suggested they turn around and continue on their journey. They had safely delivered the children and had no reason to meet their father. Myobu, whose thought process was apparently in stark contrast to his own, hopped down and handed over his bow. Kitsune followed suit, begrudgingly handing over his sword and bow.

Two men led the horses away to a nearby stable. Stripped of all their weapons and belongings, Kitsune felt vulnerable and naked. Not feeling they had a choice in the matter, he and Myobu followed the captain, an accompaniment of her subordinates, and the children through the main entrance and into Sandya.

It was like stepping into another world. A barrage of sounds and smells as innumerable citizens bustled their way about the packed streets immediately hit their senses. The mountainous stone walls of the fortress created long, claustrophobic alleyways. Huge swaths of colored fabric decorated the walls, intended to muffle the noise. It did little good, though the decoration added some cheer to what otherwise would have been a dreary, utilitarian corridor.

Amid the varied fabrics hanging from the tall walls was a network of mirrors. Their purpose confused Kitsune at first. He thought they perhaps served as a crime deterrent. Nobody but Myobu would have been able to make out the details from the reflections hanging fifty footfalls above the ground. Then he realized they reflected sunlight from above to the pathways below. Of course, lighting the pathways provided security, but it allowed merchants to line the walls with small stands from which all types of goods were sold. Of all the things available for purchase, including clothing, jewelry, and grain, it was the smell of cooked meat that cut through the rest of the sensations bombarding Kitsune. His stomach growled.

Despite the attempts to hide the utilitarian nature of the fortress, its purpose reverberated throughout the network of alleyways. After growing up around those in the military, Kitsune was used to a general feeling of readiness. He sensed it in the soldiers outside the main gate, but it also pulsed throughout the marketplace. It was in the eyes of buyers and sellers as they glanced up at the newcomers being hustled down the street. They looked as though they were reaching for knives hidden beneath folds in their garments.

It couldn't always be like this, Kitsune thought. The anxiety would fray nerves.

The captain and her soldiers led the visitors deeper into the city without any hesitation. Mountainous walls aside, the city sprawled out like a maze. The group entered and exited several building complexes along the way, climbed numerous flights of stairs, and took so many turns Kitsune swore they had gone in several circles. He wondered if there was any reason to the design or if they were being led around to be disoriented. It was a marvel anyone kept track of where they were going. Joseph's little legs eventually could not move quickly enough to keep up with the rest of them, and Myobu carried him.

As they traveled deeper into the fortress, it became more evident they were entering the living spaces of the wealthy. Fine rugs lined the halls, and far fewer people milled about. The stones making up the floors and walls were smooth to the touch, and the scent of finely prepared foods mixed with incense. Whatever kind of administrator the children's father was, his superiors kept him well compensated.

The troupe finally came to a set of tall, wooden double doors guarded by another two servicemen. Allison turned to Kitsune and Myobu. "Please remain here while I speak with my father." Then she took Joseph by the hand and slipped through the doors, accompanied by the captain.

Despite the group of people now congregating in the hallway, it was eerily quiet. Kitsune was hesitant to even shuffle about lest he break the uneasy silence. After noticing the serene look on Myobu's face, he said, "I don't understand how you're so calm."

He almost added, "This doesn't seem right," but the words he already spoke reverberated throughout the still hallway. With the others around, he didn't want to appear too anxious or suspicious.

"Really?" Myobu replied. "Why's that?"

The double doors burst open to reveal a large, bald man with a braided goatee. Draped in brown furs, he spread out his arms in a friendly gesture. His mere presence breathed life into the stone walkway, and he boomed, "My boys! I am forever in your debt! You have no idea the state I've been in this past day."

The man embraced them tightly, Kitsune blinking tufts of fur out of his eyes. "Please, come into my office so we may talk."

While Kitsune's suspicious nature spiked when the man violently swung open the doors, he finally calmed himself. This was clearly a parent joyful at the return of his offspring. Few could feign that kind of genuine emotion.

The pair followed the man back into his room, which was a large, high-ceilinged office. Bookshelves lined the walls, filled with texts from all the known lands. Kitsune even recognized a few written by Kitsunetsuki thinkers. He couldn't help but be wary again, as they were beyond the needs of a mere city administrator.

The man walked about excitedly, gesturing servants to pour drinks and retrieve food from some nearby kitchen. Allison and Joseph sat side by side in a large chair behind a massive wooden desk, grinning wildly. They were dirty and exhausted, but giddy at the sight of their boisterous father.

"What were your children doing so far out in the wilderness?" Myobu asked. "They said they were accompanied by an uncle and that he died in an attack."

"A necessary cover story," the man replied, shaking his head. He looked back at his offspring. "They were being transported here from the capital. We hoped a small guard detail would avoid attention. Though not an uncle, the group was attacked and their guard killed. Thankfully, that soldier returned the favor before passing on, then you were there to save them last night."

"Family or not, we are sorry for the loss of your man," Myobu said.

The man nodded. "My daughter tells me the two of you are journeying to the Wastelands. I can't say I recommend such an endeavor and, having no reliable knowledge of what lies beyond the border in that direction, I have nothing to offer you in gratitude for your service. I can guarantee your safety for the remainder of your travels through Odom. A contingent of my personal guard will accompany you to our northernmost outpost, which is maybe a two-and-a-half-day ride from here. Also, I can restock your supplies, adding any additional provisions you request."

"We thank you for your kindness," Myobu said, bowing in gratitude. "It is more than we deserve."

"My first instinct is to agree with you," the man said, sobering. He looked at Kitsune. "But I hold no ill will toward you. Just your father. You have returned my children and heirs, my reasons for living, aside from my beautiful wife."

Kitsune frowned. "I'm sorry, but I am at a loss and disadvantage. You seem to know of me and my family, though I know nothing of you."

"Allison told me exactly who you are, Prince Kitsune of the Asher lineage. I am Patriarch Kirby, head of Odom."

Kitsune stiffened in shock, but that gave way to a seething anger. As though in response to his feelings, the glass windows burst open and an unusually hot wind rushed in. Dust and loose papers swept up into the air. A low rumbling, like the crumbling of enormous rocks, sounded in the distance.

Before he could stop himself, he said in a steely voice, "You killed my mother."

VERANDA

Patriarch Kirby held up his hands, shielding his face as flying debris pelted him. Still, he kept his sorrowful eyes on Kitsune. His mouth opened and closed as he fumbled for words. Finally, over the cracking and rumbling noises emanating from outside, he choked out, "You...you believe that?"

Myobu reached over, placing a hand on Kitsune's shoulder. The sounds of rocks being torn asunder ceased, and the wind died down. Papers and balls of dust started their lazy descent to the floor. The anger gripping him seeped away like water after a rainfall, replaced with a more reasoned mindset.

"My apologies, Patriarch," Kitsune said, bowing his head. "I have only recently become aware my grandmother and mother met unnatural ends, and my emotions have gotten the better of me. My father's mother, a Yokai spirit, was ruthlessly drained of her powers by my grandfather, and my own mother... Well, my source for that information is questionable, but the ruling house of Odom was clearly indicated."

Kirby, no longer jovial, appeared flustered from the sudden winds that had stormed his office. He leaned against his large desk, behind which Allison and Joseph still sat, clinging to one another in confusion.

Servants who left before the confrontation returned with smiles and plates of food, puzzled at the change in the atmosphere.

"I can understand why you would believe I authorized an assassination on your mother, Prince Kitsune. It would explain your father's undertakings over the past couple of decades, for he is the originating factor behind Odom's economic state of decay. The actions of King Oni have led to the thieves and bandits ruling our roads, resulting in the evil men who nearly took the lives of my children. Without Allison and Joseph, the chances of my family surviving beyond another generation or two are slim. As the Kirby line disappears, so do the chances of a redeemed Odom.

"Rumors that Oni's manner stems from retribution for an attack on his wife are not uncommon, and I can't blame you for accepting them regardless of their source. However, I tell you I sanctioned no such action. Relations between Odom and Kitsunetsuki were friendly, and trade made us prosperous. There was no reason to jeopardize a bright future."

Kitsune nodded. He wasn't ready to trust anything anybody told him—not at face value, anyway. He felt foolish for his emotional outburst, however.

"I am curious, though," Kirby continued. He gestured for one of the servants to approach him. "Why do you think your paternal grandmother was killed by your grandfather? Did your father tell you this?"

"No," Kitsune admitted. "I learned of it through another source, though I consider this individual to be reliable."

Kirby whispered something into his servant's ear. With a quick questioning glance at the prince, the attendant left the room.

"I've sent for one of my advisors who can shed some light on the situation. Help us come to an understanding regarding all of this," Kirby said. "While we wait, though, please tell me about the circumstances surrounding your own mother's death."

Cautiously, Kitsune relayed what he knew, starting with how he previously understood she died from complications during childbirth. While growing up, there had never been reason to suspect this was not the truth. In retrospect, he realized his father could have carefully controlled or even hand-picked the people he regularly came into contact with. Teachers, trainers, and soldiers. The king may have ordered them to maintain the secret of her death. With the powerful magic Kitsune now realized his father commanded, was it even possible for him to have altered their own memories? In either case, what was the purpose of keeping the truth from him?

"You'd be surprised what a father will do to protect his children," Kirby said, looking back at his offspring. Joseph dozed in his sister's arms. "It may have started as a compassionate lie. Then, as you grew older, he may not have had the heart to reveal the truth."

Despite his respect for his father, Kitsune found nothing compassionate about that idea. He recalled the sun cycles he spent in anguish, supposing he killed his own mother through the mere act of being born. There was no scenario in which anyone should let a child believe that.

"I only learned of the alternative narrative a few days ago," Kitsune continued, looking down to the floor in sadness. "I can find no comfort in the knowledge I was not responsible for her death. The idea of her being murdered—whether it be by agents of Odom, spies from another land, or a common criminal... It is too much to bear. I wish there could be another truth."

"There is only one truth, child," said a voice from the side. They all turned to see an elderly woman standing in the doorway, dressed in fine clothes. White hair fell over broad shoulders. Even at her age, she was a handsome woman. "Your mother was murdered, plain and simple. It was not by the order of Patriarch Kirby, as you have concluded. No, only rumor fueled by Oni."

"Veranda, this is—" Kirby began, but the woman waved a dismissive hand at him.

"I recognize who this is," Veranda said, her husky voice making it difficult to discern if she was friendly or menacing. "How could I not?"

Kitsune, at a loss, stared at the elderly woman. He found something familiar about her, about the confident way she carried herself. Her light green eyes radiated with intelligence.

"Who was it, then?" he asked softly. "Who took my mother's life?"

Veranda took a few steps farther into the room. With her head held high, she was visibly trying to remain poised in the face of some terrible fact. "My child…"

Kitsune waited, assuming she was addressing him again. Veranda stared at him, her eyes pleading for him to understand. Suddenly, he did, although it made little sense. It didn't fit with what he accepted as fact.

"Your son?" he voiced.

Nodding, Veranda took a moment before speaking again. When she did, she spoke slowly, her voice wavering. "Yes, my beloved son. He was a prince then, though now he is a king."

"My father?" Kitsune whispered.

"Yes," Kirby interjected. "Somehow, the truth reached you in a split fashion. Your grandfather never murdered your grandmother. It was your father who killed his wife, your mother, blaming me afterward. This woman here—Veranda—is your grandmother, alive and well."

The emeralds around Kitsune's throat pulsed green, and the world around him disappeared.

*

A vast emptiness surrounded Kitsune—no ground beneath his feet or sky above his head. Kirby's office and all the people had vanished, leaving only white light. He felt naked and unprepared without his armaments on his back or in his hand.

"My son," came the voice of the Lady of the Mountain behind him.

Turning, he saw the Lady looking more radiant than ever before. Her usually straight hair was now up in pinned curls, and a long white gown draped her figure. The light surrounded her in an ethereal glow, and as Kitsune stared, he saw she *was* the light, and he was of her and her spirit.

"Is it true?" he asked, his wide eyes looking up into hers. He could feel tears welling up, threatening to spill down his face. "Are you my mother?"

The Lady nodded. "It is so."

Kitsune stumbled to his knees, the tears now falling from his cheeks in large, clear drops. "Did... Did you know? Did you know I was your son?"

"It was my initial suspicion," the Lady admitted. "The hoshi no tama felt familiar, and there is an obvious connection between the two of us. When I was robbed of my magic and physical self, I remember parting with a baby boy. My last thoughts were sorrowful, yes, but not out of misery of my own fate. I was mortified I was leaving my son in the hands of a monster. Then, when my consciousness resurfaced, I found you, a handsome man with beautiful eyes reminding me of those I've seen in my family."

The Lady, his mother, knelt before him. She clasped his face in her hands. "You called me 'grandmother,' and the certainty in your voice convinced me it was true. It was so close in my mind that the difference was minute. Either way, you were of me."

"You are so precious to me, Mother," Kitsune said, allowing her to wipe away his tears. "You've been my guiding star. I am proud to be your son. The difference, though, is anything but minute. At least to me."

"How so, my child? What is it that upsets you so?"

Kitsune sniffled, a second wave of tears threatening to burst forth from his eyes. "The monster that killed you was my father! The man I have always looked up to, looked to for moral guidance, and respected...murdered my mother!"

The Lady peered up into a sky that wasn't there, thoughtful for several long moments. Finally, still looking away, she said, "I am incomplete, Kitsune. My thoughts are scattered and my soul is torn with a foothold in this world and the next. For better or for worse, it is because of this I hold no anger or resentment toward my husband for taking my life. It occurs to me I really never knew the man, for the one I envisioned would never have acted with such malice. Still, while I maintain such things should never be done, I cannot say I comprehend his motives."

"Why would he steal another's magic?" Kitsune thought out loud. He recalled again what he saw while in the Boleyn Room. In particular, the large golden spheres shining so brilliantly. "Your hoshi no tama consists of emeralds. Are they all fashioned as such?"

His mother shook her head, appearing to concentrate, drawing upon fragments of memories. "Each hoshi no tama reflects the individual whose magic they originally stored and therefore come in a variety of forms and stones. There are some cases, though rare, that they consist solely of precious metals."

"I don't think you are the only one he has stripped of magic," Kitsune said darkly. "I suspect he's been collecting it for many sun cycles, storing it in orbs of gold he keeps hidden away, close to his person."

"It is possible," the Lady said, musing. "However, it wavers from my point. Yes, he's done these terrible deeds, but what is the inspiration behind them? What is the endgame?"

Kitsune frowned. "You feel anything would justify what amounts to murder? It doesn't seem right."

"Are you not yourself on a quest to kill a man who has done nothing to harm you or your kingdom?"

She asked the question inquisitively, without scolding or acerbic tones. Still, it shocked him and sent a chill up his spine.

When he didn't answer, she went on. "I clearly did not know my husband when I married him. I cannot pretend to understand him now after so many sun cycles of growth and maturation. Do not be sad you are your father's son, as you are not saddened to be mine. People change, and he could be every bit the noble king you see him as."

Kitsune felt a wave of comfort wash over him at those words. Too many of the pillars holding up his view of the world were crumbling. He was learning new details of his father since his banishment, but to lose his certainty in his father's honorable intentions would tear his mind apart. Even his newfound connection to Myobu wouldn't be able to save him.

As though sensing his thoughts turning to Myobu, the Lady said, "Find strength and comfort in those you love and who love you, my child. They will be the ones who always look out for you and save you during the times you most need it."

"Like you?" he said, standing. He held her hands, helping her up.

"My understanding of many things has been altered or destroyed," the Lady said with a hint of sadness. A small smile then graced her face. "My love for my son remains intact, though, and I will do anything I can within my limited abilities to show that."

He embraced her then. It was a hug meant to make up for a lifetime of absence and was unfit for a woman of splendor and poise, but it was one a child would give his mother. She hugged him tightly back.

"Go speak with your grandmother," the Lady whispered into his ear. "She *is* your grandmother. You won't be here for much longer, and she is a trustworthy woman."

*

"Grandmother," Kitsune said, bowing respectfully. His consciousness returned from the dreamscape back to the office, and time here had apparently not passed but a mere moment since Kirby made the introduction. "I see my father in you now. I am sorry I did not recognize it sooner."

"I see him in you as well, my child," Veranda said, clasping her hands in front of her. "Although you mostly take after your mother."

"You knew my mother?"

Veranda smiled in remembrance. "She was a lovely woman and would have made a wonderful queen to Kitsunetsuki. For the little time she was there, she endeared herself to the people of Oinari. We were all heartbroken when your father returned home from their honeymoon without her. The situation confused us, but my husband and I found some comfort in that he returned with you, our grandchild."

A wave of emotions overwhelmed Kitsune. The only family he knew growing up was his father. He was told his mother died, and since no other kin were near, he extended the same conclusion to them. Now, in a matter of days, he had been reunited with his mother and grandmother. It was oddly comforting to know the elderly woman before him now held him in her arms many sun cycles ago, rejoicing in his existence.

"Fortunately, my husband saw through the prince's treacherous lies. Not accepting that your mother died in a rock slide at Castle Verde, he concluded she had been ruthlessly slain. He sent me away from our kingdom, fearing what our son would do next. I have been in hiding here in Odom ever since."

"You've never returned?" Kitsune exclaimed.

"Not long after I arrived in Patriarch Kirby's court for protection, word arrived of my husband's death. My son was now king, and I have not gone back for fear of my life." Veranda paused, looking ashamed of herself. "I wanted to bring you with me, but my husband said that would only infuriate our son and send him after us. Still, I regret to admit I was too afraid to attempt a return to collect you."

Kitsune stepped forward, clasping her hands in his. "I was born a prince, and I was raised as such. My father never mistreated me, although I am learning with each passing day the truth kept from me. Do not be sorrowful for the past, but rejoice in that we have crossed paths now."

A growling interrupted their reunion. Kitsune looked around, then laughed with the others when they realized it was Myobu's stomach.

Kirby gestured toward a dining table where a feast was being laid out, and the six of them sat.

As they began loading their plates, Kirby said, "If you weren't traveling through Odom in search of your estranged grandmother, I must inquire as to what your meaning is."

Kitsune considered his answer. Whether or not he agreed with his father's actions or believed he had grown into a respectable man, it was imperative he not give the impression they were currently aligned in some malevolent task. Fortunately, that did not require the bending of any truth. "I was exiled from my homeland."

The revelation startled Kirby. "The king would exile his only heir? On what grounds?"

Kitsune looked over at Myobu, who quietly loaded his plate with sliced ham. The peculiar but welcome sensation of lightness in his stomach returned as they momentarily locked eyes, and the other gave him a small encouraging smile. "My father did not approve of the male company I occasionally took to my bed," he admitted sourly. "There are plans to outlaw such behavior, making it taboo. He may have thought I would eventually fall in love with another man and ascend the throne with him by my side."

Kirby and Veranda looked blankly at Kitsune, not comprehending the actions of the neighboring monarch. Apparently, King Oni was in the minority in considering that such relationships were immoral. Kitsune felt a modicum of relief in this.

"Though I do not know the reasons, my father does not approve of relations between members of the same sex. It was a sudden revelation to me, and it came simultaneously with my banishment. After being publicly humiliated, soldiers escorted me to the border where they forced me into Odom."

Veranda gasped in shock and Kirby looked dumbfounded. "The people didn't put a stop to this?"

"The king announced the reason for my alienation and his plans for the future only after I was gone. Before that, the people assumed I committed a heinous act, and I could not communicate the truth to them. Even if they knew, I doubt there would have been any kind of response. They live in fear of their king." Such fear, something Kitsune previously considered a sign of respect, was not necessarily a good thing.

"Then you will stay here with us," Veranda said, her dark mood lightening. "I can finally know my grandson!"

The patriarch replied for Kitsune. "Allison told me Sandya happened to be a convenient stop along your way to the Wastelands, though that can't be your true destination. Where are you actually journeying?"

"Myobu has agreed to help me find my way into the tribal lands," Kitsune answered, giving more thought to his words. "I wish to find the Harbinger, who I hope will help me locate Ninko, the King's Sun."

"You seek Kyubi?" Veranda said loudly, flustered for the first time. She shrank back, taking notice of her own outburst. Much quieter, she muttered, "It would be much better if you were to stay here with me."

Kirby took hold of one of her hands in a comforting grip, speaking calmly to her in a low voice. Kitsune wondered what she had against the Harbinger but didn't want to upset her now with more questions. Instead, as individual conversations broke out across the table, he turned his attention to the massive plates of food in front of him. It was hard to take part in any substantial exchange, as trying to retain a sense of decorum was difficult in the presence of such savory delights. Before he realized it, he polished off the entire leg of some fowl, cleaned out a bowl of mashed potatoes, and chomped his way through a sweet red apple.

"I trust you found the food satisfactory?" Kirby said with a smile.

"It's more food than I've eaten in the last several days," Kitsune said, pulling on a clump of his hair that had found its way into his mouth. "It was better than we could have dreamt for."

"Now I won't have to hear his stomach growl for a while!" Myobu chimed in.

Kitsune stifled a sudden yawn, covering his mouth with his hand. Kirby noticed it, chuckled, and stood up. "The food has probably robbed you of what energy your day beneath the sun left you with. It's about time we let you wash up and rest before you continue your journey."

As servants ushered Veranda, Myobu, and the children out of the office, Patriarch Kirby motioned for Kitsune to stay a moment. Once the door closed, his jovial face took on a serious look. He said, "So you seek the Harbinger. Have you any idea what to expect?"

Kitsune shook his head, admitting that, like so much else around him, he had not known of her until recently. "Is she not wise?"

"Oh, the Harbinger is reportedly very wise, and she will help you if she can," Kirby said. "You must understand, however, that wisdom does not always equate to benevolence. Keep in mind she is a Yokai. They can be fierce and loyal companions, but they are also notorious for a lack of tact. She may tell you where the King's Sun is, but she may also reveal to you the time and nature of your death."

Nodding, Kitsune was all too aware that Yokai blood flowed through his veins. He realized no one aside from his father had been aware his mother was one of the Yokai and, by blood, of his own potential. If it had been common knowledge, it was possible Kirby would not be confiding in him so much.

"There's no way for you to know this, but your grandmother Veranda saw the Harbinger once a long time ago."

Kitsune looked up, surprised. "Truly? What kind of answers was she seeking?"

"She has never said," Kirby replied, shaking his head. "However, she has spoken of other matters the Harbinger revealed. In particular, that she would unwittingly unleash a dark force upon this world that would be capable of swallowing it whole."

"My father?" Kitsune said.

Isaac Grisham

"I can only assume, seeing as he now rules over half the region," Kirby returned. "I wanted to reveal this so you will not judge her too harshly for never returning for you. She is a strong woman, but the shame she carries in her heart, the knowledge that she is responsible for birthing such a dark force into the world, has weighed her down and whittled away at her soul. It's plain to me, as I can see it in her eyes. All that just because of what the Harbinger foretold. If you find Kyubi, and she tells you something unpleasant, do not let it crush your spirit. That kind of prophecy is dangerous to the cores of those who hear it. Do you understand me?"

Kitsune nodded.

"Now, as for this King's Sun you mentioned, I have heard tell of him. Not much, but if the rumors are true, he is the kind of man who will help you to the best of his abilities."

Kitsune doubted he would be all too willing to die for him.

"What are your long-term intentions? Do you have a plan?"

"To return to Kitsunetsuki," he replied. "To eventually become king, as is my right."

The patriarch nodded, accepting this answer positively. Then, after a bit of hesitation, he said, "Prince Kitsune, Odom is a struggling land, and I admit to you alone it is on the verge of total collapse. Still, with what remains of our previously enormous wealth, we maintain a decent military might."

Though remaining silent, Kitsune raised a questioning eyebrow.

"The intention is not to attack Kitsunetsuki," Kirby assured him. "We lack sufficiently experienced and tactically minded leadership, and such an invasion would be futile. Your kingdom's military strength and prowess is legendary in lands you've not even heard of. No, our military is purely for defense."

"Defense against King Oni," Kitsune said, understanding. Like so many other things, he was beginning to comprehend the true meaning and cost of war. Just days before, he was hoping to become a leader in a noble military campaign to conquer foreign lands. What was noble

142

about that, though? Here he was now, in a land crumbling under the foreign policies of his father. Those policies had meant to make a once friendly ally weak and easy to eventually overcome.

"Your own strength and prowess are also legendary," Kirby added, surprising Kitsune. "There are many fantastical stories, but actual reports say you have never been defeated in hand-to-hand combat. Our diplomats have also reported that soldiers seem to appreciate and respect you. Most would follow you into battle, even though you have no actual practical experience."

"You are too kind, Patriarch Kirby," Kitsune said. He had not known anyone held him in such regard, and the knowledge filled him with a new respect for Kitsunetsuki's military. It also caused a surge of homesickness.

"Not my words," Kirby said dismissively. "It does, however, give me faith in your abilities. Seek the Harbinger. Find the King's Sun. Do what you feel you must to find your way back into your country. If you do not find the answers or path you seek, know there is a home here for you, just like your grandmother found." The patriarch smiled, getting to his point. "And if you could never call this home, know there is an army here that, under my direction, would follow you..."

Kirby trailed off, but Kitsune heard the unspoken words: "...into opposition against your father."

"For now, though," Kirby continued, trying to lighten the mood, "speak with your grandmother. Your stay here will be but a few hours."

"So short a stay?" Kitsune asked, unconsciously looking back at the table of food. He did not relish the idea of running low on supplies again.

"Despite the incident in which you saved my children, the road to Sandya from the south is relatively safe. Onward north, however, is far more dangerous. Thieves have taken to preying on those traveling from the northern settlements in search of work and safety. I have a detachment of soldiers scheduled to make a run of supplies to an outpost near the border of the Wastelands. They will leave in the early hours of the morning under the cover of dark."

"We should travel with them?"

"It would be the safest and quickest path for you," Kirby said. "The longer you are here, the greater the chances enemies will discover you. Leave under the cover of darkness and your last leg of the journey through Odom should be a safe one. When you depart, you'll even be fully stocked with plenty of supplies and food."

"I don't think Myobu would let me turn down such a gracious offer," Kitsune said with a laugh.

"I'll have your friend informed," Kirby said, opening the office doors. "One of my staff will take you to Veranda. Be sure to get some sleep before you leave, though. I know from my own travels you can never count on getting much while on the road."

THE NORTHERN OUTPOST

Curled up under several blankets on his bed, Kitsune stared into a fire burning in the hearth. His room for the next couple of hours was small but cozy. The stone walls would have been bleak if not for woven cloth of soothing colors decorated them. With a full belly and a warm room, he was on the verge of drifting off to sleep.

The fire reminded him of when he had awoken from his fever, Myobu hurdling away from a fireplace after igniting a large fireball. Then their gazes met, and it seemed Kitsune fell into the other's big brown eyes. He still felt that way, and he couldn't climb his way out.

Kitsune shifted beneath the covers, remembering the conversation he had with Veranda before coming to bed. She had, of course, asked about the dark-haired man. "There's something about him," she said with a subtle wink. "If my bones didn't creak as much as they do now, I'd give you some competition!"

With grandmotherly concern, Veranda begged him to stay in Sandya with her. She used all the tools at her disposal in her attempts to persuade him, even offering a place for Myobu. While her persistence touched his heart, he told her he had to follow through with what he considered to be his duty.

"Very admirable," she told him with a mixture of pride and sorrow. "Even if you aren't telling me the entire truth."

"What?" Kitsune exclaimed, startled by her bluntness.

"I may not have seen my son for many a moon, but a mother doesn't forget the habits and persona of her children," Veranda said, her voice still full of mixed emotions. "I could always tell when Oni kept something from me, even if he wasn't lying. I recognize some of the same traits in you. All the signs are there."

Kitsune hung his head. Similarities drawn between him and his father usually pleased him, especially since they were so physically different. This, however, was a reprimand.

"I know better than to even attempt to pry information out of you. Just be certain your actions bring no harm to Patriarch Kirby and Odom, or even yourself," she said, affectionately running a gnarled hand through his hair. "I will advise you to be wary of your father. As you are discovering for yourself, he is a manipulative man. He murdered his own wife, which shows there isn't a thing or person he wouldn't sacrifice to attain his desires. I do not want to lose another family member to his agendas."

Even though she promised to be present when he left the city, Veranda wouldn't let him leave her chambers without a multitude of hugs and promises he would return to Odom before too long. He happily obliged, fortunate to now have family eager to see more of him.

After closing the door to his own room, though, a sense of loneliness overwhelmed him. He spent most of his childhood in long periods of isolation, devoid of family. He usually never minded it, but this was the first time he was truly alone since passing through the Eastern Gate, and it was an unwelcome sensation.

Despite being locked, the wooden door to his room swung open. A dark figure slipped inside and pushed the door closed. Kitsune's hand involuntarily reached for the underside of the bed where he normally would have tucked away his sword. As the militia had confiscated their weapons, he had swiped a knife from the dinner table earlier.

The figure stepped into the light, and Kitsune dropped his caution.

"How did you get in here?" he exclaimed, sitting up in bed.

Myobu, now knowing there was no reason to be stealthy, leapt over the footboard and on to the mattress. With a sly look, he said, "Does it matter?"

"I suppose not," Kitsune murmured.

Brazenly, Myobu stripped his shirt from his body with liquid-like movement. Before Kitsune could object, the man settled down on the bed next to him as though he'd been there a thousand times already. The heat of desire blossomed within him.

"You were quiet during our meeting with Patriarch Kirby," Kitsune said, attempting to distract his wandering thoughts. What he wanted to do was trace a finger down Myobu's naked chest and watch as the skin broke out into goosebumps.

"It was your conversation," Myobu responded. "Just as this is your journey. I am here to support you in any way I can. You did well on your own, though. You charmed the patriarch into providing us an escort through Odom and won yourself a new grandmother."

"I think Allison did the charming for us. She has her father wrapped around her finger. The soldiers, too, I would wager. She'll make a fine matriarch to Odom someday," Kitsune said with a smile. "I will miss Veranda. There's so much of my history to learn from her."

"It was a worthwhile detour, but I missed my chance to sleep next to you by the fire last night." Myobu reached out a hand to draw Kitsune closer. Kitsune took hold of it, but he kept it at a distance.

"I know what you desire, and I hope you realize I long for that as well. What might have happened last night, what could occur right now, is how every day should end for us," Kitsune said. He shifted, buying time while he chose his next words. They needed to be said, even if it guaranteed Myobu would no longer accompany him on his mission. "There are some things I need to say. I haven't been completely honest with you."

Myobu surprised him by nodding his head. "Yes, I had a hunch you were keeping something from me."

"Truly? How could you tell?" Kitsune was astounded at hearing this twice within an hour. To successfully navigate the rest of their travels, he would need to spin the truth, if not outright lie, convincingly. Apparently, he was far worse at it than he thought.

"When you speak, you rarely look directly at me. Instead, you focus off to the side as though there is someone behind me," Myobu explained, giving a slight shrug. "While you are busy thinking of how to lay out the facts of a story, however, you look me or other people straight in the eye. It's probably an unconscious attempt to appear more convincing."

"I always look you in the eyes!" Kitsune said defensively.

"You may think you do," Myobu replied, "but your eyes drift off when you talk about things, especially your home, father, or childhood. It's like you're picturing them in your mind."

Kitsune thought it was charming someone would notice that kind of nuance about him. Then he shook his head, clearing his mind. He needed to focus on what he had to do.

"Besides, I overheard you speaking with Patriarch Kirby and Veranda while we ate," Myobu continued. He finally took his hand back out of Kitsune's grasp. "Why did you never tell me the reason behind your banishment?"

That caught Kitsune off guard. It had been in his thoughts so much he must have assumed Myobu was cognizant. Or was that really true? "I've been drawn to you since the moment we met. Before then, actually, if you want to know the truth. I would be lying if I said I hadn't wondered if you felt the same way for me. If you understood why my father exiled me, you would have guarded your heart."

"Perhaps," Myobu said, sitting up. "I doubt it would have mattered much. What else have you kept hidden from me?"

"I told you before that I sought the King's Sun because I believe he can offer me a way to end my banishment and find my way back into Kitsunetsuki," Kitsune started, not surprised Myobu knew there was more. Despite the pile of blankets, he shivered from nervousness, a chill creeping through his body. "I didn't come across that information on my own. My father told me."

"Your father pointed you to someone who might help end the banishment he himself pronounced?"

"More so an ultimatum, or a course of action to reverse my exile."

Myobu seemed to hesitate a moment before asking his next question, as if not sure he wanted the answer. "What does your father require of you?"

The nervous shaking of his body stilled, though the sickening chill remained. The fire in the hearth seemed to shrink back as Kitsune took a breath and spoke. "To take back my rightful place in Kitsunetsuki, I am to kill the King's Sun."

Myobu's body immediately stiffened, and the prince saw the armor protecting Myobu's sanguine nature was not invulnerable. His eyes were shiny, full of sadness and knowledge, as if he had expected this since the time their paths crossed.

"I see," Myobu murmured. "And you intend to carry out this course of action?"

"I do," Kitsune replied, grabbing hold of Myobu's wrist. "I must do as my father has asked. He is my king, and he comes before anything I want. I want you to stay with me, Myobu, but I could no longer keep you from the whole truth just to have you by my side. I would not continue to let you guide me down a path ending in my betraying you."

With a slow movement just as fluid as before, Myobu released himself from Kitsune's grip. He pulled his shirt on and slipped from the bed. Back at the door, he whispered, "I need to think about this."

"Myobu," Kitsune called out before the other closed the door. When the dark-haired man looked back at him, Kitsune thought he saw a tear trickling down his face, glistening in the fire's light. "I'm sorry."

With a sad smile, Myobu replied, "I know."

Then the door shut.

Kitsune did not sleep. Instead, he wept. His tears were not out of selfish pity or shame, nor were they for the hurt and pain he caused Myobu—they were of the sorrow for what might have been; for what should be between the two of them. In the dream with the cottage, Kitsune believed with absolute certainty that walking through the door would forever change his life. With the sheer giddiness coursing through him, he had assumed only positive things were in store for him and the man inside.

During the darkest moments of the night, he called out for his mother. No answer came from the chain around his neck. No flash of green light. No comforting words.

He had never been so alone.

*

"Here you go, sir," a young stable boy said quietly, jumping down off of Kitsune's cart. The youth had hitched the two horses to the wagon, and they looked far more refreshed than Kitsune felt. He was thankful for the cover of darkness, especially when saying his goodbyes to Patriarch Kirby and Veranda. When they asked where his companion was, it took all the self-control he could muster not to break down into an emotional heap. Instead, he mumbled that Myobu was under no obligation to travel with him and had probably slipped away in the night.

Kitsune climbed into the cart, dejectedly tossing his trusty backpack into the back, which was now stocked full of clothing, blankets, and food. So long as thieves didn't attack and rob him, he wouldn't have to stop for more supplies for the rest of the trip. With his recent luck, though, he wouldn't assume anything. Thankfully, his sword and bow were once again safely at his side.

He scanned the area around the main gate of Sandya, desperate to catch sight of Myobu in the moonlight. All he saw among the rocks were soldiers hurrying to their mounts or carts and the figures of those there to say goodbye.

After a final farewell wave to Kirby and Veranda, Kitsune took the reins and guided the horses into the departing caravan.

Tears stung at the back of his eyes. The loneliness that overwhelmed him mere hours before persisted, and leaving his newfound family behind only reinforced the emptiness. Even surrounded by soldiers, people he identified with, he felt alone.

A final glance back at Sandya a few tics later showed the city and its people again becoming indistinguishable from the mountains. Kitsune gave in to the fruitlessness of finding a familiar face and turned back to the long, dark road in front of him.

The prince spent most of the next two and a half days in solitude. His closest companion was Captain Bap, the assigned protector of the caravan. A soldier of few words, those he did utter carried as much enthusiasm and warmth as Captain Saxma's. The two seemed similar in temperament, though Bap lacked the vengeful malice in his eyes to complete the comparison.

As the hours ticked by, the impact of Myobu's departure became more apparent. Kitsune was depending on him to find the Harbinger. The tribal lands encompassed an immense portion of the region, and the people populating the area were disconnected from one another. It might take weeks to find a single individual among them. More likely, many months.

Even if he bypassed the Harbinger and traveled straight to the capital of Gaav, more mysteries awaited him. Kitsune knew of its general location and easily recalled basic facts about the culture and history, but he had little knowledge of the current political climate or the personalities of those he might encounter. For all he knew, Myobu was traversing the lands right now to warn the King's Sun about the impending assassination attempt.

The realizations highlighted how quickly Kitsune came to rely on the dark-haired man. How much he needed him.

The two nights spent on the road were especially lonely. The absence of Myobu's scent was made especially apparent by the food, sweat, and excrement of all those in the caravan. Kitsune tried to occupy his mind by volunteering to patrol the area for bandits while others slept. This left him tired during the daylight hours, though he had to keep an eye on his horses lest they wander too far off path.

All in all, by the time they reached the northern outpost, he was exhausted and in a foul mood.

*

"This is the end of the line for us," Captain Bap declared as the caravan made its way into the base. "I will pass on the patriarch's orders to the colonel here that he is to allow you shelter for as long as you desire and claim to any additional resources you deem necessary to your travels."

"I will depart before the sun sets," Kitsune replied, surprising even himself by speaking up. He had been so quiet during the trip that some assumed him to be mute.

"You may want to reconsider," chimed in Rori, Bap's second-in-command. She was a younger soldier and, despite her attempts to mimic her superior, had a bright personality. "There's a storm coming. I can sense it in the air."

Bap nodded his head in agreement with the assessment. "It's usually so dry in this region. This warmth and humidity that followed us from the south is just begging for a storm."

The two looked to Kitsune as though he would give a further confirmation. He shrugged, admitting he did not know much about the region's normal climate. Its stark contrast to Sandya shocked him. As they pushed north, the Argent Mountains and the green forestry thriving in their shadows gave way to rolling grasslands that farmers used to let their livestock graze. Eventually even the grass gave way to dirt and sand, and frequent strong gusts threw the silt high into the air. This forced Kitsune to pull his hood down over his eyes. He only glanced up every once in a while to make sure the horses hadn't veered off course. Even when the wind was relatively mild, enough filth hung in the air to make the sun hazy.

"It all comes from the Wastelands," one of the other travelers had said when Kitsune made a comment. "Many generations ago this was all fertile land, just like it is down south."

"What happened in the Wastelands?" Kitsune asked. He knew there had been a cataclysmic event, though he couldn't fathom what would make an entire region uninhabitable and barren. He assumed the knowledge of its cause had been lost along with all those who lived there. The traveler confirmed his ignorance, answering Kitsune's question with a shrug.

Despite the arid nature of their surroundings, the air was humid. Kitsune wouldn't have minded, having grown up lounging about on the terraces of Inari Palace in the warm, humid atmosphere, but now the moisture made all the dirt cling to his skin and clothes.

"You would suggest I stay here and ride out the storm?" Kitsune asked.

"Under normal circumstances, yes," Bap replied. "As I understand things, though, your intention is to travel west as fast as possible. The quickest route involves passing over a bridge not far from here. I traversed it myself just a month ago. It was rickety then. I'm not sure how many more storms it can weather, if it is even still there now."

A glance at Rori garnered no clue into the current condition of the bridge. "We abandoned it when trade with Ruio was cut off. Our spies take safer, less detectable routes to get into Kitsunetsuki," she explained, giving Kitsune what she probably thought was a hard, challenging stare. "The colonel would probably give you clearance to use one of them, but as the captain says, it'd take you much longer."

"I'll take the bridge," Kitsune assured, then excused himself from the caravan.

While knowing he should depart immediately, Kitsune had the inescapable urge to first visit the market. He needed something not included in the fully stocked cart, an item of great importance, though he couldn't exactly say what it was. He shook his head as though trying to rattle loose the answer. Hopefully, he'd know it when he saw it.

So Kitsune spent the next hour walking about the nearly abandoned bazaar, marveling at how the outpost differed from Sandya and Castle Nogare. Whereas those structures were grand and elaborately planned, either melting into their surroundings or magnifying the beauty of it, the construction of the outpost appeared rushed and haphazard. Instead of a castle or fortress, several administrative buildings huddled close together, surrounded by some housing for officials. Rows of tents filled the space between them and a rickety wooden wall encircling the entire encampment. While it reminded him of Kitsunetsuki's defenses, Kitsune doubted the fence would provide much protection should they come under attack.

If the outpost possessed a name, Kitsune did not know it. If so, none of the occupants or vendors advertised it. He guessed its founders had meant to facilitate relations with Ruio when the Eastern Gate closed. It probably grew considerably until Kitsunetsuki absorbed Ruio. Afterward, it fell into decay, a task helped along by the wind and sand, with only a few remaining stragglers left behind to keep watch over King Oni—or over the Wastelands.

Kitsune walked along the dusty streets, unable to suppress the moroseness weighing him down. He missed his new friend and wondered what Myobu would think of this desolate location. For the first time, Kitsune really considered his future. After he completed his mission and the king reinstated his position in Inari Palace, what did he want in life? Before, all he wanted was to take part in his father's wars. His perception of the world was changing, though, as were his intentions to take part in it. Kitsunetsuki need not rule over all, and its policies towards other kingdoms needed to change.

As did its policies towards its own people.

That seemed a grand revelation to Kitsune, but before he truly realized its importance, someone asked, "Something catch your fancy?"

Kitsune blinked in surprise, realizing he had come to a standstill along the main dirt throughway of the marketplace. As expected, vendors lined every allowable section of the street, though the owners and peddlers were not enthusiastic about venturing out and ensnaring new customers. They opted instead to remain behind their booths under the shade or a blanket. Indeed, it took Kitsune several heartbeats to find the source of the voice: a wiry old man with tanned, leathery skin. Devoid of hair or even a shirt, the elderly man sat perfectly still on a stool. Most of the wares he had for sale were old, weathered rubbish, which was why he blended in so well.

"See something you like?" the man repeated, seeing he now commanded Kitsune's attention.

Kitsune saw a plank of wood fastened above the man's booth with the painted words *Wastelands Things* in faded black. He scanned the items, wondering what had caught his eye. It all looked like junk. Broken, useless junk. Perhaps they were novelty items, and people purchased them just to possess a little piece of history.

"All these items are from the Wastelands?" Kitsune asked.

"Guaranteed" came the old man's reply.

"You've been there yourself, then?"

The man's eyes, heavily creased from squinting so much to keep the sand and dust out, shot open. "Spirits no, boy! Nobody enters the Wastelands! At least none that have lived to tell about it afterward."

From his history lessons, Kitsune recalled that a technologically advanced civilization settled there over twelve hundred sun cycles ago and the event that had transformed the land occurred roughly nine hundred cycles ago. Investigators cut short initial inquiries into what caused the decimation when some of them began dying, apparently burning from the inside out. Spiritual advisors claimed the Yokai spirits cursed the area in response to its inhabitants tampering with the fabric of nature. Scientists agreed that experimentation gone awry had caused the incident. They further surmised the event changed something in the air, making it toxic.

All governments since then forbade expeditions into the Wastelands, though the evidence of what happened was still clear in places like Odom's northern base. What had once been fertile, forested land was now a desert devoid of most life. Any remaining creatures were the subjects of horror stories told around campfires: ferocious animals with additional limbs, third eyes, or extra rows of razor-sharp teeth.

Just as he had given little stock in the stories of Yokai spirits before, Kitsune doubted the veracity of all the mystery surrounding the Wastelands. He thought, over the generations, there would have been enough adventurers or bandits brave enough to risk a trip into the quarantined areas. Or stupid enough to stumble through the poorly marked zones. Surely, if people still burnt up from the inside out or grew additional appendages, there would be documentation of numerous accounts.

Although, if such individuals simply disappeared as the old man alluded to, there would be nothing to account for.

"You seem to have a lot of items here from a land nobody has been able to get in and out of for so long," Kitsune said conversationally, trying not to sound like he was giving a stern accusation. Rather, he preferred not to be taken for a fool. He suspected the man, or at least his family, regularly crossed over into the Wastelands and took small tokens like these to sell off. Claiming they came from a land no one could enter made them more desirable.

The old man shrugged indifferently. Customers probably confronted him with the argument before. "I've been collecting them for a long time."

Kitsune nearly turned to leave when his eyes finally found what had initially caught his attention: a leather-bound book partially tucked beneath a pile of rusted gardening tools. Unlike the surrounding items, it would be the last thing to survive the ages. The leather bindings were frayed and water damaged but otherwise seemed intact. The pages in between them appeared to be in similar condition.

"What is that?" Kitsune asked, pointing.

The man pulled the book out from underneath the pile of junk, handing it over for inspection. "I have made many inquiries into the history of this volume. From what I can surmise, it is a historical account of one of the last head priests of the civilization that inhabited that once-great land. The written words are from their ancient language, which only a handful of people today can translate."

Kitsune didn't have to open the book to see the old man lied, especially about his valiant efforts to uncover its background. The one grain of truth in his story was that it came from a time when people spoke the ancient language; few in the world now read it. In Kitsunetsuki, high scholars, top military personnel, and the royal family were fluent in the language as a means of safeguarding information and knowledge. Kitsune knew it and easily deciphered the one word imprinted into the leather cover:

Journal

The prince glanced through the first few pages. True to the volume's intent, the book was a diary. Its owner, probably a woman judging by the handwriting, had carefully and neatly written short accounts, broken apart by dates. He read through the first entry.

2.20 – I cannot believe I'm back here. Right where I was two years ago. I left this forsaken city for so many reasons. They were good reasons, too.

Growing up, I did not belong to the local religious sect, though a good majority of the population were members. This made me feel somewhat like a second-class citizen even among my best friends. My father made life bearable. As an educational administrator, he was a highly respected man in the community. It's strange, I think, that even while that particular religious sect found technological and scientific advances abominable, they came to accept my father, a major player in the system that produced such imaginative and inventive thinkers.

The impression that I was somehow a minority never receded after university. In fact, it only worsened when I took my first posting. I did not work for the actual organization, but rather through a third party. It was the only way I could get through the doors of a major energy research facility. While I realize outsourcing work is standard practice, it only made me consider myself less of a person. I wasn't good enough for all the rights and privileges afforded to actual employees. That, and it paid a lot less. Most of my other friends became engineers of the physical variation, like structural. More money, and certainly more practical than theoretical energy manipulation.

I was going through a lot of emotionally charged issues at that time. The most unexpected was my father. He completely tore our family apart. After what he did, I was ashamed to be his daughter. What a contrast from growing up, when sharing his last name guaranteed a semblance of social acceptance.

I debated changing my last name, which I came to despise. In the end, I did something even more drastic. Packing my bags, I moved across the nation to an area recently acquired from the tribal lands. I began working for a lesser-known research facility. It has a reputation for inferior performance and scientific credibility. At first, I assumed this was because many of the employees are uneducated natives of the tribal lands. In reality, that facility conducts some of the most advanced research I have ever come across, most of it top secret. The natives, who perpetuate the guise of a backward people, are some of the top minds in the world today. I can't write any details in a personal diary, except that if the models cooked up there came to fruition, the energy needs of our nation—probably all the lands—would be forever sated.

Still, I was unable to shake the stigma of being a second-class citizen. Since most of the people who work at the facility and live in the area are natives, I was the outsider. Not only that, I was an outsider belonging to a people who acquired their land for use of its resources. No one thought highly of me, and my work was often regarded as substandard.

After two years, I was fed up with the area. It is beautiful to be sure, and the climate far more to my liking. I missed my own people, though. The friends I silently compete with. The family I left behind to escape my name. My father, even. While I have not forgiven him for what he did to the family, I have come to accept it as truth. My anger will reverse nothing. Besides, he continues to love me and support my decisions. Between continuing to shun him or involving him in my life, I choose having a father.

Kitsune did not understand much of the text, but her societal views and relationship with her father captivated him. While others had forced him from the upper class of his society, she placed herself among the lower classes. Despite the station she claimed to suffer, he guessed her to be well-educated, capable of travel, and able to make her own decisions. So many in Kitsunetsuki were not so privileged. If only his kingdom was more like this lost civilization.

Kitsune's mind reeled back around to a previous thought. Kitsunetsuki *could* be like this woman's culture. In fact, it could be better. It would take time. Its war-torn direction would need to change, as would its policies on social issues.

King Oni was wrong. Wrong to wage war against peaceful and economically beneficial neighbors. Wrong to force his ideals and opinions upon others, even if he was the monarch. And he was wrong to exile Kitsune for being himself.

Those were subversive thoughts, and it stunned Kitsune to come to those conclusions. He tempered this disloyalty by reaffirming his conviction to complete his mission and get an audience with his father. Only then could he attempt to reason with the king.

If only such treasonous ways had come to him before Myobu left.

"Do you want the book or not?" the old merchant interrupted. Grave concern was in his eyes.

"What's wrong?" Kitsune asked, drawing nearer.

"I have to pack up soon." The man started to fidget, throwing smaller items into larger ones. "The storm is almost upon us."

"Are you sure?" Kitsune asked, looking up again. "It's hard to see with all the dust, but I don't think there's anything heading this way. I can still make out the sun at the horizon."

"Look to the east."

Puzzled, as weather normally progressed from west to east, Kitsune turned around. He gasped sharply, taking in a lungful of sandy air. Behind the silt blurring the sky above, he easily made out the ominous wall of a powerful thundercloud spanning countless leagues. He wanted to ask how it was possible, but it was not the time for conjecture. The storm was visibly closing in on the base.

A jolt of adrenalin ran through Kitsune, and he took a step in the direction of his horses.

"Hey!" cried out the old man, pointing to the journal. "If you want the book, you have to pay!"

Without asking for a price or haggling, Kitsune reached into a pocket, pulled out a gold coin, and tossed it to the merchant. The man rubbed the polished coin with a weathered thumb, shocked at his luck in the transaction. He looked back up, intent on asking if any other items caught the customer's interest, but the man had disappeared.

TOWERS

"It looks like a giant cock."

Major Saxma looked over at Captain Pan, amused by the man's blatant vulgarity. Not even a sip of wine in him. "Indeed it does. Any idea what it's for?"

Pan shrugged. "None that have any evidence to support them."

The two men stood at the base of a four-story cylindrical tower. An egg-shaped, bulbous room sat at its peak. Crafted from stone, it did give the tower the appearance of a giant, armor-clad cock.

There was a single door on the exterior of the tower. Saxma had seen the design schematics and knew a narrow stairwell lined the interior of the tower, the only way to reach the uppermost room. No windows or arrow slits marked the spiral staircase, giving it no defensive reason for existing. Aside from King Oni's insistence that it be constructed, Saxma had no other source of information about the building.

"How many of these things are there?"

"I believe it's safe to assume the tower we saw under construction in Onger is a sister structure. And since this location will eventually become the only entrance into the kingdom from the north, I would venture to say there's probably one being built at the Western Pass,"

Pan answered. "If we accept the rumors that similar towers are going up in all the major cities, then about a dozen at this point."

Saxma took a few steps back from the tower, then turned in a full circle to get a better view of the entire military complex of which he was now in charge. The most striking features of it all were the base of what would become a twenty-five-footfall-tall barrier, a wall that would span most of the northern border of Kitsunetsuki, and the Northern Gate. Just as the wall split an otherwise tranquil and unpopulated prairieland into two halves, the gate was to be the only break in the wall itself. It would soon become the focus of what little northern traffic remained.

Though the majority of the wall was still massive piles of assorted stones, construction of the new regional military installation, a complex of dormitories, administrative centers, and mess halls, was already complete. From here, soldiers went out to patrol the border, not so much protecting it as ensuring those undertaking its construction stayed on task. The bricklayers and stonemasons were citizens of what used to be Ruio. While technically residents of Kitsunetsuki and not slaves, they weren't being treated much better. Aside from being forced into labor, their temporary housing consisted of simple tents, and allotted meals were meager at best.

This was the project given to Saxma as part of his promotion to major, his reward for delivering Prince Kitsune to Odom. Seal the north. Mind those who built the wall. Repel any assaults.

It was a menial assignment. Through Captain Pan, he kept the men and natives in line. Saxma allocated most of his time to completing administrative tasks, reviewing transfer requests, looking over communications, and the like. Tasks he had not enlisted to do. Despite this, though, there would be no complaints from him. Not after what happened with his predecessor.

Few would talk about Major Alexi. From what little information he could glean, Saxma would describe him as an honorable but stupid man. Alexi had followed his orders, but he was not shy about declaring his displeasure with them. Like Saxma, he thought the assignment to be beneath him, but he also considered the treatment of the natives unethical. Furthermore, he declared the entire venture a needless waste of Kitsunetsuki funds and resources. There was no need to protect the kingdom from a barren wasteland.

Though his officers advised him to curtail his protestations, Alexi continued his proclamations. He even petitioned King Oni to reconsider or scale back the immensity of the project. He continued to be forthright in his convictions right up until the tower's completion. The day its builders cemented the last brick into place and installed the contents being held in the bulbous room at the top, Alexi grew silent and distant. That night, he climbed atop his horse and rode north into the Wastelands. No one dared follow him, and not a soul had seen Alexi since.

Saxma stared north at the hills into which others had last seen Alexi riding off. Though he would not voice it, he agreed with his predecessor. For its stated purpose, the northern wall truly was a waste of resources. No one would attack from the north. The only thing that emerged from that region was the occasional five-legged deer. No army was crazy enough to march through it.

A more likely scenario than an invasion from the north would be a rebellion of the vast number of Ruio workers. While most couldn't handle swords and bows with any skill, many were experts with their own tools. They could kill with their trowels, picks, and axes with as much ease as Saxma could with his bare hands.

The natives didn't show any signs of protesting, though. They seemed rather content to do their work by day and return to their tents at night. Saxma found this odd behavior for a group whose people Kitsunetsuki conquered and subjugated within the past twenty sun cycles, let alone being recently forced from their homes and family to labor on a wall.

"Is it possible," he thought out loud regarding the tower, "this is somehow an extension of the king's power? That it holds or transfers whatever he uses to make others in Oinari believe in his every word with utter certainty?"

Pan's eyes widened in surprise, but it was from his commanding officer's actual suggestion of something so fantastical, not the fantastical suggestion itself. Saxma entertained some of Pan's more farfetched ideas during their conversations, but he hadn't produced many theories himself. "It's no less plausible than anything I've come up with. What makes you speculate such a thing?"

"The Boleyn Room," Saxma said under his breath.

"The throne room?" Pan's eyes went even wider. "You've seen it?"

Saxma glanced suspiciously up at the tower as though it was eavesdropping on their conversation, then jerked his thumb in the direction of the Northern Gate. They walked toward it, pretending to inspect its progress, all the while surrounded by the sounds of clinking metal and breaking rocks as masons shaped, fitted, and dressed stone.

"Of course I haven't been in the Boleyn Room," he whispered. "But I was recently present in one of its ancillary rooms when the king exited it. There was a light inside…a light too beautiful to have been created by mere flame."

The word *beautiful* felt weird in his mouth. Even Pan looked at him queerly.

"Shut up. I'm committing treason by even discussing it with you, so shut your trap. You know what I mean. It was a golden light unlike anything I've seen."

"Magic?" Pan surmised.

"Aside from whatever condition led us to accept every word King Oni said as truth, it's the most supernatural thing I've encountered. Almost forgot about it entirely. I was too focused on taking the prince into custody."

It pleased Saxma that his words did not elicit any negative response from the captain. Under his tutelage, Pan had come a long way in his training. Not so much yet that the men respected him. That would come in time so long as he didn't shy away from battle. They were cautious of him now, however, and followed orders in a timely fashion.

Pan had taken Saxma's advice and locked a man in a cell box during their march north. He hadn't been so brave as to inflict the punishment upon one of his friends. Instead, he enlisted their help one night in arresting one of the rowdier lieutenants. The man consumed too much alcohol and was making a fool of himself, unbecoming for an officer of the Kitsunetsuki military. After initially resisting detainment, Pan tranquilized the man with a persuader. Then Nasuno and Tsuzumi tossed the officer into a cell box, which remained locked for the following two days until they arrived at their current location.

Saxma still didn't think it made as great an impact that imprisoning a friend would have, but taking action over a lieutenant was still impressive. The rest of the men, no matter what rank they held, saw that much.

Even more important than Pan's personal growth as an officer were their private discussions. They spent long hours speaking of King Oni, his military campaigns, and the intent to institute new laws and ethics. Many of their ideas and theories were pure conjecture, based on rumor or discreet discussions with other men in the company, and they often circled about and negated previous notions.

Of several subjects they were certain. The king's parentage, for example, did not include the Yokai as was often rumored. Oni's father, a respected leader, never displayed special abilities beyond the reach of man. Queen Veranda, the one of whom the rumors most often cited as being Yokai, was still alive and under the protection of Patriarch Kirby. It was a little-known secret afforded by a few of the more affluent officers who traveled east before the border was closed. There existed no stories of Veranda exhibiting great power, either. If she were truly Yokai, she would have surely changed form and fled into the wilderness.

Despite this, King Oni commanded some kind of supernatural ability. They could not yet tell whether it was inborn or something foreign under his control, but it was there. Many of the officers Saxma and Pan spoke with or overheard relayed similar experiences to their own. In particular, they had questioned the king's statements and reasoning as they marched farther from Oinari. Their oaths and loyalties kept them from candidly revealing such things. One man was so distraught by the conflicts between an altered reality and his allegiance that he could no longer sleep through the night without medicinal aid.

In attempting to ascertain the origin of his king's power, Saxma had remembered the golden light from inside the Boleyn Room. "If the source of that light was also the key to his power, maybe the tower somehow channels it here?"

"Or house some of the actual source material," Pan guessed. "We'd have to look inside to know for sure."

That would be difficult to do. Saxma knew from the schematics that two heavy wooden doors separated them from the oval chamber, one being the entrance and another inside at the top of the spiral stairwell. They were both locked, and Saxma did not have the keys. They were the only doors in many leagues the major was unable to open, and no one knew who could.

"If any of this was true, why has the effect worn off from the soldiers, particularly you and me?" Saxma said, doubtful. "If the king were still persuading our thoughts, how are you and I actively having this conversation? Wouldn't he know? Wouldn't he have us arrested?"

"I think it would take more energy to enforce his will over such great distances, even with the help of the towers. The military is loyal to the royal family regardless of supernatural persuasion, so why waste it on them? Rather, if it was true, the tower here is probably to keep the Ruio builders subdued and, in the future, to keep a mental eye on the gate, to dissuade attackers."

Saxma glanced around at the workers, chipping away at and shaping stone. It was eerie how easily and happily they took to their work, forced upon them though it was. Their offbeat behavior helped support the new theory.

Still, their discussion was returning to one of pure conjecture. While speculation helped them stitch together what they already knew, it had been a painfully slow process. Much like the stonemasons, Saxma and Pan carefully chipped away at all the nonsensical maneuvers and plans of the king, parsing out true intentions from misleading words and actions. Just as the northern wall was taking shape, they were just now roughing out Oni's grand scheme. Everything done appeared to be an attempt to exert more control over the kingdom, its neighbors, and all inhabitants.

Though he could not explain why, Saxma had an uneasy feeling that something cataclysmic was about to befall Kitsunetsuki. His patience for guesswork was wearing thin. It was not his style to sit around and wait for something to happen, and planning for what might eventually turn into a full-fledged mutiny against the king was exhausting.

Equally exhausting was his body's frustratingly constant desire for sex. A limited number of women lived in the camp. Those present were of the variety few found sexually appealing.

"Spirits," Saxma muttered under his breath, realizing his eyes were running greedily over Pan's slender frame. He willed the pressure in his pants to dissipate, knowing it had been far too long since he'd been with a woman if he found a man such as Pan attractive to look upon. His subordinate preferred only the opposite sex, though that wouldn't stop Saxma from taking him if he had to. If considering rebellion taught him anything, it was that he'd do almost anything for the benefit of Kitsunetsuki.

Despite much contemplation, he couldn't conjure up a reason that forcing himself upon Pan would benefit the kingdom. It was easier to justify mutiny against the king.

"Would you look at that," Pan said, startling Saxma from his reverie.

Saxma followed Pan's gaze, looking to the northeastern horizon where dark storm clouds billowed, visible even though they were many leagues away. Curtains of rain fell, and lightning arced across the clouds and to the ground, an unnerving sight when not accompanied by the sound of thunder.

"A storm is passing into the east. What of it?" he growled.

"That's just it," Pan said. He pointed to the north and west. The skies were clear and blue. "I never saw the storm building, and it looks far too massive to have just cropped up."

"What exactly are you implying?" Saxma asked. He saw many of the builders taking notice of the menacing clouds. The sounds of metal on rock grew fainter as they refocused their attention. "The storm is heading westward? Is that even possible?"

Understanding and predicting weather patterns was one of the fundamental subjects taught in the military. Good commanders would not march their soldiers or send them into battle if a storm might result in catastrophic results or provide an enemy with an advantage. Informed soldiers dressed properly and employed tactics better suited for current environmental conditions.

A basic tenet of weather, at least in the known world, was that it moved from west to east. Exceptions existed, but those were usually ocean storms so massive that they rotated around themselves. This settlement was nowhere close to the ocean. Yet, the more they stared at the dark clouds, the more obvious it became that they were moving in a westerly direction.

"For it to defy natural patterns, it must be a strong storm," Pan commented. "Perhaps it isn't natural at all."

"Have everyone take shelter," Saxma ordered. Then, referring to the workers, "And not their tents. Cram as many as you can into the mess halls and dormitories."

Aside from the soldiers, close to five hundred able-bodied native men and women lived on-site whose work ranged from masonry to cooking and laundry. Their tent dwellings could bear the mild weather of the region. The sky above was blue now, but if the oncoming storm was as bad as it looked, these shelters would not suffice. They never intended for the permanent buildings, built of stone and lumber, to accommodate everyone at the same time. They had to try, though.

"Move it!" Saxma barked, startling all those nearby into action. They had been staring into the east, perhaps all hoping they were sharing a collective dream. With Pan now off carrying out his directives, he was alone soon enough in the middle of the main road. Or so he thought.

"Excuse me, Major," came a soft voice to Saxma's right. He looked down to find a small, willowy man. Dressed in dark rags, he had long, stringy hair and a scraggly beard.

"Jasper," Saxma said, immediately recognizing the man as one of his hired spies. With an insignificant and unassuming appearance, Jasper made a perfect scout by being invisible to the attention of most others. He possessed an unrivaled knowledge of the region's geography, using it to slip in and out of kingdoms along paths known to few. Saxma had first used the man's skills, which were never a cheap investment, to ascertain his chances of promotion to captain. More recently, he made better use of Jasper's abilities by sending him into Odom. The spy was supposed to find the whereabouts of Prince Kitsune, assuming he was still alive, and report back with any interesting movements or intents.

Saxma turned and began walking up the dusty road toward an administrative building, Jasper behind him in his shadow. The spy whispered, "I bring news of your interest in the east."

"I would hope you wouldn't return without reason," Saxma growled under his breath.

"The subject is much closer than you might think."

Glancing back at Jasper, Saxma saw the man looking at the oncoming storm. "He's there? So far north?"

"The target was traveling with a caravan toward Odom's northernmost outpost. I rode with them for much of the distance before slipping away." Jasper squinted, studying the horizon. "That storm is currently over the outpost he was heading for. By the look of those clouds—and knowing the quality of the settlement's construction—he is in considerable danger."

"They are both soldiers," Saxma mused. "Coupled with Mamori's extensive field experience, they should be more than capable of finding appropriate shelter."

"Mamori is long dead," Jasper whispered, though more to keep from being overheard than to convey a sense of remorse.

Saxma blinked at that news. It was unfortunate. Mamori was a good soldier, and Saxma had taken a modicum of comfort knowing the prince was in good, protective hands. Still, he refused to feel remorse or even responsibility for the death. Mamori had, after all, committed treason. Saxma would have been within his rights to cut him down back at the Eastern Gate.

"Who is he with now?"

"The subject has allied himself with a commoner by the name of Myobu. I cannot determine the history of the man, and all I can provide are my own observations. Though I doubt he is from Odom, he has a good grasp on how to navigate through its land and politics. He is an excellent bowman and has used his skills multiple times to defend themselves and others. Also, I believe they have fallen in love with one another."

Saxma walked around the corner of the building, stepping up to the private entrance to his office. After making sure no one was looking, he ushered the spy inside. A few moments later, they were in his office, home to a few tables and a liquor cabinet. They ignored the chairs in front of a desk. The impending storm was on their minds and would have made it difficult to relax. Jasper, however, let down a bit of his act and spoke in a manner that didn't fit his filthy attire.

"Summarize Kitsune's journey for me," Saxma said, leaning back against his desk.

Jasper admitted it had taken him a while to catch up with the prince. In his tracking, he first came across two mangled bodies and a fresh grave, the occupant of which he discovered to be Mamori. Then, after a respite at Castle Nogare, where evidence showed the prince stayed with a newcomer, he traveled north to Sandya. There he finally caught up with Kitsune and Myobu.

"The two met with Patriarch Kirby, and the prince now knows his grandmother is alive. Kitsune left Sandya alone as part of a caravan heading north, Myobu having slipped away during the night. I know not where the commoner was heading or what his intentions were."

Saxma wondered if Prince Kitsune attempted to form an alliance with the patriarch. "What is he hoping to accomplish by heading north?"

"The prince is in search of the Harbinger, a Yokai who resides in the tribal lands. From the Odom outpost, he plans to head directly west, skimming the border of Kitsunetsuki and the Wastelands. That's why I ultimately came to you. If he survives the storm, he should be traveling a stone's throw from here within two days' time."

Saxma remained silent as he mulled this over. Prince Kitsune was another sticking point in the ongoing discussions between him and Pan. Saxma argued that, if Kitsune survived his initial exposure in Odom, he would eventually seek an alliance with Patriarch Kirby and attempt a coup. The captain, however, believed the prince would use diplomacy and bargain his way back into the king's good graces. Either way, they agreed he would not sit idly by.

Of further concern was whether or not Kitsune possessed any kind of magic. Saxma now believed that the man had always displayed some form of power. That would explain how he was undefeated in combat despite his diminutive size. If this was true, had he inherited the gift from his father? Or was it possible his mother, of whom little was known, had Yokai blood?

It added up to too many questions and not enough answers. Other than installing the prince as king if they successfully deposed Oni, Saxma and Pan left him out of all militaristic scenarios they dreamt up against the monarchy. Now, though, he had a chance to gauge the man's interest and perhaps get a feel for any other coup plans underway.

Saxma's mind was made up. If he were to take any action against King Oni, the last thing he wanted or needed was interference from another operation. That might destroy any chances of either party succeeding. Instead, they could join forces and devise a two-pronged approach.

He was getting ahead of himself. First, he needed to find the prince. Second, there was Jasper to worry about. The spy might be under his employ at the moment, but nothing would keep him silent if another source offered better coin. Saxma was not yet certain on how to proceed, but if word got out that he might assist Prince Kitsune, he'd lose his head.

"If you have any business you need to attend to, do it," Saxma ordered. "Speak to no one about what we've discussed. Meet Pan by the gate in fifteen tics."

"Excuse me?" Jasper looked puzzled.

"I need Captain Pan to find our prince…*now*. Preferably alive. You are the only man who can make that possible expediently."

"But the storm!" Jasper protested. He looked as though he was about to bolt out the door.

"Consider your fee doubled," Saxma stated, knowing twice an already exorbitant amount would quiet the man's fears. The thought crossed his mind that he may have to justify the costs and reasons of his actions to his superiors later. *If* there would be a later. For the time being, he considered his actions beneficial for the kingdom.

"Go now," Saxma ordered a still-stunned Jasper, ushering him out of the building. "Take Pan to Kitsune. If he deems it necessary, help smuggle the prince back here to me."

The wind was picking up outside, and the skies overhead were turning a greenish gray color. Saxma picked up his pace, striking out to find Pan. He had a special task for the captain to complete, one to which the man would probably not take kindly.

THE HEART OF NINKO

The two old horses galloped faster than they had in sun cycles, racing down a path neither they nor their handler could clearly see. The sand and dirt permeating the air thickened as the storm bore down upon them. Kitsune could barely keep his eyes open long enough to register the horrendous landscape surrounding him.

The cart bounced violently, and Kitsune gripped the reins tightly in fear. He realized now he should never have left the outpost. Disaster was certain if he turned back, but he needed to find shelter soon. He was completely lost, though, and wholly unfamiliar with the landscape. He didn't even know if the road he was on led to the bridge he was seeking or was veering off in another direction.

A flash of lightning highlighted a gnarled-looking tree to his left. He glanced over at it, his heart pounding against his chest. When he looked forward again, he nearly jumped from the cart in terror.

Someone was sitting next to him, wrapped up in a cloak.

Kitsune spun about on the bench, bringing his right arm up to block any forthcoming attack. A hand—a small hand—appeared out of the dusty air, stretching out from the cloaked figure and coming to rest upon his arm.

The prince looked at the face shrouded by the hood, then lowered his guard. Though obscured, he would recognize the lines and features of Myobu anywhere. Before he could feel anything, let alone say something, Myobu took the reins from him.

"How can you possibly steer? I cannot see a thing!" Kitsune shouted over the howling winds, coughing violently as he inhaled a mouthful of sand.

Myobu didn't answer, instead concentrating entirely on the route in front of them. The ride became rougher, and Kitsune thought they had left the more traveled trail in favor of a lesser one. As they blindly barreled forward, Kitsune wondered how Myobu would be able to bring the horses to a stop before they all toppled over into whatever it was the bridge crossed over.

The sounds of powerful, deep growling and splintering wood reached their ears from the eastern sky. It reverberated through their bodies and was so disturbing, so vast, that neither of them wanted to acknowledge it. Kitsune looked back through squinted eyelids, shocked at how dark and sickly green the menacing sky had turned. Somewhere behind all the haze, he could just make out the silhouette of what looked like a cloud falling from the sky to the earth.

"Great spirits," he whispered. "What is that?"

As if reading his thoughts, Myobu replied, "I think it's some kind of tornado. I've never seen one like it."

The tornadic cloud gave another monstrous moan as it touched ground. Kitsune remembered the first time the Lady of the Mountain appeared to him. When his mother dislodged herself from the mountainous slope, towering above him, he felt a sense of dread like never before. She was a giant force of nature he, not knowing it was an illusion, had absolutely no control over. It was the first time he considered his life to be in danger.

As giant droplets of rain pelted Kitsune in the face, he knew this force, unlike the Lady of the Mountain, was not part of a dreamscape. He fought to keep down the panic rising in his chest, looking over at Myobu for comfort.

The cart glanced against a stony outcrop to their right, bouncing dangerously over a few rocks strewn across the path. The jolting movement tossed them both up into the air. When they crashed back down on to the bench, Kitsune felt his tailbone break.

Myobu cursed the horses as he faced forward to correct their direction. Kitsune watched helplessly as most of their new supplies bounced out of the back of the cart.

"We have to go back!" he shouted, finding it hard to keep the panic out of his voice.

"We can't!" was the response. "We won't make it!"

After another glance back, a wave of relief swept over Kitsune when he spotted his original backpack still in the cart. Reaching, he grabbed it and pulled it close. Myobu's was on the bench next to him, and he held it against his chest, burying his face into it, breathing in his scent. It was almost enough to distract him.

Myobu pulled back sharply on the reins, bringing the horses to a reluctant stop. He hauled Kitsune off the bench by the shoulder and ran forward.

Kitsune faltered, the pain from his tailbone shooting up his spine. He screamed above the yawning storm. "Where are you going? What about the horses?"

Myobu looked back, and the fear in his eyes made Kitsune's breath catch in his throat.

The wind howled, pushing the prince against his will. Myobu grabbed him by the shirt and shoved him forward. "Don't look back, and don't look down!"

Kitsune stumbled onward, stepping onto wooden planks. He froze, knowing they were now upon the bridge. Despite Myobu's warning, it was impossible not to look down. The darkness below commanded attention. It was an ominous black rivaling the sky falling to earth behind them.

The canyon below did not particularly frighten Kitsune. The bridge itself, however, gave him pause. Its design consisted of wooden planks set side by side and held in place by some dubious-looking rope. A few footfalls above the planks, two separate lengths of rope stretched out parallel to each other, acting as makeshift handrails. They were not tethered to the planks at any particular interval, so as the bridge swayed haphazardly in the wind, the planks and handrails could be several footfalls out of sync.

The icy rain came down harder, now accompanied by large chunks of hail. The horses screamed in fright as balls of ice pelted them, and they galloped away. Kitsune could sympathize, himself struggling to keep the terror from paralyzing him.

After passing Myobu his backpack, Kitsune slipped his own over his shoulders. Then, before he had time to overthink the situation, he ran out along the bridge. He knew if he gave any consideration to his actions, he would have hesitated and they would have no chance of escaping the tornado. Their odds were not favorable as it was.

Kitsune shifted his weight from left to right in sync with the bridge as it swayed, ignoring the handrails. His eyes were fixed on the path ahead as it came into view so he could identify missing or damaged boards, jumping deftly over any gaps. Twice, boards tore away from their fastenings mere moments before he would have stepped foot on them. The handrails, made of heavy rope, slapped against his body, threatening to topple him over.

The prince thought he heard Myobu screaming something from behind. It just as well could have been the storm, growling and whining as it did. There was no way he would risk looking back, lest the overpass shift in front of him and he run right off the edge.

The bridge jolted upward, tossing Kitsune up into the air. His feet and arms flailed about as he continued to run with no purchase. In horror, he watched as the planks shifted far to the left, leaving nothing but the yawning darkness of the canyon below him. As he fell, he continued to thrash about wildly, and by random chance his arm hooked around one of the handrails.

The weightlessness in his stomach made him feel sick.

As he gripped the rope with both hands, Kitsune realized the tornado had ripped the eastern moorings free. The bridge was collapsing, and he was falling toward the western side.

Time seemed to slow as Kitsune descended, leaving his mind with a few extra moments to consider his many failures. If he were to die here and now, unable to traverse a bridge, the failure to carry out King Oni's mission and prove his worthiness of being an Asher would only be the pinnacle of his father's disappointment in him. There would be no consequences of his death. No one within the walls of Inari Palace would mourn him.

On top of that, Kitsune had completely failed Myobu in every aspect, bringing the man nothing except pain and hard choices. That in return for the happiness the dark-haired man gave him, having helped open his eyes to the world and himself. No, happy did not begin to describe how he felt, especially now that they were reunited. Despite the hardships he'd endured, he had never been so deliriously joyful and alive than when he was with Myobu.

Damn his father for putting him in this position, Kitsune thought. Damn any parent.

A sudden and undefined anger took root within his mind—not toward anyone in particular, but rather, if anything, at this moment in time. He was not weak, he did not consider himself to be inconsequential, and he certainly did not want to disappoint all those he loved. He would not let this moment steal his chances to prove himself.

A rocky canyon wall visualized out of the mist, and the prince cried out in pain as the left side of his frame smashed into the jagged rocks. The fall had not been so perilously long that his body was dashed to bits, but he did momentarily lose control of his left arm. He slipped several footfalls down the rope before securing his position.

Somewhere below him, out of the dusty darkness and sound of rushing wind, came a similar cry of pain. Despite the throbbing in his extremities, Kitsune grinned, grateful beyond measure that Myobu had made it as well.

The top of the cliff wasn't an unfathomable distance above, so Kitsune pulled himself upward, putting each hand above the other. He was thankful he stored his cloak away earlier, as the wind and rain would have soaked it and thrown him off balance. As it was, the increasingly large hail continued to hit him, cracking against his head and knuckles.

When at last he reached the top and rolled over on to the ground, he didn't let his muscles and mind relax even for a moment. The earth shook violently beneath him, and when he opened his eyes, the monstrous cloud was close enough that he could see the rotational winds forming it. He wondered how it could sustain itself over the canyon or if the funnel even made it all the way to the bottom.

After a few moments, a feeble-looking hand appeared from the side of the cliff, grasping for something to hold on to. Kitsune clasped it in his own and hauled Myobu to safety. While they had made it across the bridge, he didn't think they'd last much longer. The tornado was picking up debris and spitting material out at incredible speeds. Tree limbs either splintered against rock or embedded themselves deep into the dirt. He winced as smaller slivers dug their way into his flesh.

"You've been here before, yes?" he shouted near Myobu's ear. "Do you know of a safe place we can wait out this storm?"

Nodding, Myobu pointed west, away from the cliff, and started down what Kitsune hoped was a path. In the torrents of rain, he almost lost sight of his companion. Reaching out, he grabbed a handful of clothing and allowed himself to be led.

They hadn't gone more than two hundred paces, stumbling down a steep decline and around a massive boulder, when they ran into a solid structure. Though he could barely make out the size and shape of the impediment, Kitsune recognized it immediately by touch.

"How can this possibly help us?" he cried out angrily, remembering the gray metallic building just outside of Oinari. Its walls had been smooth and featureless, and he could only assume in his current circumstances that this one shared those traits. "There's no way inside!"

His words were lost, though, and not only to the wind. Myobu had disappeared. Even the handful of clothing the prince had been clinging to dematerialized, leaving him with an empty clenched fist.

Though baffled, Kitsune had no time to process Myobu's sudden departure. In front of him, the wall of the structure melted. Ripples of metal peeled away to reveal a gaping black hole. In complete disregard to the raging storm, encroaching funnel cloud, and debris flying about at breakneck speeds, Kitsune could not help but stare, entranced at this magic.

Then, without warning, a pair of small hands reached out from the black hole. They clamped down on his shoulders and pulled him forward through the opening and into the gray building.

Once through, the rippling metal closed back up, plunging Kitsune into complete darkness and an eerie silence marked only by his beating heart and heavy breathing.

"Are you hurt?" Myobu said through the darkness. His voice was like sweet honey to Kitsune's ears.

"I'm fine," he responded, running his hands back through his drenched hair. The building was warm and musty, which suited him just fine. He'd otherwise soon be shivering beneath his wet clothing. "My tailbone snapped, I have a hundred splinters, and I will be bruised and sore in the morning, but we survived."

"I can't do anything about the tailbone, but I'll help with the splinters," Myobu said, sounding appropriately concerned.

"Never mind the splinters. Where the hell are we? What is this place? There's a similar structure not far from where I grew up, but no one has ever been able to get inside of it."

"They are relics of a time long past," Myobu said in a low, sad voice. "Standing monuments of the great civilization that once occupied what is now the Wastelands."

"You jest!" Kitsune exclaimed. By all accounts, the event that made the Wastelands uninhabitable occurred nearly nine hundred sun cycles ago, not long after the formation of the Kitsunetsuki Kingdom. He knew the building outside of Oinari was at least a couple of hundred sun cycles old and many theories attributed it to the lost civilization, but he struggled to believe anything could last so long in such pristine condition. He had seen edifices constructed and fall apart within his lifetime.

Kitsune's breath caught in remembrance. Inari Palace was probably just as old as these ancient places and was also unspoiled by time. "Are these buildings touched by magic?"

"There are many places in this world maintained by magic, but these are not." Myobu's voice came from another location in the darkness, and Kitsune turned about, willing his eyes to adjust. "From what I've been told, the society that built these places was a people of science. They engineered the materials these structures consist of to outlast themselves."

"What was their purpose?" Kitsune said. "For that matter, how do we know they still aren't performing the tasks they were built for?"

"Like many locations around the world, this place was built to channel energy. Not spiritual or magical, but raw energy. Like lightning," Myobu explained. "As for whether it is still functional…"

There was a soft clicking sound, and light burst into existence, blinding Kitsune. He crouched in alarm, shielding his eyes.

Myobu strode over and embraced him comfortingly, chuckling softly. "It's okay. We're safe now."

"Thanks to you," Kitsune replied, blinking his eyes rapidly, waiting for his eyes to adjust to the light so he could look into Myobu's dark eyes. "You are back, right? You aren't planning on leaving again?"

"My place is with you," Myobu conceded, his voice low. "If you'll have me."

The prince's heartbeat escalated. "Of course I want you. I'm sorry for denying you—denying us—beforehand. I've decided my father is wrong to deny others the opportunity to explore their love and attraction. With you by my side, I am certain we can convince him to reverse his proclamation."

The two continued to embrace each other for several moments. Kitsune wanted to kiss the man, to continue the exploration he stopped that night in Sandya, but the alien nature of the building in which they stood was perplexing. It appeared the designers used the same materials comprising the external edifice for most everything within, though the complexity of the surrounding objects contrasted the sheer simplicity of the exterior. Stairwells leading to platforms lined the walls. Pipes sprouted from the floor, forked like trees, and disappeared into the walls and ceiling. Flat panels of square and circular shapes protruded from the walls, as well as what looked like windows with no view behind them. He did not understand what they were or if they served any function at all.

The light now filling the room emanated from glowing balls floating in the air at regular intervals near the ceiling. They reminded Kitsune of the glowing orbs in the Boleyn Room, except that they were pleasant to gaze into while these hurt his eyes.

"This isn't magic?" he asked, walking in a circle as he looked around.

"Of a different kind," Myobu answered with a smile. "Anything we see but don't understand can seem like the magic of the Yokai. Here, though, the energy these structures harness can be used to create light within balls of glass. It's hard to see from here, but those light sources aren't floating. They are attached to fixtures, which in turn are connected to the ceiling. It's almost like a torch."

Kitsune knew energy existed all about him, that even a resting rock contained powerful amounts of potential energy. It was possible to tap such energy for use, like creating fire in a hearth. Scholars and researchers shared theories that this energy could be harnessed, redirected, stored, and used for purposes beyond imagination. Scientific advancement was nowhere close to testing such theories.

It was odd—Kitsunetsuki was regarded as the most advanced land. People came from nations unknown to study in its universities. As he stood inside this building, though, the prince knew those who once called the Wastelands home would probably consider his own to be backward.

"I still don't understand how we got in here," Kitsune said, looking back at the wall through which he had fallen. No evidence remained of the hole that had opened up for him, no discernable entrance of any kind.

Myobu shrugged. "I've only been inside a time or two before, and the portal has always opened up for me. The last time I was here fumbling around in the dark, I accidentally brushed up against some of those tiny levers on that desk or panel, which is how I learned to turn on these lights."

He reached out, palming the fabric of Kitsune's shirt. Heat blossomed in the prince's cheeks. It was an odd moment for Myobu to get frisky, but he wasn't about to complain.

"Ow!" Kitsune yelped as a short burst of fiery heat seared his upper arm.

"Oh, shush," Myobu chided, showing him a large splinter before tossing it into a corner.

"Ahh," Kitsune muttered, trying not to sound too disappointed.

Myobu repeated the process nearly two dozen more times, palming him across the arms, shoulders, back, and abdomen. Just prior to each shard being freed, Kitsune felt a quick flare of heat as though his companion was placing a tiny iron against his skin. The more it happened, the more comfortable and less painful he found it, as though it was further reassurance all would be well.

"Take off your shirt," Myobu ordered after he was satisfied he had removed all the major chunks. His tone was reminiscent of a physician.

Perhaps because of the tone, Kitsune did as he was told without question, watching as the other removed his cloak from the bag and spread it out across the ground. Then, at the doctor's insistence, he sat down on top of it. Myobu followed suit, sitting down across from him, a sad look suddenly appearing on his face.

Before Kitsune could say anything, Myobu reached forward and rested his palm on the left side of the prince's chest. He whispered, "Your heart beats here."

Kitsune's heart thumped, and he could see Myobu's hand move with each beat. After several heartbeats, Myobu moved his hand down to the right side of his abdomen. Kitsune looked at him peculiarly, but then the other said, "Ninko's heart beats here. Unlike yours, it is not protected by a cage of bone. It is, however, the quickest and surest way to kill him. I want to be with you, I will travel with you on your journey, and I will help you find the King's Sun. I cannot assist in attacking, so when you loose your arrow or stab with your sword, it is here that you must aim."

As he stared at his companion in disbelief, Kitsune felt a combination of shock and shame. Even in deciding to return, the dark-haired man had just made a terrible sacrifice. Kitsune had no idea how to respond. All words seemed inadequate, so he fell forward and embraced the man again.

Myobu held on tight, stroking the prince's long hair. After a while, he again adopted the manner of a physical and directed Kitsune to lie down on his stomach.

Once Kitsune was in position, Myobu immediately straddled him across the back. He massaged Kitsune's shoulders and back, being particularly careful with the more bruised left side of his body. His small hands applied the perfect amount of pressure and movement at every spot. Those hands had power in them, and Kitsune reveled at being touched by them.

Despite the somber conversation that just transpired, Kitsune was instantly aroused. Out of respect to Myobu's sacrifice, he wanted to remain quiet and compliant. What he desired, though, was to spin around, rip off the man's clothes, and take him. To keep from grinding the floor in frustration, he looked about for a distraction. His pack was an arm's length away, and he saw the top of the journal he purchased from the outpost in it. He reached out, caressing the book's leather spine.

The commonalities between Kitsune and the woman who wrote in the journal so long ago fascinated him. Both of their fathers committed acts that tore their families apart. She was struggling to forgive while Kitsune was working to be forgiven—or at least understood. Shame riddled them both. Hers stemmed from her surname being tarnished by her father, and his at being the one to tarnish the Asher lineage. Despite their disgrace, both of them decided to move forward, working to correct and mend their relationships. Their problems, no matter how small or encompassing, were universal. He found that oddly comforting. It meant the people of the Wastelands, for all their achievements, were just like them.

"Hey!" Kitsune exclaimed in surprise as Myobu grabbed his hand back from the backpack. He rolled over to face Myobu, cringing in pain as he put pressure on his tailbone.

"I didn't know I had competition for your attention," Myobu said slyly. "Should I be jealous?"

"Believe me, you have nothing to be jealous of."

"Good," he said, standing up. "Now take off your pants."

"Excuse me?" Kitsune said defiantly. He sat up, crossing his legs, wincing as he did. "I most certainly will not!"

"I need to check your legs for any remaining splinters. The last thing you want is some kind of infection taking root. Besides," Myobu said, reaching for one of the little levers on the panel, plunging the room back into darkness, "I won't be able to see a thing."

Kitsune sat flabbergasted for a moment, but then asked himself why he was being so shy. It wasn't his nature to be timid or self-conscious about being naked. He was usually the more aggressive one, getting to the pleasurable interactions as soon as possible. The difference was that before now, he didn't really care what the other person thought of him. He never truly cared about the other person at all.

Now, though, all these emotions and desires were connected to his would-be partner. He was determined not to hurt or disappoint Myobu. No more than he already had, at least.

He cared about the other man so much, and it struck him that his own hesitation was preventing both of them from furthering the exploration of their relationship. He remembered the anger he experienced while falling into the canyon, disappointed in himself at how he'd treated Myobu. His failure to follow the path of his desire now would be the true disappointment to them both. He'd be damned if he stymied the flow of either of their joy.

With a newfound confidence, he ignored the pain in the small of his back and shimmied off his pants, using them as a pillow as he laid down his head. In the darkness, he could hear the rustling of cloth as Myobu stripped himself bare as well. He regretted that the lights had been doused, as he had yet to see Myobu in the nude. It hardly seemed fair, seeing as how the other bathed him naked even before knowing his name.

Just as he must have done while cleaning Kitsune's body, Myobu began running his hands up and down Kitsune's legs. His fingers caressed and squeezed, searching for perforations. Only twice more did Kitsune suffer the sudden pinch and heat as a sliver of wood was extricated.

Once Myobu reached Kitsune's waist, he suddenly grabbed hold of his cock. Kitsune gasped in surprise and ecstasy as the other assessed the last parts of his body for damage. After Myobu deemed the prince's body clear, he tightened his grip and used it as leverage as he climbed up Kitsune's body.

"You're going to be fine," Myobu whispered in his ear once they were face to face. "I've got them all."

Unable to contain himself any longer, Kitsune grabbed the back of Myobu's head, taking hold of his thick, dark hair, and kissed him. He entered the other's mouth with his tongue, exploring, while he inhaled Myobu's scent longingly. He felt Myobu's erection brush against his own, and he moaned into the kiss. He tried to move his hips upward to grind against him, but Myobu still grasped his cock firmly, keeping him still.

"How can you be so sure?" Kitsune said shrewdly, pulling Myobu away. "I think that last part needs a closer inspection."

Kitsune imagined two fiery eyes burning with lust in the dark. Myobu shook his head loose from the prince's grasp, leaned forward for another quick kiss, then began working his way back down, offering kisses to his chest, playful bites to his nipples, and a trailing tongue down his abdomen, all of which Kitsune felt with a heightened sensitivity. He couldn't help but attempt to move, to thrust and release, but Myobu kept him still with a firm grasp.

The caressing stopped once Myobu reached his groin, leaving Kitsune with just the sound of his own heavy breathing. He looked down, wondering what his partner was doing, but could not see a thing. Then he sensed the tongue again, and he gasped sharply in pleasure. This time Myobu was licking his shaft, starting from the base and working his way upward. He squirmed, relishing the sensations.

Myobu ran his tongue over every bit of his cock as though tasting or cleaning it. Each languid movement was methodical and unhurried. It was a slow, teasing motion like nothing Kitsune had ever endured before—and he was enjoying it.

After the last thorough bit of licking, Myobu gave a knowing chuckle. Then he took all of Kitsune into his mouth.

Kitsune let loose a howl so loud he thought all the world would hear. Myobu was burning hot on his skin, and as the dark-haired man moved his head about, the heat spread throughout Kitsune's body. He needed more and never wanted it to end.

The prince thrashed about, trying to find purchase as waves of ecstasy drove through his body, so powerful he forgot about his broken tailbone. His heels beat down on the hard floor several times before he

Isaac Grisham

wrapped his legs over Myobu's back. His arms flailed about, gripping the cloak before he finally gave up any pretense of dignity and grabbed on to Myobu's head.

The heat became so much that Kitsune thought he was breathing smoke. Still, he yowled incomprehensively, his voice ricocheting off the walls, answered by only more howls. He struggled for the release he needed, squeezing his legs and pushing with his hands.

When Myobu finally released the prince's cock from his hand, Kitsune bucked his hips upward, driving himself into the other as far as he could go. He did this again and again with increasing ferocity until the heat reached a boiling point.

And everything exploded.

FORK IN THE ROAD

"The storm was of your own creation."

"Pardon?" Kitsune asked, looking to his mother. His clothing and hair had preoccupied him, as they were suspended weightlessly about his body. The two of them were caught in the dreamscape's slow-motion winds of a menacing storm. Normal dreams usually made actual scenarios far more terrifying. In this case, though, it would have been hard to top what he and Myobu barely survived. Especially with the Lady, a source of great comfort, standing a few footfalls away from him.

"You are not one of the Yokai, but as my son, you are of them," the Lady said. Still dressed in the long white gown with her hair pinned up, she was a beacon of beauty and hope within the destruction unfolding about them. "There is magic within you."

"I know that. It's how I was able to call down lightning to save myself and Mamori, even if it was an unconscious effort. But I haven't been able to reproduce the same results since."

The Lady walked around Kitsune. "Have you even tried?"

"No," Kitsune admitted. In truth, he hadn't dwelled on the subject of magic since the night he and Myobu first kissed. He hadn't even taken the time to meditate. The discovery of his paternal grandmother, finding his mother, and the fear of losing Myobu kept his mind busy.

"You must do as your love has directed," his mother said kindly. "Whether you want it or not, like it or not, the power inside you is growing. Like water coming to a boil within a kettle, your magic seeks release."

"What does that have to do with the storm?" Kitsune asked. He gestured at the raging winds about them, bringing devastation to the imaginary lands. "This is far more than a single bolt of lightning."

"I suspect your magic allows you to control certain faucets of the natural world around you. Weather, specifically. As Myobu taught you, your emotions play a major role in how your powers manifest themselves. Tell me, my son, what emotions fill your soul?"

"I don't know how to describe it," he answered honestly. His thoughts turned to Myobu, and the blood in his veins seemed to pulse faster. His equilibrium went askew, and his innards felt as though they were constricting and free floating. He wiped a bead of sweat from his temple, saying, "I guess I'm warm. Warmer than usual."

The Lady paused in thought. Her passive smile eventually returned. "Warmth. Good. To further the analogy, would you also say you feel humid?"

It was Kitsune's turn to pause as he considered. Indeed, his fascination with Myobu and the feelings stirring within him somehow permeated his being much like humid air clung to clothing, weighing porous materials down.

"The feelings you have for Myobu...they are hot and humid," the Lady said, making Kitsune squirm in embarrassment. "Through your magic, you are unwittingly affecting the world around you with these feelings, drawing the warmth and moisture from other regions to you. You are so powerful that it's overriding normal weather patterns, which would explain the storm's direction."

"I still don't understand how I can cause something so devastating without even being cognizant of it." He said nothing, but he feared for the people of the Odom outpost. If they suffered because of him, he would never forgive himself.

"The power resides within you, whether you want it or not, like it or not," the Lady repeated. "Just as your magic seeks release, it will manifest itself to the fullest extent that it can. The only thing you can do is learn to understand, control, and harness it."

"I will speak with Myobu about it tomorrow," Kitsune promised, knowing what she was hinting at.

"Learn quickly, Kitsune," the Lady almost seemed to beg.

In a sudden *whoosh*, the storm sped up. Her hair came loose; the wind tousled it and her dress about. Painfully bright flashes of lightning obscured his vision, and cold rain and wind bit at his skin.

"I sense the time is near that you will need command of all your faculties," she said.

"The King's Sun?" Kitsune shouted, cupping his hands to his mouth to be heard above the howling winds.

"You are close to him," his mother's voice bellowed out through the dark storm, low and menacing. His dreamy conversations with the Lady had always been ethereal but never nightmarish, and the sudden shift in her voice startled him awake.

*

Myobu stood at one of the building's many panels, his hand clasping one of the odd knobs sticking out of it. On a previous visit, he identified the lever that turned on the glowing balls above. He activated them now, flooding the room with harsh light. Kitsune's eyes snapped open.

"What time is it?" Kitsune asked, extricating himself from his cloak.

"Still early in the morning," Myobu replied tiredly. "The sun is probably just now rising."

"The storm?"

Myobu waved his hands as though to brush the worry from Kitsune's mind. "I took a peek earlier. The storm passed through the night."

"You appear exhausted," the prince said, concerned. "Did you sleep at all?"

"A couple of hours." It was the truth, but only technically. Sleep had been erratic. He thought that, after their harrowing adventure and subsequent physical encounter, rest would come easily. Unfortunately, every time he closed his eyes, nightmarish visions of the future pervaded. He saw Ninko, a sword or arrow sticking out of his side, falling to the ground in agony. In those dreams, Kitsune's look of victory always turned to horror at the realization of what he had just done. Myobu would jerk awake from these nightmares with considerable guilt, especially now that the prince had confessed his true intentions.

Not that he hadn't expected the news. The Harbinger told him the King's Sun must die by the hand of the individual Myobu would fall in love with. He had been furious when Kyubi presented the path to him, but he traveled it nonetheless. Kyubi's insights into the future were not always set in stone, and he thought he'd be able to devise a way to accomplish his goals via a different route. Kitsune's steadfastness to his plan, however, did not leave much room for exploration of other options.

Myobu struggled to understand Kitsune's reasoning for continuing with his quest. With the truth of his father's past now unveiled, he thought abandoning a murderous agenda was the only logical course of action. The man was not completely human, though, and Myobu knew from personal experience that humans did not easily understand the thought processes and impetuses of the Yokai. That trait also extended to their hybrid offspring. Sometimes, in excess.

After leaving the prince's quarters in Sandya, Myobu had wandered the halls of the fortress. He had been angry again—angry that Ninko's fate appeared to be sealed, that Kitsune could not see past his loyalty to his father, that he ever went to see the Harbinger in the first place.

In a moment of weakness, hoping to escape his role in all of it, Myobu reacquired his belongings and fled Sandya. He hadn't gotten more than half a league before his heart ached at the thought of leaving Kitsune behind. The man was as troubled about the whole affair as he was. His tortured expression, highlighted by firelight, would be an image Myobu would remember until death. He couldn't leave him alone, unable to find his way back to Inari Palace.

Still needing solitude, Myobu trailed the caravan from a distance as it traveled north. He was setting up camp when the storm hit. It had been sheer luck that Kitsune came barreling by a few tics later on the cart. Last night's union lifted his spirits, though in revealing the secret of Ninko's heart, he had truly betrayed that office. While it would ultimately serve Gaav, it still made him a traitor to a home he loved. That fact was the antithesis to his feelings for Kitsune, and the conflicting emotions raging within him were exhausting burdens to bear.

Other dreams had troubled Myobu's sleep, most of which concerned the Wastelands. His previous journey through was relatively uneventful. He stuck to the outer edges where he knew the air was safe enough to breathe. All one had to do was keep an eye out for the occasional twisted, malformed beast venturing out from the center of the region. Their claws, teeth, and additional appendages were the inspirational ingredients for nightmares.

Myobu had fought with such creatures on previous ventures into the Wastelands. His recollections of those times were vague, but he remembered enough not to take the trip lightly. Poisoned air and hungry predators aside, there was little to survive on. And the dust made everything exponentially more miserable. He itched at imagined dust when he did sleep. In the end, it was easier just to stay awake.

From one of his pockets, Myobu pulled out an apple. He tossed it to Kitsune.

"From our supplies?" Kitsune asked.

"All those provisions are lost to us," Myobu replied, knowing the other was thinking of all the goods they left behind on the other side of the canyon. "Thankfully, we stuffed our packs full of apples back in Sandya. Otherwise, we wouldn't have anything. I hope you like them."

Kitsune bit into the apple eagerly, chomping on the wet fruit. "Even so, these can't possibly last us long with the energy we'll be burning. Is it safe to hunt and forage in the Wastelands?"

"Historically, no. The life that survived whatever cataclysm befell this land became poison. Those that ate of it fell ill and suffered horribly until death." Myobu shrugged. "It's been many a sun cycle since anyone has recorded an actual death. Far longer than I can remember."

"We may not have a choice but to cross the border into northern Kitsunetsuki," Kitsune said, a twinge of anxiety in his voice. "I'm unsure what kind of punishment I would receive if caught. Usually, the banished who are in violation are put to death."

"I would advise against that," Myobu replied, stooping next to him to load their few remaining belongings into their packs. "I noticed an unusual amount of military presence along the border. Each time I neared it, I came across an encampment. An attempt to cross over is not worth the risk. Are you ready to go?"

With a nod, Kitsune got up off the floor, grimacing at what must have been his sore tailbone. Myobu doused the lights, plunging the room back into darkness, then shuffled his way to the outer wall. He opened the portal, a discovery not as accidental as he led Kitsune to believe. Fresh air rushed inward, replacing the stale atmosphere of the building. As he stepped out, he could feel heat as rays of sun touched his skin, and what was usually the white noise of wildlife now seemed to create an orchestra of sound.

Kitsune's senses most likely painted him a similarly serene picture, which did not prepare him for the real devastation. From the look on his face, Myobu knew the tornado's aftermath mortified the prince. The monstrous funnel cloud had torn up trees and ripped them to shreds, driving their shards deep into the ground. Even stone had not escaped the storm's wrath. It split mighty boulders in half, their innards crumbling. Gone was the path they had traversed up to the gray building. Wind had shorn away the top layer of soil, completely dispersing it. Only skeletal trees remained.

"Do you think the tornado touched down on the outpost?" Kitsune asked, but the question seemed more a musing to himself. "The casualties would have been great. Our horses probably suffered a similar fate, not knowing where to find proper shelter."

The prince's cheeks were suddenly wet, and Myobu realized the man was crying. To his own recollection, Myobu had never before cried. The confusion on Kitsune's face said he wasn't too familiar with the concept either.

"These might be my first truly genuine reactionary emotions!" Kitsune cried out as though defending his current state. "The death of Mamori could not bring me to tears. I mourn him, certainly, but his end was not of my doing. At least directly. If anything, I was angry at those who put him into a deadly situation.

"This, though," he sputtered, throwing out his hands to indicate the destroyed terrain. "This was all because of me. All because of my emotions and a magical ability I have yet to learn how to control. Any injuries or deaths that occurred from this was entirely my fault."

"How do you mean?" Myobu asked, though he had a strong hunch he already knew.

The prince wiped the tears away with a sleeve, turning away from Myobu and forging a westward path away from the gray building. Several dozen heartbeats passed before he spoke again, probably waiting until his voice would no longer waver. Finally, he cleared his throat and said, "Is it possible to continue learning magic while we travel?"

"Of course," Myobu returned, stepping carefully over a broken tree trunk. "Those who wield magic learn to do so amid all sorts of activities. If you work at it, it should become second nature to you. You won't have to stop and think about what you're doing. Why do you ask?"

"I believe I may have caused the storm."

Though Myobu had expected the revelation, he couldn't help but stop short. Kitsune did too but did not look back at him. If this was true, the implications were hard to register. The amount of influence and sheer power the prince could potentially wield was staggering.

"Then it is even more important you learn to control your powers," Myobu finally responded. "It is extremely beneficial we now know your exact specialization."

"Weather," Kitsune verified.

"Precisely. Now I know why the wind has been picking up every time you look at me."

"I do not…look at you!" Kitsune gasped. He appeared to appreciate Myobu's attempt to humor him, giving him a sly glance before moving on again.

"Of course not," Myobu teased, following him. "And I didn't do unspeakable things to you last night!"

They sighed in remembrance of the encounter. It had been an amazing, satisfying experience that left Myobu craving more. Even long after Kitsune dozed off, Myobu wanted to do more, go further. It was part of the reason he slept so poorly. Letting the prince rest was the wiser course of action, of course—they had a long way yet to travel. There would be opportunities to play around before they reached the Harbinger.

"For now, focus on the weather and how you can affect it. Only minor things," Myobu added. "We don't want another storm pushing us along. Maybe you can conjure up some of those breezes that occur when you do or do not gaze my way."

"And what if I'm able to succeed?"

"You'll be able to without any trouble," Myobu assured. "The trick will be in learning how to control and redirect it. Magic is deeply intertwined with how you emote to yourself and to the world at large.

Master your own feelings and understand how everything around you affects them. Do this and you will be able to create and disperse storms of any magnitude within moments."

*

As the sun climbed into the sky, its light only partially filtered by the branches of trees long dead, Kitsune practiced how Myobu instructed. The ravaging storm appeared to have let up shortly after they sought shelter in the gray structure the night before, and they found a well-worn path again. This made it easier for Kitsune to concentrate without fear of falling over debris.

True to Myobu's prediction, Kitsune found he could easily create light breezes. He didn't even need to look at the other man to accomplish that. The mere act of thinking about him caused his heart to flutter. Each time his pulse quickened, he reached out with his senses and felt for the air. As he became one with the surrounding molecules, something strange happened: He understood them—and the molecules understood him in return. They absorbed his characteristics, becoming agitated. As they grew more excited, they bounced about and, in mass, created the breezes he had been feeling ever since meeting Myobu.

Once, when the wind was strong enough to rustle their clothing, Kitsune seized control of it by enveloping a pocket of excited molecules with mental energy. He forced them to move about as he desired. Myobu gave him a bemused grin after the pocket of air swept around his body several times, blowing hair back from startled eyes. Then, pushing as hard as he could, Kitsune directed the air up against the nearest tree. A branch splintered off from the trunk, crashing to the ground with such force that small wildlife in the nearby underbrush fled in panic.

Like all others around it, the tree was dead, its limbs dry and brittle, although the damage still rattled Kitsune. Images of the storm that must have torn apart the outpost flitted in and out of his mind.

The rows of tents and wooden border fences would have suffered far worse a fate than the dead tree.

The prince soon found he could not create a force larger than the one that snapped the dried branch. He knew himself well enough to know it was a mental block. As much as he desired to learn how to build and control his magic—partially to prevent another incident like the storm—he was also petrified his efforts would create another catastrophic event.

"Don't be too hard on yourself," Myobu said, noticing the frustration on his face. "You're learning at a pace I've not seen before, an incredible feat for someone your age."

"Are you calling me old?" It had meant to be a teasing jest, but it came out harsher than Kitsune intended.

"Most know of their abilities early in their youth and learn to harness it as they mature," Myobu replied, nonplussed. "Many of those who discover their power later in life have troubles controlling it because they never had reason to temper their own emotions. Within the span of a morning, you've solidified what elements you can manipulate with your magic and how to keep your own emotions from overwhelming them."

Kitsune sighed. "I'm going to rest my mind for a while. I think I'm fraying my own wits. Maybe I'll try to meditate again this afternoon." In truth, he was mentally exhausted. Just as the journey was uncovering his heritage, he was discovering elements within himself. The placid demeanor he always wore and felt was shattering as a mixture of love, confusion, and anger took over. While he now understood how his feelings for Myobu caused a massive storm, he needed to be sure stray ire thoughts of his father didn't cause snowfall or some other bizarre phenomena. "How about lunch? I hear we have plenty of apples!"

When Myobu didn't reply, Kitsune turned to see Myobu looking alarmed. Then he turned back to the road ahead, immediately seeing what was so concerning.

The trail led them out of the wooded area, then forked. The right path continued westerly, probably along the border of the Wastelands. The left path traversed a steep bluff overlooking a large green plain and appeared to lead south into Kitsunetsuki.

The path they wanted to take—the one continuing through the Wastelands—was impassable. A recent rockslide, possibly caused by a small cell from last night's storm, had completely obliterated its existence. An attempt to traverse its pebble-strewn path would be treacherous.

Still, the alternative was no better. Not only did it lead into Kitsune's homeland, but its view of the border was cause for great consternation. There had been a military presence here since the annexation of Ruio, but the current number of patrolling soldiers was unheard of. They marched between countless military camps, ready for the smallest sign of trouble. Kitsune guessed this increased presence was due to what was being built.

The idea of a northern wall was a lofty goal, overreaching the expense and resources of even Inari Palace. With no natural barriers, everything would have to be manmade. A patchwork of failed efforts by past Ruio rulers dotted the northern landscape, but most had fallen into disrepair. The world looked upon them as nothing more than relics of the past.

This new attempt was no mere experiment, though. It appeared that King Oni was dedicated to sealing off the border, throwing his immense wealth and military power at completing it. For as far as Kitsune could see, a new stone wall was taking shape, rising into existence above the ground.

"Now what should we do about this?" Myobu mused, scratching at the stubble on his face with his fingers.

"I think you should listen to what we have to say before making a decision," said a new voice from behind them.

The two whipped around to face the newcomer, Kitsune reaching for his bow while Myobu armed himself with his sword. Two men stood there, one of whom was dressed in the uniform of a captain. It immediately reminded Kitsune of Captain Saxma. The shame he had felt at being marched naked through the streets of Oinari, the anger at being unceremoniously tossed through the Eastern Gate, and the sheer rage at Mamori's murder rose to the surface. They tore at his emotions like a fresh wound. Against his better judgement, he loosed an arrow aimed directly at the soldier's chest.

The man anticipated the aggressive response and had drawn his own sword before announcing himself. Now he swung it at the shaft, breaking it in half, flinching as a piece bounced off his armor.

"Stop! My prince, I beg that you listen!" the man cried out as Kitsune nocked his next arrow. It took Kitsune a moment to place the voice, but then recognized it as Mamori's fellow soldier Pan.

Kitsune calmed his anger with a wary breath. He lowered his weapon, looking at the two men. He hadn't recognized Pan earlier, wearing the captain's garb. Both that and the confident way he held himself surprised the prince, possibly even more than coming across him on this lonely road so far from their last encounter. He had liked Pan but would not have thought he possessed the mettle to be a captain. At least not the capacity to grow into it in such a short period of time. Yet here he was, apparently comfortable in his new role.

Though he thought he recognized the second man, Kitsune could not place him. The slight figure and scraggly facial hair kept cropping up in the recesses of his memory, like he had taken note of him in a large crowd.

"What do you want?" Kitsune asked cautiously. They may have been friendly before, but he knew alliances could change. The new rank could have been a reward for being a part of Kitsune's expulsion. "I have done nothing to violate Kitsunetsuki law since my banishment. I didn't truly break any beforehand."

Pan looked down the fork in the road leading into the kingdom, the only path Kitsune and Myobu could take unless they retraced their steps. He looked as though he had an endless supply of thoughts he wished to express and was trying to decide on the perfect one with which to begin.

"I wish you no harm," Pan started. "Neither does Major Saxma. At least no more than he already has."

"Tell that to Mamori!" Kitsune shouted out before he could get a handle on his anger. "He was killed—murdered by mercenaries who captured us."

"I know. They were most likely hired by one of Saxma's men," the captain said, then paused. "By one of my men. There are a number of mercenaries on the hunt for you."

An image of Mamori's body, blood flowing from a hole in his chest, came to Kitsune. He remembered the failure and shame on the soldier's face and the pitiful way he apologized before passing. His grip tightening on the bow, he snarled, "Why?"

"He was under orders from King Oni himself."

"Lies!" Kitsune bellowed. He took aim again, pulling back on the string. "My father gave me a task, a mission I take no joy in performing. If he wanted it done, why would he conspire to have me killed before I could complete it?"

"The king has been acting irrationally in all matters," Pan said, stepping forward. He pointed to the south at the construction. "He's closing off the north from a barren wasteland, spending obscene amounts of coin in the process."

"He's the king!" Kitsune defended. "He has spies and intelligence we are not privy to. There may be good reasons behind his actions."

"He banished his own son," Pan pressed. "The only heir to the throne, his only security in continuing the royal bloodline. And for what? Following your heart and desires freely just as Kitsunetsuki citizens have been privileged to do for generations? You said yourself that you broke no actual law."

"As king, he can instigate changes as he sees fit."

"No," Pan interjected, taking another few steps toward Kitsune. "While that kind of power may reside within the monarchy, so does the obligation to use it wisely or not at all. The royal family doesn't exist so its members can use the kingdom's resources to carry out their fantasies. They are there to lead their people into the best imaginable future, to protect them from dangers, and to inspire them to do great and wondrous things. I have always thought this way, and I believe Major Saxma now holds to this ideal as well.

"You may be the legitimate son of the king, Prince Kitsune, but we consider ourselves to be his family, too. All the people of Kitsunetsuki are his progenies. It is his duty to watch over each and every one of us, and he is failing to do that."

Kitsune stared at Pan in wonder. Was this the same quiet, meek man who refrained from drinking too much before going on patrol? Was Saxma responsible for the transformation into a self-assured, confident person? Kitsune didn't believe that to be a front, for it certainly had taken all of Pan's nerve to speak for a man who shot Kitsune without hesitation, most likely taking advantage of him while unconscious, then unabashedly clapping him in irons and marching him through Oinari. It was a good idea for Saxma to send Pan in his stead. Kitsune may have loosed another arrow or two before listening.

"My prince," Pan said when there was no response. "The king has another kind of power. Magic, and most likely not the kind inherited from a Yokai spirit."

Kitsune nodded absently, murmuring, "I know this."

"He is using this power to manipulate people. Make them believe things that aren't true. Behave in ways they aren't accustomed to acting."

Kitsune looked up sharply. "Why would he be doing such things?"

"Absolute control," Pan said. "But for what, we don't know."

Pan moved forward again, closing the gap between the two groups. It was a nervous and uncomfortable movement. He opened his mouth to say something but stopped when he found Myobu's sword at his throat.

"You will not come any closer to Prince Kitsune, especially while you are speaking on behalf of your major," Myobu said in a voice both calm and threatening.

The soldier stared back at Myobu. Then, deftly avoiding the sharp blade, he dropped to one knee. It wasn't out of fear, though Kitsune recognized plenty of that in his eyes. It was more of a concern for the future and a pleading to be listened to.

"My prince," Pan said, turning his gaze to Kitsune. "Both Major Saxma and I swore an oath to protect the king and his family. That includes you, banishment or not, and all the people who should be protected under his banner. King Oni has not lived up to his own royal responsibilities, and our eyes have been opened to the consequences of this. I admit to you that our thoughts have turned to mutiny."

Kitsune stared down in shock at the kneeling man. This certainly wasn't the person he had known before! If the soldier had been anyone other than Pan, he would have thought all this a ploy or joke.

"Despite knowing the punishment for treason is death, we have discussed and drawn up plans. As of yet, we have gone no further than that," Pan continued. "While I would prefer to go into greater detail, we unfortunately have little time. Others will notice my extended absence from the camp. When Saxma heard you were nearby, he sent me to find you. To pledge our service to you. In our eyes, you are the leader our kingdom needs, and we will do as you say. Tell us to march against the king, and we will march. Order us to stay here and continue building that wall while planning a strike, and we will comply. Command us to abandon all thoughts of rebellion, and we will do so, albeit reluctantly."

The group fell into silence while Kitsune considered the offer. His immediate reaction was to strike Pan down for his talk of uprising. Instead, he added his words to the knowledge he had already accumulated on his father: Oni had murdered Kitsune's mother. Oni's own mother fled the kingdom in fear of her son. Sun cycles later, after waging needless wars on neighboring kingdoms, Oni banished Kitsune for nonexistent crimes and plotted his murder.

Kitsune loved his father, but he knew these were not the actions of a wise, just, or sane king.

Still, Kitsune was not ready to rise up against his father and forsake a monarchy that had peacefully transitioned from parent to child for over nine hundred sun cycles. Even if he and Saxma could convince a portion of the military to follow their lead, a rebellion would result in thousands of deaths with no guarantee of success. He had to attempt the completion of his original mission. That would cause only one death and grant him legal admittance back into Kitsunetsuki. He'd be able to see his father again and gain a chance to sway his king's moods.

"Continue with my father's work here in the north," Kitsune ordered, noticing the immediate defeat in Pan's demeanor. He glanced over at Myobu, who was still on guard. "There are things I must do west of here. Things that will grant me admittance into Kitsunetsuki. With luck, I will return through the Western Pass within a month's time. I will then travel to your camp here, after which we shall together ride to Oinari."

"We will attempt to prepare a sizeable force for you to march with," Pan said as he returned to his feet. "Anything we do will have to be covert. We suspect the king can reach into people's minds. It's possible he can read thoughts and plant suggestions. If we prepare to march, it will likely have to be done through manipulation on our part."

"Do what you can," Kitsune instructed. He looked at Pan. "You are an adaptable individual, and Saxma is more open-minded than I would have thought. I am confident you both can accomplish most anything you put your mind to."

Myobu stepped in, sheathing his sword. He pointed down the road. "None of this matters if we can't proceed to the west. I assume we can't take the left path. If anyone discovers the prince, he could be executed. Traveling due north to avoid this rockslide could put us deep into the Wastelands, and I am not familiar enough with the dangers that lie within to risk Kitsune's life."

With a wave of Pan's hand, the second man stepped up. Kitsune was again struck with the feeling that he had seen him before, but he could not pinpoint any specific time or place.

"There's a path approximately four hundred footfalls behind us that branches off and heads northwesterly for a while before meeting up with the main path again," the dirty-looking man said. "It's obscure, mostly used by foraging goats, which is probably why you didn't spot it before. It is difficult to traverse at times, but only spans about four or five leagues. You should make it back to this road before nightfall."

"Do they face any dangers out here?" Pan inquired.

"Nothing aside from the normal wildlife. Snakes, wasps, and whatever oddity the Wastelands might send their way," he said, looking as though he wanted to slip back into the shadows. "There's little to no human presence up here anymore."

Pan looked from Kitsune to Myobu. "Do you have any questions for Jasper?"

Myobu shook his head, and Kitsune said, "Nothing off the top of my head."

"Unfortunate way of putting it," Pan said with a troubled sigh. Then, turning, he drew his sword and, with one quick swipe, beheaded the shadowy man Jasper.

Isaac Grisham

BREACH

The storm's damage to the Northern Gate encampment was simultaneously significant and trivial. As Major Saxma predicted, its strong winds had swept away all the tent dwellings. Their remains littered the landscape for several leagues. The dormitories, administrative buildings, and mess halls still stood, though many of their roofs had been torn asunder and timber sections smashed and broken. The Northern Gate, as well as the wall it would eventually allow travelers through, remained largely intact. Construction of the wall and gate was far enough along that they stood a few footfalls off the ground at most, saving them from the buffeting winds.

The loss of life was minimal, restricted mostly to individuals who didn't make it into a permanent structure before the windstorm descended upon them. There were numerous injuries, however. Roofs and walls had collapsed, resulting in innumerable cracked ribs, broken appendages, and concussions. Thankfully, many of the workers had previous medical training and could tend to the wounded.

With clear and blue skies overhead, the entire camp was moving to clean up the wreckage, repair the damage, and move forward with construction. It was a well-organized effort, a testament to Kitsunetsuki's military training and the native's dogged work ethic.

There was not much for Saxma to do. This was a good thing, as one particular subject consumed his attention.

The tower.

Fortified walls and locked doors were sufficient to keep its contents away from prying eyes, although it was not enough to protect it from the storm. The tower had taken considerable damage. While the bulbous section at the top remained whole, sections of the curved wall supporting it had crumbled away, revealing the spiral staircase Saxma knew was there from schematics. Of even more interest, a falling tree trunk had demolished the entrance. The first barrier to the tower's secrets had been breached. Was the second door at the top of the stairs still in place?

Even in its weakened state, the fortification was a foreboding sight. Despite this—or perhaps because of this—no one wanted to look at it. Workers and soldiers kept their heads down, avoiding the tower. Given its prominent location and height, this was no simple task.

Saxma wondered if his own thoughts regarding the structure were his own fear dissuading him from entering or King Oni using its contents to persuade everyone to his will. He reminded himself that he was afraid of nothing and no one, not even mystic rulers, and decided his unsettled stomach resulted from Oni's meddling. As he had over the past several days, he worried if the king could read the minds of individuals. He did not want to end up like Major Alexi, though he would not let the possibility keep him from his duty.

Hands clenched determinedly by his side, Saxma walked through the tower's ruined entrance.

Even though the crumbling walls now let in the sunlight and fresh air, the atmosphere was cold and damp, and its sense of foreboding seeped through the fabric of his uniform like a snake. He shivered as goosebumps broke out across his skin.

Much of the rubble had fallen outward, so navigating the small room to the stairwell was easy. The stairs themselves were only slightly more challenging, some of them having broken away along with the pieces of wall they had been built into. The ones remaining were solid underneath Saxma's feet, and he silently praised the engineers who designed and built the tower. It was only a few tics before he reached the upper level.

Though it was considerably darker above, he saw immediately that the second door was closed. There did not appear to be any damage to the structure up here. It had been a long shot, but finding proof of or against his king's supernatural powers would have done much to calm Saxma's uneasiness at planning a revolt. He was not confident that marching hundreds of soldiers closer to where the sovereign could easily control or manipulate their minds was a well-grounded strategic plan.

A wave of dizziness overtook the major, and he braced himself against a stone wall. He remained motionless for several heartbeats, fighting against the nausea threatening to empty his stomach. The building must not have been as stable as he imagined, and he sensed it swaying beneath his feet.

"Damn!" Saxma shouted in frustration once the dizziness passed. He turned to leave before the structure collapsed in on him, but he was suddenly compelled to physically express his agitation. Cursing again, he slammed a fist against the door.

To his immense surprise, it swung open soundlessly. Golden light spilled outward, lighting up the upper portion of the stairwell.

Saxma peered inside, and his mind reeled at what he saw. He knew the room could only be a few footfalls wider than the shaft of the tower, large enough to hold a small office. In defiance of its external proportions, however, it now appeared to be as large as a stable. Or a dungeon, with its cold stone walls. The ceiling was so far above his head that he couldn't discern it, though a multitude of golden orbs obscured his field of vision.

The orbs were the source of the golden light illuminating the tower, and they floated about the room of their own accord, bouncing off neighboring spheres. Each beam of light refracted as they, too, encountered other spheres. This gave the room an aquatic effect, like the sun's rays reflecting off a body of water.

Much of the light bore down to the floor, emphasizing a particular spot in the middle of the room. King Oni stood calmly with his hands clasped behind his back. He appeared to glow in the radiance as he stared gravely at the open door.

"My king," Saxma said automatically, dropping to one knee. His heart froze at the sight of the man, sinking deeper into his chest. The soldier had absolutely no idea how any of what he saw was possible.

"Major," Oni replied in a calm, even tone that nevertheless sent chills down Saxma's spine. "I require information from you. I believe an update is well past due."

"There was a storm," Saxma answered, keeping his eyes on the floor as he knelt. "It will not take long to recover. The wall was undamaged."

"I have gathered as much from the thoughts of other men," King Oni said. Then, much more loudly, "You know that is not what I am inquiring about."

Saxma's chest tightened, and a moment later an invisible force violently pulled him up off the floor and into the room. The door slammed shut behind him, its lock turning. At the same time, the room itself closed in around him, shrinking in size until it was just him, the king, and a few orbs floating above their heads. Despite the claustrophobic walls, Oni looked just as calm up close, though Saxma could clearly see displeasure in his eyes. Displeasure, distaste, or was it just plain hate?

"The storm that came through traveled east to west. It was not natural," Saxma gasped, finding it harder to breathe. It felt like his collar was shrinking along with the room. Then, daringly, he added, "Much like this chamber."

"Major," Oni said in a slow, chiding drawl. He gestured around at their close surroundings. The golden light glinted off his green eyes as he looked up. "You are more correct than you know. Surely you realize this room—this version of it, anyway—is only in your head? That I am in your head?"

Saxma choked as another wave of nausea hit him. He realized the chamber's door was probably fully intact and securely locked, and he was likely outside on the stairwell, eyes glazed over and drooling like an imbecile.

Perspiration broke out across Saxma's brow as the beginnings of what he could only describe as true fear took hold of him. In spite of what could happen next, Saxma was still impressed at how accurate his and Pan's deductions were.

"Do not flatter yourself," Oni said coolly. "You are not the first to become aware of my abilities. Certainly not the first to question my actions. You and your subordinate won't be the last, either. Now, where is Captain Pan?"

King Oni squinted as he appeared to analyze Saxma for several long moments. Saxma tried to keep Pan's whereabouts from his thoughts, thinking he might hide the answer like valuables in a safe, but his efforts did little good.

"On a mission to find my son, who is currently near to your location," Oni said. "Kitsune has survived longer and traveled farther than I expected. Why are you in search of him? You are, after all, the one who carried out his banishment."

The major could almost feel the answers to the king's questions slip from his mind. All his thoughts, actions, and words over the past several weeks were laid bare as the king rifled through his head as though he were thumbing through a stack of administrative papers.

"You were a good soldier, Major. I had plans for you after your work in the north was complete. There are wars to be fought, and your skill would have helped win them."

"Sir?" Saxma rasped. He was having trouble focusing, and the walls surrounding them appeared to be rotating.

"It is fascinating how I can leave an entire regiment of men to perform their duties without my influence, and yours is the mind that strays from my directive," the king said, his tone indicating anything but fascination. "I can understand Captain Pan. He comes from a curious, intellectual background. You, on the other hand…you were always so singularly focused. You had two goals: to perform your duty to the best of your abilities and to use that as a means of advancement. Those goals always aligned well with my own plans. That you've gone so far off course now as to consider mutiny is truly disappointing."

"No!" Saxma cried out, desperate. His knees gave out, and he would have fallen to the floor if not for the magical force maintaining a constricting grip within his chest. The walls spun even faster, as did the spheres above his head. "It's not true!"

"You and the captain have laid out some detailed plans on how to go about removing me from the throne," the monarch said, again perusing Saxma's memories and thoughts. "Persuading or tricking the men under your command to follow you on a march back to Oinari. Use my own weapons to lay siege against Inari Palace. Kill me outright before I strike back with supernatural strength. I would have liked to see you attempt this. The look of confusion on your face as you moved closer to my capital, closer to the source of my magic and influence, may have been worth the delays in my plans. You and your force would still have been leagues away when your minds succumbed and reverted to my will. Nothing more than dumb livestock."

It was a major flaw in any of the schemes the two soldiers came up with, Saxma knew. There didn't appear to be any way to get to the king without falling into his mind trap. Attempts to remove Oni's source of power would fail for the same reason. The one notion they had only scratched the surface of was the hopeful possibility that someone was immune to that power…or possessed an even greater magic.

If Kitsune had magic of his own, it might countermand his father's.

"You have that exactly right," Oni said, his calm exterior cracking with the lines of irritation. "I could never see into my son's mind.

Never know or control his thoughts. I knew he worshipped me, would do anything I asked of him, but I couldn't risk the possibility that he would one day turn against me. Children do that to their parents, you know." He chuckled. "They play nice while plotting deviously. No, this is about control, and I expel what I cannot control. It is why I ultimately banished my son from Kitsunetsuki."

Saxma's eyes widened, and he lifted his head to look the man in the face.

"I am a king, a warrior, and a conqueror. Do you really believe I concern myself with whom anyone takes to their bed?" the king asked. His face returned to its tranquil mask, a stark contrast to the spinning, blurred walls and the pain in Saxma's chest. "Such matters are trivial, even in regard to my son. As prince, he had every right and privilege to whore his way through the military barracks. I needed something that would vilify him, however. There had to be a reason behind his banishment. Since he was loyal to a fault, I was forced to create that reason."

"Why not just kill him?" Saxma croaked. He groaned inwardly as he realized just how much a pawn he truly was in the king's schemes. Not only had he rid the monarch of his only potential impediment, but he did so on false pretenses. "Why draw me into the charade?"

"I could have." Oni nodded. "However, I saw an opportunity to attain two desires with one action. Do not concern yourself with why, though. I have learned all I can from you. In a few moments, it will be beyond your capacity to care."

"No!" Saxma cried out as the constrictions around his throat and chest tightened.

"Just because I don't believe in the new laws as much as I have advertised doesn't make them any less relevant or the punishments for breaking them any less severe." As always, Oni spoke with a casual indifference. "Your memories have revealed that you had intercourse with my son before leaving Oinari and escorting him to the Eastern Gate."

"Of course, sir!" the major defended. He struggled in growing panic, attempting to break free of the magical grip. He found that moving his hands away from his sides brought them into contact with the walls, which ground deep into his skin as they rotated about the two men. "As you ordered, I treated him with the respect given to any traitor, which is to say I afforded him none. Admittedly, the act was a personally motivated revenge."

It surprised Saxma that, in addition to the new sensation of fear, he found himself ashamed. Not of the act of taking advantage of a traitorous man. He was still himself, after all. He was embarrassed at being so easily duped by authority into treating an honorable man like garbage. He only wished he had apologized for his actions. If Kitsune wanted his life for what he had done, so be it.

"I was not aware prisoners were treated in such a manner," the king said, the hint of a smile on his lips. "And unfortunately, as you know, that is exactly the kind of behavior I banished Kitsune for. It would not do to punish my son and then let you go with impunity."

"Sir, no!" Saxma exclaimed, preparing for the sentence he knew was coming.

"The punishment for such a transgression is death," King Oni declared, the slight smile giving way to a full grin. It looked unnatural on his face, like it wasn't used to such a gesture. "Even if it were not, your intent to rebel against the monarchy is also punishable by death."

Saxma thrashed in defiance. He felt and heard as the moving stone tore his flesh away and ground into the bones of his arms and hands.

"You will get a reprieve of sorts," Oni said. After the soldier stopped struggling and gave a hopeful look, he clarified, "Oh, no, Major Saxma. You will cease to exist. However, your sending Captain Pan to interfere with my son's journey puts my plans in jeopardy. Your mercenaries failed to kill him in Odom, so I need him to kill the son of King Marauxus. A ranking officer such as yourself could be critical in keeping that plan in motion. Or at least the vessel of a ranking officer I can control from afar."

The idea of his body walking around like a mindless meat sack revolted Saxma, and he felt bile rise in his throat. What the king intended was like being robbed, evicted, and raped at the same time. Even in death, Oni would continue using Saxma's remains to carry out a deception that made little to no sense.

"But why?" he choked, feeling defeated. He expected pain and suffering that would make his shredded extremities feel like nothing more than a scratch. He did not expect an answer to his question, but to his surprise, Oni responded.

"I suppose, without knowing the details of my past, my actions would appear to be those of a madman. It's why I do not blame you for conspiring against me. I would likely do so if I was in a comparable situation." Pain flitted across the king's face. His magical grip on Saxma did not lessen, though, and the soldier guessed the discomfort stemmed from memories. "I made a mistake when I was young. Not the kind of blunder children make as they mature and develop. There were profound consequences to my actions, and people suffered greatly for it. I have since discovered I can remedy my errors. I can take back what I did, but doing so will require an immense amount of power."

The walls emitted light as they whirled about, becoming indistinguishable from the orbs above. The light silhouetted the king's frame, and his features were lost in shadow. Except his green eyes—those glowed brightly from his dark form.

Saxma noticed several painful sensations in his head, as though a dozen or so white-hot needles were searing their way through his skull and into his brain. He knew with absolute certainty that this was his end, and his eyes bulged in terror.

"There will be many sacrifices," Oni said with no sadness or regret. "Kitsune's banishment is but a small one. Your death is another."

As expected, the pain in his head grew until the individual points overlapped, eclipsing the agony in his extremities. He wanted to move his hands to his head, to assuage the hurt, but he feared what the lighted walls would do upon contact. Instead, he howled in anguish.

"You will not be alone. Before the end, most life will be sacrificed," Oni stated. His voice remained calm, but his eyes belayed an obsessive insanity as they glowed even brighter. Saxma noticed this before the hot misery in his head expanded, causing him to go blind. It wasn't a black blindness, but one of pure white.

"Not to worry, major," King Oni said, though Saxma could barely hear him. His ears were ringing, and blood dripped down his neck. "In the end, everything will be made right, and none of this will matter. Until then, may your soul rest in the afterlife."

Major Saxma screamed anew as the agony in his head blossomed outward. Then, just as quickly as the sensation had started, everything went numb.

Like water falling over numb lips, his consciousness fell away from his body.

MARCH TO THE SEA

The blood and violence hadn't shocked Kitsune—he was used to that. It was the sheer ease with which Pan sliced off Jasper's head that caught him off guard. It was so far removed from the man he met, so timid and quiet.

It had to be done. Kitsune realized that once Pan explained the dead man's background. Jasper was a spy with no allegiances. He would sell information to the highest bidders. With knowledge regarding the Kitsunetsuki prince colluding with military personnel to overthrow the king, the spy could actively seek out said bidders. Probably even Oni himself.

Regardless, there hadn't even been a chance to halt the execution. Kitsune leapt forward in protestation, Myobu right behind him, but the body and its newly detached appendage fell to the road by the time they reached them. Pan gave his explanations, after which they hid the body behind some rocks where scavengers would likely find and eat it. Then the soldier helped find the path Jasper referenced.

Despite the reasoning, Kitsune seethed with anger—that another life was lost because of him, that Pan had and could so easily take such action. He tried his best to hide it, to trust this supposed new ally, but the rage seeped out in the form of magic. Even Myobu's warning glances and supportive gestures were not enough to keep the air from becoming thin and the sun from beating down upon them. The temperature rose by several degrees, and sweat was dripping off everyone by the time Kitsune and Myobu parted ways with the soldier.

To help keep his mind focused as they walked deeper into the Wastelands, Kitsune read entries from the ancient journal. Assuming it was genuine, it was a perfect window into the region's past. What made the diary so surprising was that Kitsune understood most everything its author wrote about. Several words like "facility" were foreign to him, but he guessed their meaning contextually. He didn't know of any theories on energy creation. The idea seemed to counter common schools of thought. But he could understand its importance.

That the woman mentioned energy at all excited Kitsune. There was a probable connection between her and the structure—facility—he and Myobu used to escape the tornado. If he continued to read, he might uncover more about the building. In turn, it could be possible to use its facsimile in Kitsunetsuki for the benefit of its people.

In spite of the rugged trail, he used his keen ears to effectively follow Myobu as he delved into the journal entries. The more he read, the more engrossed he became in the long-dead woman and the research she conducted.

3.13 — With my advanced knowledge and experience, I was able to acquire a position at the research facility I worked at a few years ago. This time, though, I am an actual employee, not an external. The company put me on a project similar to the one I was working on in the tribal lands, creating a source of power so great it could solve all of our energy problems before they even exist. It's a prestigious station, and it pays well! It seems my years of perseverance are finally paying off.

Aside from work and family and friends, I must admit there is one additional subject that drew me back to where I grew up: Damian.

The first time I saw Damian was about two years ago, just before I moved away. I glimpsed him one night while out drinking with some friends and thought him to be the most handsome man I'd ever seen. So handsome, in fact, that I could not introduce myself. Instead of taking a chance, maybe at least making a new friend, I succumbed to my shyness and feelings of inadequacy. Then I left the area.

While I was away, my friends gave me periodic updates on him. I pieced together that he was not a high-ranking man of science, politics, or religion. Nor was he rich by any means. He was an artist. Mostly doing portraits, he immortalized people on canvas, always making them appear their best. Not just physically. He could make anyone look honest, successful, or loving. It is the kind of occupation one undertakes because they are passionate about it and not drawn to power, money, and fame. This attribute I saw in him, his pursuit to better others around him as well as himself, touched and inspired me.

Now that I'm back and feeling far more confident in myself, I decided I should try to meet him. I don't expect anything romantic to happen. Even if we don't become friends, I might get my portrait painted. I had a common acquaintance contact him on my behalf to see about getting a consultation. I have learned he no longer works in an established studio. His mother passed away recently, and he has been busy sorting through her estate. My friend showed him a photograph of me. I'm not sure which one she used, but it was apparently good enough for him to make a private appointment with me. If I am to believe my friend, he said I was cute!

Anyway, the "appointment" is tonight. He is coming over to my place to examine what would be his subject, so to speak. And he's bringing dinner! I picked up some wine.

3.15 – What was supposed to be a simple artistic consultation and dinner ended up being a three-day and two-night date. Damian just now left, and I miss him already.

He showed up the other night with some pasta from a local restaurant. I could immediately tell he'd been through a recent emotional ordeal. There are events like the untimely passing of a loved one that will etch themselves onto one's face, and I saw it on his. He looked much more serious and mature than the first time he caught my eye.

Still, Damian did not let his mother's death dampen the mood. We didn't even broach the subject. He was charming with a disarming laugh and eyes so soulful that I could stare into them forever. We had dinner, after which he carefully studied my face. He cut my hair, giving me a new style that better suited me. It was a talent I didn't know some portrait artists possessed. So methodical he was while cutting, so intense, that it was like he was sculpting a statue out of stone. I could see that this process of creation was his passion, and I wondered how much he missed it.

Wine came next, and we drank several glasses on my settee. We played a couple of films, but we didn't pay any attention, opting instead for increasingly silly conversation. It was during the second film that he surprised me with a kiss. It was long and deep, and I stared at his face as it continued on.

By the end of the night, Damian was far too intoxicated to go home. He stayed over with me. There was no sex. I'm not one to sleep with someone after just having met them, but I had a desire for him so intense that it would have been impossible to say no if he requested it. Regardless, it was a pleasure to be curled up next to him in bed, and I slept better than I had in a long time.

We spent much of the next day shopping. He helped pick out some new clothes for me, updating my fashion. I fear I fell behind while in the tribal lands, where functionality wins out over style. That's not a bad thing, but I was eager to look the part at my new job, appear my best for a portrait, and keep Damian's eye.

That evening played out similar to the first, eating dinner on the settee with a film playing in the background. We shared more wine and conversation, and he spent the night again.

Damian had to leave this morning. Not that he wanted to, but he needed to meet with a lawyer regarding his mother's estate. He also figured he'd stop by his home and pick up a fresh set of clothes!

I sensed an instant connection and attraction, and it was hard to let him leave and return to my normal, mundane life. Solitude doesn't have the comfort it usually supplies and eating alone now just seems pathetic. At least tomorrow I'll be back at work, which will keep my mind off him until next we meet.

Over the next several entries, the author continued to write of trivial matters. She mentioned a tasty sandwich she ate for lunch one day and a decorative knickknack she picked up at a shop. True to her word, she did not reveal any useful insights into her work. This was unfortunate, as those were exactly what Kitsune was hoping to glean.

How she gravitated toward Damian in nearly all conversation, while not enlightening, brought a smile to Kitsune's lips. He didn't like to fall asleep because it was time spent away from Myobu, so he saw a bit of himself in her. Just a little, for he did not understand her proactively withholding sex. Unlike how his budding relationship with Myobu changed his concept of how two people could continually interact with one another, she took the same stance to every previous partner!

Kitsune shook his head in amusement, wondering at the complexities of individuals as he read on.

__3.24__ – The past week has flown by. What an exciting time! My research team made some extraordinary developments before my hire, and some of my experimental models have been instrumental in producing actual results. I think we could create a working prototype within weeks, something I had previously not thought possible for several decades. If all goes well, I believe we'll be able to interface with the power grid already in place.

Damian and I communicated with each other throughout the week before meeting up again over the weekend. In contrast to our previous excursion, we went out to a bar and danced. By dance, I mean we downed a few drinks and ended up making out in a corner. With the musical beat, the flashing lights, and the throngs of people, it was magical. He kept laughing, opening his eyes to find me staring at him.

I also met one of his friends, another artist named James. It was a rite of passage, I think. I had to meet James' "approval" before Damian could continue to see me. I liked James. He was a jittery fellow, but amiable. Still, I didn't understand why his opinion of me mattered so.

Nevertheless, I must have passed the inspection. Damian and I made love last night. It was sweet and tender. He seemed a little self-conscious, going shy. I found it strange from such an attractive man, yet I also thought it endearing.

I know it's only been eleven days and I'm crazy for saying this, but I think I'm falling in love with Damian. He's helped me to realize how absurd I've been for attempting to emulate my friends and family. I've been trying so hard to fall in line and march forward in step with society, not realizing most everyone is doing the same thing. We march, march, march in unison, but do we really know where we are trying to go? It's like we're all trying to reach the shore at the end of land to step into the sea and play, not knowing the sea is death to the soul.

Damian has pulled me out of that line, and I will follow him instead.

Not everything is perfect, so I know I'm not being entirely naïve. I may have to be aggressive in bed, which is not something I am used to. There's no shortage of things to talk about, and I enjoy every moment I'm with him. That and he's just so damn cute!

Can't wait to see him again.

4.10 – *As much as my father has let me down, angering me to the point that I considered excommunicating him, I cannot imagine my life without the man. Therefore, it goes without saying that even the mere consideration of my mother passing away brings me to tears. I cannot yet say what it feels like to lose a parent, so it would be ignorant to claim I understand how Damian is suffering after the sudden death of his mother. He seemed to be doing all right. We barely discussed the matter.*

That changed two nights ago, when I was visiting his place for the first time. It had belonged to his mother, and he moved in for convenience and to save money after she died. As he gave me a tour, he told humorous stories about the oddest things. An antique couch and why his mother reupholstered it in a particular pattern. The hardwood floors in the loft which he admitted to installing himself and not doing a good job of it.

Eventually, we came across an old photo of his mother. She looked young and was beautiful with long hair. With a cigarette in one hand and wisps of smoke clouding up the air, I would go so far as to describe her as glamorous. He stared at the photo, which hung on the wall, and lost his words. I watched as large tears welled up in his eyes and fell down his perfect face. I moved to give him a hug, and he fell appreciatively into my arms.

Damian loved his mother and had maintained a relationship with her so close that I felt terrible for not having spoken to my mother in at least a week. I understood only then that his life and heart was experiencing an intense emptiness no one could possibly fill. While I could not even hope to replace that type of bond, I knew being alone in his mother's old home would not help his state of mind. So I invited him to pack a bag and stay at my place for as long as needed.

The response was immediate. With some clothes, toiletries, and a fancy coffee pot in tow, we returned to my apartment. He has yet to leave.

Kitsune wondered what the journal's writer was like face to face. While her notes made her seem flakey and singularly focused, her chosen profession meant she was also intelligent. She probably rivaled or surpassed modern scientists in wit and intellect. If they were to cross paths, which would be apparent—the intelligent or emotionally embroiled woman?

By the same token, he wondered how the people he and Myobu came across viewed him. Did others see a loyal prince struggling to obey his king's wishes, or did they see his heart, pounding heavily at the sight of the one it longed for? Was the subject of nearly all his thoughts obvious, or was he able to partake in casual conversation?

The prince glanced over at Myobu, asking himself if the other's calm exterior indicated a still heart and mind or if the man suffered from the same turmoil.

4.19 – Damian and I have passed by the one-month anniversary of our first meeting, and I have broken the news to my family that I am seeing someone. My two siblings were the most ecstatic, asking question after question until I invited Damian to dinner with them. In contrast, my father politely acknowledged my announcement, and my mother expressed concern that I was moving too fast.

In many ways, I fear my mother is correct. I know this is all ridiculously crazy, and I can logically explain my feelings as chemical reactions in my brain. It's euphoria, and I am seeing only all the good things in Damian.

There's more to it, however. For the first time in my life, I feel like everything is as it should be. Everything is just right in the world. I am where I belong, and I belong. I couldn't be more confident.

There's even been conversation about officially moving into a place together. Once he sorts out his mother's estate, we can wait until the lease on my place is up and then find a place downtown. He has some connections, so we could get some nice furniture on the cheap. He can open a studio, and I could take the train to work.

On the subject of work, the prototype performed exactly as expected, and initial simulations show that the technology should integrate with the power grid constructed over the past few years. We will make a proposal to the council within the next few weeks!

5.2 *– The veil of perfection was destined to collapse at some point, I suppose. It's a terrible feeling when the curtain falls and you see past how you view a person and see who they might actually be. Don't get me wrong, I'm still head over heels for Damian, but my heart got a taste of what my brain already knew: he is still just a human being.*

With James in tow, we were visiting his friend Matt up north. The original plan was to go out dancing. In a spectacular display of forgetfulness, however, I completely forgot to bring along my identification papers. Since I wouldn't have been able to get into any bars without them, we ended up drinking at Matt's place. I had a fine time myself, and while everyone else seemed to have fun, I can't speak for them.

I cannot recall how the topic of spectacles came up, but we were discussing fashionable eyewear. I pointed mine out as an example. They're six years old, but they weren't cheap when I purchased them, and I think they have held up well. Damian gave me a look of pity. Drunken pity, but still a look that didn't suit his handsome face. Someone commented that the spectacles were not designer, that they were so old they lost that status. That's preposterous. I may never stand at the forefront of the fashion world, but I'm certain a designer label is always a designer label.

Furthermore, who cares? We are all adults, and I think adults should be beyond denigrating others because of their eyewear.

If I went to bed grumpy, everyone else woke up in a foul mood. Things were quiet, and we spent the trip back home listening to music. Of course, my overactive imagination read into each and every song played, and they all spelled out doom.

Damian didn't stay over that night. He was exhausted, which I understood after the previous evening's debauchery, and needed a good night's rest. He was meeting with his lawyer the next day to discuss his mother's will, something I could not argue against. We gave the usual kisses and hugs before he left, but there was an unusual distance between the two of us.

I look forward to seeing him again, to clearing away the twinge of unease between us. He has pulled me out of the marching line, and I would follow him anywhere. Preferably, though, I'd like to walk alongside him.

__5.11__ – Damian and I had a chat earlier this week. He came back over the evening after his appointment with the lawyer. I mentioned how hurtful the comments about my spectacles were, and he seemed distraught about it, claiming that the last thing he wanted was to hurt me. Alcohol was to blame, naturally.

He talked more about his mother and his continuing difficulty with coming to terms with her death. It had been a sudden neurological event, and he felt cheated that she was taken from him. He spoke so lovingly and passionately about his mother that, despite never having met her, I took a liking to the woman. It is strange how one can form a kind of bond with another who is no long around to speak to.

Otherwise, things are back to normal. Our latest adventures include touring local architectural highlights. My favorite was a small home designed with the idea that function was beautiful in and of itself and that other frills were unnecessary. Its defining feature was its exterior walls, which were entirely glass. While they kept the elements at bay, everything inside was laid bare.

The small house reminded me of the power relays comprising much of our nation's electrical infrastructure. While those buildings are considerably larger and the walls not transparent, the simplicity and function of the design mirror each other.

The council has given us the go-ahead. My team and I will visit each of those relay stations, retrofitting them to handle the new technology. Odd that things have progressed so, but I suppose the company wants to stay ahead of the competition. With this kind of energy and power at our fingertips, there's no time to lose.

5.25 – It has been an exhausting couple of weeks. We've been out visiting each of the power relays, verifying that each can handle a retrofit. The idea that any of them would not is absurd, as they are all identical, but the council insists on it, citing safety precautions. I suppose I can understand, especially after training some staff at these facilities. While I'd prefer to oversee all hardware installations personally, the additional time spent at each building would push the schedule back another couple of weeks. Instead, we leave the necessary equipment behind for them to install.

The only downside of this trip is that I haven't seen Damian at all. We communicate with each other every day electronically, but it's not the same after being in such proximity! Another week of this and I will return home to his face.

5.33 – I arrived home from my trip last night. I hadn't even begun unpacking when I called up Damian. We spoke the day before, and I was excited for the dinner plans we made. He didn't answer the phone, but I received an electronic message from him before I could even set mine back down.

It read: You're a good person, but I can't be with anyone right now.

In shock, I berated him with several calls. He never answered. In my frantic need to understand what was happening, to figure out what I did wrong and stop this terrible landslide, I did the craziest thing possible and drove over to his house. My hysterical knocks were unanswered, so I let myself in with the key he gave me weeks earlier. He wasn't home and, not knowing if I'd ever be welcome there again, I walked around in the dim light, trying to memorize all the small details. A few of my items were strewn about, especially in the bedroom. I left them where they lay, hoping they might help change his mind.

Sleep was scarce when I returned home. Curled up in bed, I went through an entire box of tissues trying to stem the flow of tears. The situation caught me off guard. There had been no sign we were having problems.

My greatest issue, the thing causing me the most pain, was that everything we shared and built meant absolutely nothing to him. It was so easy to end it, so easy that he didn't even bother to do it in person.

Kitsune was ashamed to say he found the author's life more interesting once drama chipped away at the perfect façade of her and Damian's relationship. He chided himself, remembering the events were real. Nearly a millennium ago, the woman was caught off guard, her heart broken.

Personally, though he had no idea what "spectacles" were, he wouldn't have associated with a group of people who belittled others for their fashion or belongings. There were always better subjects to discuss, drunk or sober.

In a strange way, it made him appreciate his and Myobu's first rift had come so quickly and been one of substance. The color or quality of their cloaks did not matter to each other. Their morals and goals, as well as the lengths they would go to uphold and achieve them, were what counted.

Kitsune continued to read through the entries.

5.34 – This all must be a mistake. It's like I'm living through a nightmare, and I can't wake up.

After leaving a multitude of messages in a variety of forms asking for a face-to-face conversation or even a good explanation, he sent me a message tonight saying I could come over to his place for a bit. I packed up all his belongings, including the coffee pot and any gifts he gave me, and drove straight over. The first thing he said upon my arrival still confounds me. He didn't express regret for breaking my heart, and he didn't say sorry for doing it in such a terrible fashion. Instead, he apologized in advance for smiling or giggling during our conversation. Apparently, he reacted to grief and bad situations in such a way.

Funny, he never smiled or chuckled when speaking of his mother's death.

No new explanations came to me. Despite my wailing for the truth, all he'd say was that I was too good for him and he didn't want to hurt me. I think he just wanted me to collect my belongings, which he had tossed unceremoniously into a box by the door, and leave.

6.2 – I think work is the only thing keeping me sane right now. If it wasn't for the looming pressure and deadline, my mind would be free to dwell on the more depressing aspects of my life.

Damian seems to have gone off the grid. Admittedly, having driven by his home a few times and checked up on his network of friends, a fair share of stalking has taken place on my part. I haven't seen or heard from him since the other night, which I would not mind so much if I just knew he was okay. I get so worried about him.

Thoughts and questions about what I did wrong have plagued me. I must remember that Damian is going through a lot of issues right now. He needs time and space to sort out his life.

__6.8__ – I've missed several days of work, and the team is getting frustrated with me. We're under such a tight deadline and everyone else is putting in a lot of overtime. Unfortunately, I can't bring myself to get out of bed. The mere thought of even getting up to make coffee makes me sick to my stomach.

During my usual stalking routine earlier this week, I came across some recent photographs of Damian. He was out and about, smiling joyfully, his arm wrapped around an old girlfriend. I could not have been more shocked. It was not what I expected to see. For not being able to be with anyone, he appeared to be having a grand time with her. Perhaps she has helped him past his pain. Maybe it's a good thing for him.

The worst, though, was his response to my many requests to see him. I know we aren't together. I know I wasn't good for him in the ways a partner should be. I hoped we could retain a friendship. That way, it wouldn't all be for naught. His reply was: I will not meet you for a drink. I will not see you at all. Quit messaging me.

I received the message while on a bus. So many people were witness to a total emotional unraveling. I was shaking and crying so badly that a complete stranger had to help me off the vehicle at my stop. Never have I been so embarrassed.

6.25 – *I have returned to work, at least sporadically. I don't want to leave my bed and go in, but it is one of the few things keeping me tethered to the real world. Otherwise, I have withdrawn from most forms of social life. I can't take the concerned questions or pitying looks anymore. Certainly, they are not deserved by me.*

I sent Damian one last message. It was an apology for my childish behavior, which has been unbecoming and embarrassing to see. Were the world mine, he would still be working as an artist. That would mean the troubles of the past year would not have befallen him, and he would be living a more carefree life.

6.32 – *My god is the same god as those in the religious sect I grew up around. Yet, we all perceive our god in vastly different ways. In my mind, he's less strict, far more loving, and has a sense of humor. Even with my self-serving, friendlier version, I have never been the most faithful follower. Certainly, there have been many days in a row when my mind never turned to religion. Still, this is the first time I have consciously not spoken to my god. Not only would my prayers consist of pleas for help, a purely selfish act, but I am no longer worthy of any kind of unearthly attention.*

It is morally wrong to treat another human being the way Damian has treated me. People cannot disappear from each other's lives with no explanation and such a lack of empathy. Even supplications for help from the homeless, sick, and lost are answered while mine are summarily ignored. The only explanation I can come up with is that I am wholly substandard. I am that second-class person I fought so hard and so long to rise above. No, I am worse than that. I am more like a rabid dog, feral and foaming at the mouth. Damian saw who I am, adorned in my second-rate spectacles, and he fled from me.

7.30 – *The undercurrent of all things is far more revealing than what lies on the surface. It is the topical that matters to me, however. It is what people see and believe.*

My brain seems to have had enough of my dark introspection and has turned off the faucet of my emotions. I just…don't feel. There's no happiness, though I'm used to that. The sadness and desperation, however, have also disappeared. This is probably the contributing factor to my improved reliability and sociability at work. It allows me to focus on the present.

There is another reason I've thrown even more of myself into the project. It's hard for me to put into words. There have been several moments lately when I've been struck with the realization that I'm on the verge of understanding…everything. It is as though all the answers to all the mysteries of the universe that have eluded mankind are surrounding us, silently taunting us with their invisible presence. Truly, I feel I could reach out my hand, brush aside an imperceptible curtain sewn into the fabric of space and time, and discover it all. It's all right there, like a giant, clanking, brass machine. Absolutely everything. Just out of reach.

Somehow, I think my work with energy could be the key to unlocking these mysteries.

10.2 – *It has been several weeks since I've pulled out my journal and documented my thoughts. Similar to my friends and family, I've grown tired of my sour attitude and self-loathing conversation. I have nothing positive to say, and I don't wish to ruminate on my own difficulties anymore.*

The time warrants a quick entry, however, for I will not be returning to write anything else again. This will be my final record.

With much fanfare, we have successfully completed the project's testing phase. Everyone is excited to move forward. The team, the council, the research facility, and the entire nation are waiting with great anticipation. If the other governments of the world knew what we were about to bring them, they too would be astounded and rejoice.

Everything is in place, and we will go into production mode at the main energy plant today. With just a few flipped switches and pushed buttons, our world's energy limitations will vanish.

Unfortunately, so will everything else.

I was finally able to brush that cosmic curtain aside and peek at the secrets the universe has been hiding from us. For the briefest of moments, understanding was in my grasp. I knew absolutely everything. Before I could do anything with that knowledge, however, I lost hold of it. The vacuum it left behind in my mind was frustrating, making me feel yet even smaller. There was one thing I held on to: There is something wrong with the project. It might be a design flaw in the technology, an oversight in the mathematical equations, or even a simple cog that wasn't fastened tightly enough. I cannot recall which piece of the massive puzzle doesn't fit. All I can say is that when we try to force it into place, it will all come to an end.

All the energy we've been hoping to harness will instead be expelled. The destruction and loss of life will be devastating.

Surprisingly, my first reaction was not to alert the team or council. That only occurred to me as a logical course of action much later. Instead, my initial response was to just let things run their course. After much consideration, that's exactly what I will do.

Throughout my entire life, I have marched in line with society, striving for others to accept me as an equal and love me for who I am. Each time I made an advancement, though, other people brought me back down. I came to realize the march to the sea was death, and I stepped out of line for Damian. Such actions instigate all sorts of conflict, and Damian only helped me to realize that the ideals of love and equality are unattainable for me because I am neither lovable nor equal. I am undeserving of them.

Damian tried to put me back in my place, marching to the sea. That line is death. All lines are death.

I cannot live with myself knowing I am the thing I've run from for so long. The emotional depth necessary to care about the fate of others has disappeared as well. At least, it has for all but one person, and I have made arrangements for him to be far, far away from this place today.

I love you, Damian. I hate myself more than anything for still loving you. I do, though, and I always will.

Goodbye.

"Dear spirits," Kitsune said aloud, stopping short.

Myobu turned back, a look of concern on his face. Not seeing any danger, he asked, "What's wrong?"

"I believe I know what happened to these people," Kitsune answered, pointing down to the journal. "I think I know what created the Wastelands!"

233

THE TRIBAL LANDS

The room was cozy. Window drapes were open, revealing a winter forest covered by several finger lengths of new snow. Inside, though, a fire warmed the hearth, several candles created a warm glow, and large blankets and pillows lay strewn about. It provided a comfortable contrast.

Though he couldn't be certain, Kitsune suspected he was now relaxing in the same cottage he saw in a previous dreamscape. In that occurrence, he knew someone—Myobu—was waiting inside for him. The Lady had then appeared, assuring him that going inside was the right thing to do.

"You were anxious then," his mother said from a small sofa opposite the one he was nestled in. "How do you feel now?"

Kitsune looked about the room, allowing the fire and dark décor to relax him. He remembered walking through the door in the previous vision, then waking up to Myobu tumbling out of a smoky fireplace. The house wasn't real, obviously, but he had walked into a relationship with the other man. He was comfortable in that bond. It gave him a sense of home.

"Like I'm part of a family," he replied. "Many have seen me, some have known me, but only a precious few have cared so much that they've helped me know myself. I only hope I am a positive force in their lives as well."

"You freed me from a mountain. Myobu adores you, agreeing to help you on a quest against someone he holds in high regard," the Lady said. "You've even positively influenced Major Saxma's actions."

"I had nothing to do with the major's actions. Nor Pan's," Kitsune defended, shuddering again at the callous murder of Jasper, necessary or not.

"The major could have ordered Pan to kill you back at the fork, and your friend is apparently adept enough with a sword to have done so before you even knew he was there," his mother said, looking calmly at him. "You may not like the major. More than likely, he doesn't care for you either. He respects you, though, and probably finds you to be honorable. If he didn't, he would not have bothered with you at all, instead proceeding with his doomed plans of dethroning the king."

"You believe a plot to remove my father from power to be hopeless?" Kitsune asked, surprised.

"It is without you," she replied, her eyes and voice so sincere that Kitsune was further taken aback. "Both your power and familial connection to the king will be necessary in overpowering him."

"My power?" Kitsune scoffed. "My magic is about as useful as an empty canteen on a hot day."

Throughout the days of traveling across the Wastelands, Kitsune continued his efforts at meditation as well as controlling and using his powers. He grew increasingly aware of what he could do. The great storm he accidentally conjured was nothing compared to what he saw himself doing in his mind's eye. However, aside from heating the air when Pan beheaded Jasper, his efforts at using his magic yielded nothing more than gentle winds.

"It is far easier to outwardly show emotions when they are roiling about inside of you," the Lady said, knowing his thoughts. "Not so much when your mind is at peace."

"I know. And I am progressing in my development at an exceptionally quick pace. I am grateful I can control myself and have caused no further disasters," he said, regurgitating the words she and Myobu had spoken to him many times over the past several days. "You warned me that I will soon need to use the full range of my powers. I am only trying to heed your words."

The Lady looked at him silently. Then, tilting her head slightly, she said, "Though you are becoming more aware of them, you don't yet know or appreciate all of your abilities. I believe it is time for that to change."

"How exactly do we gauge my capabilities?"

"The single greatest barrier holding you back is your fear of creating another disaster. You've proven capable of controlling your power, but that control stems from an instinctual terror that you will unwittingly cause the death of others. Possibly even people you love. You can practice here with me, where you can let down your guard."

Kitsune nodded in agreement. He had feared he would harm Myobu, especially while they were sleeping. He now knew it was possible to unconsciously influence things with magic. What was to keep the same thing from happening while dreaming? He voiced that concern, not wanting to experiment and awaken later to a new victim.

"This dream state is self-contained," his mother said, shaking her head. "It can look like the physical world, and it will react to you as such, but your actions will affect nothing outside of it. If I were alive in the typical sense, it would be possible for me to let our interactions here seep into the waking world. That requires magic, though, and is now beyond my abilities."

"You are certain I can practice here and not affect the physical world, even though I am alive and possess magic?" he asked, still hesitant. After her insistent assurances that her control over the dreamscape was whole, he continued, "What do I do?"

"The same thing you always do, then push further," she replied. "Push as far as you can. You can't hurt me, even if you tried."

Kitsune sat upright and, deciding to start simple, thought of Myobu and the first kiss they shared. In response, a gentle breeze picked up around them. His mother's hair, usually so perfectly straight and tidy, moved about in every direction.

The prince pushed a little further, recalling the first time he and Myobu had lain naked together, Myobu caressing every portion of his body with his glorious hands. The touching ended on his cock. Then, with his mouth, Myobu had—

The wind picked up considerably, snuffing out the fire in the hearth and all the candles. The draperies flapped, and any loose material kicked up into the air. A spark of fear penetrated Kitsune's consciousness as he realized he had created a small cyclone within the confines of the room. It was a miniscule version of the terror he unleashed before, but he now knew how easy it was to create them in all sizes. That fear, coupled with embarrassment from thinking of Myobu sexually while in the presence of his mother, caused a retraction in his will. The wind died down.

But then the Lady's words came back to him: Learn quickly, Kitsune. I sense the time is near that you will need command of all your faculties.

The prince heeded the warning, embracing all his feelings for Myobu. The sexual experiences were there, but so was the gratitude for being saved, the astonishment at being accepted, and wonderment at being part of a family. He simultaneously reached out with his mind, searching for the wind, accepting and encouraging it. It swirled about mother and son with such increased ferocity that planks of wood ripped up from the floor, doors pulled from their hinges, and all items tossed about and smashed.

Then he encapsulated all the swirling energy in a mental bubble. The house was eerily silent for just a moment before he expelled all the energy outward in a destructive blast. Furniture splintered, walls collapsed, and the windows blew out.

The prince waited for silence to fall over them again, but he was surprised to hear a low whistling sound. He also realized the floor wasn't level, and he keeled to his left as his equilibrium went askew. As he did, he caught a glimpse out the window. The trees and the skyline were all there, though they appeared unusual. The branches were too far away.

But not by much.

And they were getting closer.

Kitsune suddenly understood that the cyclone of air he created had not been limited to the cottage. It had become a full-fledged tornado, picking up the small home as though it weighed nothing and lifting it into the air. Now, with the magic dispelled, they were falling straight back to the ground.

Instincts guided his actions, and Kitsune used one hand to steady himself while reaching out toward the ground below with the other. He sought the air below them, making a fist and pulling upward.

It made no difference. Kitsune remained calm, though, making another fist and thrusting up to the sky above them, careful to keep his body aligned as the structure rotated. As the whistling wind grew louder and higher pitched, he thought they were only descending faster. Then the structure lurched dramatically, throwing everything, including Kitsune and his mother, against one wall.

The increased pitch in the wind was the house meeting the upward flow of air he was causing. Even as the downward descent of the cottage slowed, the noise continued, the draft flowing at a rate strong enough to fight against gravity. Kitsune kept his hand extended up, his fingers now splayed out, desperately willing any last gusts of air to lessen their fall.

The house was well built. It had made it this far without disintegrating entirely. Still, it was falling apart around them, a few bricks and planks all that remained of solid walls and floors. Even if the building made it to the ground, it would surely collapse. With all the loose debris kicked up by the tornado obscuring the view from the windows or ragged holes in the walls, there was no way to discern where they were in relation to their final destination. Mental and physical exertion exhausted him, and he was aware he could not keep summoning this level of magical force.

"The scenario would almost certainly have ended in death."

Kitsune blinked. The house around them was gone, any trace of its existence erased. He lay in a patch of green grass surrounded by trees, most likely where the house should have been standing. One of his arms braced his body against the ground while the other still reached to a sunny and calm sky.

"What?" he asked, blinking again in confusion.

"You did admirably," the Lady said. She stood to his side, looking down on him benignly. "You were able to consciously create a tornadic event, albeit stronger than even you thought at first."

Kitsune was about to rebuff any praise, but his mother held out a hand to silence him. "Faced with certain doom, you continued to act. You understood what was happening, calculated what you needed to do, and then did it. Not only did you create an updraft to slow our descent, but you stabilized the cottage's motion."

"But we still would have died?"

"Indeed," she replied. "Many Yokai and other magical creatures have died exploring the limit of their powers. This makes a dreamscape the perfect area to test them. Forgive me for not thinking of it earlier."

"Do not concern yourself with that!" he exclaimed. "Forgive me if I scared you with that little stunt."

"I am no longer capable of fear," the Lady said, though for once Kitsune did not entirely believe her. The demonstration of his powers had not scared her, but something else possibly had.

If he was being honest, he was scared as well. He had sensed something within himself during the descent. Something beyond the wind and the rain and the lightning he was used to feeling. It was dark as coal and had the potential to reshape... everything. In the brief moment his consciousness caressed this unknown magic, he knew he didn't want it. Had his mother sensed this, too?

"What you accomplished today is more than most with magic could ever dream of doing," his mother continued. "And you should realize that your actions to slow the cottage's descent were not destructive, but those of a savior. Not the first you've displayed, but an important step in realizing you are capable of more than just destruction. I foresee you will rain upon thirsty crops, hold back devastating floods, and put out destructive fires. Even if you never appreciate your gifts, thousands of others will.

"You should know," the Lady said, holding her hands out to grasp his. She smiled widely, and though the look was odd to see on her face, Kitsune knew it was a genuine one. "More than anything else, I appreciate and am proud of you, my son."

*

"What are you smiling at?" Myobu asked as Kitsune opened his eyes. "And why were you sleeping? We stopped for a quick rest and apple snack, not a nap."

Kitsune brought the half-eaten apple, still in his hand, up to his mouth and took a big bite. He chewed for a long while, looking his companion over. After he swallowed, he said, "I was dreaming of you, of course."

Throughout all their traveling, long talks, and revelations, Kitsune had yet to speak of the Lady of the Mountain to Myobu. He was not ashamed or embarrassed by the fact that his mother hung from around his neck, watching all that transpired—though it seemed an odd family dynamic if he thought about it long enough. Neither did he think the other would consider him crazy, as the two of them now knew enough of the supernatural that the idea of a hoshi no tama seemed downright mundane.

The opportunity to socialize with his mother for the first time, especially in such a surreal fashion, was an extraordinarily personal thing. Kitsune was not ready to let anyone else in on this cherished time. He would have to speak of it eventually with Myobu. Until now, their discussions into family had been limited to King Oni and Myobu's vague recollections of his deceased parents. Myobu would surely pose questions, and Kitsune would not perpetuate the lie that his mother died giving birth to him. Well, at least not entirely died.

Myobu was observant, though, and already knew Kitsune wore the hoshi no tama. The dark-haired man noticed it while washing the prince's naked body and had undoubtedly seen it each time they'd lain together without clothes. Though it glowed green with magic, he was sensitive enough not to ask any probing questions.

"You were definitely dreaming of something," Myobu snorted, tossing the last remains of his apple core into a bush.

Kitsune remembered his dreamscape erection and guessed he had physically reacted as well. In a playfully defensive tone, he replied, "I can't help what I do when I'm sleeping!"

"I'm going to help you out later, whether or not you're asleep," Myobu said, though his voice grew serious.

Kitsune looked up, seeing that Myobu had turned his attention to the west. A line of trees marked the edge of a vast forest as well as the border of the tribal lands.

Unlike the eastern side of the Wastelands, where the transition between what was uninhabitable and civilization blurred well into Odom's borders, the line of demarcation on this side was definite. Within the span of two thousand footfalls, ground incapable of sustaining life gave way to a sea of green grass and trees. Kitsune guessed the difference had to do with the weather. Whatever the author of the journal did to cause such a massive calamity had found its way into the atmosphere and dispersed unevenly into the east.

"A part of me is hesitant to enter the forest," Kitsune said, acknowledging his own fears. "We've been traveling for days in this barren, open land, and the trees make me claustrophobic."

"Imagine traveling out of that," Myobu responded. "Both Gaav and the tribal lands are predominantly forested. For me, entering the

Wastelands made me feel vulnerable and unprotected. True, you can spot dangers from great distances, but there are few places to hide from those threats."

As they trekked through the Wastelands for eight days, they kept as close to the southern border as possible. The path they initially started out on eventually disappeared, its existence forgotten hundreds of sun cycles ago. From there, Myobu retraced his previous journey as best he could, keeping them close to dried-up creek beds where the occasional remains of ancient trees still stood, providing shade and protection if needed.

Though there had been distant animal howls and the random carcass, no threats ever presented themselves. This suited Kitsune just fine. The hollers they heard sounded anguished and hungry, and the emaciated remains they came across were twisted, warped, and deformed. The heat and sun explained some of it, causing flesh and tissue to contract as they decayed. It did not justify, however, additional appendages or disproportionately sized limbs.

The heat of the days, coupled with constant windstorms kicking dust into the air in such quantities that the folks at the Odom outpost would have been grateful for their lot, made this part of the expedition miserable. The temperature would then drop dramatically as the sun descended, and the two clung to each other for warmth over several sleepless nights.

Sometimes, when the wind wasn't howling and visibility was decent, they could see ancient cities. The communities must have been great centers of trade, wealth, and science, for they not only took up leagues of land, but stretched into the sky. Their giant structures had not been chiseled from mountains, built into existing natural features, or constructed on a wide base for support. Theirs jutted straight up into the sky like spears. Only the skeletal remains of these buildings endured, and even those were bent and broken. Kitsune imagined they had once been so tall they disappeared into the clouds that hung above the earth.

"We are close to where I emerged from the tribal lands on my trip east," Myobu mused. "We should come across a small tribe before nightfall. Their name translates roughly to the Purple People, though I am uncertain why. They are friendly and will give us shelter for the night."

"I would be happy enough with some water to bathe in," Kitsune said, having long ago given up on brushing the dirt from his clothes, arms, and face. He and Myobu were so soiled that they were unrecognizable. "And something to eat besides apples!"

"The Purple People make some great food," Myobu replied, his voice dreamy and eyes glazing over as he thought back to a previous meal. "More importantly, assuming we don't dawdle in the morning and the Harbinger hasn't moved on to a new location, we should reach her by late afternoon tomorrow."

"We're that close? I envisioned us hacking our way through overgrown jungle for weeks!" Kitsune exclaimed. He jumped up from the ground, his healing tailbone giving only moderate protest, and grabbed his pack. "Let's go! We don't want to be late!"

They moved into the woods, quickly finding a path Myobu recognized. As they traveled due west, they stopped only twice before they came across the Purple People. The first break occurred when they discovered a high creek bed, the first clean water they'd seen since leaving Odom. They drank their fill, then stripped down to clean their bodies and clothes.

As the dirt washed off, their spirits rose. They were in a far more hospitable environment, so long as they did not come across a hostile tribe. They were safe from the sun and would probably find something to eat other than apples. This was especially enticing. Even though Captain Pan had partially supplemented their foodstuffs, they were running dangerously low. What remained appeared withered and unappetizing.

With their bodies clean, though, they felt more presentable to themselves and anyone they would come across.

"How are you doing?" Kitsune asked coyly, wading through the water toward Myobu. Due to the miserable conditions of the Wastelands, holding conversations with each other had been difficult. Even more challenging was attempting anything frisky. With gritty sand invading every private nook of his body, the thought of anything more than hugging each other for body heat at night was uninviting. Now, though, with clean slates, Kitsune felt his usual urges returning.

Myobu shook his head in warning. "Not now. Not here. We're being watched. Nothing to be concerned over. They are most likely scouts or hunters from the tribe I mentioned." He began ringing water from his clothes and pulling them on, but he stopped momentarily to give Kitsune a wicked smile. "Unless you're an exhibitionist."

Kitsune laughed at him but was inwardly furious with himself. As he pulled his own damp clothing back on, he surveyed their surroundings until he spotted the voyeurs—two of them, and nothing purple about them. Their hair was brown and their skin appeared green, though he couldn't tell if the traits were natural or some kind of tint they applied. Their clothing was finely woven but minimal, a testament that they were close to their home. The overall effect was an excellent camouflage, but not so good that Kitsune shouldn't have been able to spot them earlier. He had been unacceptably lazy in his duty. If he couldn't protect himself, he wouldn't be able to complete his mission or keep Myobu safe.

Later in the afternoon, they stopped along the trail for the second time. A perfectly circular patch of burned grass, about fifty footfalls in diameter, captured their attention.

"A campfire that got out of control?" Myobu surmised, walking the perimeter.

"I don't believe so," Kitsune answered, trying especially hard now to use his observational skills. He brushed at the charred outer bark of a tree with his thumb. The side of the trunk facing the center of the burnt circle was blackened while the opposite side was far less injured. As the crisped bark fell away, healthy wood appeared. "An actual fire would have caused far more damage than this. Even if it was—and those who built it had worked to put it out—the affected area is far too symmetric. The fire would have spread farther on one side as they put it out on the other."

"You're right," Myobu said, frowning as he continued to pace.

"It's as though intense heat burst forth from this point," Kitsune said, standing at the center of the circle. "Then it disappeared."

While an intriguing mystery, it was unrelated to their quest, and they soon moved on. They continued uninterrupted at a brisk pace until, just as the sun was setting, they came upon the village Myobu had spoken of.

It was difficult to judge how large the settlement was or how many inhabitants lived there. The structures consisted of timber, mud, leaves, and rocks, making them blend into the forest. They were spaced far apart from one another, possibly to help prevent the spread of fire if one were to break out.

A trio of elderly villagers greeted Kitsune and Myobu at the edge of the community. The prince could immediately identify one of them as a soldier. She was not dressed for it, but he could see it in her eyes. The way she eyed them as they approached, sizing them up, cataloging their weapons and other potential dangers to her people.

Another of them appeared to be a carpenter. Though past his prime sun cycles of construction, he was apparently not ready to fully retire. A leather belt was slung around his waist from which rudimentary tools were secured. It looked as though their arrival had interrupted a project.

The third greeter was a jovial man of greater size than the others. Kitsune might have guessed he was the villager's leader if not that his clothing was of poorer quality than the others. He may have been a cook or, with his energetic personality, a social organizer.

All three had brown hair and the same green tinge to their skin Kitsune witnessed earlier on the scouts. Though they spoke a language foreign to him, they were friendly and appeared to recognize Myobu.

They made exaggerated smiles and pointed at the dark-haired man. Myobu shrugged at first in response, then seemed to catch on to what they were saying. He tilted his head to Kitsune, giving a large smile himself.

"Apparently, I look much happier than the last time I passed through here," he explained as the elders looked at one another, smiled, and nodded their heads.

"I'm glad to have been a positive influence," Kitsune replied in wonderment.

By using simple gestures, Myobu communicated to the elders their need for food and shelter, promising they would be back on the road at first light. Though they were now clean from their bath, it was clear enough from their ragged clothing and light packs that they possessed little to offer in return. Still, the jovial man led them to a shelter, and later brought bowls of meaty stew.

"Are all the tribes of this land this peaceful?" Kitsune asked, looking out across the encampment. Their hut, like most others, was neither large nor fully enclosed. A waist-high wall of dried mud and rock surrounded a pile of bedding. Several intertwined logs and branches then supported a roof of long leaves above them. Anyone walking by could look right in. Privacy was another reason Kitsune supposed the huts were spaced widely apart.

"Definitely not," Myobu replied, spooning up the remainder of his stew. "Some of them are even more benevolent, though naively so. Others are aggressive and intolerant, attacking and enslaving rival tribes. A lack of true leadership leads to instability within the tribes as they grow larger, and they break apart as they fight among themselves."

Kitsune continued to watch the night's nearby activities unfold by firelight. He knew this community was more than just a collection of people, and he strove to understand them better. One or two families clustered around each of the huts. Adults socialized by the fires, stitching clothing together, keeping food warm, and watching the nearby children at play. The younger youth stuck close to their families while the older ones dashed in and out of the shadows, playing some kind of game.

The camp's elderly, including those who had greeted Kitsune and Myobu, made their way through the village, making conversation with individuals and families. Every time one of them showed up by a fire, those around it would respectfully acknowledge him or her with their undivided attention and discussion. Though Kitsune couldn't hear or even understand their words, it looked like a relaxed method of spreading news, information, and friendly gossip.

There did not seem to be a clear leader Kitsune could identify. Instead, it looked as though the elders formed an unofficial yet active council, facilitating and participating in all the daily events. Everyone appeared to revere them, going to them for counsel and hanging on to their every word. The elders regarded the younger generations with equal amounts of respect, wanting—needing—them to absorb their knowledge and experience. It was necessary that they know each other, understand one another, so they could act as one and survive.

Kitsune began to truly understand what Pan had said about leaders being the head of a family, protecting and nurturing them, and he grudgingly gave the man credit.

"I really hope the Purple People survive," he said thoughtfully.

"They've been around for dozens of sun cycles. Even before them, other tribes inhabited this area. They watch over an ancient pyramid," Myobu replied, pointing to a crumbling ruin far off on the horizon. Its edifice was so degraded it was hardly distinguishable from the surrounding forest. "It is neither the grandest nor most famous of the pyramids in this area, but stories claim it to be home to an artifact of great value. Researchers and plunderers have searched it many times, of course, but they have found nothing. Regardless, this road provided the Purple People and their predecessors a kind of sanctuary, as traders protected by soldiers passed through often enough from Gaav, Kitsunetsuki, and Odom. The more aggressive tribes were hesitant to engage with men armed with superior weaponry. Now that trading has all but ceased, it is only a matter of time before those tribes encroach into this area."

"I love you," Kitsune said. He hadn't expected the words to tumble out of his mouth, but they hadn't surprised him. He turned to look at Myobu, who stared back at him with wide eyes.

"Wha... What?" was all he could say.

"You just fell into my life, and it's as though I'm feeling for the first time with my heart and soul. Everything has changed because of you. How I emote. How I think. You've influenced me, and all for the better."

Myobu continued to stare back at Kitsune in shock for several moments before collecting his bearings. Then he reached out and took his hand, enveloping and squeezing it.

"I was completely blindsided by you as well," Myobu said in a voice as soft as Kitsune had ever heard. He paused for a moment as though he wanted to say something, then decided to go down a different path. "I've been watching you come into your own along our journey. I've seen _you_. I've kissed and held you, sleeping so close to you I can recognize your scent."

"I don't know what all your dreams are," Kitsune murmured. "But I want to be there with you as you chase them down. I want to help make them unfold just so I can see you smile more."

Myobu gave a goofy grin. "What I'd really like is to spend a lifetime with you."

Kitsune pulled Myobu to him, holding him tight as their lips met in a fervent kiss. It was exactly what he needed to hear and feel. All the miserable time spent in the Wastelands, where they didn't speak much and intimacy was out of the question, had left him with plenty of time to think. Not only did he dwell on his father, which only stoked a growing anger at all the truths he uncovered about the king's past, but also his situation with Myobu. He had questions about their future and what Myobu's intentions were, out of which he unreasonably concluded the other man would disappear once they found the Harbinger or the King's Sun.

With just a few words and a kiss, though, overwhelming joy dispelled and replaced those fears. Myobu was his. They were together and always would be. He knew it with a concrete certainty and assuredness he had not known before.

Kitsune moved his hands down Myobu's sides. Then, slipping them under his shirt, he pulled the fabric upward, feeling the warmth on his clean, smooth skin. They stopped kissing long enough for the shirt to be completely removed and tossed to the side.

They moved to the bedding, and Kitsune gave Myobu a playful push so that he landed on his back upon it. The prince climbed on too, kissing him several more times, pulling gently at Myobu's lip with his teeth until the other man moaned.

With his tongue, Kitsune traced a line down Myobu's chin, neck, and chest. The destination was obvious, and the dark-haired man made no moves to stop him.

"Anyone can see us, you know," Myobu said coyly, even though they had lit no fire. Someone would have to walk up to the side of the hut to make out anything.

"Perhaps I am a...what did you call it? An exhibitionist?" Kitsune was playing with the outline of Myobu's cock through his pants with his mouth, so the words came out muffled. Then he looked up, concerned. "Would this be an affront to them?"

With a laugh, Myobu pushed Kitsune's head back down to his crotch. "They won't mind a bit. They gave us a particularly secluded hut for good reason."

Kitsune moaned as Myobu twitched beneath his face. He tugged Myobu's pants down, watching in delight as his cock emerged, hard and sensitive. He licked at it a few times, loving how it jerked in reaction to his every touch, then moved down toward Myobu's feet as he removed the man's pants.

"Why am I the only one with no clothes on?" Myobu began to ask, but even as the words left his mouth, Kitsune was removing his own garments.

"You were saying?" Kitsune responded, kneeling by Myobu's feet. Despite their long travels, they were smooth and soft. He particularly loved how they were a little smaller, matching their hand counterparts. He caressed them, massaging and kissing them, teasing his lover with gentle tickles.

Taking hold of Myobu's legs from under the knees, Kitsune moved back upward, lifting Myobu's feet up and exposing his buttocks.

"You're quite flexible," he said as he reached Myobu's face. After a few heavy kisses, he indicated Myobu should take hold of his own feet. "Hang on to these for a bit."

Then Kitsune worked his way down Myobu's beautiful body again, probing at the man with his tongue, taking it particularly slow along the tender areas. Myobu gasped and moaned, wriggling in pleasure as Kitsune's tongue hit erogenous areas.

The short, audible gasps Myobu gave were so beguiling that Kitsune thought he would climax before even getting to the intended stage. After giving Myobu one last good, lubricating lick, he spit into his hand and wet his own cock. He inched forward, pressing himself against the man.

"Are you ready?" Kitsune asked, looking into Myobu's deep brown eyes.

Myobu let go of his feet, letting his legs hook around Kitsune's shoulders. The muscles were trembling slightly, a mixture of nervousness and exertion. Several moments passed during which Myobu bit down on his lower lip before his body grew more relaxed.

"Yes," he whispered, staring back at Kitsune with a look of longing. "I'm ready."

The prince leaned down, kissing Myobu as he entered him. He could feel and hear the other as he moaned into the kiss. The sensation was new to Kitsune, engaging with someone he truly loved. Both were vulnerable to one another, naked and exposed, yet completely trusting and honest.

Moving in and out, Kitsune feared at first he was hurting Myobu. He felt the other man against him, though—the expected hardness and warmth, and he knew they were both enjoying this.

The night air was cool, but they broke out in perspiration. They swayed back and forth together in unison, their hands and limbs sliding across each other's slick skin. As the ecstasy grew, they became united, became one. The mission, the journey, the Purple People, and the hut all fell away and disappeared, and all they knew were each other in that moment.

And when they came, that glorious moment lasted forever.

THE KING'S SUN

"I could get used to that," Kitsune practically sang as he and Myobu made their way down the path. It was the twelfth time during their long day of travel that he referenced their activities from the night before. The giddiness helped stay the growth of fear and anger in his heart. That darkness pulsed there in response to an impending assassination and a father who had assigned him as executioner. Kitsune clung to the positive emotion like a child to a new toy.

"It was something special," Myobu replied with exaggerated exasperation, though a giant grin stretched across his face.

"After all the noise you made last night, do you think the Purple People will ever welcome us back?" Kitsune joked. In truth, the two of them had awoken to another delicious meal and a hot drink akin to coffee. The same elders who greeted them the day before sent them on their way with two days' worth of food, smiles, and what they guessed were good blessings.

"What, no response to that?" Kitsune said when he heard no reply. He turned to look at his partner. Upon seeing him, Kitsune stopped in his tracks. "What's wrong?"

Myobu was standing rigidly, staring at a few downed trees lining the path's right-hand side. The color drained from his face, giving him a sickly look. Kitsune could clearly see the whites of his eyes, and the pupils dilated so dramatically that the brown irises were barely visible. With his mouth hanging slightly open, the fear emanating from Myobu was palpable.

Kitsune grabbed his bow, nocking an arrow while turning back around. His sharp eyes scanned the tree line, looking for any recognizable human shapes lurking in the shadows. He discerned nothing ominous. Thinking Myobu's sharper eyes had picked up on something he couldn't, he whispered, "What is it?"

No answer was forthcoming, but Kitsune realized Myobu hadn't seen something through the vegetation. Rather, he saw the trees themselves and what they appeared to form. The trunks to the right of the path had not fallen but defied nature and grown horizontally. A long line of trees had grown in a similar fashion alongside the road, clumping together to form a short wall of sorts. This odd growth pattern created an empty swath in the canopy above them, giving a rare clear glimpse of the sky above. Kitsune looked ahead, noticing that the further away the wall, the more upright the trees forming it became. Farther back, they matched the surrounding canopy in height, but then the wall of trees grew taller and thicker.

The oddity terminated at what Kitsune earlier interpreted as a hill, although there was no rise in elevation. The trees just grew taller. Furthermore, he could identify two additional walls of thick trunks stemming away from a common focal point, and he guessed there was a fourth on the other side that he couldn't see. The forest in between these walls was also taller, though not as drastically and appearing to slope gradually. What once looked like a hill was now more akin to a giant green tent.

Kitsune saw nothing natural about this formation, which made it some kind of structure. It swayed gently in the breeze, reminding Kitsune of the circus that came through Oinari once every few sun cycles. The circus folk would always construct a large tent in which they performed live theatre, exhibited exotic animals, and displayed amazing physical feats. The tent itself was a canvas material, held up by great wooden poles dug deep into the ground. There were four sides and one enormous entrance, which was meant to catch interest and draw in a crowd. He always thought the canvas looked too heavy for the poles to hold up, expecting the wood to snap under the weight at any moment. Despite their heft, the enormous sheets of cloth billowed about in the wind, just as the branches and leaves making up this structure did now.

Just like the entrance to the circus tent, a gaping entryway opened the side of the leafy tent closest to them, and it definitely caught Kitsune's interest.

"Have I disappointed you?"

Myobu's voice startled Kitsune, and the question puzzled him. Looking back, he said, "Pardon?"

"Have I let you down?" he replied, looking as though he were on the verge of tears.

"Of course not!" Kitsune exclaimed, frowning at Myobu's sudden emotional transformation. He had witnessed him display many sentiments, including gloominess and absolute dread, but this was by far the most disconcerting. The arrow still nocked and pointed up the path, Kitsune backed up to the dark-haired man.

"I...I just feel guilty." Myobu choked, looking like he was about to throw up.

Upon reaching him, Kitsune let down his guard, placing the arrow back into its quiver. He reached out, holding the side of Myobu's face and neck with his hand. "You have nothing to feel guilty about, my love. You've stood with me on this journey at great personal cost. It is I who has let you down, saddened your heart. I have asked much of you."

Myobu looked up at him, and Kitsune could see the fading sun reflected in his teary eyes. "I love you, my pretty prince."

Kitsune's heart simultaneously tightened and swelled. His breathing became the only sound in the forest, as the noise of insects, birds, and rustling trees hushed at Myobu's admittance. Though each had admitted much the night before, including Kitsune's feelings and

Myobu's desires, no admission of love escaped Myobu's lips. This was Myobu at his most vulnerable, as portrayed by his large, seeking eyes, and the words were true.

"I love you, too," Kitsune replied, then pulled Myobu into a long kiss. Myobu wrapped his arms around Kitsune, holding him tightly. Any time Kitsune would pull out of the kiss, even for just a short breath, Myobu would let out an irresistible moan, clearly not satiated.

The sun had disappeared behind the tree tent by the time they let loose of one another. Watching Myobu run a hand through his thick hair, damp with sweat, Kitsune said, "I meant what I said yesterday. You've changed my life. I'm no longer ashamed of who I am. There are so many things I want to do now. Changing my father's mind about…about people…is just one of those goals."

"But you still want to kill Ninko, don't you?"

A flash of anger swept through Kitsune, so strong he almost lashed out. He did not understand where it stemmed from, for he had begun to consider alternative courses of actions. Perhaps it was all the internal conversations he had with himself while traveling through the Wastelands, or maybe it was just the miserable sandy onslaught, but it finally dawned upon him that King Oni's actions were truly, inarguably wrong. It was so evident that even those as bullishly loyal as Major Saxma considered revolution.

"I don't know," he admitted. "I mean…I don't want to kill him. I haven't since you've spoken of him. Since then, I've rationalized the act as a way of gaining entrance into Kitsunetsuki, but I'm coming to believe no one should have to die at my father's whim. Is that what this is all about?"

"No," Myobu answered softly, shaking his head. Then, motioning ahead at the tree structure, he said, "We're here. This is where the Harbinger lives."

"I thought it might be, but it's so quiet," Kitsune said. "Where is everyone?"

"Everyone?" Myobu questioned. "It is only Kyubi."

Kitsune looked back at the giant trees. Despite its resemblance to a tent, what lay underneath the towering canopy was still mostly forest. There were no long hallways and rooms for guests and servants. "I just imagined, especially given her age, that she'd have staff."

With a wry smile, Myobu retorted, "You should know by now, given your own demeanor, that the Yokai are a solitary race. They may become attached to a single individual, but otherwise they prefer seclusion. It's why so many people don't believe the Yokai even exist."

"I suppose I've found the individual to whom I have become attached." He reached for Myobu's hand and, once their fingers intertwined, said, "Let us be done with this."

As they walked side by side for the remaining distance, Kitsune recalled what little he knew about the Harbinger, chiding himself for not questioning Myobu for more details beforehand. One of the oldest living of the Yokai, she would be as powerful as she was wise. Through her magical abilities of sight, she could have known of Kitsune since his birth. Possibly even beforehand.

Despite her purported wisdom, the Harbinger was not necessarily selfless in nature. She was still of the Yokai, and the Yokai had strange motives and were known to play tricks. Myobu came to her in an effort to better serve Gaav, and she sent him down a path leading to his assistance in the assassination of one of that kingdom's most influential advisors. Kitsune's grandmother Veranda came across her long ago and received knowledge that would hollow out her soul.

Kitsune stopped short at the grand entrance, taking a moment to feel the presence of his grandmother. She too walked this path, maybe even stepping through this same grove of trees. He wished he had more knowledge about her visit. Had she arrived at the same late hour as they? Was she in good company or was she traveling alone? Veranda seemed a stately, independent woman, and Kitsune imagined she would have been able to handle herself perfectly well here in the tribal lands.

"Has the darkness come to swallow me up?" came a silky voice from the shadows just inside the tree tent, interrupting Kitsune's reverie. He jumped in surprise, reaching for his sword hilt, but he kept himself from drawing the weapon when he saw Myobu was not startled. In fact, he looked as though he had been expecting it.

The owner of the silky voice stepped out into the open. Light from the stars above penetrated through the leaves, bathing the woman in luminescence. With her pale, flawless skin, angular facial features, and trim body, the woman's mere presence and beauty were captivating. She reminded Kitsune of his mother, and he knew this woman was of the Yokai.

Two key differences separated the Lady of the Mountain and the newcomer, who Kitsune assumed was the Harbinger. The first was their hair. His mother's was as black as pitch while the Harbinger's was snowy white. More interesting was how she pulled it back from her face and bound it together in nine separate sections, giving her the appearance of having nine voluminous tails.

The second difference was the eyes. The Lady's eyes usually matched her serene smile. There was a broken, sad confusion in them as she tried to piece together the memories and feelings remaining with her. While the Harbinger smiled tranquilly, her eyes were anything but unclear. She knew exactly who she was, and her eyes relayed that with cunning and shrewdness.

The Harbinger scanned Kitsune and Myobu with her knowing gaze, then answered her own question. "No, not yet, I suppose."

"Kyubi," Myobu greeted, bowing respectfully. Kitsune followed suit.

"Myobu," she returned in her smooth, seductive voice. With a tilt of her head to indicate Kitsune, she continued, "I see you found the answer to your question, that you followed the path I laid out for you."

"I followed your suggestion, though it went against every fiber of my being." Despite the negative words, Myobu looked affectionately over at Kitsune. "I have not regretted that decision."

"You never shall," Kyubi assured. Then she turned to address Kitsune. "Prince Kitsune, son of Oni. It is good Myobu found you."

Kitsune was puzzled. The Harbinger directed Myobu toward the Eastern Gate as part of his quest to serve Gaav, he knew, and the two of them joked the prince was the result. But Kitsune never took that seriously. He hadn't even broached the subject of Myobu's pursuit since revealing his ultimate plan to kill the King's Sun. It seemed an indelicate thing to do.

Had their flirtatious joking been based in truth?

"Please, come inside. I'll put some tea on the fire," Kyubi invited, gesturing into the grove of trees like it was a parlor. It may not have been a traditional home, but it was her domain. A host of fireflies shined brightly from the air, ground, and tree trunks, illuminating a clear path to the center. There, a small fire burst into existence, revealing a kettle and fallen logs upon which to sit.

"Your friend came to me not long ago, wanting advice on how best to aid his adopted home," she continued conversationally, leading them toward the fire. Her nine bundles of hair bounced about lively. She turned her head to gaze at Kitsune with one eye.

"I was aware of that. It was his confidence in your words that brought us here to you."

"Are you aware of what I revealed to him?"

Kitsune looked at Myobu, who appeared heavenly under the light of a thousand fireflies. "Not specifically."

Her serene looks contorted into a small sneer, and she said mockingly, "I told him he would need to fall in love."

A small pulse of anger surged through Kitsune. He would not allow her to disparage what he and Myobu had with each other. He wouldn't let his father do it, and he wouldn't let her. He tried his best to suppress the fury, inquiring, "You don't believe in what you told him? Or don't you believe in love?"

"I tell nothing but the truth in what I see," she answered matter-of-factly, her placid demeanor returning. Once they reached the fire, she poured three cups of tea from the kettle as they took their seats on the logs. Kitsune noticed his tailbone no longer pained and briefly wondered if one of Kyubi's gifts was healing.

"Love is certainly real," the Harbinger continued, handing them their cups. Warm steam rose from each even though the fire had only just started. "I see it all the time."

"Just not for you," he guessed, accepting an offered tea. Though he held the mug close to his body, he refrained from drinking. Tea was either a stimulant or a sedative, and he did not desire the latter. Despite the late hour, he did not intend to stay the night. The tree structure, fascinating as it was, unsettled him, and the Harbinger had a way of exacerbating his already frayed nerves.

"On the contrary!" Kyubi exclaimed, her eyes widening with delight. "I've been in love no less than two dozen times throughout my long life, resulting in many marriages and countless children."

As she handed Myobu his own mug of tea, she explained how she believed love was as much a destructive force as it was a source of attraction. Yes, she'd witnessed the usual crumbling of relationships and broken hearts. It often went beyond that, though, like a disease with dark tendrils. It drove people insane, which led some to be malicious or even violent toward others.

"When I was young, I saw firsthand how the love of one person utterly destroyed an entire civilization," she concluded, eyeing Kitsune as though she knew of the journal stowed away in his pack.

"We did not come here to ask about love," Myobu interrupted gently, not looking up from his tea. Unlike Kitsune, he seemed to enjoy his drink, cradling it in his hands, inhaling the aroma, and taking small sips. "While I'm not in any hurry to continue down my path, I believe Kitsune desires to push on further before a new day even begins."

"You may not have come to ask about love, but you arrived because of it. Your love. My love. King Oni's love," Kyubi snapped. She looked irritated, though this suddenly morphed into an expression of sorrow so profound it caught Kitsune off guard. That passed as well, and she continued evenly, if not dismissively, "Yes, of course. Please, Kitsune, inquire of me what you wish to know."

"You perceive much and no doubt are wise, Kyubi," Kitsune said, choosing his words carefully. "This is evidenced by the fact that you know my name and parentage without ever having laid eyes on me. However, despite Myobu's faith in you, I question how much I can trust your reliability. You gave Myobu instructions on how best to serve his home, and that advice led him to me. What I had been planning— what I may still have to do—would in no way be good for Gaav."

"I gave you a cup of tea despite knowing you would not taste a drop," the Harbinger said slyly, taking a sip of her drink. "I do not wish to appear rude."

"I'm not sure I understand what one has to do with the other."

"You do not know because you do not see," she replied. "You are but a child, too young to understand the effects of unfolding events through the passage of time."

Kitsune's chest tightened in frustration, and he hoped his annoyance wasn't as plainly visible as hers. The vague conversations gnawed at his patience, especially since he had done nothing to rein them in. Kyubi had asked for his question, and he delayed it himself. Her belittling comments did nothing to quell the ire.

"The decimation of an entire civilization is, by itself, a terrible event," she continued, growing visibly agitated. Her hands shook, causing the tea in her mug to splash. She set it down. "However, its disappearance may have allowed for the continued survival of the rest of the lands. Likewise, the murder of Ninko, the King's Sun—while a horrific act with terrible consequences—may end up being beneficial down the road of time."

"You cannot seriously be justifying a murder based upon what you see in the future!" Kitsune sputtered, so aghast that her knowledge of his plans didn't surprise him.

His plans. Even if he was no longer sure he'd be able to follow through with his plans, his words and his initial intentions did not mix well. He felt even more shame for having ever intended to carry them out at all.

The Harbinger leapt from the log with an agility no creature a thousand sun cycles old could possess, staring at him through wide, penetrating eyes. "But that's exactly what you are planning to do! It's exactly what you must do. Take the life of one of the Yokai. One of my brethren! It is for the benefit of all people."

"I…I… What?" he stuttered, trying to process. He wanted to say he had not known Ninko was of the Yokai, but that really would have vindicated nothing. And was she truly condoning the murder of one of her kind?

"He is a fire wielder! Of course he is one of my kind," Kyubi cried out in indignation, apparently either reading his mind or his facial expression. She paced back and forth rapidly, the light of the fire flickering across her bare feet. "You need to kill him so you can find your way back to your father. He sent you because he doesn't have the power to do it himself."

"My father could rip your magic away from you! I'd say that's a type of power, but he is not one of you!" Kitsune exploded, jumping from his seat. It was a far less graceful movement than Kyubi's, and the mug he'd been holding spilled. Myobu stood up as well. His eyes wide at what was transpiring, he took a few steps away from the fire.

"Oni wields more power than any one being should," she said, evading Kitsune's point. She looked pained, as though she was holding something back, saying one thing while meaning another. "And you wish to help him?"

"Yes!" He realized how terrible he sounded. "Of course I want to help him. Not to hurt others, but to be a better person."

Kyubi sneered. "The actions of Oni, subtle though they may be, have been nothing but malicious. He's an evil man, used to malevolent ways. I'm afraid there is only one path to changing his entire demeanor."

"He's made some awful choices. I can attest to that. My father can be saved, though." Kitsune's defense of, love, and loyalty to his father grew in equal amounts to the confusion flooding his body. "I must save him. There has to be a way other than taking another's life."

"How else do you propose accomplishing that? You have not seen the future as I have, what terrible things are about to transpire. How do you save a man who has buried himself under such wickedness?"

"I just need to talk to him. I will raise an army, march to Oinari, and confront him. Plans are already underway. If I can speak with him, I can reason with him."

The Harbinger barked a laugh. "Regardless of what transpires here today, you will lead an army to Kitsunetsuki. However, you cannot reason with people like Oni. What will you do if he refuses to change? What will you do when he won't listen to your words? Will you do what is necessary?"

"I will not kill my father!" Kitsune yelled, catching the implication. He suddenly found his bow in his hand, and he brandished it toward her like a club. "Do not ask such a thing of me! If he refuses, I will remove him from the throne. My army will be of an unprecedented size, and it will ensure the end of his rule."

"A military force of that size will lead to casualties. Many more than just the one. How else can you gain access to Oni?"

"You already know I must kill the King's Sun to gain legal admittance into Kitsunetsuki," Kitsune said. "Only when I complete that deed will my father address me in person."

The anxiety, anger, and resentment evaporated from Kyubi's face so quickly it might have all been an act. "Then ask me what you wish to know."

He opened his mouth to ask how he could get to his father. Her answer was evident from their conversation, though. The thought of parroting Myobu's question, asking how he could best serve his beloved kingdom, crossed his mind. He had a hunch the answer would be the same. Without realizing he was speaking aloud, he said, "Just tell me where he is. Tell me so I can do what is necessary."

The Harbinger's face drained of all color. She covered her mouth with both hands; her eyes bulged in shock.

"What?" he shouted, tired of her theatrics and fearing yet another delay or trick. "What is it?"

"Dear spirits," she whispered. "He's right behind you."

In one fluid motion, Kitsune swung around, grabbing an arrow from its quiver and nocking it in the bow. When his turn was complete, the projectile was aimed squarely at the chest of a man he had never seen before. The middle-aged stranger had dark hair, a well-groomed mustache, and a goatee. His finely tailored robes and headdress of red and black revealed him to be of high rank, though wearing such garb out here in the wilderness was as foolish as it was ludicrous. Aside from a staff carved out of wood, the man was unarmed.

"Are you him?" Kitsune asked feverishly. He wanted to blurt out everything. That he had been sent to kill him. That though he took to the task initially, he no longer believed it to be a right course. Perhaps the man would forgive him. Maybe he would even offer a new perspective into Kitsune's troubles, sage guidance on how best to proceed.

Most of all, though, Kitsune just wanted this misadventure to be over. He was so tired of the debates, internal and external, and he wanted this to be done so he could move on with his relationship with Myobu and persuade his father to amend his beliefs. It occurred to Kitsune that he could have just loosed the nocked arrow. A part of him wanted to, but he held back.

"Are you Ninko?" he asked again. "The King's Sun?"

In response, the man thrust out his chest and lifted his arms up parallel to the ground. He squeezed his eyes shut and bellowed out a magnificent roar. The head of his staff burst into white-hot flames.

The man could control fire, and he was about to attack. That was all Kitsune needed. He lowered his aim to the right side of Ninko's abdomen, where Myobu said the man's heart beat, and let the arrow fly.

The moment the arrow left Kitsune's grip, Ninko's staff shimmered and faded from existence. The fine clothing melted away. As the headdress and facial hair disappeared, a shorter, younger person appeared.

Myobu stood where Ninko had been only a moment before, his eyes closed and arms held out in a self-sacrificing gesture.

"NO!" Kitsune screamed. He shot his hand out, extending his magic to get a sense for the arrow's wooden shaft.

THWACK.

Myobu stumbled back a step, dropped his arms, and looked down to his stomach. The projectile had buried itself deep within his abdomen. It visibly twitched as the heart it pierced gave its last few beats.

Kitsune dropped his bow, rushing forward to catch Myobu as he collapsed. He barely registered a silver fox with nine tails leaping away into the brush.

"Stay with me, Myobu! I'm here for you," Kitsune cried out, lowering him to the ground. "I'm so sorry. Oh spirits, I'm so sorry!"

Myobu reached out with a weak hand, and Kitsune took hold of it in both of his.

"Ky…Kyubi saw this ending…before you and I even began," Myobu said with great effort. His eyes shifted out of focus and his face grew pale as blood flowed from his wound. "You truly have been the one for me."

After one final labored breath, Myobu's body fell limp and his dark brown eyes went vacant.

As Kitsune stared in disbelief, the hoshi no tama broke loose from around his neck. It fell and shattered upon a small rock. Green smoke rose from the remains before dissipating into the air.

"No! No!" Kitsune repeated the words over and over. He shook Myobu's body and beat upon his chest. "I love you! I cannot live without you! Come back to me. I don't care who you are!"

With his magic, he frantically probed Myobu's body for any sense of life. If he was still there, if he had just fallen unconscious, there might still be time to seal the wound and revive him. He had done nothing like that, had no idea if healing was within his power, but he needed to try.

To his own surprise, Kitsune immediately sensed something. Without thinking, he reached for it with his mind and pulled. He pulled with all his might, hoping to bring it to the surface, hoping it would bring the light back into Myobu's eyes.

Myobu's body bucked, but it was not from new life. Flames erupted from his mouth and eyes, streaming up into Kitsune's face. The fire blinded him and burned his throat as it worked its way deep into his body, responding to the magical pull. He staggered back in pain, accidentally ripping the arrow from Myobu's abdomen.

With the flames came specific memories not his own. He saw an image of a burnt circle in the woods. Perfectly round, the edges of crisped foliage still smoked and glowed orange. The flash fire that caused this phenomenon had been the resultant emotional outburst of confusion and rage at Kyubi's vision.

Kitsune then saw Rhinecourt burning, set afire by devastating magic. An impatient anger, overriding logic and reason, had called upon the power. The ire stemmed from the failed expectation of finding something or someone. Its destructive force seared its way through the abandoned village, further obliterating evidence of friendship between Odom and Kitsunetsuki.

Rhinecourt faded away, replaced with an image of a large hearth. A bundle of tinder burst into a hot blaze, taking him by surprise. A desire to protect had created this fire, and that feeling was stronger than expected.

The view moved away from inside the hearth and toward another individual—a naked man with fine features and long hair standing beside a makeshift bed of hay. The protective feelings grew, accompanied by an abrupt burst of lust.

Kitsune reeled in confusion, realizing he was staring at himself. It was the moment he'd first seen Myobu in Castle Nogare. Somehow, he was experiencing Myobu's memories through Myobu's eyes.

The last images were a mixture of the times they were intimate with each other. Kitsune saw smallish hands pawing, grabbing, and groping at his own body, greedily pulling off clothes. In an awfully odd moment, he felt what it was like to both take himself into his mouth and feel himself thrusting deep into his body.

As Kitsune experienced the last memories, he saw how close Myobu had come to losing control of a fiery magic. In the lust, sweat, and heat of those moments, the power nearly bubbled over and exploded outward. Myobu just barely kept himself from succumbing to a fiery ecstasy, and Kitsune understood that had been the extreme, unearthly heat he'd felt.

The memories ceased, but Kitsune cried out and wept in anguish as the flames continued to pour out of Myobu's body and into his. Any tears that would have fallen instead immediately evaporated. He tried to reverse the flow of magic, pushing instead of pulling, but it continued steadfastly and unabated.

At last, the final tendrils of fiery power exited Myobu, appearing to trail lazily through the air for several moments, and disappeared into Kitsune's eyes and mouth. Both of their bodies dropped to the ground. Myobu's was still, but Kitsune's writhed in tortured agony as it attempted to understand what it just ingested.

Kitsune did not know how to control fire. He barely knew how to control his own powers. The two of them, combined with his distraught confusion and sorrow, proved too much.

The night erupted into a cyclone of flame. Swirling walls of fire rose around Kitsune, leaving him relatively untouched as though he were in the eye of a tornado. Leaves sizzled, and the limbs and trunks of giant trees cracked open under the heat. The canopy above incinerated, giving way to the open sky.

Kitsune screamed in agony. He screamed at what he had done, at what he had lost. He screamed in anger at the betrayal.

Myobu was gone. The Lady was gone. Even the Harbinger, from whom Kitsune would no longer seek answers, had disappeared.

He was alone, and everything was burning.

THE WESTERN PASS

The sun rose from the horizon the next morning as it always did, unknowing and uncaring of what transpired during the night. Its warming rays of light, unencumbered by any cloud cover, gave radiant birth to a new day.

Full consciousness did not immediately come to Kitsune. As time passed, his senses became more receptive to the surroundings. Kitsune's eyes eventually opened, revealing he had not rested while the moon passed overhead. Though having fallen unconscious from mental and physical exhaustion, his body walked itself away unscathed from the fiery events. He had been walking within the current of a shallow river, letting the flow do much of the work for him.

It was afternoon by the time hunger forced Kitsune to think. Plenty of bushes and trees close to the river bore fruit, but much of it would be poison to his body. As he picked his way through berries and apples, his brain scoured the lexicon of plant life his childhood studies had forced him to memorize. After calming his stomach, he filled his bag with a small supply and then continued down the river.

As the sun began its descent in the west, Kitsune became aware of his location and where he was heading. The tribal lands were northwest of his homeland. Most streams and rivers fed into the Rout, which would lead him to Kitsunetsuki's Western Pass. A legion of soldiers would be there, and they would escort him to Oinari. Once at the capital, he would report to the king that his mission was complete.

Questions presented themselves as the day drew to a close. Kitsune left the river, intent on building a fire, and he asked himself why he was in the tribal lands to begin with. To complete an assignment, yes, but what about it brought him here? What exactly was his task?

A nagging suspicion that he was missing something crept over him. He checked his pack again and again, searching for the absence of some obvious object, but he couldn't come up with what it was.

It wasn't until Kitsune went to light some kindle he collected that the mental walls his brain had carefully constructed around particular memories collapsed. Instead of using flint to start the fire, he closed his eyes, reached out with his mind, and felt for the tinder. As he had been taught, he sought the anger from within himself and used it to conjure up a flame hot enough to ignite the dry twigs and leaves.

How had he done that? Through magic. Fire wielding wasn't the power he was born with, though. It was Myobu's. Who was Myobu? Myobu was the man he loved. Myobu was also the King's Sun, the man Kitsune once swore to kill. Kitsune killed the man he loved and then absorbed his power.

The small flame he had created burst outward as remembrance flooded Kitsune. He bellowed out Myobu's name as the fireball threw him back, his clothing and hair singed. Then his brain reasserted control over the situation, and he fell into darkness.

*

The following day unfolded similarly, as did the next, and the one after that. Kitsune would wake to find himself traveling down an increasingly turbulent waterway. As the sun made its way through the sky, his mind would let down its guard. He would avoid dangers as best he could, nourish his body with fruit from his pack, then collapse again at dusk while building a fire and remembering.

It wasn't until the fourth night that he clung to the memories, refusing to be shepherded back into the recesses of his mind. The fire raged about him and bolts of lightning lit up the sky as he fought to gain control of his emotions. He wept and beat the ground until he was too weak to do anything else. His energy eventually depleted, the phenomena subsided, and he lay on the ground and slept.

*

It had been a betrayal. Yes, Myobu may have loved him, but that hadn't kept the man from drawing Kitsune into a scripted act ending in tragedy.

Kitsune awoke in a normal fashion, lying still on the ground and fully aware of himself and where he was. He felt a miserable wretch, wanting nothing more than to curl up into a tight ball and fall asleep. Instead, he forced himself to eat. He threw it up, but he drank some water and ate again.

Though suffering from constant headaches, he was now walking steadily along a well-used road following the Rout River, intent on making it to the Western Pass by nightfall. He was mildly surprised he hadn't come to it the day before. He and Myobu had not traveled far into the tribal lands to see the Harbinger. In his state of shock, his pace of traveling must have been excruciatingly slow.

It was shock he was suffering from, and he knew he was lucky to have come out of it alive. He could just as easily have drowned in any of the streams or rivers he came across, walked right off a cliff, or fallen prey to a carnivorous beast. The spirits were with him.

A flash of fire erupted around him at the mere thought of the Yokai spirits. Thinking of them—whether it be Myobu, his mother, or the Harbinger—immediately conjured pain and resentment. Those feelings built up within him until they overflowed into the new form of magic he had little control over.

Unfortunately, the Yokai consumed him. His solitary walk to the pass left him with plenty of time to think, and in that span he pieced together a more complete story of the past.

The King's Sun

Ninko, the King's Sun and Marauxus' greatest advisor, had left the Kingdom of Gaav some time ago on a personal quest. His allegiance to his adopted king and country was strong, and he desired to know what he could do to be a better servant. This quest led him to the Harbinger.

Kyubi, one of the oldest and wisest of the Yokai, lived up to her kind's qualities. She gave answers to those who brought questions, but often layered them in extraneous detail or conversation. Whether or not the intention behind her spoken words was benign or malicious, Kitsune did not know. He suspected the answer was somewhere in between.

The finest way for Ninko to serve Gaav was to die. Not just any death—he couldn't drown in a river, walk off a cliff, or let a ferocious animal eat him.

Ninko had to die by the hand of the one he loved.

It wasn't truly important if the Harbinger specifically said Prince Kitsune would be the individual Ninko would come to love or if that man or woman would become clear in time. Her instructions, though, included traveling into Odom. In particular, Rhinecourt.

The King's Sun trusted in her word and traversed the lands until he reached the Eastern Gate. How long he waited, Kitsune could not guess. Long enough to become impatient. Even angry. In some type of tantrum, Ninko lashed out with his power, burning the small village to the ground. Kitsune had arrived with Mamori not long afterward.

Ninko may have been in the shadows, watching as bandits captured Kitsune and Mamori. Or he may have wandered off after scorching the abandoned village. Either way, he found the prince in time to save his life, taking him to Castle Nogare and nursing him back to health. Perhaps it had been an act of kindness for a stranger in need, or maybe the feelings of lust were already starting to creep in at that point. The excess of fire he conjured in the castle's hearth made Kitsune believe some kind of inner turmoil occurred.

Kitsune essentially knew the rest. Ninko took on the guise of Myobu, and the two had traveled together, shared stories, lain with each other, and fallen in love. Without a doubt, there had been love. There had also been lies, conceit, and an overarching plan to move every character into place for the story's inevitable ending.

Had Ninko been elated when Kitsune revealed his plans to murder him back in Sandya, or had he been hoping his impending death by his love would be accidental?

What truly consumed Kitsune, what made him angrier with each step he took, was that their relationship was not enough. Ninko's feelings may have been genuine, but that hadn't stopped him from leading Kitsune down a path of destruction. It hadn't made him stop and think perhaps King Marauxus and Gaav were doing just fine with how he was currently serving them, and maybe he could pursue other means of personal satisfaction. Instead, Ninko continued to act out in a scripted fashion that would create monstrous storms and leave Kitsune alone.

It made Kitsune feel like an animal, no better than a family pet that had to be abandoned for one trivial reason or another.

I am more like a rabid dog, feral and foaming at the mouth. Myobu saw who I really was, and he fled from me.

Kitsune shook his head as nearby plants singed in reaction to his raw emotions. Those weren't his words. They belonged to a long-dead woman who wrote them in a journal. He began to understand her pain, to see how her lover Damian unraveled her mind.

Did those words truly pertain to him as well? Had Kitsune been so focused on his own murderous agenda, unable to see the truth in front of him, that Ninko continued forward to his own death just to escape him?

"Hey! Hey there," a voice called out. "Stay right there!"

Kitsune froze, though more out of surprise than from compliance. It took him several moments to identify the source of the voice. In front of him was a large, rocky hill. He had presumed the path would detour to the right, hugging the river. Upon closer inspection, however, the road ran straight into the base of the mount.

It was the Western Pass. Built centuries ago, it was not known for sheer size and scale like the Eastern Gate. Its ingenuity was in its simple design. The original builders burrowed straight through the rock to the other side of the hill, not an easy accomplishment even with current technology and building methods. When Kitsunetsuki took possession of the pass, a series of gates had been installed within the tunnel to prohibit unauthorized travel and a guard tower built upon the side of the hill. It was from within that tower that the voice came.

"Don't move!" the man shouted again. Kitsune could see even from below that he was young, clearly new to the role of gatekeeper, and had not been particularly well-trained for his duty. "Who are you?"

"I am Prince Kitsune of the Asher Lineage," he responded in a clear, commanding voice. Inside, however, he was seething at the man's incompetence. What if he had been a diplomat? Such a greeting was rude, and it gave a poor impression of Kitsunetsuki's people.

"Aahhh…" The man trailed off, unsure of how to respond to what must have seemed an outlandish claim. "The prince was banished from the kingdom."

"Hence why I am standing on this side of the border," Kitsune confirmed.

"The king sent him into Odom. Rumors say mercenaries killed him."

"I have traveled in the meantime, and I have escaped death more than once while doing so," Kitsune said. "My father, King Oni, banished me under particular terms. If I completed a task, one he revealed to me before I left, he would end my banishment. I am here today to announce I have successfully carried out that task."

"Oh!" the gatekeeper cried out in sudden clarity, apparently remembering something important. He turned and disappeared from view.

Kitsune sighed, wondering if the man drank too much the night before and was still suffering the aftereffects. It didn't matter much to him so long as he could get through the pass. In gratitude, he would forgive this man's lack of regard for his post.

The gatekeeper reappeared a few moments later, eying Kitsune with a more cautious look. As he unraveled a scroll, he said, "This communication arrived from Oinari just yesterday. I haven't read it yet, but the seal is broken, so the men down below have seen it."

"The men below" was a reference to the military encampment on the opposite side of the barrier, a second line of defense if hostile forces were to attack the pass. Military code demanded they share and discuss all communication from the capital with the gatekeeper so his decisions on letting people in or out of the kingdom were better justified. Kitsune could not forgive their disregard for the law.

The man read through the scroll, his head moving from side to side. He would glance at Kitsune after every few lines. About halfway through, he asked, "Did you really murder this man? Advisor—err—Ninko?"

Kitsune nodded. "That was the task my father gave me."

"Ah, no," the gatekeeper disagreed, looking back down at the parchment. He read through some bits again, tracing them with a finger. "This confirms your exile, but it makes no mention of a mission or task given to you by King Oni. Actually, it suggests you've most likely become unhinged, a result most likely stemming from your condition."

"My 'condition'?" Kitsune said, his patience slipping. "What is that supposed to mean?"

"Doesn't say here what it is," the man said, pausing a moment to see if Kitsune would volunteer the information. "Just that you sought and killed this foreigner in a misguided attempt to gain favor with the king."

"Let me in," Kitsune demanded. "Let me in now so I can sort this out."

"Um, no," the gatekeeper said, again consulting the paper. "Says here you have acted against the king's wishes, both before and after banishment, and that under no circumstances are you to be granted re-entry into Kitsunetsuki."

Kitsune's stomach dropped. He staggered forward a few steps, opening his mouth to argue. To his surprise, no words arose.

"If you are to show up at any official entrance to the kingdom or be stopped by an officer," he continued, reading parts he had not yet skimmed, "you are to be...killed on sight."

The man's eyes drifted away from the scroll and down to Kitsune. With an apologetic smile, he said, "I don't suppose you'd stay put while I went and got my bow?"

"No," Kitsune said in a low voice. It wasn't an answer to the gatekeeper's question, but a reaction to what he was hearing. The last pieces of the story were falling into place. His father had used him. There was never any intention of bringing him back into the fold.

King Oni was looking to start another military campaign. Kitsune had suspected it for some time, and the information Pan passed along all but solidified that notion. Against which kingdom, though? Kitsunetsuki's military was exceptionally well-trained and organized, but the king would fail if he attempted a two-pronged war against Odom and Gaav.

The answer, most likely, was to put certain elements into play and see what panned out. The main element was Kitsune. Oni had secretly tasked him with a job. The success of that mission—the unprovoked murder of the King's Sun—would likely cause Gaav to declare war on Kitsunetsuki. However, if mercenaries had hanged Prince Kitsune outside an Odom city, Oni might have used that as an excuse to attack his eastern neighbor.

Kitsune always wanted to be at the forefront of his father's next campaign. In a bizarre twist of fate, he truly was. His banishment wasn't because of his sexuality. The king didn't care if he slept with a man or woman, human or Yokai. It had been to start a war.

King Oni used Kitsune's own loyalty against him. Myobu used his love against him. And because Kitsune was so inept and easily deceived, his mother gave up on him, escaping into the open arms of true death.

"No," Kitsune repeated, louder and with more malice. The headache pounded fiercely against his skull, and there was a sharp buzzing in his ears. He ignored the pain. No longer would he be controlled or taken advantage of by another force, be it a headache, magic, lover, or king. He would work for and be loyal to his people, not his father. His love would be for his kingdom, not for any one individual. Those who would attempt to dissuade him or use him for their own agendas would be stricken down.

"Go. Go tell King Oni his son, Prince Kitsune, is coming for him. Tell him that when I reach Oinari, I will take the crown for myself and throw him into a dungeon so far below Inari Palace the light of day will never bless his eyes again."

The gatekeeper stood still, not exactly believing he had correctly heard Kitsune. A nervous giggle escaped him.

Kitsune didn't hear the laugh. He barely heard anything. He was reaching deep within himself to tap into a power he had yet to scratch the surface of. Topically, he sensed his fury. Below that, his newly gained and barely controlled ability to wield fire roiled. In response to his consciousness brushing against that power, a dozen or so small fires burst into existence around him. He delved deeper still into his core. Past his inborn power to manipulate the weather, which was now causing quick strikes of lightning, was the dangerous ability to reshape the ground beneath them. This was the magic he had only briefly glimpsed while practicing within his mother's imaginary world. He didn't know what it was then, and it had scared him. It scared even her.

The stone floor beneath the gatekeeper's feet suddenly cracked and pulled apart. Startled, he jumped away. Then he looked about in panic as the sound of crumbling rock grew.

"Go! Now!" Kitsune bellowed.

The man needed no further encouragement. The ground was shaking now, and the sounds of the earth collapsing beneath him were loud enough to drown out any words. With a final look of terror at the prince, the gatekeeper darted out the back of the guard tower.

Wanting the man to survive his descent down the other side of the hill, Kitsune focused his attention on the tunnel running underneath it. His mental tendrils filled it, felt for the rock and soil that surrounded it, then, clenching his fists, collapsed it. A thunderous noise emanated at the movement of so much earth, and plumes of debris and dust exploded from what used to be the entrance.

Encouraged by his success, Kitsune used his anger to fuel more action. He picked random points within the mass of the hill and forced all the matter there upward to the surface. Trees exploded and splintered as the dirt beneath them was thrown into the air. The atmosphere became dirty and hard to see through, reminding Kitsune of the northern Odom camp. This caused his heart to ache and the buzzing sound in his ears to grow louder. Just before setting off for that dirty outpost, Kitsune thought Myobu deserted him. He returned, though. He returned and, touching Kitsune on the chest and abdomen, revealed where to strike at Ninko, how to kill himself.

CRACK!

Kitsune knew he had split the hill into two horizontal sections, although he couldn't see it. He reached out his hands, helping to focus his energies in pushing the top half of the hill over into the Rout River. The guard tower collapsed entirely as its foundation became unstable, then fell away. Gusts of dirt spewed into the surroundings until Kitsune could only sense the remains of the hill with his magic. Shrill shrieking sounds ripped through the air as large sheets of stone scraped over one another.

Though unable to see anything, he reveled as he felt the sheer volume of earth sliding into the water. He could hear the boulders as they sent out massive waves—just as the Lady of the Mountain had in his first vision of her.

He could be terrifying, too. He could destroy. He possessed the power to end everything.

Kitsune stopped at that thought. His arms dropped back to his sides, and he stared with dull eyes into nowhere. His mind wandered backward nearly a millennium to a time when the cruel actions of a man named Damian drove a woman mad. Her reaction was to utilize a power of her own. Not magic like his, but one based on science. She used her power to obliterate the society that had raised her, putting her into a mental and physical place to be enraptured and then hurt by a horrible, unfeeling man.

Kitsune didn't want to erase anything. Not his homeland or his beloved people. Throwing every last granule of the hill into the river would disrupt the flow of water, if not block it entirely from his kingdom. It would affect the livelihoods of all those in the villages lining the river, taking away sources of food and water for irrigation of fields. Means of living would disappear and entire families could go hungry.

He would not let his own anguish extend to and affect his people.

A sliver of sunlight pierced through the dust, and in it Kitsune saw the enormous, noisy, brass machine the journal writer wrote about. For the briefest instant, he understood everything. He felt a clarity like he had never known.

The light disappeared, and he blinked in frustration as much of what he just felt slipped from his grasp. The only thing left to him was a confirmation of a reality that had already revealed itself, a cold world devoid of meaningful love, and the only way to survive it. Command and conquer.

Kitsune turned and walked away from the wreckage of the Western Pass. He knew exactly what he had to do.

EPILOGUE

The exhalation of Myobu's last breath marked his death. Conversely, as the air left his lungs, his consciousness expanded with new life.

Though he could no longer physically sense anything, Myobu was hyperaware of his surroundings. There was cognizance, but he also understood everything he was becoming a part of. He was the soil, the enormous evergreen trees growing from it, and the insects living within. He was the water in a nearby stream, and he was the rocks the water flowed over. He was the air all the wildlife breathed, and he was all the wildlife. He was the Harbinger.

He was Kitsune.

As soon as Myobu was a part of Kitsune, he understood him. As soon as he understood him, he experienced sorrow. Even devoid of a physical vessel, confusion, regret, and betrayal weighed him down. It was a mixture of hysteria, and he could feel his—Kitsune's—very being shift and crumble.

Myobu wanted to reach out and envelop Kitsune, comfort and calm him. Yet his own consciousness continued to expand outward unabated. His level of comprehension and appreciation on how the natural world operated grew exponentially as they coalesced. Soon, Kitsune became a small and inconsequential part of himself. All the people of all the lands, including the Yokai, were soon trivial to him. Every individual, all realms, all joys and tragedies were mere pinpricks in the fabric of space and time. They were neither important nor unimportant.

As his mind stretched out and he became one with all that was, Myobu's sense of self thinned. His own identity and history became lost in the swath of mental growth. The name *Myobu* came to have no meaning, and it was forgotten.

Eventually, having consumed all the knowledge and comprehended all the land and water offered, his progression continued outward spherically. He learned of other planets, moons, and extraterrestrial objects spinning around a giant red star and knew how intricately they all affected one another, allowing one to be hospitable to life while another was barren.

From there he went on to see other solar systems, finding they too interacted with one another. Along with other interstellar phenomena like black holes, quasars, and novae, they formed the larger entity of a galaxy. He saw the planet—no, the system—he hailed from was itself as miniscule and irrelevant as the life forms it supported.

As his awareness extended beyond the beautiful golden lights of his galaxy, he knew he would eventually encounter others. He surmised that they were all involved in a similar dance with one another, affecting everything in the cosmos as though they were all interconnected with invisible twine. For now, though, an inky blackness surrounded him, sprinkled with the light of a trillion stars and galaxies. Most were white, yet some shined blue or red.

One of the lights moved.

Everything in the universe moved. He now understood even light traveled at a particular speed. The source of this light, which had a brilliant green shine, moved out of step in the universal dance, coming closer to his consciousness.

He yearned to learn more about this emerald light. Its behavior indicated a purpose, which in turn suggested a consciousness. If it was, would it be similar to his own, far from the simple, inconsequential life forms now a part of him? They could join, become one, and know all.

It occurred to him that this hopeful longing for another like himself resulted from loneliness. Being one with everything he encountered was not enough to fulfill him. Strangely, the more homogenous he became with what he happened upon, the emptier he felt. He wished he could stop growing.

Thankfully, between the rate of his outward growth and the impressive speed of the mysterious green light, he didn't have to wait long before the two converged. The moment they overlapped, he stilled.

While he could sense another mind, they remained distinct, flowing over one another like a consciousness and subconsciousness. This contact gave him select information and understanding, such as how to cease his unfurling, which he did immediately. Also, he learned the identity of the green light.

"Greetings, Mother," he transmitted to her.

"No, I am not your mother," came the reply in a calm, soothing voice. "I am the progenitor of Kitsune."

He considered that for a moment, searching for the meaning of the name. "Kitsune is of me, and I am of Kitsune. You are our mother."

"No," the voice said again, filled with patience. From the light, a woman emerged. Clad in a long dress of earthly green colors, her beauty was striking. With porcelain skin and long black hair, her visage was marred only by her eyes, which told of a haunted past and fear for the future.

She was the Lady of the Mountain, and he could apperceive the broken slopes of the mount she had once been a part of within himself.

"How are you doing that," he asked, indicating her new form. Then, after a confused moment wondering what shape he would take if he could, he said, "Who am I?"

"In one way or another, I have been in death far longer than you have. I have learned to do many things in this state," she said. "Let me help you understand."

The Lady reached her hand to the heavens. The stars, while continuing to shine brightly from the otherwise blackness of space, were also something other than stars. He understood that they were now representations of memories, thoughts, and ideals.

Then the Lady plucked three lights from their place in the universe and held them in her cupped hands. A broken emotion filled her eyes, one he thought he should be able to identify but couldn't. Then, looking back up at him, she opened her hands and let the stars fall through her fingers.

As he watched the spots of light descend, he identified what each represented. One was Kitsune, offspring of the Lady and a part of himself. Another was Myobu, a name that seemed familiar.

The third star was by far the largest and brightest. It shown with not one color but radiated all colors with a fierce intensity. It was the light of love.

The three stars fell into a pool of water he had not known was there, creating ripples across the previously serene surface. He observed as the currents washed across him, fancying in the distorted reflections of the other stars above. As the lights refracted, he saw what they represented. Within moments, he viewed hundreds of thousands of faces from many of the worlds within himself. He also processed their memories, emotions, and political and religious persuasions.

One individual stood out from the rest. He was an old but lively man with more hair on his face than he had on his head. Dressed in layers of long furs, he gestured about wildly as though he was telling an exciting story.

The man was Patriarch Kirby of Odom, and he recalled how the old leader revealed to Kitsune more truth about the prince's past and origins than anyone else alive. He remembered standing in the patriarch's office, listening to the conversation but gazing longingly over at Kitsune. He and the prince hadn't known each other long, had in fact just shared their first kiss the night before, but he knew he loved him.

"Myobu," whispered the Lady.

The rippling water had all but subsided. Before they disappeared altogether, he saw a man with a heart-shaped face framed with thick, dark brown hair. It was a glimpse of himself—slender, toned, with smaller hands. That seemed an important detail.

"I was...am Myobu," he said, noticing he had taken on the man's form.

"You are," she said softly.

"Kitsune?" he cried out, remembering their last moments together. Myobu did not need to search within himself for Kitsune to know the other was in great pain.

"Do you love my son?"

"More than anything, I love Kitsune."

"And King Marauxus and the Kingdom of Gaav?"

"Of course," Myobu admitted. Though he knew the answer right away, it took him several moments to consider the meaning behind those names. "It is a different kind of love."

"Naturally," the Lady said. After a long moment, her expression turned dark. "You must return to my son immediately."

The idea filled Myobu with great joy and anticipation, but her change in demeanor stifled them. That, and the fact he had been shot in the heart with an arrow and was dead. Many questions arose within him, but his first ones were for Kitsune. "Why? What is wrong?"

"Kitsune no longer has an anchor for his emotions, and they are running rampant." Her voice rose with anxiety. "He has yet to learn control over all his own powers, let alone the one he absorbed from you."

He whispered, "Fire."

"Everything will burn. Mountains will be blasted into dust, rivers and oceans will dry up, and entire cities will be decimated. Mostly, though, everything will burn." The Lady was on the verge of tears. "My beautiful son would be remembered as a monster if anyone were to survive his wrath."

"We must return to him immediately!"

"No," was the quiet reply, and Myobu witnessed a tear glide down her cosmic cheek.

"Why not?"

"The dead returning to life is not natural, and doing so requires a great deal of magic," the Lady explained. "The magic of the Yokai follows them after death. It allows our consciousness to expand into all things, for conversations like this to transpire, and, in circumstances like these, return a soul to its original vessel."

Myobu waited expectantly, still not understanding.

"The magic is consuming," she continued. "I am incomplete, but there is enough of my life force in this realm to enact the process. Once finished, I will no longer...be."

"You'll die?"

"We are already in death," she said with a wry smile. "I will no longer exist on any plane."

"There must be another way!" Myobu objected. "There has to be another source of magic. If there isn't, I can be the one to send you back. You should be the one to return to your son!"

"You may have commanded great power during your life, but you would have much to learn in death before you could perform such a deed. Even if you could, I have no vessel to return to."

"Another source of magic, then?" he pleaded, not wanting to deprive Kitsune of his mother, even if they only came together in the far future after he, too, passed from life.

"I have no vessel to return to," she repeated, "and yours is decaying as we speak. I must return you to it now before it can no longer support your life force."

"But..."

Holding up a hand to stop him from speaking, the previous tranquil look returned to the Lady's face, accompanied by peace and a sense of knowing. She said, "I willingly sacrifice myself for my son. You, too, have sacrificed, and you will have to do so again. Kitsune will have done terrible things by the time you rejoin him, but your love may be strong enough to save him. To save everything."

A glowing golden-green light permeated through her being, and she gave the widest, most honest smile Myobu had ever seen. With a joyous laugh, the Lady of the Mountain said her last words: "Give my prince a hug from his mother, and tell him I love him."

The Lady's human form dematerialized into the ball of green light and sped forward into him. At many times the speed of light, she flew back into the galaxy whence they came, back to their solar system, and, whizzing past planets, back to their world. Without ever reducing speed, she tore through the atmosphere, closed in on the tribal lands, then exploded in a dazzling display over a corpse in the burnt remains of a forest.

Then she was no more.

Myobu waited for what came next. Nothing happened at first, so he looked inward at himself. The corpse in the woods was at the center of his being—it was his body. He reached out to it with his mind, wondering if they had waited too long and it would no longer sustain life.

He observed a heartbeat. His own heartbeat.

The moment he sensed life returning to his body, he felt as though he were dying. His expanded consciousness began to collapse into itself, being pulled back into a material brain. He was no longer the galaxy, its hundreds of billions of stars and tens of billions of solar systems. The memories, thoughts, and emotions of countless creatures were ripped from him, and scientific models that seemed so simplistic escaped his understanding. It made him feel empty, alone, and claustrophobic.

He tried to slow his inward descent, mentally grasping at celestial objects, but everything slipped from him like it had all been a dream. At the last moment, he gave in, turning and examining his home world. He saw Patriarch Kirby and Allison and Joseph. He saw King Marauxus and all the others he loved in Gaav. He saw his longtime friends Tod and Kensie. He even saw King Oni, sitting alone in an egg-shaped room.

Most importantly, Myobu saw Kitsune, his pretty prince. He grew concerned, wondering exactly what Kitsune was doing on the outskirts of the Purple People's village.

Then his essence was stuffed back into his physical head.

With a rasping gasp for breath, Myobu opened his eyes.

Thanks for reading *The King's Sun*. Find me online at:

WEBSITE

www.isaacgrisham.com

TWITTER

@isaacgrisham

FACEBOOK

@AuthorIsaacGrisham

Instagram

isaac.grisham

Made in the USA
Monee, IL
17 November 2021